Stare .... *appears or not, I am a woman in the world. I have buried my father, and shall soon know how to make my grandpa up in stone.*
Alice Walker
"A Sudden Trip Home in the Spring"

"Please," Alice said. "Please, Liz, listen. I don't know how he can do those things. I doubt if even *he* knows for sure. He might not mean to do you any harm, but he already is. He's made you love him by knowing every secret thing you want and need, and that's not love at all. That's rape."
Stephen King
"I Know What You Need"

Robert Benard, a graduate of Yale University, lives and works in New York City. He is the author of the novel *A Catholic Education* (Laurel-Leaf, 1987).

QUANTITY SALES

INDIVIDUAL SALES

Laurel-Leaf Library of American Literature

ALL PROBLEMS ARE SIMPLE
and Other Stories

Nineteen Views
of the
College Years

Edited by
Robert Benard

LAUREL-LEAF BOOKS bring together under a single imprint outstanding works of fiction and nonfiction particularly suitable for young adult readers, both in and out of the classroom. Charles F. Reasoner, Professor Emeritus of Children's Literature and Reading, New York University, is consultant to this series.

Published by
Dell Publishing
a division of
The Bantam Doubleday Dell Publishing Group, Inc.
1 Dag Hammarskjold Plaza
New York, New York 10017

Laurel-Leaf Library ® TM 766734, Dell Publishing, a division of the Bantam Doubleday Dell Publishing Group, Inc.

ISBN: 0-440-20164-0

RL: 6.2

Printed in the United States of America

September 1988

10 9 8 7 6 5 4 3 2 1

KRI

For their invaluable help in compiling this anthology, I thank Knox Burger and Bob Wyatt; for her tireless efforts in assembling permissions, I thank Cary Fisher; and for his faith in and enthusiasm for this volume, I thank my editor, George Nicholson.

—R.B.

CONTENTS

INTRODUCTION

The college years mark the passage to adult responsibility; they present, if only embryonically at times, all the thorny problems that constitute the human condition.

What is this world? Why are we here and what do we want? Whether it's the would-be writer colliding with the real thing in "1939," or the discoverer of romance where he least suspects it in "Christmas Poem," the people in these nineteen stories explore—as those in all good stories do—these fundamental questions.

Chosen for the precision of their telling detail, the beauty of their making and their truthfulness about the human heart, each of these stories renders a reality where questions of value resound: the heedless cruelty of a suitor in "A Different Set of Rules"; the fierce, lonely passion of the artist in "The Anatomy Lesson"; the confusion of love and power in stories by Stephen King and F. Scott Fitzgerald; and the poignant comedy of bravado in "Houseparty" and "The Famous Toboggan of Laughter."

By transplanting us into their worlds, these stories speak directly to us about ourselves; show that actions have consequences; and identify the small, careless gesture or remark that can change life utterly and forever.

Some of America's finest short story writers are here. In "The Christian Roommates," John Updike portrays the fascinated revulsion of the programmed for the natural. In "The Echo," Paul Bowles dramatizes frightened love gone cruel. And in "The Tea Time of Stouthearted Ladies," Jean Stafford captures indelibly a world so oppressive that a young woman must escape any way she can.

These stories invite comparison and contrast. For example, compare the "bourgeois scruples" of Updike's Orson with the "maniacal respectability" that makes Stafford's Kitty need to run; then measure both against the hardened heart of Bowles's

Aileen. Each is a great story and each shows the courage that freedom requires.

In different ways all these stories point to freedom—freedom from fear and hypocrisy, freedom to love, *self*-liberation—as a lodestar that can indeed suggest that all problems are simple.

I Am Twenty-one

by Mary Robison

I heard ringing, and I realized that what I had done was continued my answer to Essay Question I—"What effect did the discovery of the barrel vault have on the architecture of 13th century cathedrals?"—writing clockwise in the left, top, and right-hand margins of page one in my exam book. I had forgotten to move along to page two or to Essay Question II. The ringing was coming from in me—probably from overdoing it with diet pills or from the green tea all last night and from reading so much all the time.

I was doing C work in all courses but this one—"The Transition from Romanesque to Gothic." I needed to blast this course on its butt, and that was possible because for this course I knew it all. I needed only time and space to tell it. My study notes were 253 pencil sketches from slides we had seen and from plates in books at the Fine Arts Library and some were from our text. I had sixty-seven pages of lecture notes that I had copied over once for clarity. Everything Professor Williamson had said in class was recorded in my notes—practically even his throat clearings and asides about the weather. It got to the point where if he rambled, I thought, yeah, yeah, cut the commercial and get back to the program.

Some guy whose hair I could've ripped out was finished with his exam. He was actually handing it to the teaching assistant. How could he be *finished,* have given even a cursory treatment to the three questions? He was a quitter, a skimmer, I decided; a person who knew shit about detail.

I was having to stop now and then, really too often, to skin the tip of my pencil with the razor blade I had brought along. I preferred a pencil because it couldn't dry up or leak. But this was a Number 2 graphite and gushy-gummy and I was writing the thing away. The eraser was just a blackened nub. Why hadn't I brought a damn *box* of pencils?

The teaching assistant was Clark—Clark Something or Something Clark, I didn't know. He was baggy and sloppy, but happy-looking. He had asked me out once for Cokes, but I had brushed him off. That was maybe stupid because he might've been in charge of grading exams.

I decided to ignore Essay Question II, pretend I hadn't even seen it. I leaned hard into Question III, on church decoration, windows, friezes, flora, fauna, bestiaries, the iconography in general. I was quoting Honorius of Autun when the class bell fired off.

I looked up. Most people were gone.

"Come on, everyone!" Clark called. "Please. Come on now. Miss Bittle? Mr. Kenner, please. Miss Powers?"

"Go blow, Clark," I said right out loud. But I slapped him my exam booklet and hurried out of Meverett, feeling let down and apathetic all of a sudden, and my skin going rubbery cold.

I biked home with a lot of trouble. I went on the sidewalks. I was scared that in the streets I'd get my ringing confused with car warnings.

I was still ringing.

Last semester I had had a decorating idea for my apartment, this monastic idea of strict and sparse. I had stripped the room down to a cot, a book table, one picture. The plaster walls were a nothing oatmeal color, which was okay. But not okay was that some earlier renter had gooped orange—unbelievably— paint on the moldings and window frames. So where I lived looked not like a scholar's den, finally, but more like a bum's sleepover, like poverty.

My one picture up wasn't of a Blessed Virgin or a detail from Amiens of the King of Judah holding a rod of the Tree of Jesse. Instead, it was an eight-by-ten glossy of Rudy and Leslie, my folks. Under the backing was written *Gold Coast, the first cool day.* The photo had been shot out on North Lake Shore Drive around 1964, I'd say, when I was three. Leslie, my mom, was huddled into Rudy, sharing his lined leather jacket. They appeared, for all the eye sparkle, like people in an engagement-ring ad. I kept the picture around because, oddly, putting away the *idea* of my folks would've been worse than losing the real them. In the photo, they at least *looked* familiar.

They had been secret artists. Rudy was a contractor for a living, Leslie a physical therapist. So they worked all their art urges out on me—on my school projects, for instance, which they hurled themselves into. One project "I did" for seventh grade that they helped me with was, I swear, good enough for a world's fair. It was a kind of three-dimensional diorama triptych of San Francisco Bay with both bridges—Oakland and Golden Gate—that may have even lit up or glowed in the dark. We had to borrow a neighbor's station wagon just to get the thing safely over to Dreiser Junior High—it lined up as long as an ironing board.

I got my bike tugged inside, left it leaning against the wall under the photograph. I clapped a kettle onto the midget stove in my kitchen part of the apartment, and paced, waiting for the water to heat. The pitch of the steam when it got going was only a quarter tone below the ringing in my head.

My folks were two and a half years gone.

I used to drive out to the site of their accident all the time—a willow tree on Route 987. The last time I went, the tree was still healing. The farmlands were a grim powdery blond in the white sun, and the earth was still ragged from winter. I sat there in my tiny Vega on the broken crumbly shoulder. The great tree and the land around—flat as a griddle for miles and miles—didn't seem as fitting as I had once thought, not such a poetic place for two good lives to have stopped.

I had my tea now and grieved about the exam. Leaving a whole essay question unanswered! How could I expect to get better than a C?

Just before my first sip of tea, my ringing shut off as though somebody had punched a button, said, "Enough of that for her."

I decided it was time to try for sleep, but first I used a pen with a nylon point to tattoo a P on the back of my hand. This meant when I woke up I was to eat some protein—shrimp or eggs or a green something.

On the cot I tried, as a sleep trick, to remember my answer to Essay Question I—word for fucking word.

1939

by Peter Taylor

Twenty years ago, in 1939, I was in my senior year at Kenyon College. I was restless, and wasn't sure I wanted to stay on and finish college. My roommate at Kenyon was Jim Prewitt. Jim was restless, too. That fall, he and I drove to New York City to spend our Thanksgiving holiday. Probably both of us felt restless and uneasy for the same reasons that everyone else did in 1939, or for just the obvious reasons that college seniors always do, but we imagined our reasons to be highly individual and beyond the understanding of the other students.

It was four o'clock on Wednesday afternoon when we left Gambier, the little Ohio village that gives Kenyon its post office address. We had had to wait till the four o'clock mail was put in the Gambier post office, because each of us was expecting a check from home. My check came. Jim's did not. But mine was enough to get us to New York, and Jim's would be enough to get us back. "Enough to get back, *if* we come back!" That became our motto for the trip. We had both expressed the thought in precisely the same words and at precisely the same moment as we came out of the post office. And during the short time it took us to dash back across the village street, with its wide green in the center, and climb the steps up to our room in Douglass House and then dash down again with our suitcases to the car, we found half a dozen excuses for repeating our motto.

The day was freakishly warm, and all of our housemates were gathered on the front stoop when we made our departure. In their presence, we took new pleasure in proclaiming our motto and repeating it over and over while we threw our things into the car. The other boys didn't respond, however, as we hoped they would. They leaned against the iron railing of the stoop, or sat on the stone steps leaning against one another, and refused to admit any interest in our "childish" insinuation: *if* we came back. All seven of them were there and all seven were in agreement on the "utter stupidity" of our long Thanksgiving trip as well as that of our present behavior. But they didn't know our incentive, and they couldn't be expected to understand.

For two years, Jim and I had shared a room on the second floor of old Douglass House. I say "old" because at Kenyon in those days there was still a tendency to prefix that adjective to the name of everything of any worth on the campus or in the village. Oldness had for so many years been the most respected attribute of the college that it was natural for its prestige to linger on a few years after what we considered the new dispensation and the intellectual awakening. Old Douglass House *was* an oldish house, but it had only been given over for use as a dormitory the year that Jim and I—and most of our friends— came to Kenyon. The nine of us moved into it just a few weeks after its former occupants—a retired professor and his wife, I believe—had moved out. And we were to live there during our three years at Kenyon (all of us having transferred from other colleges as sophomores)—to live there without ever caring to inquire into the age or history of the house. We were not the kind of students who cared about such things. We were hardly aware, even, of just how quaint the house was, with its steep white gables laced with gingerbread work, and its Gothic windows and their arched window blinds. Our unawareness—Jim's and mine—was probably never more profound than on that late afternoon in November, when we set out for New York. Our plan was to spend two days in Manhattan and then go on to Boston for a day with Jim's family, and our only awareness was of that plan.

During the previous summer, Jim Prewitt had become engaged to a glorious, talented girl with long flaxen hair, whom he had met at a student writers' conference somewhere out West. And I, more attached to things at home in St. Louis than Jim was to things in Boston—*I* had been "accepted" by an

equally glorious dark-eyed girl in whose veins ran the Creole
blood of old-time St. Louis. By a happy coincidence both of
these glorious girls were now in New York City. Carol Crawford, with her flaxen hair fixed in a bun on the back of her neck
and a four-hundred-page manuscript in her suitcase, had
headed East from the fateful writers' conference in search of a
publisher for her novel. Nancy Gibault had left St. Louis in
September to study painting at the National Academy. The two
girls were as yet unacquainted, and it was partly to the cor-
recting of this that Jim and I meant to dedicate our Thanksgiving holiday.

The other boys at Douglass House didn't know our incentive, and when we said goodbye to them there on the front steps
I really felt a little sorry for them. Altogether, they were a sad,
shabby, shaggy-looking lot. All of us who lived at Douglass
House were, I suppose. You have probably seen students who
look the way we did—especially if you have ever visited Bard
College or Black Mountain or Rollins or almost any other college nowadays. Such students seem to affect a kind of hungry,
unkempt look. And yet they don't really know what kind of
impression they want to make; they only know that there are
certain kinds they *don't* want to make.

Generally speaking, we at Douglass House were reviled by
the rest of the student body, all of whom lived in the vine-
covered dormitories facing the campus, and by a certain pro-
portion of the faculty. I am sure we were thought of as a group
as closely knit as any other in the college. We were even considered a sort of fraternity. But we didn't see ourselves that way.
We would have none of that. Under that high gabled roof, we
were all independents and meant to remain so. Housing us
"transfers" together this way had been the inspiration of the
dean or the president under the necessity of solving a problem
of overflow in the dormitories. Yet we did not object to his
solution, and of our own accord we ate together in the Commons, we hiked together about the countryside, we went together to see girls in nearby Mount Vernon, we enrolled in the
same classes, flocked more or less after the same professors, and
met every Thursday night at the creative writing class, which

we all acknowledged as our reason for being at Kenyon. But think of ourselves as a club, or as dependent upon each other for companionship or for anything else, we would not. There were times when each of us talked of leaving Kenyon and going back to the college or university from which he had come—back to Ann Arbor or Olivet, back to Chapel Hill, to Vanderbilt, to Southwestern, or back to Harvard or Yale. It was a moderately polite way each of us had of telling the others that *they* were a bunch of Kenyon boys but that *he* knew something of a less cloistered existence and was not to be confused with their kind. We were so jealous of every aspect of our independence and individuality that one time, I remember, Bruce Gordon nearly fought with Bill Anderson because Bill, for some strange reason, had managed to tune in, with his radio, on a Hindemith sonata that Bruce was playing on the electric phonograph in his own room.

Most of us had separate rooms. Only Jim Prewitt and I shared a room, and ours was three or four times as big as most dormitory cubicles. It opened off the hall on the second floor, but it was on a somewhat lower level than the hall. And so when you entered the door, you found yourself at the head of a little flight of steps, with the top of your head almost against the ceiling. This made the room seem even larger than it was, as did the scarcity and peculiar arrangement of the furniture. Our beds, with our desks beside them, were placed in diagonally opposite corners, and we each had a wobbly five-foot bookshelf set up at the foot of his bed, like a hospital screen. The only thing we shared was a little three-legged oak table in the very center of the room, on which were a hot plate and an electric coffeepot, and from which two long black extension cords reached up to the light fixture overhead.

The car that Jim and I were driving to New York did not belong to either of us. It didn't at that time belong to anybody, really, and I don't know what ever became of it. At the end of our holiday, we left it parked on Marlborough Street in Boston, with the ignition key lost somewhere in the gutter. I suppose Jim's parents finally disposed of the car in some way or other.

It had come into our hands the spring before, when its last
owner had abandoned it behind the college library and left the
keys on Jim's desk up in our room. He, the last owner, had
been one of us in Douglass House for a while—though it was,
indeed, for a very short while. He was a poor boy who had been
at Harvard the year that Jim was there, before Jim transferred
to Kenyon, and he was enormously ambitious and possessed
enough creative energy to produce in a month the quantity of
writing that most of us were hoping to produce in a lifetime. He
was a very handsome fellow, with a shock of yellow hair and
the physique of a good trackman. On him the cheapest department store clothes looked as though they were tailor-made, and
he could never have looked like the rest of us, no matter how
hard he might have tried. I am not sure that he ever actually
matriculated at Kenyon, but he was there in Douglass House
for about two months, clicking away on first one typewriter and
then another (since he had none of his own); I shall never
forget the bulk of manuscript that he turned out during his
stay, most of which he left behind in the house or in the trunk
of the car. The sight of it depressed me then, and it depresses
me now to think of it. His neatly typed manuscripts were in
every room in the house—novels, poetic dramas, drawing-room
comedies, lyrics, epic poems, short stories, scenarios. He wasn't
at all like the rest of us. And except for his car he has no place
in this account of our trip to New York. Yet since I have di-
gressed this far, there is something more that I somehow feel I
ought to say about him.

Kenyon was to him only a convenient place to rest awhile
(for writing was not work to him) on his long but certain journey from Harvard College to Hollywood. He used to say to us
that he wished he could do the way we were doing and really
dig in at Kenyon for a year or so and get his degree. The place
appealed to him, he said, with its luxuriant countryside, and its
old stone buildings sending up turrets and steeples and spires
above the treetops. If he stayed, he would join a fraternity, so
he said, and walk the Middle Path with the other fraternity
boys on Tuesday nights, singing fraternity songs and songs of
old Kenyon. He said he envied us—and yet he hadn't himself

time to stay at Kenyon. He was there for two months, and while he was there he was universally admired by the boys in Douglass House. But when he had gone, we all hated him. Perhaps we were jealous. For in no time at all stories and poems of his began appearing in the quarterlies as well as in the popular magazines. Pretty soon one of his plays had a good run on Broadway, and I believe he had a novel out even before that. He didn't actually go to Hollywood till after the war, but get there at last he did, and now, I am told, he has a house in the San Fernando Valley and has the two requisite swimming pools, too.

To us at Kenyon he left his car. It was a car given to him by an elderly benefactor in Cambridge, but a car that had been finally and quite suddenly rendered worthless in his eyes by a publisher's advance, which sent him flying out of our world by the first plane he could get passage on. He left us the car without any regret, left it in the same spirit that American tourists left their cars on the docks at European ports when war broke out that same year. In effect, he tossed us his keys from the first-class deck of the giant ship he had boarded at the end of his plane trip, glad to know that he would never need the old rattletrap again and glad to be out of the mess that all of us were in for life.

I have said that I somehow felt obliged to include everything I have about our car's last real owner. And now I know why I felt so. Without that digression it would have been impossible to explain what the other boys were thinking—or what we thought they were thinking—when we left them hanging about the front stoop that afternoon. They were thinking that there was a chance Jim and I had had an "offer" of some kind, that we had "sold out" and were headed in the same direction that our repudiated brother had taken last spring. Perhaps they did not actually think that, but that was how we interpreted the sullen and brooding expressions on their faces when we were preparing to leave that afternoon.

Of course, what their brooding expressions meant made no difference to Jim or me. And we said so to each other as, with Jim at the wheel, we backed out of the little alleyway beside the

house and turned into the village street. We cared not a hoot in
hell for what they thought of us or of our trip to New York.
Further, we cared no more—Jim and I—for each other's ap-
proval or disapproval, and we reminded each other of this then
and there.

We were all independents in Douglass House. There was no
spirit of camaraderie among us. We were not the kind of students who cared about such things as camaraderie. Besides, we
felt that there was more than enough of that spirit abroad at
Kenyon, among the students who lived in the regular dormitories and whose fraternity lodges were scattered about the
wooded hillside beyond the village. In those days, the student
body at Kenyon was almost as picturesque as the old vine-clad
buildings and the rolling countryside itself. So it seemed to us,
at least. We used to sit on the front stoop or in the upstairs
windows of Douglass House and watch the fops and dandies of
the campus go strolling and strutting by on their way to the
post office or the bank, or to Jean Val Dean's short-order joint.
Those three establishments, along with Dicky Doolittle's filling
station, Jim Lynch's barber shop, Jim Hayes's grocery store,
Tom Wilson's Home Market, and Mrs. Titus's lunchroom and
bakery (the Kokosing Restaurant), constituted the business district of Gambier. And it was in their midst that Douglass
House was situated. Actually, those places of business were
strung along just one block of the village's main thoroughfare.
Each was housed in its separate little store building or in a
converted dwelling house, and in the spring and in the fall,
while the leaves were still on the low-hanging branches of the
trees, a stranger in town would hardly notice that they were
places of business at all.

From the windows of Douglass House, between the bakery
and the barber shop, we could look down on the dormitory
students who passed along the sidewalk, and could make our
comment on what we considered their silly affectations—on
their provincial manners and their foppish, collegiate clothing.
In midwinter, when all the leaves were off the trees, we could
see out into the parkway that divided the street into two lanes
—and in the center of the parkway was the Middle Path. For

us, the Middle Path was the epitome of everything about Kenyon that we wanted no part of it. It was a broad gravel walkway extending not merely the length of the village green; it had its beginning, rather, at the far end of the campus, at the worn doorstep of the dormitory known as Old Kenyon, and ran the length of the campus, on through the village, then through the wooded area where most of the faculty houses were, and ended at the door of Bexley Hall, Kenyon's Episcopal seminary. In the late afternoon, boys on horseback rode along it as they returned from the polo field. At noon, sometimes, boys who had just come up from Kenyon's private airfield appeared on the Middle Path still wearing their helmets and goggles. And after dinner every Tuesday night the fraternity boys marched up and down the path singing their fraternity songs and singing fine old songs about early days at Kenyon and about its founder, Bishop Philander Chase:

> The first of Kenyon's goodly race
> Was that great man Philander Chase.
> He climbed the hill and said a prayer
> And founded Kenyon College there.

> He dug up stones, he chopped down trees,
> He sailed across the stormy seas,
> And begged at ev'ry noble's door,
> And also that of Hannah Moore.

> He built the college, built the dam,
> He milked the cow, he smoked the ham;
> He taught the classes, rang the bell,
> And spanked the naughty freshmen well.

At Douglass House we wanted none of that. We had all come to Kenyon because we were bent upon becoming writers of some kind or other and the new president of the college had just appointed a famous and distinguished poet to the staff of the English Department. Kenyon was, in our opinion, an obscure little college that had for more than a hundred years slept the sweet, sound sleep that only a small Episcopal college can ever afford to sleep. It was a quaint and pretty spot. We recognized that, but we held that against it. That was not what we were looking for. We even collected stories about other people who had resisted the beauties of the campus and the surrounding countryside. A famous English critic had stopped here on his way home from a long stay in the Orient, and when asked if he did not admire our landscape he replied, "No. It's too rich for my blood." We all felt it was too rich for ours, too. Another English visitor was asked if the college buildings did not remind him of Oxford, and by way of reply he permitted his mouth to fall open while he stared in blank amazement at his questioner.

Despite our feeling that the countryside was too rich for our blood, we came to know it a great deal better—or at least in more detail—than did the polo players or the fliers or the members of the champion tennis team. For we were nearly all of us walkers. We walked the country roads for miles in every direction, talking every step of the way about ourselves or about our writing, or if we exhausted those two dearer subjects, we talked about whatever we were reading at the time. We read W. H. Auden and Yvor Winters and Wyndham Lewis and Joyce and Christopher Dawson. We read *The Wings of the Dove* (aloud!) and *The Cosmological Eye* and *The Last Puritan* and *In Dreams Begin Responsibilities.* (Of course, I am speaking only of books that didn't come within the range of the formal courses we were taking in the college.) On our walks through the country —never more than two or three of us together—we talked and talked, but I think none of us ever listened to anyone's talk but his own. Our talk seemed always to come to nothing. But our walking took us past the sheep farms and orchards and past some of the old stone farmhouses that are scattered throughout that township. It brought us to the old quarry from which most of the stone for the college buildings and for the farmhouses had been taken, and brought us to Quarry Chapel, a long since deserted and "deconsecrated" chapel, standing on a hill two miles from the college and symbolizing there the failure of Episcopalianism to take root among the Ohio country people.

Sometimes we walked along the railroad track through the valley at the foot of the college hill, and I remember more than once coming upon two or three tramps warming themselves by a little fire they had built or even cooking a meal over it. We would see them maybe a hundred yards ahead, and we would get close enough to hear them laughing and talking together. But as soon as they noticed us we would turn back and walk in the other direction, for we pitied them and felt that our presence was an intrusion. And yet, looking back on it, I remember how happy those tramps always seemed. And how sad and serious we were.

Jim and I headed due East from Gambier on the road to Coshocton and Pittsburgh. Darkness overtook us long before we ever reached the Pennsylvania state line. We were in Pittsburgh by about 9 P.M., and then there lay ahead of us the whole long night of driving. Nothing could have better suited our mood than the prospect of this ride through the dark, wooded countryside of Pennsylvania on that autumn night. This being before the days of the turnpike—or at least before its completion—the roads wound about the great domelike hills of that region and through the deep valleys in a way that answered some need we both felt. We spoke of it many times during the night, and Jim said he felt he knew for the first time the meaning of "verdurous glooms and winding mossy ways." The two of us were setting out on this trip not in search of the kind of quick success in the world that had so degraded our former friend in our eyes; we sought, rather, a taste—or foretaste—of "life's deeper and more real experience," the kind that dormitory life seemed to deprive us of. We expressed these yearnings in just those words that I have put in quotation marks, not feeling the need for any show of delicate restraint. We, at twenty, had no abhorrence of raw ideas or explicit statement. We didn't hesitate to say what we wanted to be and what we felt we must have in order to become that. We wanted to be writers, and we knew well enough that before we could write we had to have "mature and adult experience." And, by God, we *said* so to each other, there in the car as we sped through towns like Turtle Creek and Greensburg and Acme.

I have observed in recent years that boys the age we were then and with our inclinations tend to value ideas of this sort above all else. They are apt to find their own crude obsession with mere ideas the greatest barrier to producing the works of art they are after. I have observed this from the vantage ground of the college professor's desk, behind which the irony of fate has placed me from time to time. From there, I have also had the chance to observe something about *girls* of an artistic bent or temperament, and for that reason I am able to tell you more about the two girls we were going to see in New York than I could possibly have known then.

At the time—that is, during the dark hours of the drive East —each of us carried in his mind an image of the girl who had inspired him to make this journey. In each case, the image of the girl's face and form was more or less accurate. In my mind was the image of a brunette with dark eyes and a heart-shaped face. In Jim's was that of a blonde, somewhat above average height, with green eyes and perhaps a few freckles on her nose. That, in general, was how we pictured them, but neither of us would have been dogmatic about the accuracy of his picture. Perhaps Carol Crawford didn't have any freckles. Jim wasn't sure. And maybe her eyes were more blue than green. As for me, I wouldn't have contradicted anyone who said Nancy Gibault's face was actually slightly elongated, rather than heart-shaped, or that her hair had a decided reddish cast to it. Our impressions of this kind were only more or less accurate, and we would have been the first to admit it.

But as to the talent and the character and the original mind of the two glorious girls, we would have brooked no questioning of our concepts. Just after we passed through Acme, Pennsylvania, our talk turned from ourselves to these girls—from our inner yearnings for mature and adult experience to the particular objects toward which we were being led by these yearnings. We agreed that the quality we most valued in Nancy and Carol was their "critical" and "objective" view of life, their unwillingness to accept the standards of "the world." I remem-

ber telling Jim that Nancy Gibault could always take a genuinely "disinterested" view of any matter—"disinterested in the
best sense of the word." And Jim assured me that, whatever
else I might perceive about Carol, I would sense at once the
originality of her mind and "the absence of anything commonplace or banal in her intellectual makeup."

It seems hard to believe now, but that was how we spoke to
each other about our girls. That was what we thought we believed and felt about them then. And despite our change of
opinions by the time we headed back to Kenyon, despite our
complete and permanent disenchantment, despite their unkind
treatment of us—as worldly and as commonplace as could be—
I know now that those two girls were as near the concepts we
had of them to begin with as any two girls their age might be,
or should be. And I believe now that the decisions *they* made
about *us* were the right decisions for *them* to make. I have only
the vaguest notion of how Nancy Gibault has fared in later life.
I know only that she went back to St. Louis the following
spring and was married that summer to Lon Havemeyer. But
as for Carol Crawford, everybody with any interest in literary
matters knows what became of her. Her novels are read everywhere. They have even been translated into Javanese. She is, in
her way, even more successful than the boy who made the long
pull from Harvard College to Hollywood.

Probably I seem to be saying too much about things that I
understood only long after the events of my story. But the need
for the above digression seemed no less urgent to me than did
that concerning the former owner of our car. In his case, the
digression dealt mostly with events of a slightly earlier time.
Here it has dealt with a wisdom acquired at a much later time.
And now I find that I am still not quite finished with speaking
of that later time and wisdom. Before seeing me again in the car
that November night in 1939, picture me for just a moment—
much changed in appearance and looking at you through gold-
rimmed spectacles—behind the lectern in a classroom. I stand
before the class as a kind of journeyman writer, a type of whom
Trollope might have approved, but one who has known neither
the financial success of the facile Harvard boy nor the reputa-

tion of Carol Crawford. Yet this man behind the lectern is a
man who seems happy in the knowledge that he knows—or
thinks he knows—what he is about. And from behind his lectern he is saying that any story that is written in the form of a
memoir should give offense to no one, because before a writer
can make a person he has known fit into such a story—or any
story, for that matter—he must do more than change the real
name of that person. He must inevitably do such violence to
that person's character that the so-called original is forever lost
to the story.

The last lap of Jim's and my all-night drive was the toughest.
The night had begun as an unseasonably warm one. I recall
that there were even a good many insects splattered on our
windshield in the hours just after dark. But by the time we had
got through Pittsburgh the sky was overcast and the tempera-
ture had begun to drop. Soon after 1 A.M. we noticed the first
big, soft flakes of snow. I was driving at the time, and Jim was
doing most of the talking. I raised one finger from the steering
wheel to point out the snow to Jim, and he shook his head
unhappily. But he went on talking. We had maintained our
steady stream of talk during the first hours of the night partly
to keep whoever was at the wheel from going to sleep, but from
this point on it was more for the purpose of making us forget
the threatening weather. We knew that a really heavy snowstorm could throw our holiday schedule completely out of gear.
All night long we talked. Sometimes the snow fell thick and
fast, but there were times, too, when it stopped altogether.
There was a short period just before dawn when the snow
turned to rain—a cold rain, worse than the snow, since it began
to freeze on our windshield. By this time, however, we had
passed through Philadelphia and we knew that somehow or
other we would make it on to New York.

We had left Kenyon at four o'clock in the afternoon, and at
eight the next morning we came to the first traffic rotary outside New York, in New Jersey. Half an hour later we saw the
skyline of the city, and at the sight of it we both fell silent. I
think we were both conscious at that moment not so much of
having arrived at our destination as of having only then put

Kenyon College behind us. I remember feeling that if I glanced over my shoulder I might still see on the horizon the tower of Pierce Hall and the spires of Old Kenyon Dormitory. And in my mind's eye I saw the other Douglass House boys—all seven of them—still lingering on the stone steps of the front stoop, leaning against the iron railing and against one another, staring after us. But more than that, after the image had gone I realized suddenly that I had pictured not seven but *nine* figures there before the house, and that among the other faces I had glimpsed my own face and that of Jim Prewitt. It seemed to me that we had been staring after ourselves with the same fixed, brooding expression in our eyes that I saw in the eyes of the other boys.

Nancy Gibault was staying in a sort of girls' hotel, or rooming house, on 114th Street. Before she came down from her room that Thanksgiving morning, she kept me waiting in the lobby for nearly forty-five minutes. No doubt she had planned this as a way of preparing me for worse things to come. As I sat there, I had ample time to reflect upon various dire possibilities. I wondered if she had been out terribly late the night before and, if so, with whom. I thought of the possibility that she was angry with me for not letting her know what day I would get there. (I had had to wait on my check from home, and there had not been time to let her know exactly when we would arrive.) I reflected, even, that there was a remote chance she had not wanted me to come at all. What didn't occur to me was the possibility that *all* of these things were true. I sat in that dreary, overheated waiting room, still wearing my overcoat and holding my hat in my lap. When Nancy finally came down, she burst into laughter at the sight of me. I rose slowly from my chair and said angrily, "What are you laughing at? At how long I've waited?"

"No, my dear," she said, crossing the room to where I stood. "I was laughing at the way you were sitting there in your overcoat with your hat in your lap like a little boy."

"I'm sweating like a horse," I said, and began unbuttoning my coat. By this time Nancy was standing directly in front of me, and I leaned forward to kiss her. She drew back with an expression of revulsion on her face.

"Keep your coat on!" she commanded. Then she began giggling and backing away from me. "If you expect me to be seen with you," she said, "you'll go back to wherever you're staying and shave that fuzz off your lip."

For three weeks I had been growing my first mustache.

I had not yet been to the hotel where Jim and I planned to stay. It was a place that Jim knew about, only three or four blocks from where Nancy was living, and I now set out for it on foot, carrying my suitcase. Our car had broken down just after we came up out of the Holland Tunnel. It had been knocking fiercely for the last hour of the trip, and we learned from the garage man with whom we left it that the crankcase was broken. It seems we had burned out a bearing, because we had forgotten to put any oil in the crankcase. I don't think we realized at the time how lucky we were to find a garage open on Thanksgiving morning and, more than that, one that would have the car ready to run again by the following night.

After I had shaved, I went back to Nancy's place. She had gone upstairs again, but this time she did not keep me waiting so long. She came down wearing a small black hat and carrying a chesterfield coat. Back in St. Louis, she had seldom worn a hat when we went out together, and the sight of her in one now made me feel uncomfortable. We sat down together near the front bay window of that depressing room where I had waited so long, and we talked there for an hour, until it was time to meet Jim and Carol for lunch.

While we talked that morning, Nancy did not tell me that Lon Havemeyer was in town from St. Louis, much less that she had spent all her waking hours with him during the past week. I could not have expected her to tell me at once that she was now engaged to marry him, instead of me, but I did feel afterward that she could have begun at once by telling me that she had been seeing Lon and that he was still in town. It would have kept me from feeling quite so much at sea during the first hours I was with her. Lon was at least seven or eight years older than Nancy, and for five or six years he had been escorting debutantes to parties in St. Louis. His family were of German origin and were as new to society there as members of Nancy's family were old to it. The Havemeyers were also as rich nowadays as the Gibaults were poor. Just after Nancy graduated from Mary Institute, Lon had begun paying her attentions. They went about together a good deal while I was away at college, but between Nancy and me it had always been a great joke. To us, Lon was the essence of all that we were determined to get away from there at home. I don't know what he was really like. I had heard an older cousin of Nancy's say that Lon Havemeyer managed to give the impression of not being dry behind the ears but that the truth was he was "as slick as a newborn babe." But I never exchanged two sentences with him in my life—not even during the miserable day and a half that I was to tag along with him and Nancy in New York.

It may be that Nancy had not known that she was in love with Lon or that she was going to marry him until she saw me there, with the fuzz on my upper lip, that morning. Certainly I must have been an awful sight. Even after I had shaved my mustache, I was still the seedy-looking undergraduate in search of "mature experience." It must have been a frightful embarrassment to her to have to go traipsing about the city with me on Thanksgiving Day. My hair was long, my clothes, though quite genteel, were unpressed, and even rather dirty, and for some reason I was wearing a pair of heavy brogans. Nancy had never seen me out of St. Louis before, and since she had seen me last, she had seen Manhattan. To be fair to her, though, she had seen something more important than that. She had, for better or for worse, seen herself.

We had lunch with Jim and Carol at a little joint over near Columbia, and it was only after we had left them that Nancy told me Lon Havemeyer was in town and waiting that very moment to go with us to the Metropolitan Museum. I burst out laughing when she told me, and she laughed a little, too. I don't remember when I fully realized the significance of Lon's presence in New York. It wasn't that afternoon, or that night, even. It was sometime during the next day, which was Friday. I suppose that I should have realized it earlier and that I just wouldn't. From the time we met Lon on the museum steps, he was with us almost continuously until the last half hour before I took my leave of Nancy the following night. Sometimes I would laugh to myself at the thought of this big German oaf's trailing along with us through the galleries in the afternoon and then to the ballet that night. But I was also angry at Nancy from the start for having let him horn in on our holiday together, and at various moments I pulled her aside and expressed my anger. She would only look at me helplessly, shrug, and say, "I couldn't help it. You really have got to try to see that I couldn't help it."

After the ballet, we joined a group of people who seemed to be business acquaintances of Lon's and went to a Russian nightclub—on Fourteenth Street, I think. (I don't know exactly where it was, for I was lost in New York and kept asking Nancy what part of town we were in.) The next morning, about ten, Nancy and I took the subway down to the neighborhood of Fifty-seventh Street, where we met Lon for breakfast. Later we looked at pictures in some of the galleries. I don't know what became of the afternoon. We saw an awful play that night. I know it was awful, but I don't remember what it was. The events of that second day are almost entirely blotted from my memory. I only know that the mixture of anger and humiliation I felt kept me from ducking out long before the evening was over—a mixture of anger and humiliation and something else, something that I had begun to feel the day before when Nancy and I were having lunch with Jim and Carol Crawford.

Friday night, I was somehow or other permitted to take Nancy home alone from the theater. We went in a taxi, and neither of us spoke until a few blocks before we reached 114th Street. Finally I said, "Nancy." And Nancy burst into tears.

"You won't understand, and you will never forgive me," she said through her tears, "but I am so terribly in love with him."

I didn't say anything till we had gone another block. Then I said, "How have things gone at the art school?"

Nancy blew her nose and turned her face to me, as she had

not done when she spoke before. "Well, I've learned that I'm not an artist. They've made me see that."

"Oh," I said. Then, "Does that make it necessary to—"

"It makes everything in the world look different. If I could only have known in time to write you."

"When did you know?"

"I don't know. I don't know when I knew."

"Well, it's a good thing you came to New York," I said. "You almost made a bad mistake."

"No," she said. "You mustn't think I feel that about you."

"Oh, not about me," I said quickly. "About being an artist. When we were at lunch yesterday, you know, with Jim and his girl, it came over me suddenly that you weren't an artist. Just by looking at you I could tell."

"What a cruel thing to say," she said quietly. All the emotion had gone out of her voice. "Only a child could be so cruel," she said.

When the taxi stopped in front of her place, I opened the door for her but didn't get out, and neither of us said goodbye. I told the driver to wait until she was inside and then gave him the address of my hotel. When, five minutes later, I was getting out and paying the driver, I didn't know how much to tip him. I gave him fifteen cents. He sat with his motor running for a moment, and then, just before he pulled away, he threw the dime and the nickel out on the sidewalk and called out to me at the top of his voice, "You brat!"

The meeting between Nancy and Carol was supposed to be one of the high points of our trip. The four of us ate lunch together that first day sitting in the front booth of a little place that was crowded with Columbia University students. Because this was at noon on Thanksgiving Day, probably not too many restaurants in that neighborhood were open. But I felt that every student in the dark little lunchroom was exulting in his freedom from a certain turkey dinner somewhere, and from some particular family gathering. We four had to sit in the very front booth, which was actually no booth at all but a table and two benches set right in the window. Some people happened to be getting up from that table just as we came in and Carol, who had brought us there, said, "Quick! We must take this one." Nancy had raised up on her tiptoes and craned her neck, looking for a booth not quite so exposed.

"I think there may be some people leaving back there," she said.

"No," said Carol in a whisper. "Quick! In here." And when we had sat down, she said, "There are some dreadful people I know back there. I'd rather die than have to talk to them."

Nancy and I sat with our backs almost against the plate-glass window. There was scarcely room for the two of us on the bench we shared. I am sure the same was true for Jim and Carol, and they faced us across a table so narrow that when our sandwiches were brought, the four plates could only be arranged in one straight row. There wasn't much conversation while we ate, though Jim and I tried to make a few jokes about our drive through the snow and about how the car broke down. Once, in the middle of something Jim was saying, Carol suddenly ducked her head almost under the table. "Oh, God!" she gasped. "Just my luck!" Jim sat up straighter and started peering out into the street. Nancy and I looked over our shoulders. There was a man walking along the sidewalk on the other side of the broad street.

"You mean that man way over there?" Nancy asked.

"Holy God, yes," hissed Carol. "Do please stop gaping at him."

Nancy giggled. "Is he dreadful, too?" she asked.

Carol straightened and took a sip of her coffee. "No, he's not exactly dreadful. He's the critic Melville Bland." And after a moment: "He's a full professor at Columbia. I was supposed to have dinner today with him and his stupid wife—she's the playwright Dorothy Lewis and really *awfully* stupid—at some chichi place in the East Sixties, and I told them an awful lie about my going out to Connecticut for the day. I'd rather be shot than talk to either of them for five minutes."

I was sitting directly across the table from Carol. While we were there, I had ample opportunity to observe her, without her seeming to notice that I was doing so. My opportunity came each time anyone entered the restaurant or left it. For nobody could approach the glass-front door, either from the street or from inside, without Carol's fastening her eyes upon that person and seeming to take in every detail of his or her appearance. Here, I said to myself, is a real novelist observing people—*objectively* and *critically*. And I was favorably impressed by her obvious concern with literary personages; it showed how committed she was to a life of writing. Carol seemed to me just the girl that Jim had described. Her blond hair was not really flaxen. (It was golden, which is prettier but which doesn't sound as interesting as flaxen.) It was long and carelessly arranged. I believe Jim was right about its being fixed in a knot on the back of her neck. Her whole appearance showed that she cared as little about it as either Jim or I did about ours . . . Perhaps *this* was what one's girl really ought to look like.

When we got up to leave, Nancy lingered at the table to put on fresh lipstick. Carol wandered to the newspaper stand beside the front door. Jim and I went together to pay our bills at the counter. As we waited for our change, I said an amiable, pointless "Well?"

"Well what?" Jim said petulantly.

"Well, they've met," I said.

"Yeah," he said. "They've met." He grinned and gave his head a little shake. "But Nancy's just another society girl, old man," he said. "I had expected something more than that." He suddenly looked very unhappy, and rather angry, too. I felt the blood rising in my cheeks and knew in a moment that I had turned quite red. Jim was much heavier than I was, and I would have been no match for him in any real fight, but my impulse was to hit him squarely in the face with my open hand. He must have guessed what I had in mind, for with one movement he jerked off his horn-rimmed glasses and jammed them into the pocket of his jacket.

At that moment, the man behind the counter said, "Do you want this change or not, fellows?"

We took our change and then glared at each other again. I had now had time to wonder what had come over Jim. Out of the corner of my eye I caught a glimpse of Carol at the news-stand and took in for the first time, in that quick glance, that she was wearing huaraches and a peasant skirt and blouse, and that what she now had thrown around her shoulders was not a topcoat but a long green cape. "At least," I said aloud to Jim, "Nancy's not the usual bohemian. She's not the run-of-the-mill arty type."

I fully expected Jim to take a swing at me after that. But, instead, a peculiar expression came over his face and he stood for a moment staring at Carol over there by the newsstand. I recognized the expression as the same one I had seen on his face sometimes in the classroom when his interpretation of a line of poetry had been questioned. He was reconsidering.

When Nancy joined us, Jim spoke to her very politely. But once we were out in the street there was no more conversation between the two couples. We parted at the first street corner, and in parting there was no mention of our joining forces again. That was the last time I ever saw Carol Crawford, and I am sure that Jim and Nancy never met again. At the corner, Nancy and I turned in the direction of her place on 114th Street. We walked for nearly a block without either of us speaking. Then I said, "Since when did you take to wearing a hat everywhere?"

Nancy didn't answer. When we got to her place, she went upstairs for a few minutes, and it was when she came down again that she told me Lon Havemeyer was going to join us at the Metropolitan. Looking back on it, I feel that it may have been only when I asked that question about her hat that Nancy decided definitely about how much Lon and I were going to be seeing of each other during the next thirty-six hours. It is possible, at least, that she called him on the telephone while she was upstairs.

I didn't know about it then, of course, but the reception that Jim Prewitt found awaiting him that morning had, in a sense, been worse even than mine. I didn't know about it and Jim didn't tell me until the following spring, just a few weeks before our graduation from Kenyon. By that time, it all seemed to us

like something in the remote past, and Jim made no effort to
give me a complete picture of his two days with Carol. The
thing he said most about was his reception upon arriving.

He must have arrived at Carol's apartment, somewhere on
Morningside Heights, at almost the same moment that I arrived at Nancy's place. He was not, however, kept waiting for
forty-five minutes. He was met at the door by a man whom he
described as a flabby middle-aged man wearing a patch over
one eye, a T-shirt, and denim trousers. The man did not intro-
duce himself or ask for Jim's name. He only jerked his head to
one side, to indicate that Jim should come in. Even before the
door opened, Jim had heard strains of the Brandenburg Concerto from within. Now, as he stepped into the little entryway,
the music seemed almost deafening, and when he was led into
the room where the phonograph was playing, he could not
resist the impulse to make a wry face and clap his hands over
his ears.

But although there were half a dozen people in the room,
nobody saw the gesture or the face he made. The man with the
patch over his eye had preceded him into the room, and everyone else was sitting with eyes cast down or actually closed.
Carol sat on the floor tailor fashion, with an elbow on each
knee and her face in her hands. The man with the patch went to
her and touched the sole of one of her huaraches with his foot.
When she looked up and saw Jim, she gave him no immediate
sign of recognition. First she eyed him from head to foot with
an air of disapproval. Jim's attire that day, unlike my own, was
extremely conventional (though I won't say he ever looked conventional for a moment). At Kenyon, he was usually the most
slovenly and ragged-looking of us all. He really went about in
tatters, sometimes even with the soles hanging loose from his
shoes. But in his closet, off our room, there were always to be
found his "good" shoes, his "good" suit, his "good" coat, his
"good" hat, all of which had been purchased for him at Brooks
Brothers by his mother. Today he had on his "good" things.
Probably it was that that made Carol stare at him as she did.
At last she gave him a friendly but slightly casual smile, placed
a silencing forefinger over her lips, and motioned for him to

come sit down beside her and listen to the deafening tones of the concerto.

While the automatic phonograph was changing records, Carol introduced Jim to the other people in the room. She introduced him and everyone else—men and women alike—by their surnames only: "Prewitt, this is Carlson. Meyer, this is Prewitt." Everyone nodded, and the music began again at the same volume. After the Bach there was a Mozart symphony. Finally Jim, without warning, seized Carol by the wrist, forcibly led her from the room, and closed the door after them. He was prepared to tell her precisely what he thought of his reception, but he had no chance to. "Listen to me," Carol began at once—belligerently, threateningly, all but shaking her finger in his face. "I have sold my novel. It was definitely accepted three days ago and is going to be published in the spring. And two sections from it are going to be printed as stories in the *Partisan Review.*"

From that moment, Jim and Carol were no more alone than Nancy and I were. Nearly everywhere they went, they went with the group that had been in Carol's apartment that morning. After lunch with us that first noon, they rejoined the same party at someone else's apartment, down in Greenwich Village. When Jim told me about it, he said he could never be sure whose apartment he was in, for they always behaved just as they did at Carol's. He said that once or twice he even found himself answering a knock at the door in some strange apartment and jerking his head at whoever stood outside. The man with the patch over his eye turned out to be a musicologist and composer. The others in the party were writers whose work Jim had read in New Directions anthologies and in various little magazines, but they seemed to have no interest in anything he had to say about what they had written, and he noticed that their favorite way of disparaging any piece of writing was to say, "It's *so* naïve, *so* undergraduate." After Jim got our car from the garage late Friday afternoon, they all decided to drive to New Jersey to see some "established writer" over there, but when they arrived at his house the "established writer" would not receive them.

Jim said there were actually a few times when he managed to get Carol away from her friends. But her book—the book that had been accepted by a publisher—was Carol's Lon Have-meyer, and her book was always with them.

Poor Carol Crawford! How unfair it is to describe her as she was that Thanksgiving weekend in 1939. Ever since she was a little girl on a dairy farm in Wisconsin she had dreamed of becoming a writer and going to live in New York City. She had not merely dreamed of it. She had worked toward it every waking hour of her life, taking jobs after school in the wintertime, and full-time jobs in the summer, always saving the money to put herself through the state university. She had made herself the best student—the prize pupil—in every grade of grammar school and high school. At the university she had managed to win every scholarship in sight. Through all those years she had had but one ambition, and yet I could not have met her at a worse moment in her life. Poor girl, she had just learned that she *was* a writer.

Driving to Boston on Saturday, Jim and I took turns at the wheel again. But now there was no talk about ourselves or about much of anything else. One of us drove while the other slept. Before we reached Boston, in mid-afternoon, it was snowing again. By night, there was a terrible blizzard in Boston.

As soon as we arrived, Jim's father announced that he would not hear of our trying to drive back to Kenyon in such weather and in such a car. Mrs. Prewitt got on the telephone and obtained a train schedule that would start us on our way early the next morning and put us in Cleveland sometime the next night. (From Cleveland we would take a bus to Gambier.) After dinner at the Prewitts' house, I went with Jim over to Cambridge to see some of his prep-school friends who were still at Harvard. The dinner with his parents had been painful enough, since he and I were hardly speaking to each other, but the evening with him and his friends was even worse for me. In the room of one of these friends, they spent the time drinking beer and talking about the undergraduate politics at Harvard and about the Shelley Poetry Prize. One of the friends was editor of the *Crimson,* I believe, and another was editor of the *Advocate* —or perhaps he was just on the staff. I sat in the corner pretending to read old copies of the *Advocate.* It was the first time I had been to Boston or to Cambridge, and ordinarily I would have been interested in forming my own impressions of how people like the Prewitts lived and of what Harvard students were like. But, as things were, I only sat cursing the fate that had made it necessary for me to come on to Boston instead of returning directly to Kenyon. That is, my own money having been exhausted, I was dependent upon the money Jim would get from his parents to pay for the return trip.

Shortly before seven o'clock Sunday morning, I followed Jim down two flights of stairs from his room on the third floor of his family's house. A taxi was waiting for us in the street outside. We were just barely going to make the train. In the hall I shook hands with each of his parents, and he kissed them goodbye. We dashed out the front door and down the steps to the street. Just as we were about to climb into the taxi, Mrs. Prewitt came rushing out, bareheaded and without a wrap, calling to us that we had forgotten to leave the key to the car, which was parked there in front of the house. I dug down into my pocket and pulled out the key along with a pocketful of change. But as I turned back toward Mrs. Prewitt I stumbled on the curb, and the key and the change went flying in every direction and were lost from sight in the deep snow that lay on the ground that morning. Jim and Mrs. Prewitt and I began to search for the key, but Mr. Prewitt called from the doorway that we should go ahead, that we would miss our train. We hopped in the taxi, and it pulled away. When I looked back through the rear window I saw Mrs. Prewitt still searching in the snow and Mr. Prewitt moving slowly down the steps from the house, shaking his head.

On the train that morning Jim and I didn't exchange a word or a glance. We sat in the same coach but in different seats, and we did not go into the diner together for lunch. It wasn't until almost dinnertime that the coach became so crowded that I had either to share my seat with a stranger or to go and sit beside

Jim. The day had been long, I had done all the thinking I
wanted to do about the way things had turned out in New
York. Further, toward the middle of the afternoon I had begun
writing in my notebook, and I now had several pages of uncom-
monly fine prose fiction, which I did not feel averse to reading
aloud to someone.

I sat down beside Jim and noticed at once that *his* notebook
was open, too. On the white, unlined page that lay open in his
lap I saw the twenty or thirty lines of verse he had been working on. It was in pencil, quite smudged from many erasures,
and was set down in Jim's own vigorous brand of progressive-
school printing.

"What do you have there?" I said indifferently.

"You want to hear it?" he said with equal indifference.

"I guess so," I said. I glanced over at the poem's title, which
was "For the Schoolboys of Douglass House," and immediately
wished I had not got myself into this. The one thing I didn't
want to hear was a preachment from him on his "mature experience" over the holiday. He began reading, and what he read
was very nearly this (I have copied this part of the poem down
as it later appeared in *Hika,* our undergraduate magazine at
Kenyon):

> Today while we are admissibly ungrown,
> Now when we are each half boy, half man,
> Let us each contrast himself with himself,
> And weighing the halves well, let us each regard
> In what manner he has not become a man.

> Today let us expose, and count as good,
> What is mature. And childish peccadillos
> Let us laugh out of our didactic house—
> The rident punishment one with reward
> For him bringing lack of manliness to light.

But I could take no more than the first two stanzas. And I
knew how to stop him. I touched my hand to his sleeve and

whispered, "Shades of W. B. Yeats." And I commenced reciting:

> Now that we're almost settled in our house
> I'll name the friends that cannot sup with us
> Beside a fire of turf in th' ancient tower . . .

Before I knew it, Jim had snatched my notebook from my hands, and began reading aloud from it:

> She had told him—Janet Monet had, for some inscrutable reason which she herself could not fathom, and which, had he known—as she so positively and with such likely assurance thought he knew—that if he came on to New York in the weeks ensuing her so unbenign father's funeral, she could not entertain him alone. . . .

Then he closed my notebook and returned it to me. "I can put it into rhyme for you, Mr. Henry James," he said. "It goes like this:

> She knew that he knew that her father was dead.
> And she knew that he knew what a life he had led—

While he was reciting, with a broad grin on his face and his eyes closed, I left him and went up into the diner to eat dinner. The next time we met was in the smoking compartment, at eight o'clock, an hour before we got into Cleveland.

It was I who wandered into the smoking compartment first. I went there not to smoke, for neither Jim nor I started smoking till after we left college, but in the hope that it might be empty, which, oddly enough, it was at that moment. I sat down by the window, at the end of the long leather seat. But I had scarcely settled myself there and begun staring out into the dark when the green curtain in the doorway was drawn back. I saw the light it let in reflected in the windowpane, and I turned around. Jim was standing in the doorway with the green curtain draped back over his head and shoulders. I don't know why, but it was only then that I realized that Jim, too, had been jilted. Perhaps it was the expression on his face—an expression of disappointment at not finding the smoking compartment empty, at being deprived of his one last chance for solitude before returning to Douglass House. And now—more than I had all day—I hated the sight of him. My lips parted to speak, but he literally took the sarcastic words out of my mouth.

"Ah, you'll get over it, little friend," he said.

Suddenly I was off the leather seat and lunging toward him. And he had snatched off his glasses, with the same swift gesture he had used in the restaurant, and tossed them onto the seat. The train was moving at great speed and must have taken a sharp turn just then. I felt myself thrown forward with more force than I could possibly have mustered in the three or four steps I took. When I hit him, it was not with my fists, or even my open hands, but with my shoulder, as though I was blocking in a game of football. He staggered back through the doorway and into the narrow passage, and for a moment the green curtain separated us. Then he came back. He came at me just as I had come at him, with his arms half folded over his chest. The blow he struck me with his shoulders sent me into the corner of the leather seat again. But I, too, came back.

Apparently neither of us felt any impulse to strike the other with his fist or to take hold and wrestle. On the contrary, I think we felt a mutual abhorrence and revulsion toward any kind of physical contact between us and if our fight had taken any other form than the one it did, I think that murder would almost certainly have been committed in the smoking compartment that night. We shoved each other about the little room for nearly half an hour, with ever-increasing violence, our purpose always seeming to be to get the other through the narrow doorway and into the passage—out of sight behind the green curtain.

From time to time, after our first exchange of shoves, various would-be smokers appeared in the doorway. But they invariably beat a quick retreat. At last one of them found the conductor and sent him in to stop us. By then it was all over, however.

The conductor stood in the doorway a moment before he spoke, and we stared at him from opposite corners of the room. He was an old man with an inquiring and rather friendly look on his face. He looked like a man who might have fought game-cocks in his day, and I think he must have waited that moment in the doorway in the hope of seeing something of the spectacle that had been described to him. But by then each of us was drenched in sweat, and I know from a later examination of my arms and chest and back that I was covered with bruises.

When the old conductor was satisfied that there was not going to be another rush from either of us, he glanced about the room to see if we had done any damage. We had not even upset the spittoon. Even Jim's glasses were safe on the leather seat. "If you boys want to stay on this train," the conductor said finally, "you'll hightail it back to your places before I pull that emergency cord."

We were only thirty minutes out of Cleveland then, but when I got back to my seat in the coach I fell asleep at once. It was a blissful kind of sleep, despite the fact that I woke up every five minutes or so and peered out into the night to see if I could see the lights of Cleveland yet. Each time, as I dropped off to sleep again, I would say to myself what a fine sort of sleep it was, and each time it seemed that the wheels of the train were saying: *Not yet, not yet, not yet.*

After Cleveland there was a four-hour ride by bus to Gam-bier. Sitting side by side in the bus, Jim and I kept up a continu-ous flow of uninhibited and even confidential talk about our-selves, about our writing, and even about the possibility of going to graduate school next year if the army didn't take us. I don't think we were silent a moment until we were off the bus and, as we paced along the Middle Path, came in sight of Douglass House. It was 1 A.M., but through the bare branches of the trees we saw a light burning in the front dormer of our room. Immediately our talk was hushed, and we stopped dead still. Then, though we were as yet two hundred feet from the house and there was a blanket of snow on the ground, we began running on tiptoe and whispering our conjectures about what was going on in our room. We took the steps of the front stoop two at a time, and when we opened the front door, we were met by the odor of something cooking—bacon, or perhaps ham. We went up the long flight to the second floor on tiptoe, being careful not to bump our suitcases against the wall or the banisters. The door to our room was the first one at the top of the stairs. Jim seized the knob and threw the door open. The seven whom we had left lolling around the stoop on Wednesday were sprawled about our big room in various stages of undress, and all of them were eating. Bruce Gordon and Bill Anderson were in the center of the room, leaning over my hot plate.

Jim and I pushed through the doorway and stood on the doorstep looking down at them. I have never before or since seen seven such sober—no, such frightened-looking—people. Most eyes were directed at me, because it was my hot plate. But when Jim stepped down into the room, the two boys lounging back on his bed quickly stood up.

I remember my first feeling of outrage. The sacred privacy of that room under the eaves of Douglass House had been violated; this on top of what had happened in New York seemed for a moment more than flesh and blood could bear. Then, all of a sudden, Jim Prewitt and I began to laugh. Jim dropped his suitcase and went over to where the cooking was going on and said, "Give me something to eat. I haven't eaten all day."

I stood for a while leaning against the wall just inside the door. I was thinking of the tramps we had seen cooking down along the railroad track in the valley. Finally I said, "What a bunch of hoboes!" Everyone laughed—a little nervously, perhaps, but with a certain heartiness, too.

I continued to stand just inside the door, and presently I leaned my head against the wall and shut my eyes. My head swam for a moment. I had the sensation of being on the train again, swaying from side to side. It was hard to believe that I was really back in Douglass House and that the trip was over. I don't know how long I stood there that way. I was dead for sleep, and as I stood there with my eyes closed I could still hear the train wheels saying *Not yet, not yet, not yet.*

A Sudden Trip Home in the Spring

by Alice Walker

For the Wellesley Class

Sarah walked slowly off the tennis court, fingering the back of her head, feeling the sturdy dark hair that grew there. She was popular. As she walked along the path toward Talfinger Hall her friends fell into place around her. They formed a warm jostling group of six. Sarah, because she was taller than the rest, saw the messenger first.

"Miss Davis," he said, standing still until the group came abreast of him, "I've got a telegram for ye." Brian was Irish and always quite respectful. He stood with his cap in his hand until Sarah took the telegram. Then he gave a nod that included all the young ladies before he turned away. He was young and good-looking, though annoyingly servile, and Sarah's friends twittered.

"Well, open it!" someone cried, for Sarah stood staring at the yellow envelope, turning it over and over in her hand.

"Look at her," said one of the girls, "isn't she beautiful! Such eyes, and hair, and *skin*!"

Sarah's tall, caplike hair framed a face of soft brown angles, high cheekbones and large dark eyes. Her eyes enchanted her friends because they always seemed to know more, and to find more of life amusing, or sad, than Sarah cared to tell.

Her friends often teased Sarah about her beauty; they loved dragging her out of her room so that their boyfriends, naive and worldly young men from Princeton and Yale, could see her. They never guessed she found this distasteful. She was gentle with her friends, and her outrage at their tactlessness did not show. She was most often inclined to pity them, though embarrassment sometimes drove her to fraudulent expressions. Now she smiled and raised eyes and arms to heaven. She acknowledged their unearned curiosity as a mother endures the prying impatience of a child. Her friends beamed love and envy upon her as she tore open the telegram.

"He's dead," she said.

Her friends reached out for the telegram, their eyes on Sarah.

"It's her father," one of them said softly. "He died yesterday. Oh, Sarah," the girl whimpered, "I'm so sorry!"

"Me too." "So am I." "Is there anything we can do?"

But Sarah had walked away, head high and neck stiff.

"So graceful!" one of her friends said.

"Like a proud gazelle," said another. Then they all trooped to their dormitories to change for supper.

Talfinger Hall was a pleasant dorm. The common room just off the entrance had been made into a small modern art gallery with some very good original paintings, lithographs and collages. Pieces were constantly being stolen. Some of the girls could not resist an honest-to-God Chagall, signed (in the plate) by his own hand, though they could have afforded to purchase one from the gallery in town. Sarah Davis's room was next door to the gallery, but her walls were covered with inexpensive Gauguin reproductions, a Rubens ("The Head of a Negro"), a Modigliani and a Picasso. There was a full wall of her own drawings, all of black women. She found black men impossible to draw or to paint; she could not bear to trace defeat onto blank pages. Her women figures were matronly, massive of arm, with a weary victory showing in their eyes. Surrounded by Sarah's drawings was a red SNCC poster of a man holding a small girl whose face nestled in his shoulder. Sarah often felt she was the little girl whose face no one could see.

To leave Talfinger even for a few days filled Sarah with fear. Talfinger was her home now; it suited her better than any home she'd ever known. Perhaps she loved it because in winter there was a fragrant fireplace and snow outside her window. When hadn't she dreamed of fireplaces that really warmed, snow that almost pleasantly froze? Georgia seemed far away as she packed; she did not want to leave New York, where, her grand-

A Sudden Trip Home in the Spring

father had liked to say, "the devil hung out and caught young gals by the front of their dresses." He had always believed the South the best place to live on earth (never mind that certain people invariably marred the landscape), and swore he expected to die no more than a few miles from where he had been born. There was tenacity even in the gray frame house he lived in, and in scrawny animals on his farm who regularly reproduced. He was the first person Sarah wanted to see when she got home.

There was a knock on the door of the adjoining bathroom, and Sarah's suite mate entered, a loud Bach concerto just finishing behind her. At first she stuck just her head into the room, but seeing Sarah fully dressed she trudged in and plopped down on the bed. She was a heavy blond girl with large milk-white legs. Her eyes were small and her neck usually gray with grime.

"My, don't you look gorgeous," she said.

"Ah, Pam," said Sarah, waving her hand in disgust. In Georgia she knew that even to Pam she would be just another ordinarily attractive *colored* girl. In Georgia there were a million girls better looking. Pam wouldn't know that, of course; she'd never been to Georgia; she'd never even seen a black person to speak to, that is, before she met Sarah. One of her first poetic observations about Sarah was that she was "a poppy in a field of winter roses." She had found it weird that Sarah did not own more than one coat.

"Say listen, Sarah," said Pam, "I heard about your father. I'm sorry. I really am."

"Thanks," said Sarah.

"Is there anything we can do? I thought, well, maybe you'd want my father to get somebody to fly you down. He'd go himself but he's taking Mother to Madeira this week. You wouldn't have to worry about trains and things."

Pamela's father was one of the richest men in the world, though no one ever mentioned it. Pam only alluded to it at times of crisis, when a friend might benefit from the use of a private plane, train, or ship; or, if someone wanted to study the characteristics of a totally secluded village, island or mountain,

she might offer one of theirs. Sarah could not comprehend such
wealth, and was always annoyed because Pam didn't look more
like a billionaire's daughter. A billionaire's daughter, Sarah
thought, should really be less horsey and brush her teeth more
often.

"Gonna tell me what you're brooding about?" asked Pam.

Sarah stood in front of the radiator, her fingers resting on the
window seat. Down below girls were coming up the hill from
supper.

"I'm thinking," she said, "of the child's duty to his parents
after they are dead."

"Is that all?"

"Do you know," asked Sarah, "about Richard Wright and
his father?"

Pamela frowned. Sarah looked down at her.

"Oh, I forgot," she said with a sigh, "they don't teach
Wright here. The poshest school in the U.S., and the girls come
out ignorant." She looked at her watch, saw she had twenty
minutes before her train. "Really," she said almost inaudibly,
"why Tears Eliot, Ezratic Pound, and even Sara Teacake, and
no Wright?" She and Pamela thought e.e. cummings very
clever with his perceptive spelling of great literary names.

"Is he a poet then?" asked Pam. She adored poetry, all poetry. Half of America's poetry she had, of course, not read, for
the simple reason that she had never heard of it.

"No," said Sarah, "he wasn't a poet." She felt weary. "He
was a man who wrote, a man who had trouble with his father."
She began to walk about the room, and came to stand below the
picture of the old man and the little girl.

"When he was a child," she continued, "his father ran off
with another woman, and one day when Richard and his
mother went to ask him for money to buy food he laughingly
rejected them. Richard, being very young, thought his father
Godlike. Big, omnipotent, unpredictable, undependable and
cruel. Entirely in control of his universe. Just like a god. But,
many years later, after Wright had become a famous writer, he
went down to Mississippi to visit his father. He found, instead
of God, just an old watery-eyed field hand, bent from plowing,

his teeth gone, smelling of manure. Richard realized that the most daring thing his 'God' had done was run off with that other woman."

"So?" asked Pam. "What 'duty' did he feel he owed the old man?"

"So," said Sarah, "that's what Wright wondered as he peered into that old shifty-eyed Mississippi Negro face. What was the duty of the son of a destroyed man? The son of a man whose vision had stopped at the edge of fields that weren't even his. Who was Wright without his father? Was he Wright the great writer? Wright the Communist? Wright the French farmer? Wright whose white wife could never accompany him to Mississippi? Was he, in fact, still his father's son? Or was he freed by his father's desertion to be nobody's son, to be his own father? Could he disavow his father and live? And if so, live as what? As whom? And for what purpose?"

"Well," said Pam, swinging her hair over her shoulders and squinting her small eyes, "if his father rejected him I don't see why Wright even bothered to go see him again. From what you've said, Wright earned the freedom to be whoever he wanted to be. To a strong man a father is not essential."

"Maybe not," said Sarah, "but Wright's father was one faulty door in a house of many ancient rooms. Was that one faulty door to shut him off forever from the rest of the house? That was the question. And though he answered this question eloquently in his work, where it really counted, one can only wonder if he was able to answer it satisfactorily—or at all—in his life."

"You're thinking of his father more as a symbol of something, aren't you?" asked Pam.

"I suppose," said Sarah, taking a last look around her room. "I see him as a door that refused to open, a hand that was always closed. A fist."

Pamela walked with her to one of the college limousines, and in a few minutes she was at the station. The train to the city was just arriving.

"Have a nice trip," said the middle-aged driver courteously, as she took her suitcase from him. But for about the thousandth time since she'd seen him, he winked at her.

Once away from her friends she did not miss them. The school was all they had in common. How could they ever know her if they were not allowed to know Wright, she wondered. She was interesting, "beautiful," only because they had no idea what made her, charming only because they had no idea from where she came. And where they came from, though she glimpsed it—in themselves and in F. Scott Fitzgerald—she was never to enter. She hadn't the inclination or the proper ticket.

2

Her father's body was in Sarah's old room. The bed had been taken down to make room for the flowers and chairs and casket. Sarah looked for a long time into the face, as if to find some answer to her questions written there. It was the same face, a dark Shakespearean head framed by gray, woolly hair and split almost in half by a short, gray mustache. It was a completely silent face, a shut face. But her father's face also looked fat, stuffed, and ready to burst. He wore a navy-blue suit, white shirt and black tie. Sarah bent and loosened the tie. Tears started behind her shoulder blades but did not reach her eyes.

"There's a rat here under the casket," she called to her brother, who apparently did not hear her, for he did not come in. She was alone with her father, as she had rarely been when he was alive. When he was alive she had avoided him.

"Where's that girl at?" her father would ask. "Done closed herself up in her room again," he would answer himself.

For Sarah's mother had died in her sleep one night. Just gone to bed tired and never got up. And Sarah had blamed her father.

Stare the rat down, thought Sarah, surely that will help. *Perhaps it doesn't matter whether I misunderstood or never understood.*

"We moved so much looking for crops, a place to *live,*" her father had moaned, accompanied by Sarah's stony silence. "The moving killed her. And now we have a real house, with *four* rooms, and a mailbox on the *porch,* and it's too late. She gone. *She* ain't here to see it." On very bad days her father would not eat at all. At night he did not sleep.

Whatever had made her think she knew what love was or was not?

Here she was, Sarah Davis, immersed in Camusian philosophy, versed in many languages, a poppy, of all things, among winter roses. But before she became a poppy she was a native Georgian sunflower, but still had not spoken the language they both knew. Not to him.

Stare the rat down, she thought, and did. The rascal dropped his bold eyes and slunk away. Sarah felt she had, at least, accomplished something.

Why did she have to see the picture of her mother, the one on the mantel among all the religious doodads, come to life? Her mother had stood stout against the years, clean gray braids shining across the top of her head, her eyes snapping, protective. Talking to her father.

"He called you out your name, we'll leave this place today. Not tomorrow. That be too late. Today!" Her mother was magnificent in her quick decisions.

"But what about your garden, the children, the change of schools?" Her father would be holding, most likely, the wide brim of his hat in nervously twisting fingers.

"He called you out your name, we go!"

And go they would. Who knew exactly where, before they moved? Another soundless place, walls falling down, roofing gone; another face to please without leaving too much of her father's pride at his feet. But to Sarah then, no matter with what alacrity her father moved, foot-dragging alone was visible.

The moving killed her, her father had said, *but the moving was also love.*

Did it matter now that often he had threatened their lives with the rage of his despair? That once he had spanked the crying baby violently, who later died of something else altogether . . . and that the next day they moved?

"No," said Sarah aloud, "I don't think it does."

"Huh?" It was her brother, tall, wiry, black, deceptively

calm. As a child he'd had an irrepressible temper. As a grown man he was tensely smooth, like a river that any day will over-flow its bed.

He had chosen a dull gray casket. Sarah wished for red. Was it Dylan Thomas who had said something grand about the dead offering "deep, dark defiance"? It didn't matter; there were more ways to offer defiance than with a red casket.

"I was just thinking," said Sarah, "that with us Mama and Daddy were saying NO with capital letters."

"I don't follow you," said her brother. He had always been the activist in the family. He simply directed his calm rage against any obstacle that might exist, and awaited the conse-quences with the same serenity he awaited his sister's answer. Not for him the philosophical confusions and poetic observa-tions that hung his sister up.

"That's because you're a radical preacher," said Sarah, smil-ing up at him. "You deliver your messages in person with your own body." It excited her that her brother had at last imbued their childhood Sunday sermons with the reality of fighting for change. And saddened her that no matter how she looked at it this seemed more important than Medieval Art, Course 201.

3

"Yes, Grandma," Sarah replied. "Cresselton is for girls only, and *no,* Grandma, I am not pregnant."

Her grandmother stood clutching the broad wooden handle of her black bag, which she held, with elbows bent, in front of her stomach. Her eyes glinted through round wire-framed glasses. She spat into the grass outside the privy. She had in-sisted that Sarah accompany her to the toilet while the body was being taken into the church. She had leaned heavily on Sarah's arm, her own arm thin and the flesh like crepe.

"I guess they teach you how to really handle the world," she said. "And who knows, the Lord is everywhere. I would like a whole lot to see a Great-Grand. You don't specially have to be married, you know. That's why I felt free to ask." She reached into her bag and took out a Three Sixes bottle, which she proceeded to drink from, taking deep swift swallows with her head thrown back.

"There are very few black boys near Cresselton," Sarah explained, watching the corn liquor leave the bottle in spurts and bubbles. "Besides, I'm really caught up now in my painting and sculpting. . . ." Should she mention how much she admired Giacometti's work? No, she decided. Even if her grandmother had heard of him, and Sarah was positive she had not, she would surely think his statues much too thin. This made Sarah smile and remember how difficult it had been to convince her grandmother that even if Cresselton had not given her a scholarship she would have managed to go there anyway. Why? Because she wanted somebody to teach her to paint and to sculpt, and Cresselton had the best teachers. Her grandmother's notion of a successful granddaughter was a married one, pregnant the first year.

"Well," said her grandmother, placing the bottle with dignity back into her purse and gazing pleadingly into Sarah's face, "I sure would 'preshate a Great-Grand." Seeing her granddaughter's smile, she heaved a great sigh, and, walking rather haughtily over the stones and grass, made her way to the church steps.

As they walked down the aisle, Sarah's eyes rested on the back of her grandfather's head. He was sitting on the front middle bench in front of the casket, his hair extravagantly long and white and softly kinked. When she sat down beside him, her grandmother sitting next to him on the other side, he turned toward her and gently took her hand in his. Sarah briefly leaned her cheek against his shoulder and felt like a child again.

4

They had come twenty miles from town, on a dirt road, and the hot spring sun had drawn a steady rich scent from the honeysuckle vines along the way. The church was a bare, weather-beaten ghost of a building with hollow windows and a sagging door. Arsonists had once burned it to the ground, light-

ing the dry wood of the walls with the flames from the crosses
they carried. The tall spreading red oak tree under which Sarah
had played as a child still dominated the churchyard, stretching
its branches widely from the roof of the church to the other
side of the road.

After a short and eminently dignified service, during which
Sarah and her grandfather alone did not cry, her father's casket
was slid into the waiting hearse and taken the short distance to
the cemetery, an overgrown wilderness whose stark white
stones appeared to be the small ruins of an ancient civilization.
There Sarah watched her grandfather from the corner of her
eye. He did not seem to bend under the grief of burying a son.
His back was straight, his eyes dry and clear. He was simply
and solemnly heroic; a man who kept with pride his family's
trust and his own grief. *It is strange,* Sarah thought, *that I never
thought to paint him like this, simply as he stands; without anon-
ymous meaningless people hovering beyond his profile; his face
turned proud and brownly against the light.* The defeat that had
frightened her in the faces of black men was the defeat of black
forever defined by white. But that defeat was nowhere on her
grandfather's face. He stood like a rock, outwardly calm, the
comfort and support of the Davis family. The family alone
defined him, and he was not about to let them down.

"One day I will paint you, Grandpa," she said, as they
turned to go. "Just as you stand here now, with just"—she
moved closer and touched his face with her hand—"just the
right stubborn tenseness of your cheek. Just that look of Yes
and No in your eyes."

"You wouldn't want to paint an old man like me," he said,
looking deep into her eyes from wherever his mind had been.
"If you want to make me, make me up in stone."

The completed grave was plump and red. The wreaths of
flowers were arranged all on one side so that from the road
there appeared to be only a large mass of flowers. But already
the wind was tugging at the rose petals and the rain was making dabs of faded color all over the green foam frames. In a
week the displaced honeysuckle vines, the wild roses, the grape-

vines, the grass, would be back. Nothing would seem to have changed.

5

"What do you mean, come *home*?" Her brother seemed genuinely amused. "We're all proud of you. How many black girls are at that school? Just *you*? Well, just one more besides you, and she's from the North. That's really something!"

"I'm glad you're pleased," said Sarah.

"Pleased! Why, it's what Mama would have wanted, a good education for little Sarah; and what Dad would have wanted too, if he could have wanted anything after Mama died. You were always smart. When you were two and I was five you showed me how to eat ice cream without getting it all over me. First, you said, nip off the bottom of the cone with your teeth, and suck the ice cream down. I never knew *how* you were supposed to eat the stuff once it began to melt."

"I don't know," she said, "sometimes you can want something a whole lot, only to find out later that it wasn't what you *needed* at all."

Sarah shook her head, a frown coming between her eyes. "I sometimes spend *weeks,*" she said, "trying to sketch or paint a face that is unlike every other face around me, except, vaguely, for one. Can I help but wonder if I'm in the right place?"

Her brother smiled. "You mean to tell me you spend *weeks* trying to draw one face, and you still wonder whether you're in the right place? You must be kidding!" He chucked her under the chin and laughed out loud. "You learn how to draw the face," he said, "then you learn how to paint me and how to make Grandpa up in stone. Then you can come home or go live in Paris, France. It'll be the same thing."

It was the unpreacherlike gaiety of his affection that made her cry. She leaned peacefully into her brother's arms. She wondered if Richard Wright had had a brother.

"You are my door to all the rooms," she said. "Don't ever close."

And he said, "I won't," as if he understood what she meant.

6

"When will we see you again, young woman?" he asked later, as he drove her to the bus stop.

"I'll sneak up one day and surprise you," she said.

At the bus stop, in front of a tiny service station, Sarah hugged her brother with all her strength. The white station attendant stopped his work to leer at them, his eyes bold and careless.

"Did you ever think," said Sarah, "that we are a very old people in a very young place?"

She watched her brother from a window of the bus; her eyes did not leave his face until the little station was out of sight and the big Greyhound lurched on its way toward Atlanta. She would fly from there to New York.

7

She took the train to the campus.

"My," said one of her friends, "you look wonderful! Home sure must agree with you!"

"Sarah was home?" Someone who didn't know asked. "Oh, *great,* how was it?"

"Well, how was it?" went an echo in Sarah's head. The noise of the echo almost made her dizzy.

"How was it?" she asked aloud, searching for, and regaining, her balance.

"How was it?" She watched her reflection in a pair of smiling hazel eyes.

"It was fine," she said slowly, returning the smile, thinking of her grandfather. "Just fine."

The girl's smile deepened. Sarah watched her swinging along toward the back tennis courts, hair blowing in the wind.

Stare the rat down, thought Sarah; *and whether it disappears or not, I am a woman in the world. I have buried my father, and shall soon know how to make my grandpa up in stone.*

The Anatomy Lesson

by Evan Connell

North Fayer Hall stood on the final and lowest hill of the university, a little askew from the other buildings as if it were ashamed of its shabbiness and had turned partly away. Its windowsills were pocked by cigarette burns and the doors of its green tin lockers had been pried open for so many years that few of them would lock anymore; the creaking floors were streaked and spattered with drops of paint, dust lay upon the skylights, and because the ventilating system could not carry off so many fumes it seemed forever drenched in turpentine. Mercifully the little building was hidden each afternoon by the shadows of its huge, ivy-jacketed companions.

Just inside the front door was the office and studio of Professor A. B. Gidney, head of the art department, who taught ceramics, bookbinding, fashion design, and lettering. Professor Gidney's door was always open, even when he was teaching class somewhere else in the building, and in his studio were teacups and cookies and a hot plate which the students were free to use whenever they pleased. There was also a record player and a soft maple cabinet containing albums of operettas and waltzes; every afternoon punctually at five the music started.

Behind his office were the student ateliers, each with twenty or thirty short-legged chairs placed in a semicircle around the model's platform, and at the extreme rear of the building next to the fire escape, and reached by a dim corridor which multiplied every footstep, stood the studio of the other instructor.

This final studio was shaped like an up-ended coffin. In the rafters which surrounded its skylight spiders were forever weaving, and because the window had not been opened in years

the air was as stale as that of an attic, always cold in December
and always close in July. The window as a matter of fact could
not even be seen because of the magazines and newspapers
heaped atop a huge, ironbound trunk with a gibbous lid. In one
corner of the room a board rack held rows of somber oil paintings, each nearly the same: marshes in the center of which one
hooded figure was standing with head bowed. The first few
strokes of another such painting rested on an easel in the center
of the room, and around this easel a space had been cleared, but
the material that was banked against the walls and rose all the
way to the ceiling threatened to engulf it at any moment. There
were gilt picture frames, some as large as a door; there were
crocks and pails half filled with coagulated liquids, cartons,
milk bottles, splintered crates covered with layers of dust and
tobacco crumbs, rolls of linen canvas with rectangles ripped
out, jugs of varnish and turpentine lined up on an army cot
with a broken leg, brushes, rags, tubes, apple cores, wrappers of
chocolate bars, Brazil nuts, toothpicks, and pictures everywhere—glued on the walls or on boxes or, it seemed, on whatever was closest: pictures of madonnas, airplanes, zebras, rapi-
ers, gargoyles, schooners, adobe pueblos, and a host of others.
There seemed to be no plan or preference; a solarized print of a
turkey feather had been stuck to the trunk so that it half oblit-
erated a sepia print of the Bosporus. The glue pot itself could be
traced by its smell to a cobwebbed corner where, because it had
cracked and was leaking, it sat on a piece of wrapping paper.
On this paper was an inscription, printed at one time in red
Conté but now almost invisible. Beneath the glue and ashes the
letters read:

> I am here,
> I have traversed the Tomb,
> I behold thee,
> Thou who art strong!

Here and there on the floor lay bits of what looked like chalk
but which were the remains of a little plaster cast of Michelangelo's *Bound Slave*. The fragments suggested that the statuette

had not fallen but had been thrown to the floor. Also scattered about were phonograph records; most of them looked as if someone had bitten them. Several rested on the collar of a shaggy overcoat which in turn was draped over a stepladder. The phonograph itself lay on its side, the crank jutting up like the skeleton of a bird's wing and the splintered megaphone protruding from beneath one corner of a mattress like some great ear. In the middle of the night when the university campus was totally deserted there would occasionally come from the rear of North Fayer Hall the muffled sound of plainsong or Gregorian chant, to which was sometimes added for a few bars a resonant bass voice in absolute harmony, that of the instructor whose name was printed in gold on the studio door, a door that was always locked: ANDREV ANDRAUKOV, DRAWING & PAINTING.

Nothing interested Andraukov except paint. Each thing he saw or heard or touched, whether it writhed like a sensuous woman or lay cold as an empty jug, did not live for him until he, by his own hand, had given it life. Wherever he happened to be, in a class or outside, he paced back and forth like a tiger, and when with hands laced into a knot at the tail of his sack-like tweed coat and his huge, bony head bowed as if in prayer he stalked the corridors of North Fayer Hall, or the streets of Davenport below the university, he created a silence. Always he walked with his head bowed, and so far had his slanting eyes retreated into their sockets that few people had met his gaze. His teeth were as yellow and brown as his leathery skin and it seemed as if flesh were too much of a luxury for his bones to endure.

It was his habit to start each drawing class in the still-life room, a damp, chill studio with shelf upon shelf of plaster and bronze casts. He always took his students there the first morning; they stood about uncertainly, their young faces rosy from the September air, clean pencils and papers and new drawing boards clutched in their arms.

"Here," he would say, unrolling a long, cold finger. "Rome. Egypt. Greece. Renaissance. You will copy."

The students looked at him, a haggard old man whose head

by daylight could be no more than a skull in a leather bag, and one by one they settled themselves before a statue. Around and around behind them went Andrev Andraukov, taking from awkward fingers the pencils or sticks of charcoal, drawing with incredible delicacy tiny explanatory sketches in a corner of the paper. When he leaned down to inspect the drawings of the girls they stiffened and held their breath fearing he might somehow contaminate them. To them he might have been the Genghis Khan. Slowly and with a kind of infinite patience he wandered from one to another, shaking his head, trying to explain, never taking from his mouth the stub of a brown cigarette which protruded from his drooping and streaked mustache like an unfortunate tooth. The moment he heard the chimes which ended each class he halted his explanation even though in the middle of a sentence, and without a single word or another look he went out. The sound of his footsteps echoing in the corridor ended with what seemed like the closing of a hundred distant doors.

When he saw that his students were losing interest in the plasters and so could gain nothing more, he took them into the life atelier. On the walls of this room were tacked reproductions of masterful paintings. Helter-skelter stood drawing boards and student paintings, and on a platform rested an electric heater and a stool. Here, in this studio, he commenced his instruction of the living human body: on the blackboard he drew diagrams and explained for several days, as best he could through the net of language, how it was that men and women functioned. Then he got his students a model. Each morning one would arrive carrying a little satchel in which there was a robe or a cloak to wear during the rest periods and sometimes an apple or cigarettes or even a book.

Generally the models did as others had done for three thousand years before them, so there faced the class each morning a noble though somewhat shopworn pose. With earnest faces the students copied, bending down close to their paper the better to draw each eyelash and mole, their fingers clutching the charcoal as if they were engraving poetry on the head of a pin, and one after another they discovered that if charcoal was rubbed it would shine. In two days every drawing gleamed like the top of a candy box. All the while their instructor, a cigarette fixed in his smelly mustache, paced the back of the room or walked up and down the corridor.

Although the students did not know it, he was waiting. Year after year as students flowed by him this old man watched and waited; he waited for the one who might be able to understand what it meant to be an artist, one student, born with the instinct of compassion, who could learn, who would renounce temporal life for the sake of billions yet unborn, just one who cared less for himself than for others. But there were good foods to eat, dear friends to chat with, and pretty girls to be seduced, so many fascinating things to be done and discussed, thus Andrev Andraukov could only watch and wait.

It was as if a little play never ended, wherein, to his eternal question, *Is it not important?*, the young people answered, *Yes! Yes! There must be one who cares!* And he asked, *Will it be you, then?* But they replied, *Ah, no! Not me! Someone else. You see, I have so awfully many things to do. . . .*

One November morning the members of Andraukov's class found lettered on the blackboard in his square hand, TODAY: ANATOMY. As a result they did not open their lockers but sat in a semicircle facing the model stand and waited. Andraukov hurried in several minutes late; beside him walked a strange model who went behind the Japanese screen in the corner and began to undress.

Indicating a six-foot plaster man, stripped of skin and flesh, Andraukov asked two of the students to lift it onto the model stand. Next he pointed to the wooden cabinet where a skeleton dangled by a bolt through its skull, and said, "Mr. Bones." Two more students carried the rattling skeleton onto the stand. There was a half-smoked cigarette clamped in the jaws. Andraukov patiently removed it, as he had removed hundreds of others.

"Now," he said, "Miss Novak, please."

His model walked out from behind the screen and stepped onto the platform where she stood between the skeleton and the cut-away. She was a huge peasant girl with tubular limbs and coarse red hair that hung down her back like a rug. Between her great breasts was the tattoo of a ship. Her Slavic eyes were expressionless.

Andraukov took up a position behind the semicircle of students. From one of his coat pockets—which was more of a pouch—he brought up a crooked brown cigarette. After he had held two matches under it the cigarette began to sputter, flame, and finally emit blasts of terra-cotta smoke. Now Andraukov was ready to begin the lecture; he walked a few steps in each direction and then blew from his nostrils such a cloud that he nearly hid himself.

"Well," he began, "here is girl. Young woman. Who does not agree?" He walked out of the smoke, looked around, and then walked back into it. "Good. We progress. On street I look at woman first the head, then down, so we will do here. Who can tell what is the shape of human head? Mr. Sprinkle will tell us."

Sprinkle stood up and fingered his lower lip while he thought. Finally he answered that the human head was shaped like a ball.

"So? Miss Vitale will tell us."

Alice Vitale said it looked like an egg.

"Miss Novak, please to turn around. We will see back of head."

The model gathered her hair and lifted it until the class could see her neck and the base of the skull.

"Mr. Bondon, now, please."

Michael Bondon had begun to grow sideburns, and because his father was very rich he was not afraid to cross his legs and shrug.

Andraukov watched him for several seconds and then without expression continued, "Ball. Egg. Who is correct?" He explained that from the front the human head does resemble an egg and from the rear a ball or a melon, but, he cautioned, the artist must not look at what he sees so much as what he cannot see, and holding up one hand he demonstrated that the students, seeing his palm with their eyes, must also see his knuckles with their minds. He said that the artist must see around corners and through walls, even as he must see behind smiles, behind looks of pain.

"For to what use you shall employ knowledge?" he asked, walking to the window and gazing out at the slopes covered with wet snow. "For what you shall be artist? To draw such as all the world can see? Pussycat? Nice bouquet of lily? Little boy in sailor suit? Then bring to this class a camera. No! Not to this class. Go elsewhere." He looked out the window again at the soggy clouds which were settling on the university buildings, and then with his cigarette pinched between thumb and forefinger as if it were alive and about to jump, he walked slowly across the room, where he stopped with his back to the students. "You people, you wish to be artist. Why? That a stranger on the street will call you by name? You would be famous? You would have money? Or is it you have looked at your schedule and said, 'Ah, this is hard! I need now something easy. Yes, I will take drawing.'"

He turned around, looked at the faces of the men, his gaze resting on each for a number of seconds. "You have thought, 'I will take drawing because in studio will be pretty girl without dress!' So? This is reason? Or perhaps in this room—in this room perhaps now there sits young man who in this world discovers injustice. He would be conscience of the world. Mr. Dillon will now stand up. Mr. Dillon, you would draw picture which is to say, 'Behold! Injustice!'? You would do that?"

"No, sir," Dillon murmured.

"You will not be conscience of the world?"

"No, sir."

"If not you," Andraukov asked, gazing at the boy, "then who?" He carefully licked the under side of his mustache and pushed the cigarette deeper into his mouth. His knuckles were yellow and hard as stone. From the town of Davenport the sound of automobile horns came faintly up to the university hills; but for these noises and the creak of the instructor's shoes the life studio was quiet.

Andraukov walked to the stand, where he flattened his thumb against the neck of the cut-away. "Sterno-mastoid. Favorite muscle. Favorite muscle of art student." He asked his model to look at the skeleton and as she turned her head the sterno-mastoid stretched like a rope between ear and collarbone.

"*Beatrice d'Este,* how many know this painting, painting by Leonardo da Vinci? Three? Three hands? Disgrace! Now I tell you: In *Beatrice* is no sterno-mastoid. And why? Leonardo da Vinci is painting young woman, is not painting tackle of football team." He looked down on the faces turned attentively toward him and did not think they understood, but he did not know how to phrase it any more clearly. He decided to tell a joke. With a piece of green chalk he sketched on the blackboard a grotesque profile. He peered at it and shouted, "Young man after my daughter. Look like this! No, no—" He had confused the grammar. "Would have daughter, such young man like this." The class did not know what he was doing.

Andraukov felt he should explain his joke. He pulled on his mustache for a while and tried again but there was still only a confused tittering. He decided to continue with the lecture. Having become a trifle warm, he unbuttoned his vest and hooked both thumbs in the pockets.

"Well, below head is neck. Below neck is breast. You are afraid of this word. Why? This is God's word. Why everybody —all the young girls say 'bust'? Bust is for firecracker. Not for woman. No! Everybody—class entire together—now say correct word."

He listened to the class uneasily repeat the word and he nodded with satisfaction. "So! Not to be 'bust' again. I do not like that word. For drawing; art student draw like balloon. This is wrong. Not balloon, but is bag to rest on rib cage. Is part of body like ear is part of head, like peanut butter of sandwich, not to be alone. Who does not understand? Who has question?" No hands were raised.

Andraukov asked his model to face him with her heels together, legs straight, and hands at her sides. He stared. He was pleased with the way she stood.

"Class. Class, consider Miss Novak, fine model, head high. Is good to be proud of body. Yes. This is true!" He struck himself with a stony fist. "No scent on earth is so putrid as shame.

Good students, do not fear to be proud." He paused to medi-
tate. "Well, on rib who can tell status of breast? Nobody? There
is nobody to speak? There is fear?" He looked around. "Ah!
Brave student. Mr. Zahn will speak. Mr. Zahn stands to tell
instructor of breast. Good. Speak." With head bowed he prepared to listen, but almost immediately held up one hand. "No,
no! I would know direction. I would know angle. Yes, angle. On
breast does nipple look ahead like nose on face?"

Logan Zahn was a thin, heavily bearded young man who sat
in corners whenever possible. He was older than the other students and wore glasses so thick that his eyes seemed to bulge.
There were rumors that he was writing a book about something.

"No," he answered in a surprisingly high voice.

"The nipple, it will look down, perhaps?"

"No."

"Then where?"

"Up."

"And?"

"Out."

"Good!"

Zahn and the model looked at each other, both expressionless.

"You will tell instructor amount of angle. The left breast
now, to where it is looking?"

"At the print of Cézanne's apples on the wall."

"And the right?"

Logan Zahn was not afraid. He pointed out the window. "At
the Episcopal church."

Andraukov looked at the model and then toward the church.
"That is correct." He tugged from his vest a heavy watch and
studied it, pursing his lips. Why, he asked, tucking away the
watch, why was it that men wished to touch women? To allow
time for his question to penetrate he folded his arms across his
chest and began wandering about the studio. He picked a bit of
chalk off the floor, he opened a window an inch, he stroked a
dusty bronze on a shelf, he went back to close the window, and
when at last he felt that every student should have been able to

consider his question and speak of it properly he invited answers. Nobody volunteered.

"I will tell you," he said. "No, I will not tell you. Mr. Van Antwerp will stand."

Van Antwerp, who was the university's wrestling champion, scratched his scalp and grinned. Andraukov's face did not move.

Van Antwerp grinned some more. "They're fat," he said.

"Man is not fat? Yes, but different. Well, on woman where it is most thick?"

Van Antwerp began to stand on his other foot. He blushed and sniggered. The class was silent. For a few moments Andraukov stood with eyes closed and head cocked to one side as if listening to something beyond the range of other ears, but abruptly he strode across the room to Van Antwerp's green tin locker and wrenched it open.

"These material, it belong to you? Take it now. You will not return! Who else now—who else—" But not being able to phrase what he wished to say, he stood facing a shelf while Van Antwerp collected his things and left, slamming the door. Andraukov looked over his shoulder at the students. He turned all the way around and the color began to come back into his face.

"We speak of shape. Shape, yes. Is caused by many things. There is fat, placed by God, to protect child of womb. There is pelvic structure—so broad!" His bony hands gripped an imaginary pelvis. "There is short leg, spinal curve so deep. There is, too, the stance of woman. All these things, these things are not of man. You will not draw man and on him put balloons, lipstick, hair, and so to say, 'Here is woman!' No!"

He continued that woman was like the turtle, born to lie in the sun and sometimes to be turned over. Woman, he told them, was passive. She was not to smoke tobacco, to swear, to talk to man, to dance with man, to love like a drunken sailor; she was to brush her hair and wait. As he thought about the matter Andrev Andraukov stalked back and forth cutting the layers of smoke left by his cigarette.

"Trouser! Crop hair! Drink beer! For ten thousand years woman is correct: gentle, quiet, fat. Now?" He paused to stare at the floor, then lifting his head, said, "Well, today is good model. Consider limbs: not little to break in pieces but big and round like statue of Egyptian goddess, like statue in concrete like *Girl Holding Fruit* of Clodion. This piece, how many know? This Clodion?" He looked over the class and seeing only two hands, pinched the bridge of his nose in a sudden, curious gesture and closed his eyes. He instructed them all to go to the library that afternoon and find a picture of the statue. Around the studio he wandered like a starved and shabby friar, the cuffs of his fraying trousers dusting the paint-stained boards and the poor coat dangling from the knobs of his shoulders. The laces of his shoes had been broken and knotted many times, the heels worn round. He stopped in a corner beside a cast of *St. George* by Donatello and passed his fingertips across the face as if he were making love to it. He licked the drooping corner hairs of his mustache. He swung his Mongol head toward the class.

"You do not know Clodion! You do not know Signorelli, Perugino, Hokusai, Holbein! You do not even know Da Vinci, not even Cranach or Dürer! How, then, how I can teach you? Osmosis? You will look inside my head? Each day you sit before the model to draw. I watch. There is ugly model, I see on your face nothing. Not pity, not revolt, not wonder. Nothing. There is beautiful model, like today. I see nothing. Not greed, not sadness, not even fever. Students, have you love? Have you hate? Or these things are words to you? As the artist feels so does he draw. I look at you, I do not need to look at the drawing."

There was no sound but the footsteps of the old instructor. Dust motes whirled about him as he walked through a bar of winter sunlight.

"Good students, why you have come to me? You do not know what is crucifixion, the requiem, transfiguration. You do not even know the simple ecstasy. These things I cannot teach. No. I teach the hand. No man can teach the heart." Holding up his own hand for them all to see, he went on. "This is not the home of the artist. Raphael does not live here." Tapping himself on the chest, he said, "The home of Raphael is here."

The little sunlight faded so that all the sky was mushroom

gray, somehow auguring death and the winter. A wind rose, rattling the windows. The studio's one radiator began to knock and send up jets of steam. Andraukov snapped on the lights. He walked toward the motionless Slavic woman, his eyes going up and down her body as he approached.

"Who can find for instructor, sartorius?"

A girl went to the plaster cast and spiraled one finger down its thigh.

"Now on the model."

She touched the crest of the hip and inside the knee.

"What Miss Grodsky does not say is, ilium to tibia. But is all right because she tries. She will learn."

He asked if anybody knew why the muscle was named sartorius, but nobody knew; he told them it came from the word *sartor,* which meant tailor, and that this muscle must be used in order to sit cross-legged as years ago the tailors used to sit. He asked for the patella and his student laid one finger on the model's kneecap but did not know what the word meant. It meant a little pan, he said, as he drew its outline on the model's skin with a stick of charcoal. He asked next for the scapula; she hesitated and then touched the collarbone. He shook his head, saying, "Not clavicle, not the key." She guessed at the ankle and he shook his head again, placing her finger behind the model's shoulder. There with charcoal he outlined the scapula, saying as he finished it, "So! And Miss Grodsky can sit down. Mr. Zahn will find for instructor, pectoralis major."

Logan Zahn got up again and pointed.

Andraukov said, "Miss Novak does not bite." He watched as Zahn placed a fingertip outside and then inside her breast. "Correct. Easy question." With charcoal he drew the pectoralis on her skin. "Now for instructor, gluteus medius." He watched Zahn touch the side of her hip.

"Gastrocnemius."

He patted the calf of her leg.

"Masseter."

He touched her jaw.

Andraukov looked at him intently. "You are medical student?"

"No."

"Find for me—find pectoralis minor."

With his hands Zahn indicated that it lay deeper in the body.

"So. Where you have learn what you know?"

"Library," Zahn answered in his squeaky voice.

"I have told you to study anatomy in library?"

"No."

"But you have gone?"

"Yes."

Andraukov's nostrils dilated and he blew a cloud of smoke dark enough to have come from a ship; he stood in the middle of it, nearly hidden. When he emerged he began to speak of the differences between men and women; placing both hands on the model's forehead, he stretched the skin above her drugged eyes until the class saw how smooth the skull appeared, and for comparison he pointed to the ridge of bone like that of an ape's on the bleached skeleton. He pointed to the angle of the model's jawbone and next to the more acute angle on the skeleton. Below the pit of her neck he drew an outline of the sternum and compared it to the skeleton's longer, straighter bone. He said that the woman's neck seemed longer because the clavicle was shorter, thus narrowing the shoulders, that the elbow looked higher because the female humerus was short, that the reason one could not judge the height of seated women was because they possessed great variations in the length of the leg, that female buttocks were of greater diameter than male because of protective fat and because the sacrum assumes a greater angle. He turned the skeleton about on its gallows and placed his model in the same position. He drew the sacrum on her skin, and the vertebrae rising above it. She arched her back so that he could lay his hand on the sloping shelf. Why, he asked, why was it thus? And he answered himself, saying that the spine of man was straighter. Then for what reason did the spine of woman curve? For what reason did the pelvis tilt? Who would explain to him?

But again he answered himself. "Cushion!" A cushion for the foetus. From a cupboard he brought a length of straight wire and stabbed it at the floor; the wire twanged and vibrated from the shock, but after he had bent it into an *S* the wire bounced. He flung it into a corner and walked back and forth rubbing his hands as he lectured. The belly protrudes because there resides the viscera of the human body. Fashion magazines do not know about viscera, they print pictures of young girls who cannot eat because they have no stomach, who cannot walk because they have no maximus, who seem to stand on broken ankles. Although paper was flat the students must draw as if it were round; they must draw not in two dimensions but in three. A good artist could draw in three dimensions, a master could draw in four.

He stopped to consider the attentive looks on their faces and asked who understood, but did not wait for an answer. He spoke of how Rembrandt painted a young woman looking out an open window and said to them that she did not live three hundred years ago, no, she was more than one young woman, she was all, from the first who had lived on earth to the one yet unborn who would be the final. He told them that some afternoon they would glance up by chance and see her; then they would know the meaning of Time—what it could destroy, what it could not. But for today, he said, his voice subsiding, three dimensions would be enough. From his baggy vest he extracted a silver thimble. He held it between two fingers.

"For belly, three dimensions. It is not, like paper, flat. So navel is not black dot. It is deep. It is the eye of God. You are going to see." Bending down, he pushed the thimble steadily into the model's navel.

Every little noise in the studio ceased. There was no movement. It seemed an evil spell had been thrown by the thimble which retreated and advanced toward the students in brief, glittering arcs.

Andraukov licked his yellow mustache. "Good students, you will forget again?"

The class was still paralyzed. Waves of shock swept back and forth across the room; with the elongated senses of the mystic Andraukov caught them.

"Good students," he said simply. "Listen. Now I speak. You have come to me not to play. You have come to learn. I will teach. You will learn. Good students, each time in history that people have shame, each time in history that people hide from what they are, then in that age there is no meaning to life. There is imitation. Nothing more. There is nothing from which the little generation can learn. There is no weapon for the son to take from the hands of his father to conquer the forces of darkness and so to bring greatness to the people of earth."

Andrev Andraukov put the thimble back in his vest pocket. The thin soles of his pointed, paint-spattered shoes flapped on the boards as he walked to the cast of *St. George* and stood for a time gazing absently beyond it.

Suddenly he asked, "Will you like to hear a story?" and immediately began telling it.

Eleven years ago he had taught another drawing class much like their own where the students drew stiff, smudgy pictures of Greek warriors and made spaghetti of Michelangelo's muscles. But they, too, had worked hard, it had been a good class, and so one day he brought them into the life studio and gave them a woman. He left them alone that first morning and when he returned at noon they lined their drawing boards up against the wall and waited for his criticism.

In regard to the first drawing he observed that the head looked as big as a watermelon and he explained that the human head was nearly the same length as the foot; immediately the class members discovered they had drawn the feet too small. The hand, he told them, demonstrating, would more than cover the face; the class laughed at the tiny hands on all the drawings. How could they have made such mistakes! Well, they would learn.

At the second piece of work he stood facing them with hands at his sides and in a few moments the class discovered what he was doing: they had not drawn the arms long enough. He explained the various uses of the human arm, suggesting that if they would learn to speak truly of function then their drawings would be correct. He looked at their faces and saw the struggle to comprehend. It was a good class.

The next drawing was a tiny thing but when he bent down to peer at it he discovered the streaks which were meant to be veins in the back of the model's hand. He held out his own hand with its great veins of red and green twine.

"These are important?" he asked them, and as he lifted his hands high in the air the class watched the veins recede.

So one by one he criticized those first works. When he came to the final drawing he found the figure had been covered by a bathing suit. He thought it was a joke. He turned to the class with a puzzled smile, but seeing their faces he knew it was not a joke.

"Who has drawn this?" he asked. No hand was raised. He returned to the first drawing and asked its owner to leave the studio; he stopped at the second drawing and asked its owner to leave. One by one the students walked out and finally he was left with two drawings but only one student.

"Miss Hugasian," he said, "you draw this morning two pictures?"

She pointed to the first.

"Well, then, this final drawing?"

Her eyes were brilliant with fright but he was patient and at last she said it had been done by Patricia Bettencourt.

"Miss Bettencourt? She is here today?" Then he left the studio and walked up and down the corridor opening each door until finally in the still-life room, seated between the casts of *Night* and *Day* with a handkerchief held over her face he saw Patricia Bettencourt. Looking down on her he wondered.

She did not move.

"You are ill?" he asked, bringing a bench close to her and sitting down. "For me today you make very nice drawing, but the bathing suit—"

Andraukov paused in telling the story of Patricia Bettencourt, but he did not stop pacing, so the eyes of the students swung steadily back and forth. Once again the only sounds in the atelier were the creak of his shoes and the knocking radiator. From time to time the electric heater on the model's platform hummed faintly. Rain trickled down the windowpanes and, finding cracks in the ancient putty, seeped and dripped to the floor, where puddles were spreading. Before continuing with the story, he walked to the door and opened it.

"Miss Bettencourt speaks. 'I did not know model was to
be—' This sentence she cannot finish because she weeps. I finish for her. I ask, 'Nude?' She does not answer. Shadow like
shroud drops on cast of Michelangelo."

Andraukov tasted his mustache and nodded to himself. He
walked to the window, where he stood with his back to the
class; they could see only the thin hair on his skull and his
yellow fingers tied into a knot at the tail of his coat.

"Good pupils, the artist is not 'nice.' No, that cannot be. He
shall hear at times the voice of God, at times the shriek of each
dwarf in the heart and in the soul, and shall obey those voices.
But the voice of his fellow man? No. That cannot be. I think he
who would create prepares his cross. Yes! It is so. But at his feet
no Magdalen. Who, then, shall accuse: 'You are evil!'? 'You are
sublime!'? There is no one to speak these words. Miss Bettencourt is in this room? Go now. I do not wish to see your
face."

The door to the corridor stood open. Andraukov remained at
the window with his back to the students.

"Then I will teach you. I teach of the human body and of the
human soul. Now you are young, as once even I was. Even as
yours were my nostrils large. Now you shall learn what is the
scent of life, and with fingers to touch, with ears to listen. Each
fruit you shall taste, of honey and grape, and one day persim-
mon. I, too, have kissed the hot mouth of life, have shattered
the night with cries, have won through such magic millions of
years. You will listen now! God is just. He gives you birth. He
gives you death. He bids you to look, to learn, and so to live."

The chimes of the university chapel had begun to toll. Wrapping his fingers once again into a knot at the tail of his coat,
Andrev Andraukov walked out the door. The anatomy lesson
was over.

A Different Set of Rules

by Daniel Menaker

Ben was walking down the stairs from the commons room above the dining hall. A girl with a bandage over one eye was walking up. Ben stood on the landing and watched her ascend toward him. She would not meet his eyes, but kept her head forward. Like a soldier in drill, Ben thought.

"So you're the one," Ben said as the girl reached the landing. She stopped and turned to face him, and smiled broadly.

"Yes," she said, "I'm the one." She was a short but substantial girl, with ample hips and square shoulders. She had wide cheekbones and a full mouth with even, very white teeth. Her forehead was broad, and her hair was straw-colored and boyishly short. Her unbandaged eye, large and blue-gray, like a clear, cold solitaire, was so beautiful that Ben had to look away.

"I read about you in the *Phoenix* this morning," he said, surveying the line of students at the foot of the stairs outside the dining room. "Is it going to be O.K.?"

"The patch comes off tomorrow," she said.

"Good," he said, forcing himself to look at her again. "That whole Freshman Serenade thing is pretty tribal, anyway."

"Oh, I don't know," she said.

"You mean you enjoyed getting thrown around in the mud by a bunch of jocks?"

"Until I got kicked," she said, and giggled. "Anyway, you're a jock yourself."

She knew who he was. He felt pride wash through him like strong liquor, and he blushed. "Not that kind of jock," he said. "I just can't understand how you could like getting pawed that way."

"What kind *are* you, then?" she said.

"I eschew categories," he said, self-mockingly. "Just because I play soccer doesn't mean I have to play soccer with a girl's face." He paused. "I read your name, but I've forgotten it."

"Stephanie McCullough. People call me Stevie."

"I'm Ben Jaffe."

"I know."

"Well, if it's as pretty as the other one, I can't wait to see it," Ben said, gesturing toward the bandage.

"Oh, it's even prettier."

Ben laughed. "I'm on my way to lunch," he said. "I want to finish in time to see Kennedy. Have you eaten already?" His own invitation took him by surprise, which was what he wanted, so that it would seem casual to himself as well as to her. But his heart like a traitor started pounding almost immediately.

"No, I already have," she said.

"Maybe some other time," he said quickly. "Well, so long. I hope—"

"I would look forward to it," she said.

"I hope that you're O.K." He backed down a couple of steps. "Keep an eye out for me," he said, and shrugged apologetically.

Ben met his friend Jed Cooper in the dining room, and after lunch they strolled together down the wide, oak-lined walk that split the college's spacious front lawn in two. It was a bright, early-October Friday afternoon, genial and comfortable in the sun, but a little chilly in the deep, sharp shadows of trees and buildings. Every now and then, a vortex of leaves swirled around the feet of the two young men as they walked. Nearby, the college maintenance crew was burning a big pile of leaves. The smoke drifted across the walk, at one point so thickly that it made Ben's eyes sting.

"We'd better hurry up," Ben said as they reached the railroad tracks that lay at the foot of the campus and divided it from the small college town. He could see the crowds that had already formed on the sidewalks of the town's main street. "I want to get a good look at this glamour boy."

"You rich Northerun fellahs always in a rush," Jed said, exaggerating his natural Kentucky drawl. He was tall and slim, like Ben, but he was also lanky and slow, while Ben was contained and tense. Their friendship, like their physical appearance, was a mixture of complement and contrast. They were both juniors and both studying in the Honors program. Ben was majoring in English, Jed in physics. They were both good athletes. Ben found his friends mainly among those students who considered themselves bohemians; Jed belonged to a fraternity. In the limited, idyllic world of a small Quaker college, both of them received wide admiration.

"I met the best-looking girl in the freshman class today," Ben said as they crossed the tracks. "I think I'll ask her to the movies tomorrow night."

"What's her name?" Jed said.

"You know, that one who hurt her eye in the Freshman Serenade Wednesday and got written up in the paper this morning. Stevie Something."

"McCullough," Jed said, "and she respectfully declines your kind offer."

"What are you talking about?"

"Well, she can't go to the movies with both of us, now, can she?" Jed said, grinning evilly, like a Halloween pumpkin.

"You son of a bitch," Ben said.

The motorcade, moving quickly in dappled sunlight, came into view half a mile down the road from the town. It slowed when it reached the edges of the crowd. The first few convertibles carried mainly nondescript, paunchy men, who Dave assumed were local Democratic officials. The fourth open car—as long and sleek as a boat—carried John Kennedy and his wife. The Senator stood to greet the crowd, waving with one hand and balancing himself by holding on to the back of the front seat with the other. He had a yellowish suntan and seemed slightly stooped. He was extremely handsome. For an instant, Ben met his eyes. His throat tightened, and he shivered a little. Then the car had passed, and the crowd's cheering first diffused and then died entirely, as if quenched by the hollow silence that took its place.

* * *

It was Sunday morning, and Ben was in his room, reading. He did well in all his studies—a success that he attributed to not much more than discipline and stubbornness. If a concept resisted him, he assaulted it relentlessly, first from this position, then from that, until it yielded.

"Was she hot!" Jed said loudly as he opened the door to Ben's room. He walked to the bed and fell onto it facedown.

"Come on in," Ben said.

Jed turned over, flinging his arms and legs over the sides of the bed, and rolled his eyes up into his head.

"Listen, I've got some work to do, if you don't mind," Ben said.

"You wouldn't be jealous, now would you?" Jed got up. "Actually, you're golden," he said, losing his manic expression.

"What do you mean?"

"She knew we lived on the same hall. All she did was ask about you—where you're from, what you're like, why you dress like some kind of refugee. It was disgusting."

"Are you serious? That's terrific!"

"Of course, I felt obliged to tell her about your liaison with the old nigra chambermaid." Jed got up and went toward the door. "Are you going to lunch?"

"Just a second," Ben said. He got up and straightened his desk, taking care, before he closed his book, to underline the passage he had been working on. He put on his green deck coat and walked into the hall. Jed was already outside. Ben walked out the dormitory's side door into the bright sunlight. Whooping and screeching as if in a panic, he ran to catch up with his friend. When he did, he jumped up onto his back, nearly knocking him over.

Ben put his hands on the back of Stevie's skirt while he kissed her. As if in one of those Oriental disciplines that hover between ballet and violence, she raised her arms up under his and opened them outward, pulling his hands away from her. He placed them high on her ribs, just touching the sides of her breasts. She held his wrists and leaned toward him, so that his hands finally rested on her back.

It was the end of their first date, a week after they had met. At Jed's invitation, they had gone to a dance given by his fraternity. Now they were standing under a lamppost outside Stevie's dormitory. The weather had turned quite cold, and Stevie shivered a little as a gust of wind swept past, pulling a rain of leaves down around them. She tilted her head back and looked at Ben. "You go pretty fast for a first date," she said.

"I'm sorry. It's just that I find you irresistible."

"Oh, sure."

"Listen, I really am sorry. I didn't mean to rush you or anything. But I do like you."

"I like you too," Stevie said, slipping away from his embrace. She took his hand and started walking toward the dormitory's entrance. "It's just that—"

"I know, I know," Ben interrupted. "We've only just met."

She tried to hit him, but he danced away.

Over the next few weeks, Ben saw Stevie as much as he could. He went to the registrar's office and looked up her course schedule, so that he could be wandering by in the hall when her classes let out. He would make sure that she saw him, and then, if she failed to approach him, he would pretend to discover her. When they did not have supper together, he would wait for her outside the dining room. Then they would go upstairs to commons, or sit and talk on the main building's front porch, or walk together down to the library.

Before September, Stevie said, she had never known a Jew. Her family was Episcopalian and so was she ("a believer," she called herself), and they lived just outside Tacoma, Washington. Her father, whom she admired very much, was the senior vice-president of a gigantic lumber company ("It's a cartel, you know," Ben said). He had been very unhappy about her going East to college. Her world in the West had been made of skiing trips, clamming in Puget Sound, square dances, golden retrievers (thinking about her dogs was one of the few things that made her homesick, she said), and two "pesky" younger brothers.

Challenged by such innocence, Ben found himself playing up the differences between their backgrounds. He mentioned casually that his parents had been radicals during the thirties and forties. He told her that his father, a Jew, and his mother, from an old New York Presbyterian family, had given up religion when they were young, and that he himself had never been inside a church except for school field trips. He spoke skeptically about government and other institutions, including the college, whose restrictive rules he and all the upperclassmen he knew found oppressive and hypocritical. When Ben spoke, he often did not look at Stevie, but instead sent his words out into the empty air, as if he were addressing some invisible assemblage. Stevie watched him attentively, and he could not tell whether what he said impressed her or shocked her. In her presence, he learned that his own words could taste bitter even as he spoke them.

Each morning Ben would order himself to stay away from Stevie that day, but in the evening he usually sought her out. He had had girl friends before, in high school and college, but, he now thought, they had been so much like him that they might just as well have been his sisters. They were sarcastic and conceited, in training to replace their enervated, brittle mothers. Although Stevie was just as bright, she did not wield her intelligence like a weapon. She seemed direct and clear, like a child. And though her simplicity often made Ben uncomfortable, he loved her for it. It was almost as if he hoped she might redeem in him the very faults that she made him so conscious of.

Many evenings, they would have coffee at the college snack bar. There they would chat for an hour or so, and Ben's friends often joined them. Kathy Gauss, who played the dulcimer and swore like a truckdriver; Kodji, a taciturn Ugandan who was captain of the soccer team and who was said to receive monthly supplies of powdered rhinoceros horn from home; A. T. Taylor, a beatnik girl from Paoli who was having a sonnet cycle published in the spring; Jim Peterson, a tall, blond Swede from

Minnesota, who, people whispered, would be *teaching* at the
Institute for Advanced Studies next year. One night, as he listened while Fergus Clancy, the congenial campus anarchist,
dissected the Kennedy family, Ben caught Stevie staring at
him, her eyes shining.

"Aren't you ever afraid that I'll fall in love with one of your
beautiful geniuses?" she said after Fergus had left.

"I guess I hope they'll help you fall in love with me," Ben
said.

"You don't need any help," Stevie said, her eyes lowered.

"What?" Ben said. Then he blushed, because of both the
sudden new intimacy itself and his obtuse reaction to it. "I
couldn't believe . . . Listen, I am in love with you too. I think
. . . I was surprised . . ."

Stevie looked up. "Well," she said, her eyes dancing, *"that's*
settled, anyway."

Later that week Stevie started staying overnight in Ben's
room. She was reluctant at first, because she was afraid of getting caught. When she finally agreed, Ben felt vaguely let down,
he did not understand why.

Naked, they would lie together on his narrow bed. Cold au-
tumn-night breezes from the slightly open window would brush
over them, and at first they would shiver against each other,
laughing quietly. Once together for a few minutes, they were
warm, and they would touch each other, delighting in how
finely made they were. He tried to tell her how he loved her,
but he could not trust his words not to crack into foolishness.
He would simply stare at her, astonished, and tears would
sometimes sting his eyes. She would not permit him to enter
her, and he was relieved that she would not—again he did not
know why. They both had orgasms, though, sometimes simply
from embracing. Then they would talk for hours, about other
people on campus whom they liked or didn't like, about professors, about high school and home, and about themselves.

On Election Night, along with twenty or so other students,
they watched the returns on a television set that Ben had set up
in his dorm's parlor. He had also procured a pint of scotch, and

by the time Illinois finally fell to Kennedy, he and Stevie were a little drunk. Afterward, in Ben's room, Stevie tried half-heartedly to hold him away from her, but he was so funny ("Und chust how long haff ve had zis little problem mit zex?" he asked her, in a tyrannical analyst's voice) that she finally yielded. It was his first time, and as he penetrated her, he felt at the heart of his intoxication a sadness as sharp as a nettle.

A week later, Ben was standing with Jed on the porch of the main building. They were waiting for Stevie to have lunch with them after her twelve o'clock philosophy class. The weather had been gray for days, and now a strong wind blew out of the east, stripping away most of the leaves that remained on the tall oaks on the front campus and promising a cold, sullen rain.

"What are you going to do with Mackler?" Jed said.

"I don't know," Ben said. "I called another meeting for after lunch. Yesterday, Mackler swore he hadn't been cheating, but Professor Prentice says he saw his crib sheet."

"What do you think?" Jed said.

"Oh, guilty, no question. He was really squirming. Anyway, some girl who sat next to him in the exam is going to testify this afternoon. I think she's going to back up Prentice."

From the corner of his eye, Ben saw Stevie walking toward the steps leading up to the porch; he did not greet her.

"You going to expel him?" Jed said.

"The guy is basically O.K. My committee wants to fire him, but I think I can talk them out of it," Ben said. He cupped his hands around Jed's pipe while Jed tried to get it lit for the fifth or sixth time. The wind blew the match out. "Jesus, Jed, when are you going to give up this silly-ass pipe? Next thing you know, you'll start wearing corduroy jackets with leather patches on the elbows."

Jed lighted his pipe. "We've got a visitor," he said.

Stevie, from behind Ben, covered his eyes with her hands.

"You're late," Ben said.

"I'm sorry," Stevie said. "I was arguing with Ginny about the mind-body problem after class."

"Yeah, Ginny's got a problem in both areas," Jed said.

"I remember those arguments in Phil. I," Ben said. "What a bunch of garbage."

"Oh, I don't know," Stevie said. "The class was pretty exciting today."

"Exciting, shmexciting," Ben said. "First of all, no freshman —Ahh, forget it."

"Big-shot junior," Stevie said, putting her arm around Ben's waist. He acted oblivious of her touching him, and she took her arm away. "What's wrong?" she said.

"Nothing," Ben said. "It's cold out here. Let's go in and eat."

As he started walking toward the door, he caught the glance that passed between Jed and Stevie, and he saw Jed put both hands out, palms up, and shrug his shoulders. He learned that from me, Ben thought.

"We suspended Mackler for two weeks—until after vacation," Ben reported to Jed later that afternoon in the locker room, as they were dressing for practice. "The girl saw the crib sheet, too."

Jed turned away from the full-length mirror, in front of which he had been striking menacing-lineman poses. He nodded his head, and Ben pounded his shoulder pads into place with his fists.

"You won, then," Jed said seriously, sitting down on a bench to lace his shoes.

"Yeah, but it took some time. Prentice was furious because the guy lied, and he wanted to kick him out. But I gave them all some crap about ruining somebody's future for one mistake."

Jed finished with his shoes, and he and Ben walked through the soccer team's section of the locker room and out toward the practice fields. It was raining now, a drizzle as fine and silvery as needles.

"Don't you think you've been a little rough with Stevie lately?" Jed said as they started jogging to keep warm.

"I know, I know," Ben said. "Since last week—maybe we

shouldn't have done it. Sometimes I feel this . . . contempt, or something."

"Well, whatever it is, you're showing it."

"She's pretty tough, in a funny kind of way."

"It's you I'm worried about."

"Oh, sure."

"I just think you're in some kind of trouble," Jed called after Ben, who had veered away from him, toward the soccer field.

Near the end of scrimmage against the junior varsity later on, Ben threw himself forward, about two feet above the ground and parallel to it, and headed the sodden ball toward the goal. He had angled it well, just beyond the goaltender's reach, and it skidded into the net. He lay in the mud uninjured but shaken; the center fullback, in trying to clear the ball, had barely missed kicking Ben full in the face.

In the dim light cast by the streetlamp outside his window, Ben could just see Stevie smiling at him, her face hovering above him like a moon.

"There," she said. "That ought to take some of the grouch out of you." She rolled onto her back.

"I haven't given you any trouble since Tuesday," Ben said.

"You haven't given me much fun, either. You just needed me to relax you a little." She paused. "Are you sure it's still a good idea for me to go home with you Thanksgiving?"

"Of course. Just don't try to say grace, or anything."

"Don't you look up all your old girl friends when you go home?"

"No. Why? Are you thinking about Rick, or whatever his name is?"

"I was just teasing."

"Maybe *you* don't want to go anymore. Maybe you want to go skiing or spelunking, or something."

"No. I want to be with you."

Ben sat up on the edge of the bed and put his feet on the floor. "Did you ever make love with Rick?" He was surprised by his own question—as surprised as he would have been if a stranger had at that moment broken down the door to his room.

"What difference does it make?" Stevie said, folding her arms over her breasts.

"Did you?"

"It's not your business. It doesn't make any difference."

"It makes a *difference*," Ben said. Ben heard that his voice had now turned into a peculiar rasp.

"You are so smart; how can you be so stupid?"

"I just want to know."

"It doesn't matter what I did before. You are the most interesting boy I've ever met."

"You did, didn't you?"

"Yes. Once. The night before I left for college. We both knew that everything would be changing. It was just good-bye."

Ben was silent. He stood up and turned and looked at Stevie. Her arms still covered her breasts, and when she saw him looking at her, she drew her knees up. He thought of her lying with someone else, and he felt physically sick.

"Good-bye!" he said finally. "It's not like kissing someone on the cheek, you know. You don't use it to say good-bye with. Except *you* do. You would."

"Oh, Benny, stop."

"God! You're so naïve. You really mean that stuff about saying good-bye. Nothing has any . . . dimensions with you. Everything is only what it is. You don't see any edges, any shadows."

"What do you mean?"

"Listen, you'd better leave." He felt as if he might faint.

Stevie stood up and dressed. He expected her to cry, but she didn't. She left without saying a word.

Toward dawn, after hours of wakefulness, Ben fell into a short, fitful sleep. He dreamed that he was conversing pleasantly with Stevie before a huge plate-glass window in the drawing room of an elegant house. Suddenly, he knew, without knowing how he knew, that a fire had started upstairs, in one of the house's many bedrooms. The fire spread to other bedrooms, but still no smoke or heat was perceptible downstairs in the

room where he and Stevie were talking. Stevie seemed completely unaware of the danger they were in. Ben tried to continue the conversation, to avoid alarming her, but his apprehen-
sion grew within him, like the fire itself. Finally, the acrid smell
of smoke reached him, and he realized that the fire now threatened to consume the entire structure. Without a word, he threw
himself forward, shattering the window into thousands of silvery needles of glass, and landed unhurt on the hard, frozen
ground outside.

The morning was brilliant but frigid, a hard edge of deep
winter protruding backward into November. Ben was in front
of Stevie's dormitory at eight forty-five. As he entered the
lobby, the dizziness he had felt the night before returned, blur-
ring his vision. He called Stevie's hall on the lobby phone, and
asked the girl who answered if Stevie was there. After a minute
or so, Ginny, Stevie's roommate, came through the door that
separated the lobby from the rest of the dormitory. She walked
over to where Ben stood.

"She doesn't want to see you," Ginny said. "She is devastated."

"'Devastated,'" Ben said.

"Yes, devastated, Mister Sarcasm," Ginny said, tossing her
short, mousy hair indignantly. Ben had a vision of this unattractive, theatrical girl carrying emotional freight from one person to another for the rest of her life.

"I'll wait for her," Ben said.

"She says you must leave her alone," Ginny said. Ben heard
an echo of Stevie's firmness in these words. "And in my personal opinion," Ginny said, lapsing back into melodrama, "you
are a son of a bitch."

Ben looked at the dead receiver, which he was still holding.
He did not hang up but put the receiver down beside the phone
and went out into the cold, bright air.

He walked to the library. He meant to try to study, but
instead he sat down, bewildered, on the steps that led up to the
building's entrance. After a while, he saw Jed coming toward

him. Look at the way he walks, Ben thought—like some kind
of cowboy. He felt a sudden surge of affection for his friend.

"You look terrible," Jed said when he reached the steps.
"Why are you sitting out here?"

Ben stood up. "Because I've read everything in there," he
said, his voice breaking. He rested one arm on Jed's shoulder
and bowed his head. "You were right," he said, now crying. "I
am in trouble."

Christmas Poem

by John O'Hara

Billy Warden had dinner with his father and mother and sister. "I suppose this is the last we'll see of you this vacation," said his father.

"Oh, I'll be in and out to change my shirt," said Billy.

"My, we're quick on the repartee," said Barbara Warden. "The gay young sophomore."

"What are *you*, Bobby dear? A drunken junior?" said Billy.

"Now, I don't think that was called for," said their mother.

"Decidedly *un*-called for," said their father. "What *are* your plans?"

"Well, I was hoping I could borrow the chariot," said Billy.

"Yes, we anticipated that," said his father. "What I meant was, are you planning to go away anywhere? Out of town?"

"Well, that depends. There's a dance in Reading on the twenty-seventh I'd like to go to, and I've been invited to go skiing in Montrose."

"Skiing? Can you ski?" said his mother.

"All Dartmouth boys ski, or pretend they can," said his sister.

"Isn't that dangerous? I suppose if you were a Canadian, but I've never known anyone to go skiing around here. I thought they had to have those big—I don't know—scaffolds, I guess you'd call them."

"You do, for jumping, Mother. But skiing isn't all jumping," said Billy.

"Oh, it isn't? I've only seen it done in the newsreels. I never really saw the point of it, although I suppose if you did it well it would be the same sensation as flying. I often dream about flying."

"I haven't done much jumping," said Billy.

"Then I take it you'll want to borrow the car on the twenty-seventh, and what about this trip to Montrose?" said his father.

"I don't exactly know where Montrose is," said Mrs. Warden.

"It's up beyond Scranton," said her husband. "That would mean taking the car overnight. I'm just trying to arrange some kind of a schedule. Your mother and I've been invited to one or two things, but I imagine we can ask our friends to take us there and bring us back. However, we only have the one car, and Bobby's entitled to her share."

"Of course she is. Of course I more or less counted on her to, uh, to spend most of her time in Mr. Roger Taylor's Dort."

"It isn't a Dort. It's a brand new Marmon, something I doubt you'll ever be able to afford."

"Something I doubt Roger'd ever be able to afford if it took any brains to afford one. So he got rid of the old Dort, did he?"

"He never had a Dort, and you know it," said Bobby.

"Must we be so disagreeable, the first night home?" said Mrs. Warden. "I know there's no meanness in it, but it doesn't *sound* nice."

"When would you be going to Montrose?" said Mr. Warden. "What date?"

"Well, if I go it would be a sort of a house party," said Billy.

"In other words, not just overnight?" said his father. "Very well, suppose you tell us how many nights?"

"I'm invited for the twenty-eighth, twenty-ninth, and thirtieth," said Billy. "That would get me back in time to go to the Assembly on New Year's Eve."

"What that amounts to, you realize, is having possession of the car from the twenty-seventh to the thirtieth or thirty-first," said his father.

"Yes, I realize that," said Billy.

"Do you still want it, to keep the car that long, all for yourself?" said his father.

"Well, I didn't have it much last summer, when I was working. And I save you a lot of money on repairs. I ground the valves, cleaned the spark plugs. A lot of things I did. I oiled and greased it myself."

"Yes, I have to admit you do your share of that," said his father. "But if you keep the car that long, out of town, it just means we are without a car for four days, at the least."

There was a silence.

"I really won't need the car very much after Christmas," said Bobby. "After I've done my shopping and delivered my presents."

"Thank you," said Billy.

"Well, of course, not driving myself, I never use it," said Mrs. Warden.

"That puts it up to me," said Mr. Warden. "If I were Roger Taylor's father I'd give you two nice big Marmons for Christmas, but I'm not Mr. Taylor. Not by about seven hundred thousand dollars, from what I hear. Is there anyone else from around here that's going to Montrose?"

"No."

"Then it isn't one of your Dartmouth friends?" said Mr. Warden. "Who will you be visiting?"

"It's a girl named Henrietta Cooper. She goes to Russel Sage. I met her at Dartmouth, but that's all. I mean, she has no other connection with it."

"Russel Sage," said his mother. "We know somebody that has a daughter there. I know who it was. That couple we met at the Blakes'. Remember, the Blakes entertained for them last winter? The husband was with one of the big electrical companies."

"General Electric, in Schenectady," said Mr. Warden. "Montrose ought to be on the Lehigh Valley, or the Lackawanna, if I'm not mistaken."

"The train connections are very poor," said Billy. "If I don't go by car, Henrietta's going to meet me in Scranton, but heck, I don't want to ask her to do that. I'd rather not go if I have to take the train."

"Well, I guess we can get along without the car for that long. But your mother and I are positively going to have to have it New Year's Eve. We're going to the Assembly, too."

"Thank you very much," said Billy.

"It does seem strange. Reading one night, and then the next day you're off in the opposite direction. You'd better make sure the chains are in good condition. Going over those mountains this time of year."

"A house party. Now what will you do on a house party in Montrose? Besides ski, that is?" said Mrs. Warden. "It sounds like a big house, to accommodate a lot of young people."

"I guess it probably is," said Billy. "I know they have quite a few horses. Henny rides in the Horse Show at Madison Square Garden."

"Oh, my. Then they must be very well-to-do," said his mother. "I always wanted to ride when I was a girl. To me there's nothing prettier than a young woman in a black riding habit, riding side-saddle. Something so elegant about it."

"I wouldn't think she rode side-saddle, but maybe she does," said Billy.

"Did you say you wanted to use the car tonight, too?" said his father.

"If nobody else is going to," said Billy.

"Barbara?" said Mr. Warden.

"No. Roger is calling for me at nine o'clock," said Barbara. "But I would like it tomorrow, all day if possible. I have a ton of shopping to do."

"I *still* haven't finished wrapping all *my* presents," said Mrs. Warden.

"I haven't even *bought* half of mine," said Barbara.

"You shouldn't leave everything to the last minute," said her mother. "I bought most of mine at sales, as far back as last January. Things are much cheaper after Christmas."

"Well, I guess I'm off to the races," said Billy. "Dad, could you spare a little cash?"

"How much?" said Mr. Warden.

"Well—ten bucks?"

"I'll take it off your Christmas present," said Mr. Warden.

"Oh, no, don't do that. I have ten dollars if you'll reach me my purse. It's on the sideboard," said Mrs. Warden.

"You must be flush," said Mr. Warden.

"Well, no, but I don't like to see you take it off Billy's Christmas present. That's as bad as opening presents ahead of time," said Mrs. Warden.

"Which certain people in this house do every year," said Barbara.

"Who could she possibly mean?" said Billy. "I opened one present, because it came from Brooks Brothers and I thought it might be something I could wear right away."

"And was it?" said his mother.

"Yes. Some socks. These I have on, as a matter of fact," said Billy. "They're a little big, but they'll shrink."

"Very snappy," said Barbara.

"Yes, and I don't know who they came from. There was no card."

"I'll tell you who they were from. They were from me," said Barbara.

"They were? Well, thanks. Just what I wanted," said Billy.

"Just what you asked me for, last summer," said Barbara.

"Did I? I guess I did. Thank you for remembering. Well, goodnight, all. Don't wait up. I'll be home before breakfast."

They muttered their goodnights and he left. He wanted to—almost wanted to—stay; to tell his father that he did not want a Marmon for Christmas, which would have been a falsehood; to tell his mother he loved her in spite of her being a nitwit; to talk to Bobby about Roger Taylor, who was not good enough for her. But this was his first night home and he had his friends to see. Bobby had Roger, his father and mother had each other; thus far he had no one. But it did not detract from his feeling for his family that he now preferred the livelier company of his friends. *They* all had families, too, and *they* would be at the drugstore tonight. You didn't come home just to see the members of your family. As far as that goes, you got a Christmas vacation to celebrate the birth of the Christ child, but except for a few Catholics, who would go anywhere near a church? And besides, he could not talk to his family en masse. He would like to have a talk with his father, a talk with his sister, and he would enjoy a half hour of his mother's prattling. Those conversations would be personal if there were only two present,

but with more than two present everyone had to get his say in
and nobody said anything much. Oh, what was the use of making a lot of excuses? What was wrong with wanting to see your
friends?

The starter in the Dodge seemed to be whining, "No . . .
no . . . no . . ." before the engine caught. It reminded him of
a girl, a girl who protested every bit of the way, and she was not
just an imaginary girl. She was the girl he would telephone as
soon as he got to the drugstore, and he probably would be too
late, thanks to the conversation with his family. Irma Hipple,
her name was, and she was known as Miss Nipple. She lived up
the hill in back of the Court House. The boys from the best
families in town made a beeline for Irma as soon as they got
home from school. Hopefully the boys who got a date with her
would make a small but important purchase at the drugstore,
because you never knew when Irma might change her mind. A
great many lies had been told about Irma, and the worst liars
were the boys who claimed nothing but looked wise. Someone
must have gotten all the way with Irma sometime, but Billy did
not know who. It simply stood to reason that a girl who allowed so many boys to neck the hell out of her had delivered
the goods sometime. She was twenty-one or -two and already
she was beginning to lose her prettiness, probably because she
could hold her liquor as well as any boy, and better than some.
In her way she was a terrible snob. "That Roger Taylor got
soaked to the gills," she would say. "That Teddy Choate thinks
he's a cave man," or "I'm never going out with that Doctor
Boyd again. Imagine a doctor snapping his cookies in the
Stagecoach bar." Irma probably delivered the goods to the
older men. Someone who went to Penn had seen her at the
L'Aiglon supper club in Philadelphia with George W. Josling,
who was manager of one of the new stock brokerage branches
in town. There was a story around town that she had bitten
Jerome Kuhn, the optometrist, who was old enough to be her
father. It was hard to say what was true about Irma and what
wasn't. She was a saleswoman in one of the department stores;
she lived with her older sister and their father, who had one leg
and was a crossing watchman for the Pennsy; she was always

well dressed; she was pretty and full of pep. That much was true about her, and it was certainly true that she attracted men of all ages.

The telephone booth in the drugstore was occupied, and two or three boys were queued up beside it. Billy Warden shook hands with his friends and with Russell Covington, the head soda jerk. He ordered a lemon phosphate and lit a cigarette and kept an eye on the telephone booth. The door of the booth buckled open and out came Teddy Choate, nodding. "All set," he said to someone. "Everything is copacetic. I'm fixed up with the Nipple. She thinks she can get Patsy Lurio for you."

Billy Warden wanted to hit him.

"Hello, there, Billy. When'd you get in?" said Teddy.

"Hello, Teddy. I got in on the two-eighteen," said Billy.

"I hear you're going to be at Henny Cooper's house party," said Teddy.

"Jesus, you're a busybody. How did you hear that?"

"From Henny, naturally. Christ, I've known her since we were five years old. She invited me, but I have to go to these parties in New York."

"Funny, she told me she didn't know anybody in Gibbs-ville," said Billy.

"She's a congenital liar. Everybody knows that. I saw her Friday in New York. She was at a tea dance I went to. You ever been to that place in Montrose?"

"No."

"They've got everything there. A six-car garage. Swimming pool. Four-hole golf course, but they have the tees arranged so you can play nine holes. God knows how many horses. The old boy made his money in railroad stocks, and he sure did spend it up there. Very hard to get to know, Mr. Cooper. But he was in Dad's class at New Haven and we've known the Coopers since the Year One. I guess it was really Henny's grandfather that made the first big pile. Yes, Darius L. Cooper. You come across his name in American History courses. I suppose he was an old crook. But Henny's father is altogether different. Very con-servative. You won't see much of him at the house party, if he's there at all. They have an apartment at the Plaza, just the right size, their own furniture. I've been there many times, too."

"Then you do know them?" said Billy.

"Goodness, haven't I been telling you? We've known the Cooper family since the Year *One*," said Teddy. "Well, you have to excuse me. I have to whisper something to Russ Covington. Delicate matter. Got a date with the Nipple."

"You're excused," said Billy. He finished his phosphate and joined a group at the curbstone.

"What say, boy? I'll give you fifty to forty," said Andy Phillips.

"For how much?" said Billy.

"A dollar?"

"You're on," said Billy. They went down the block and upstairs to the poolroom. All the tables were busy save one, which was covered with black oilcloth. "What about the end table?" said Billy.

"Saving it," said Phil, the house man. "Getting up a crap game."

"How soon?"

"Right away. You want to get in?"

"I don't know. I guess so. What do you think, Andy?"

"I'd rather shoot pool," said Andy.

"You're gonna have a hell of a wait for a table," said Phil. "There's one, two, three, four—four Harrigan games going. And the first table just started shooting a hundred points for a fifty-dollar bet. You're not gonna hurry *them*."

"Let's go someplace else," said Andy.

"They'll all be crowded tonight. I think I'll get in the crap game," said Billy.

Phil removed the cover from the idle pool table and turned on the overhead lights, and immediately half a dozen young men gathered around it. "Who has the dice?" someone asked.

"I have," said Phil, shaking them in his half-open hand.

"Oh, great," said someone.

"You want to have a look at them?" said Phil. "You wouldn't know the difference anyway, but you can have a look. No? All right, I'm shooting a dollar. A dollar open."

"You're faded," said someone.

"Anybody else want a dollar?" said Phil.

"I'll take a dollar," said Billy Warden.

"A dollar to you, and a dollar to you. Anyone else? No? Okay. Here we go, and it's a nine. A niner, a niner, what could be finer. No drinks to a minor. And it's a five. Come on, dice, let's see that six-three for Phil. And it's a four? Come on, dice. Be nice. And it's a—a nine it is. Four dollars open. Billy, you want to bet the deuce?"

"You're covered," said Billy.

"You're covered," said the other bettor.

"Anybody else wish to participate? No? All right, eight dollars on the table, and—oh, what do I see there? A natural. The big six and the little one. Bet the four, Billy?"

"I'm with you," said Billy.

"I'm out," said the other bettor.

"I'm in," said a newcomer.

"Four dollars to you, four dollars to Mr. Warden. And here we go, and for little old Phil a—oh, my. The eyes of a snake. Back where you started from, Billy. House bets five dollars. Nobody wants the five? All right, any part of it."

"Two dollars," said Billy.

When it came his turn to take the dice he passed it up and chose instead to make bets on the side. Thus he nursed his stake until at one time he had thirty-eight or -nine dollars in his hands. The number of players was increasing, and all pretty much for the same reason: most of the boys had not yet got their Christmas money, and a crap game offered the best chance to add to the pre-Christmas bankroll.

"Why don't you drag?" said Andy Phillips. "Get out while you're ahead?"

"As soon as I have fifty dollars," said Billy.

The next time the shooter with the dice announced five dollars open, Billy covered it himself, won, and got the dice. In less than ten minutes he was cleaned, no paper money, nothing but the small change in his pants pocket. He looked around among the players, but there was no one whom he cared to borrow from. "Don't look at me," said Andy. "I have six bucks to last me till Christmas."

"Well, I have eighty-seven cents," said Billy. "Do you still want to spot me fifty to forty?"

"Sure. But not for a buck. You haven't got a buck," said Andy. "And I'm going to beat you."

They waited until a table was free, and played their fifty points, which Andy won, fifty to thirty-two. "I'll be big-hearted," said Andy. "I'll pay for the table."

"No, no. Thirty cents won't break me," said Billy. "Or do you want to play another? Give me fifty to thirty-five."

"No, I don't like this table. It's too high," said Andy.

"Well, what shall we do?" said Billy.

"The movies ought to be letting out pretty soon. Shall we go down and see if we can pick anything up?"

"Me with fifty-seven cents? And you with six bucks?"

"Well, you have the Dodge, and we could get a couple of pints on credit," said Andy.

"All right, we can try," said Billy. They left the poolroom and went down to the street and re-parked the Warden Dodge where they could observe the movie crowd on its way out. Attendance that night was slim, and passable girls in pairs no-where to be seen. The movie theater lights went out. "Well, so much for that," said Billy. "Five after eleven."

"Let's get a pint," said Andy.

"I honestly don't feel like it, Andy," said Billy.

"I didn't mean you were to buy it. I'll split it with you."

"I understood that part," said Billy. "Just don't feel like drinking."

"Do you have to *feel* like drinking at Dartmouth? Up at State we just drink."

"Oh, sure. Big hell-raisers," said Billy. "Kappa Betes and T.N.E.'s. 'Let's go over to Lock Haven and get slopped.' I heard all about State while I was at Mercersburg. That's why I didn't go there—one of the reasons."

"Is that so?" said Andy. "Well, if all you're gonna do is sit here and razz State, I think I'll go down to Mulhearn's and have a couple beers. You should have had sense enough to quit when you were thirty-some bucks ahead."

"Darius L. Cooper didn't quit when he was thirty bucks ahead."

"Who? You mean the fellow with the cake-eater suit? His name wasn't Cooper. His name is Minzer or something like that. Well, the beers are a quarter at Mulhearn's. We could have six fours are twenty-four. We could have twelve beers apiece. I'll lend you three bucks."

"No thanks," said Billy. "I'll take you down to Mulhearn's and then I think I'll go home and get some shut-eye. I didn't get any sleep on the train last night."

"That's what's the matter with you? All right, disagreeable. Safe at last in your trundle bed."

"How do you know that? That's a Dartmouth song," said Billy.

"I don't know, I guess I heard *you* sing it," said Andy. "Not tonight, though. I'll walk to Mulhearn's. I'll see you tomorrow."

"All right, Andy. See you tomorrow," said Billy. He watched his friend, with his felt hat turned up too much in front and back, his thick-soled Whitehouse & Hardy's clicking on the sidewalk, his joe-college swagger, his older brother's leather coat. Life was simple for Andy and always would be. In two more years he would finish at State, a college graduate, and he would come home and take a job in Phillips Brothers Lumber Yard, marry a local girl, join the Lions or Rotary, and play volleyball at the Y.M.C.A. His older brother had already done all those things, and Andy was Fred Phillips all over again.

The Dodge, still warm, did not repeat the whining protest of a few hours earlier in the evening. He put it in gear and headed for home. He hoped his father and mother would have gone to bed. "What the hell's the matter with me?" he said. "Nothing's right tonight."

He put the car in the garage and entered the house by the kitchen door. He opened the refrigerator door, and heard his father's voice. "Is that you, son?"

"Yes, it's me. I'm getting a glass of milk."

His father was in the sitting-room and made no answer. Billy drank a glass of milk and turned out the kitchen lights. He went to the sitting-room. His father, in shirtsleeves and smoking a pipe, was at the desk. "You doing your bookkeeping?" said Billy.

"No."

"What *are* you doing?"

"Well, if you must know, I was writing a poem. I was trying to express my appreciation to your mother."

"Can I see it?"

"Not in a hundred years," said Mr. Warden. "Nobody will ever see this but her—if she ever does."

"I never knew you wrote poetry."

"Once a year, for the past twenty-six years, starting with the first Christmas we were engaged. So far I haven't missed a year, but it doesn't get any easier. But by God, the first thing Christmas morning she'll say to me, 'Where's my poem?' Never speaks about it the rest of the year, but it's always the first thing she asks me the twenty-fifth of December."

"Has she kept them all?" said Billy.

"That I never asked her, but I suppose she has."

"Does she write you one?" said Billy.

"Nope. Well, what did you do tonight? You're home early, for you."

"Kind of tired. I didn't get much sleep last night. We got on the train at White River Junction and nobody could sleep."

"Well, get to bed and sleep till noon. That ought to restore your energy."

"Okay. Goodnight, Dad."

"Goodnight, son," said his father. "Oh, say. You had a long-distance call. You're to call the Scranton operator, no matter what time you get in."

"Thanks," said Billy. "Goodnight."

"Well, aren't you going to put the call in? I'll wait in the kitchen."

"No, I know who it is. I'll phone them tomorrow."

"That's up to you," said Mr. Warden. "Well, goodnight again."

"Goodnight," said Billy. He went to his room and took off his clothes, to the bathroom and brushed his teeth. He put out the light beside his bed and lay there. He wondered if Henrietta Cooper's father had ever written a poem to her mother. But he knew the answer to that.

I Know What You Need

by Stephen King

"I know what you need."

Elizabeth looked up from her sociology text, startled, and saw a rather nondescript young man in a green fatigue jacket. For a moment she thought he looked familiar, as if she had known him before; the feeling was close to déjà vu. Then it was gone. He was about her height, skinny, and . . . twitchy. That was the word. He wasn't moving, but he seemed to be twitching inside his skin, just out of sight. His hair was black and unkempt. He wore thick horn-rimmed glasses that magnified his dark brown eyes, and the lenses looked dirty. No, she was quite sure she had never seen him before.

"You know," she said, "I doubt that."

"You need a strawberry double-dip cone. Right?"

She blinked at him, frankly startled. Somewhere in the back of her mind she *had* been thinking about breaking for an ice cream. She was studying for finals in one of the third-floor carrels of the Student Union, and there was still a woefully long way to go.

"Right?" he persisted, and smiled. It transformed his face from something over-intense and nearly ugly into something else that was oddly appealing. The word "cute" occurred to her, and that wasn't a good word to afflict a boy with, but this one was when he smiled. She smiled back before she could roadblock it behind her lips. This she didn't need, to have to waste time brushing off some weirdo who had decided to pick the worst time of the year to try to make an impression. She still had sixteen chapters of *Introduction to Sociology* to wade through.

"No thanks," she said.

"Come on, if you hit them any harder you'll give yourself a headache. You've been at it two hours without a break."

"How would you know that?"

"I've been watching you," he said promptly, but this time his gamin grin was lost on her. She already had a headache.

"Well, you can stop," she said, more sharply than she had intended. "I don't like people staring at me."

"I'm sorry." She felt a little sorry for him, the way she sometimes felt sorry for stray dogs. He seemed to float in the green fatigue jacket and . . . yes, he had on mismatched socks. One black, one brown. She felt herself getting ready to smile again and held it back.

"I've got these finals," she said gently.

"Sure," he said. "Okay."

She looked after him for a moment pensively. Then she lowered her gaze to her book, but an afterimage of the encounter remained: *strawberry double-dip.*

When she got back to the dorm it was 11:15 P.M. and Alice was stretched out on her bed, listening to Neil Diamond and reading *The Story of O.*

"I didn't know they assigned that in Eh-17," Elizabeth said.

Alice sat up. "Broadening my horizons, darling. Spreading my intellectual wings. Raising my . . . Liz?"

"Hmmm?"

"Did you hear what I said?"

"No, sorry, I—"

"You look like somebody conked you one, kid."

"I met a guy tonight. Sort of a funny guy, at that."

"Oh? He must be something if he can separate the great Rogan from her beloved texts."

"His name is Edward Jackson Hamner. Junior, no less. Short. Skinny. Looks like he washed his hair last around Washington's birthday. Oh, and mismatched socks. One black, one brown."

"I thought you were more the fraternity type."

"It's nothing like that, Alice. I was studying at the Union on the third floor—the Think Tank—and he invited me down to the Grinder for an ice-cream cone. I told him no and he sort of slunk off. But once he started me thinking about ice cream, I couldn't stop. I'd just decided to give up and take a break and there he was, holding a big, drippy strawberry double-dip in each hand."

"I tremble to hear the denouement."

Elizabeth snorted. "Well, I couldn't really say no. So he sat down, and it turns out he had sociology with Professor Branner last year."

"Will wonders never cease, lawd a mercy. Goshen to Christmas—"

"Listen, this is really amazing. You know the way I've been sweating that course?"

"Yes. You talk about it in your sleep, practically."

"I've got a seventy-eight average. I've got to have an eighty to keep my scholarship, and that means I need at least an eighty-four on the final. Well, this Ed Hamner says Branner uses almost the same final every year. And Ed's eidetic."

"You mean he's got a whatzit . . . photographic memory?"

"Yes. Look at this." She opened her sociology book and took out three sheets of notebook paper covered with writing.

Alice took them. "This looks like multiple-choice stuff."

"It is. Ed says it's Branner's last year's final *word for word.*"

Alice said flatly, "I don't believe it."

"But it covers all the material!"

"Still don't believe it." She handed the sheets back. "Just because this spook—"

"He isn't a spook. Don't call him that."

"Okay. This little *guy* hasn't got you bamboozled into just memorizing this and not studying at all, has he?"

"Of course not," she said uneasily.

"And even if this is like the exam, do you think it's exactly ethical?"

Anger surprised her and ran away with her tongue before she could hold it. "That's great for you, sure. Dean's List every semester and your folks paying your way. You aren't . . . Hey, I'm sorry. There was no call for that."

Alice shrugged and opened *O* again, her face carefully neutral. "No, you're right. Not my business. But why don't you study the book, too . . . just to be safe?"

"Of course I will."

But mostly she studied the exam notes provided by Edward Jackson Hamner, Jr.

When she came out of the lecture hall after the exam he was sitting in the lobby, floating in his green army fatigue coat. He smiled tentatively at her and stood up. "How'd it go?"

Impulsively, she kissed his cheek. She could not remember such a blessed feeling of relief. "I think I aced it."

"Really? That's great. Like a burger?"

"Love one," she said absently. Her mind was still on the exam. It was the one Ed had given her, almost word for word, and she had sailed through.

Over hamburgers, she asked him how his own finals were going.

"Don't have any. I'm in Honors, and you don't take them unless you want to. I was doing okay, so I didn't."

"Then why are you still here?"

"I had to see how you did, didn't I?"

"Ed, you didn't. That's sweet, but—" The naked look in his eyes troubled her. She had seen it before. She was a pretty girl.

"Yes," he said softly. "Yes, I did."

"Ed, I'm grateful. I think you saved my scholarship. I really do. But I have a boyfriend, you know."

"Serious?" he asked, with a poor attempt to speak lightly.

"Very," she said, matching his tone. "Almost engaged."

"Does he know he's lucky? Does he know how lucky?"

"I'm lucky, too," she said, thinking of Tony Lombard.

"Beth," he said suddenly.

"What?" she asked, startled.

"Nobody calls you that, do they?"

"Why . . . no. No, they don't."

"Not even this guy?"

"No—" Tony called her Liz. Sometimes Lizzie, which was even worse.

He leaned forward. "But Beth is what you like best, isn't it?"

She laughed to cover her confusion. "Whatever in the world—"

"Never mind." He grinned his gamin grin. "I'll call you Beth. That's better. Now eat your hamburger."

Then her junior year was over, and she was saying good-bye to Alice. They were a little stiff together, and Elizabeth was sorry. She supposed it was her own fault; she *had* crowed a little loudly about her sociology final when grades were posted. She had scored a ninety-seven—highest in the division.

Well, she told herself as she waited at the airport for her flight to be called, it wasn't any more unethical than the cramming she had been resigned to in that third-floor carrel. Cramming wasn't real studying at all; just rote memorization that faded away to nothing as soon as the exam was over.

She fingered the envelope that poked out of her purse. Notice of her scholarship-loan package for her senior year—two thousand dollars. She and Tony would be working together in Boothbay, Maine, this summer, and the money she would earn there would put her over the top. And thanks to Ed Hamner, it was going to be a beautiful summer. Clear sailing all the way.

But it was the most miserable summer of her life.

June was rainy, the gas shortage depressed the tourist trade, and her tips at the Boothbay Inn were mediocre. Even worse, Tony was pressing her on the subject of marriage. He could get a job on or near campus, he said, and with her Student Aid grant, she could get her degree in style. She was surprised to find that the idea scared rather than pleased her.

Something was *wrong*.

She didn't know what, but something was missing, out of whack, out of kilter. One night late in July she frightened herself by going on a hysterical crying jag in her apartment. The only good thing about it was that her roommate, a mousy little girl named Sandra Ackerman, was out on a date.

The nightmare came in early August. She was lying in the bottom of an open grave, unable to move. Rain fell from a white sky onto her upturned face. Then Tony was standing over her, wearing his yellow high-impact construction helmet.

"Marry me, Liz," he said, looking down at her expressionlessly. "Marry me or else."

She tried to speak, to agree; she would do anything if only he would take her out of this dreadful muddy hole. But she was paralyzed.

"All right," he said. "It's or else, then."

He went away. She struggled to break out of her paralysis and couldn't.

Then she heard the bulldozer.

A moment later she saw it, a high yellow monster, pushing a mound of wet earth in front of the blade. Tony's merciless face looked down from the open cab.

He was going to bury her alive.

Trapped in her motionless, voiceless body, she could only watch in dumb horror. Trickles of dirt began to run down the sides of the hole—

A familiar voice cried, "Go! Leave her now! *Go!*"

Tony stumbled down from the bulldozer and ran.

Huge relief swept her. She would have cried had she been able. And her savior appeared, standing at the foot of the open grave like a sexton. It was Ed Hamner, floating in his green fatigue jacket, his hair awry, his horn-rims slipped down to the small bulge at the end of his nose. He held his hand out to her.

"Get up," he said gently. "I know what you need. Get up, Beth."

And she could get up. She sobbed with relief. She tried to thank him; her words spilled out on top of each other. And Ed only smiled gently and nodded. She took his hand and looked down to see her footing. And when she looked up again, she was holding the paw of a huge, slavering timber wolf with red hurricane-lantern eyes and thick, spiked teeth open to bite.

She woke up sitting bolt upright in bed, her nightgown drenched with sweat. Her body was shaking uncontrollably. And even after a warm shower and a glass of milk, she could not reconcile herself to the dark. She slept with the light on.

A week later Tony was dead.

* * *

She opened the door in her robe, expecting to see Tony, but it was Danny Kilmer, one of the fellows he worked with. Danny was a fun guy; she and Tony had doubled with him and his girl a couple of times. But standing in the doorway of her second-floor apartment, Danny looked not only serious but ill.

"Danny?" she said. "What—"

"Liz," he said. "Liz, you've got to hold on to yourself. You've . . . *ah, God!*" He pounded the jamb of the door with one big-knuckled, dirty hand, and she saw he was crying.

"Danny, is it Tony? Is something—"

"Tony's dead," Danny said. "He was—" But he was talking to air. She had fainted.

The next week passed in a kind of dream. The story pieced itself together from the woefully brief newspaper account and from what Danny told her over a beer in the Harbor Inn.

They had been repairing drainage culverts on Route 16. Part of the road was torn up, and Tony was flagging traffic. A kid driving a red Fiat had been coming down the hill. Tony had flagged him, but the kid never even slowed. Tony had been standing next to a dump truck, and there was no place to jump back. The kid in the Fiat had sustained head lacerations and a broken arm; he was hysterical and also cold sober. The police found several holes in his brake lines, as if they had overheated and then melted through. His driving record was A-1; he had simply been unable to stop. Her Tony had been a victim of that rarest of automobile mishaps: an honest accident.

Her shock and depression were increased by guilt. The fates had taken out of her hands the decision on what to do about Tony. And a sick, secret part of her was glad it was so. Because she hadn't wanted to marry Tony . . . not since the night of her dream.

She broke down the day before she went home.

She was sitting on a rock outcropping by herself, and after an hour or so the tears came. They surprised her with their fury. She cried until her stomach hurt and her head ached, and when the tears passed she felt not better but at least drained and empty.

And that was when Ed Hamner said, "Beth?"

She jerked around, her mouth filled with the copper taste of fear, half expecting to see the snarling wolf of her dream. But it was only Ed Hamner, looking sunburned and strangely defenseless without his fatigue jacket and blue jeans. He was wearing red shorts that stopped just ahead of his bony knees, a white T-shirt that billowed on his thin chest like a loose sail in the ocean breeze, and rubber thongs. He wasn't smiling and the fierce sun glitter on his glasses made it impossible to see his eyes.

"Ed?" she said tentatively, half convinced that this was some grief-induced hallucination. "Is that really—"

"Yes, it's me."

"How—"

"I've been working at the Lakewood Theater in Skowhegan. I ran into your roommate . . . Alice, is that her name?"

"Yes."

"She told me what happened. I came right away. Poor Beth." He moved his head, only a degree or so, but the sun glare slid off his glasses and she saw nothing wolfish, nothing predatory, but only a calm, warm sympathy.

She began to weep again, and staggered a little with the unexpected force of it. Then he was holding her and then it was all right.

They had dinner at the Silent Woman in Waterville, which was twenty-five miles away; maybe exactly the distance she needed. They went in Ed's car, a new Corvette, and he drove well—neither showily nor fussily, as she guessed he might. She didn't want to talk and she didn't want to be cheered up. He seemed to know it, and played quiet music on the radio.

And he ordered without consulting her—seafood. She thought she wasn't hungry, but when the food came she fell to ravenously.

When she looked up again her plate was empty and she

laughed nervously. Ed was smoking a cigarette and watching her.

"The grieving damosel ate a hearty meal," she said. "You must think I'm awful."

"No," he said. "You've been through a lot and you need to get your strength back. It's like being sick, isn't it?"

"Yes. Just like that."

He took her hand across the table, squeezed it briefly, then let it go. "But now it's recuperation time, Beth."

"Is it? Is it really?"

"Yes," he said. "So tell me. What are your plans?"

"I'm going home tomorrow. After that, I don't know."

"You're going back to school, aren't you?"

"I just don't know. After this, it seems so . . . so trivial. A lot of the purpose seems to have gone out of it. And all the fun."

"It'll come back. That's hard for you to believe now, but it's true. Try it for six weeks and see. You've got nothing better to do." The last seemed a question.

"That's true, I guess. But . . . Can I have a cigarette?"

"Sure. They're menthol, though. Sorry."

She took one. "How did you know I didn't like menthol cigarettes?"

He shrugged. "You just don't look like one of those, I guess."

She smiled. "You're funny, do you know that?"

He smiled neutrally.

"No, really. For you of all people to turn up . . . I thought I didn't want to see anyone. But I'm really glad it was you, Ed."

"Sometimes it's nice to be with someone you're not involved with."

"That's it, I guess." She paused. "Who are you, Ed, besides my fairy godfather? Who are you really?" It was suddenly important to her that she know.

He shrugged. "Nobody much. Just one of the sort of funny-looking guys you see creeping around campus with a load of books under one arm—"

"Ed, you're not funny-looking."

"Sure I am," he said, and smiled. "Never grew all the way out of my high-school acne, never got rushed by a big frat, never made any kind of splash in the social whirl. Just a dorm rat making grades, that's all. When the big corporations interview on campus next spring, I'll probably sign on with one of them and Ed Hamner will disappear forever."

"That would be a great shame," she said softly.

He smiled, and it was a very peculiar smile. Almost bitter.

"What about your folks?" she asked. "Where you live, what you like to do—"

"Another time," he said. "I want to get you back. You've got a long plane ride tomorrow, and a lot of hassles."

The evening left her relaxed for the first time since Tony's death, without that feeling that somewhere inside a mainspring was being wound and wound to the breaking point. She thought sleep would come easily, but it did not.

Little questions nagged.

Alice told me . . . poor Beth.

But Alice was summering in Kittery, eighty miles from Skowhegan. She must have been at Lakewood for a play.

The Corvette, this year's model. Expensive. A backstage job at Lakewood hadn't paid for that. Were his parents rich?

He had ordered just what she would have ordered herself. Maybe the only thing on the menu she would have eaten enough of to discover that she was hungry.

The menthol cigarettes, the way he had kissed her good night, exactly as she had wanted to be kissed. And—

You've got a long plane ride tomorrow.

He knew she was going home because she had told him. But how had he known she was going by plane? Or that it was a long ride?

It bothered her. It bothered her because she was halfway to being in love with Ed Hamner.

I know what you need.

Like the voice of a submarine captain tolling off fathoms, the words he had greeted her with followed her down to sleep.

* * *

He didn't come to the tiny Augusta airport to see her off, and waiting for the plane, she was surprised by her own disappointment. She was thinking about how quietly you could grow to depend on a person, almost like a junkie with a habit. The hype fools himself that he can take this stuff or leave it, when really—

"Elizabeth Rogan," the PA blared. "Please pick up the white courtesy phone."

She hurried to it. And Ed's voice said, "Beth?"

"Ed! It's good to hear you. I thought maybe . . ."

"That I'd meet you?" He laughed. "You don't need me for that. You're a big strong girl. Beautiful, too. You can handle this. Will I see you at school?"

"I . . . yes, I think so."

"Good." There was a moment of silence. Then he said, "Because I love you. I have from the first time I saw you."

Her tongue was locked. She couldn't speak. A thousand thoughts whirled through her mind.

He laughed again, gently. "No, don't say anything. Not now. I'll see you. There'll be time then. All the time in the world. Good trip, Beth. Goodbye."

And he was gone, leaving her with a white phone in her hand and her own chaotic thoughts and questions.

September.

Elizabeth picked up the old pattern of school and classes like a woman who has been interrupted at knitting. She was rooming with Alice again, of course; they had been roomies since freshman year, when they had been thrown together by the housing-department computer. They had always gotten along well, despite differing interests and personalities. Alice was the studious one, a chemistry major with a 3.6 average. Elizabeth was more social, less bookish, with a split major in education and math.

They still got on well, but a faint coolness seemed to have grown up between them over the summer. Elizabeth chalked it up to the difference of opinion over the sociology final, and didn't mention it.

The events of the summer began to seem dreamlike. In a funny way it sometimes seemed that Tony might have been a boy she had known in high school. It still hurt to think about him, and she avoided the subject with Alice, but the hurt was an old-bruise throb and not the bright pain of an open wound.

What hurt more was Ed Hamner's failure to call.

A week passed, then two, then it was October. She got a student directory from the Union and looked up his name. It was no help; after his name were only the words "Mill St." And Mill was a very long street indeed. And so she waited, and when she was called for dates—which was often—she turned them down. Alice raised her eyebrows but said nothing; she was buried alive in a six-week biochem project and spent most of her evenings at the library. Elizabeth noticed the long white envelopes that her roommate was receiving once or twice a week in the mail—since she was usually back from class first— but thought nothing of them. The private detective agency was discreet; it did not print its return address on its envelopes.

When the intercom buzzed, Alice was studying. "You get it, Liz. Probably for you anyway."

Elizabeth went to the intercom. "Yes?"

"Gentleman door-caller, Liz."

Oh, Lord.

"Who is it?" she asked, annoyed, and ran through her tattered stack of excuses. Migraine headache. She hadn't used that one this week.

The desk girl said, amused, "His name is Edward Jackson Hamner. *Junior,* no less." Her voice lowered. "His socks don't match."

Elizabeth's hand flew to the collar of her robe. "Oh, God. Tell him I'll be right down. No, tell him it will be just a minute. No, a couple of minutes, okay?"

"Sure," the voice said dubiously. "Don't have a hemorrhage."

Elizabeth took a pair of slacks out of her closet. Took out a short denim skirt. Felt the curlers in her hair and groaned. Began to yank them out.

Alice watched all this calmly, without speaking, but she looked speculatively at the door for a long time after Elizabeth had left.

He looked just the same; he hadn't changed at all. He was wearing his green fatigue jacket, and it still looked at least two sizes too big. One of the bows of his horn-rimmed glasses had been mended with electrician's tape. His jeans looked new and stiff, miles from the soft and faded "in" look that Tony had achieved effortlessly. He was wearing one green sock, one brown sock.

And she knew she loved him.

"Why didn't you call before?" she asked, going to him.

He stuck his hands in the pockets of his jacket and grinned shyly. "I thought I'd give you some time to date around. Meet some guys. Figure out what you want."

"I think I know that."

"Good. Would you like to go to a movie?"

"Anything," she said. "Anything at all."

As the days passed it occurred to her that she had never met anyone, male or female, that seemed to understand her moods and needs so completely or so wordlessly. Their tastes coincided. While Tony had enjoyed violent movies of the *Godfather* type, Ed seemed more into comedy or nonviolent dramas. He took her to the circus one night when she was feeling low and they had a hilariously wonderful time. Study dates were real study dates, not just an excuse to grope on the third floor of the Union. He took her to dances and seemed especially good at the old ones, which she loved. They won a fifties Stroll trophy at a Homecoming Nostalgia Dance. More important, he seemed to understand when she wanted to be passionate. He didn't force her or hurry her; she never got the feeling that she had with some of the other boys she had gone out with—that there was an inner timetable for sex, beginning with a kiss good night on Date 1 and ending with a night in some friend's bor-

rowed apartment on Date 10. The Mill Street apartment was
Ed's exclusively, a third-floor walk-up. They went there often,
and Elizabeth went without the feeling that she was walking
into some minor-league Don Juan's passion pit. He didn't push.
He honestly seemed to want what she wanted, when she
wanted it. And things progressed.

When school reconvened following the semester break, Alice
seemed strangely preoccupied. Several times that afternoon before Ed came to pick her up—they were going out to dinner—
Elizabeth looked up to see her roommate frowning down at a
large manila envelope on her desk. Once Elizabeth almost
asked about it, then decided not to. Some new project probably.

It was snowing hard when Ed brought her back to the dorm.
"Tomorrow?" he asked. "My place?"
"Sure. I'll make some popcorn."
"Great," he said, and kissed her. "I love you, Beth."
"Love you, too."
"Would you like to stay over?" Ed asked evenly. "Tomorrow
night?"
"All right, Ed." She looked into his eyes. "Whatever you
want."
"Good," he said quietly. "Sleep well, kid."
"You, too."
She expected that Alice would be asleep and entered the
room quietly, but Alice was up and sitting at her desk.
"Alice, are you okay?"
"I have to talk to you, Liz. About Ed."
"What about him?"
Alice said carefully, "I think that when I finish talking to
you we're not going to be friends anymore. For me, that's giv-
ing up a lot. So I want you to listen carefully."
"Then maybe you better not say anything."
"I have to try."
Elizabeth felt her initial curiosity kindle into anger. "Have
you been snooping around Ed?"
Alice only looked at her.

"Were you jealous of us?"

"No. If I'd been jealous of you and your dates, I would have moved out two years ago."

Elizabeth looked at her, perplexed. She knew what Alice said was the truth. And she suddenly felt afraid.

"Two things made me wonder about Ed Hamner," Alice said. "First, you wrote me about Tony's death and said how lucky it was that I'd seen Ed at the Lakewood Theater . . . how he came right over to Boothbay and really helped you out. But I never saw him, Liz. I was never near the Lakewood Theater last summer."

"But . . ."

"But how did he know Tony was dead? I have no idea. I only know he didn't get it from me. The other thing was that eidetic-memory business. My God, Liz, he can't even remember which socks he's got on!"

"That's a different thing altogether," Liz said stiffly. "It—"

"Ed Hamner was in Las Vegas last summer," Alice said softly. "He came back in mid-July and took a motel room in Pemaquid. That's just across the Boothbay Harbor town line. Almost as if he were waiting for you to need him."

"That's crazy! And how would you know Ed was in Las Vegas?"

"I ran into Shirley D'Antonio just before school started. She worked in the Pines Restaurant, which is just across from the playhouse. She said she never saw anybody who looked like Ed Hamner. So I've known he's been lying to you about several things. And so I went to my father and laid it out and he gave me the go-ahead."

"To do what?" Elizabeth asked, bewildered.

"To hire a private detective agency."

Elizabeth was on her feet. "No more, Alice. That's it." She would catch the bus into town, spend tonight at Ed's apartment. She had only been waiting for him to ask her, anyway.

"At least *know*," Alice said. "Then make your own decision."

"I don't have to know anything except he's kind and good and—"

"Love is blind, huh?" Alice said, and smiled bitterly. "Well, maybe I happen to love you a little, Liz. Have you ever thought of that?"

Elizabeth turned and looked at her for a long moment. "If you do, you've got a funny way of showing it," she said. "Go on, then. Maybe you're right. Maybe I owe you that much. Go on."

"You knew him a long time ago," Alice said quietly.

"I . . . what?"

"P.S. 119, Bridgeport, Connecticut."

Elizabeth was struck dumb. She and her parents had lived in Bridgeport for six years, moving to their present home the year after she had finished the second grade. She *had* gone to P.S. 119, but—

"Alice, are you sure?"

"Do you remember him?"

"No, of course not!" But she *did* remember the feeling she'd had the first time she had seen Ed—the feeling of déjà vu.

"The pretty ones never remember the ugly ducklings, I guess. Maybe he had a crush on you. You were in the first grade with him, Liz. Maybe he sat in the back of the room and just . . . watched you. Or on the playground. Just a little nothing kid who already wore glasses and probably braces and you couldn't even remember him, but I'll bet he remembers you."

Elizabeth said, "What else?"

"The agency traced him from school fingerprints. After that it was just a matter of finding people and talking to them. The operative assigned to the case said he couldn't understand some of what he was getting. Neither do I. Some of it's scary."

"It better be," Elizabeth said grimly.

"Ed Hamner, Sr., was a compulsive gambler. He worked for a top-line advertising agency in New York and then moved to Bridgeport sort of on the run. The operative says that almost every big-money poker game and high-priced book in the city was holding his markers."

Elizabeth closed her eyes. "These people really saw you got a full measure of dirt for your dollar, didn't they?"

"Maybe. Anyway, Ed's father got in another jam in

Bridgeport. It was gambling again, but this time he got mixed up with a big-time loan shark. He got a broken leg and a broken arm somehow. The operative says he doubts it was an accident."

"Anything else?" Elizabeth asked. "Child beating? Embezzlement?"

"He landed a job with a two-bit Los Angeles ad agency in 1961. That was a little too close to Las Vegas. He started to spend his weekends there, gambling heavily . . . and losing. Then he started taking Ed Junior with him. And he started to win."

"You're making all of this up. You must be."

Alice tapped the report in front of her. "It's all here, Liz. Some of it wouldn't stand up in court, but the operative says none of the people he talked with would have a reason to lie. Ed's father called Ed his 'good luck charm.' At first, nobody objected to the boy even though it was illegal for him to be in the casinos. His father was a prize fish. But then the father started sticking just to roulette, playing only odd-even and red-black. By the end of the year the boy was off-limits in every casino on the strip. And his father took up a new kind of gambling."

"What?"

"The stock market. When the Hamners moved to L.A. in the middle of 1961, they were living in a ninety-dollar-a-month cheese box and Mr. Hamner was driving a '52 Chevrolet. At the end of 1962, just sixteen months later, he had quit his job and they were living in their own home in San Jose. Mr. Hamner was driving a brand-new Thunderbird and Mrs. Hamner had a Volkswagen. You see, it's against the law for a small boy to be in the Nevada casinos, but no one could take the stock-market page away from him."

"Are you implying that Ed . . . that he could . . . Alice, you're crazy!"

"I'm not implying anything. Unless maybe just that he knew what his daddy needed."

I know what you need.

It was almost as if the words had been spoken into her ear, and she shuddered.

"Mrs. Hamner spent the next six years in and out of various mental institutions. Supposedly for nervous disorders, but the operative talked to an orderly who said she was pretty close to psychotic. She claimed her son was the devil's henchman. She stabbed him with a pair of scissors in 1964. Tried to kill him. She . . . Liz? Liz, what is it?"

"The scar," she muttered. "We went swimming at the University pool on an open night about a month ago. He's got a deep, dimpled scar on his shoulder . . . here." She put her hand just above her left breast. "He said . . ." A wave of nausea tried to climb up her throat and she had to wait for it to recede before she could go on. "He said he fell on a picket fence when he was a little boy."

"Shall I go on?"

"Finish, why not? What can it hurt now?"

"His mother was released from a very plush mental institution in the San Joaquin Valley in 1968. The three of them went on a vacation. They stopped at a picnic spot on Route 101. The boy was collecting firewood when she drove the car right over the edge of the dropoff above the ocean with both her and her husband in it. It might have been an attempt to run Ed down. By then he was nearly eighteen. His father left him a million-dollar stock portfolio. Ed came east a year and a half later and enrolled here. And that's the end."

"No more skeletons in the closet?"

"Liz, aren't there enough?"

She got up. "No wonder he never wants to mention his family. But you had to dig up the corpse, didn't you?"

"You're blind," Alice said. Elizabeth was putting on her coat. "I suppose you're going to him."

"Right."

"Because you love him."

"Right."

Alice crossed the room and grabbed her arm. "Will you get that sulky, petulant look off your face for a second and *think*! Ed Hamner is able to do things the rest of us only dream about.

He got his father a stake at roulette and made him rich playing the stock market. He seems to be able to will winning. Maybe he's some kind of low-grade psychic. Maybe he's got precognition. I don't know. There are people who seem to have a dose of that. Liz, hasn't it ever occurred to you that he's forced you to love him?"

Liz turned to her slowly. "I've never heard anything so ridiculous in my life."

"Is it? He gave you that sociology test the same way he gave his father the right side of the roulette board! He was never enrolled in any sociology course! I checked. He did it because it was the only way he could make you take him seriously!"

"Stop it!" Liz cried. She clapped her hands over her ears.

"He knew the test, and he knew when Tony was killed, and he knew you were going home on a plane! He even knew just the right psychological moment to step back into your life last October."

Elizabeth pulled away from her and opened the door.

"Please," Alice said. "Please, Liz, listen. I don't know how he can do those things. I doubt if even *he* knows for sure. He might not mean to do you any harm, but he already is. He's made you love him by knowing every secret thing you want and need, and that's not love at all. That's rape."

Elizabeth slammed the door and ran down the stairs.

She caught the last bus of the evening into town. It was snowing more heavily than ever, and the bus lumbered through the drifts that had blown across the road like a crippled beetle. Elizabeth sat in the back, one of only six or seven passengers, a thousand thoughts in her mind.

Menthol cigarettes. The stock exchange. The way he had known her mother's nickname was Deedee. A little boy sitting at the back of a first-grade classroom, making sheep's eyes at a vivacious little girl too young to understand that—

I know what you need.

No. No. No. I do love him!

Did she? Or was she simply delighted at being with someone who always ordered the right thing, took her to the right movie, and did not want to go anywhere or do anything she didn't? Was he just a kind of psychic mirror, showing her only what she wanted to see? The presents he gave were always the right presents. When the weather had turned suddenly cold and she had been longing for a hair dryer, who gave her one? Ed Hamner, of course. Just happened to see one on sale in Day's, he had said. She, of course, had been delighted.

That's not love at all. That's rape.

The wind clawed at her face as she stepped out on the corner of Main and Mill, and she winced against it as the bus drew away with a smooth diesel growl. Its taillights twinkled briefly in the snowy night for a moment and were gone.

She had never felt so lonely in her life.

He wasn't home.

She stood outside his door after five minutes of knocking, nonplussed. It occurred to her that she had no idea what Ed did or whom he saw when he wasn't with her. The subject had never come up.

Maybe he's raising the price of another hair dryer in a poker game.

With sudden decision she stood on her toes and felt along the top of the doorjamb for the spare key she knew he kept there. Her fingers stumbled over it and it fell to the hall floor with a clink.

She picked it up and used it in the lock.

The apartment looked different with Ed gone—artificial, like a stage set. It had often amused her that someone who cared so little about his personal appearance should have such a neat, picture-book domicile. Almost as if he had decorated it for her and not himself. But of course that was crazy. Wasn't it?

It occurred to her again, as if for the first time, how much she liked the chair she sat in when they studied or watched TV. It was just right, the way Baby Bear's chair had been for Goldilocks. Not too hard, not too soft. Just right. Like everything else she associated with Ed.

There were two doors opening off the living room. One went to the kitchenette, the other to his bedroom.

The wind whistled outside, making the old apartment building creak and settle.

In the bedroom, she stared at the brass bed. It looked neither too hard nor too soft, but just right. An insidious voice smirked: *It's almost too perfect, isn't it?*

She went to the bookcase and ran her eye aimlessly over the titles. One jumped at her eyes and she pulled it out: *Dance Crazes of the Fifties.* The book opened cleanly to a point some three-quarters through. A section titled "The Stroll" had been circled heavily in red grease pencil and in the margin the word BETH had been written in large, almost accusatory letters.

I ought to go now, she told herself. I can still save something. If he came back now I could never look him in the face again and Alice would win. Then she'd really get her money's worth.

But she couldn't stop, and knew it. Things had gone too far.

She went to the closet and turned the knob, but it didn't give. Locked.

On the off chance, she stood on tiptoe again and felt along the top of the door. And her fingers felt a key. She took it down and somewhere inside a voice said very clearly: *Don't do this.* She thought of Bluebeard's wife and what she had found when she opened the wrong door. But it was indeed too late; if she didn't proceed now she would always wonder. She opened the closet.

And had the strangest feeling that this was where the real Ed Hamner, Jr., had been hiding all the time.

The closet was a mess—a jumbled rickrack of clothes, books, an unstrung tennis racket, a pair of tattered tennis shoes, old prelims and reports tossed helter-skelter, a spilled pouch of Borkum Riff pipe tobacco. His green fatigue jacket had been flung in the far corner.

She picked up one of the books and blinked at the title. *The Golden Bough.* Another. *Ancient Rites, Modern Mysteries.* Another. *Haitian Voodoo.* And a last one, bound in old, cracked leather, the title almost rubbed off the binding by much handling, smelling vaguely like rotted fish: *Necronomicon.* She opened it at random, gasped, and flung it away, the obscenity still hanging before her eyes.

More to regain her composure than anything else, she reached for the green fatigue jacket, not admitting to herself that she meant to go through its pockets. But as she lifted it she saw something else. A small tin box . . .

Curiously, she picked it up and turned it over in her hands, hearing things rattle inside. It was the kind of box a young boy might choose to keep his treasures in. Stamped in raised letters on the tin bottom were the words "Bridgeport Candy Co." She opened it.

The doll was on top. The Elizabeth doll.

She looked at it and began to shudder.

The doll was dressed in a scrap of red nylon, part of a scarf she had lost two or three months back. At a movie with Ed. The arms were pipe cleaners that had been draped in stuff that looked like blue moss. Graveyard moss, perhaps. There was hair on the doll's head, but that was wrong. It was fine white flax, taped to the doll's pink gum-eraser head. Her own hair was sandy blond and coarser than this. This was more the way her hair had been—

When she was a little girl.

She swallowed and there was a clicking in her throat. Hadn't they all been issued scissors in the first grade, tiny scissors with rounded blade, just right for a child's hand? Had that long-ago little boy crept up behind her, perhaps at nap time, and—

Elizabeth put the doll aside and looked in the box again. There was a blue poker chip with a strange six-sided pattern drawn on it in red ink. A tattered newspaper obituary—Mr. and Mrs. Edward Hamner. The two of them smiled meaninglessly out of the accompanying photo, and she saw that the same six-sided pattern had been drawn across their faces, this time in black ink, like a pall. Two more dolls, one male, one female. The similarity to the faces in the obituary photograph was hideous, unmistakable.

And something else.

She fumbled it out, and her fingers shook so badly she almost dropped it. A tiny sound escaped her.

It was a model car, the sort small boys buy in drugstores and hobby shops and then assemble with airplane glue. This one

was a Fiat. It had been painted red. And a piece of what looked
like one of Tony's shirts had been taped to the front.

She turned the model car upside down. Someone had hammered the underside to fragments.

"So you found it, you ungrateful bitch."

She screamed and dropped the car and the box. His foul
treasures sprayed across the floor.

He was standing in the doorway, looking at her. She had
never seen such a look of hate on a human face.

She said, "You killed Tony."

He grinned unpleasantly. "Do you think you could prove
it?"

"It doesn't matter," she said, surprised at the steadiness of
her own voice. "I know. And I never want to see you again.
Ever. And if you do . . . anything . . . to anyone else, I'll
know. And I'll fix you. Somehow."

His face twisted. "That's the thanks I get. I gave you everything you ever wanted. Things no other man could have. Admit
it. I made you perfectly happy."

"*You killed Tony!*" She screamed it at him.

He took another step into the room. "Yes, and I did it for
you. And what are you, Beth? You don't know what love is. I
loved you from the first time I saw you, over seventeen years
ago. Could Tony say that? It's never been hard for you. You're
pretty. You never had to think about wanting or needing or
about being lonely. You never had to find . . . other ways to
get the things you had to have. There was always a Tony to give
them to you. All you ever had to do was smile and say please."
His voice rose a note. "*I* could never get what I wanted that
way. Don't you think I tried? It didn't work with my father. He
just wanted more and more. He never even kissed me good
night or gave me a hug until I made him rich. And my mother
was the same way. I gave her her marriage back, but was that
enough for her? She hated me! She wouldn't come near me! She
said I was unnatural! I gave her nice things but . . . Beth,
don't do that! Don't . . . *dooon't—*"

She stepped on the Elizabeth doll and crushed it, turning her
heel on it. Something inside her flared in agony, and then was

gone. She wasn't afraid of him now. He was just a small, shrunken boy in a young man's body. And his socks didn't match.

"I don't think you can do anything to me now, Ed," she told him. "Not now. Am I wrong?"

He turned from her. "Go on," he said weakly. "Get out. But leave my box. At least do that."

"I'll leave the box. But not the things in it." She walked past him. His shoulders twitched, as if he might turn and try to grab her, but then they slumped.

As she reached the second-floor landing, he came to the top of the stairs and called shrilly after her: "Go on then! But you'll never be satisfied with any man after me! And when your looks go and men stop trying to give you anything you want, you'll wish for me! You'll think of what you threw away!"

She went down the stairs and out into the snow. Its coldness felt good against her face. It was a two-mile walk back to the campus, but she didn't care. She wanted the walk, wanted the cold. She wanted it to make her clean.

In a queer, twisted way she felt sorry for him—a little boy with a huge power crammed inside a dwarfed spirit. A little boy who tried to make humans behave like toy soldiers and then stamped on them in a fit of temper when they wouldn't or when they found out.

And what was she? Blessed with all the things he was not, through no fault of his or effort of her own? She remembered the way she had reacted to Alice, trying blindly and jealously to hold on to something that was easy rather than good, not caring, not caring.

When your looks go and men stop trying to give you anything you want, you'll wish for me! . . . I know what you need.

But was she so small that she actually needed so little?

Please, dear God, no.

On the bridge between the campus and town she paused and threw Ed Hamner's scraps of magic over the side, piece by piece. The red-painted model Fiat went last, falling end over end into the driven snow until it was lost from sight. Then she walked on.

The Christian Roommates

by John Updike

Orson Ziegler came straight to Harvard from the small South Dakota town where his father was the doctor. Orson, at eighteen, was half an inch under six feet tall, with a weight of 164 and an I.Q. of 152. His eczematous cheeks and vaguely irritated squint—as if his face had been for too long transected by the sight of a level horizon—masked a definite self-confidence. As the doctor's son, he had always mattered in the town. In his high school he had been class president, valedictorian, and captain of the football and baseball teams. (The captain of the basketball team had been Lester Spotted Elk, a full-blooded Chippewa with dirty fingernails and brilliant teeth, a smoker, a drinker, a discipline problem, and the only boy Orson ever had met who was better than he at anything that mattered.) Orson was the first native of his town to go to Harvard, and would probably be the last, at least until his son was of age. His future was firm in his mind: the pre-med course here, medical school either at Harvard, Penn, or Yale, and then back to South Dakota, where he had his wife already selected and claimed and primed to wait. Two nights before he left for Harvard, he had taken her virginity. She had cried, and he had felt foolish, having, somehow, failed. It had been his virginity, too. Orson was sane, sane enough to know that he had lots to learn, and to be, within limits, willing. Harvard processes thousands of such boys and restores them to the world with little apparent damage. Presumably because he was from west of the Mississippi and a Protestant Christian (Methodist), the authorities had given him as a freshman roommate a self-converted Episcopalian from Oregon.

When Orson arrived at Harvard on the morning of Registra-

tion Day, bleary and stiff from the series of airplane rides that
had begun fourteen hours before, his roommate was already
installed. "H. Palamountain" was floridly inscribed in the upper of the two name slots on the door of Room 14. The bed by
the window had been slept in, and the desk by the window was
neatly loaded with books. Standing sleepless inside the door,
inertly clinging to his two heavy suitcases, Orson was conscious
of another presence in the room without being able to locate it;
optically and mentally, he focused with a slight slowness.

The roommate was sitting on the floor, barefoot, before a
small spinning wheel. He jumped up nimbly. Orson's first impression was of the wiry quickness that almost magically
brought close to his face the thick-lipped, pop-eyed face of the
other boy. He was a head shorter than Orson, and wore, above
his bare feet, pegged sky-blue slacks, a lumberjack shirt whose
throat was dashingly stuffed with a silk foulard, and a white
cap such as Orson had seen before only in photographs of Pan-
dit Nehru. Dropping a suitcase, Orson offered his hand. Instead
of taking it, the roommate touched his palms together, bowed
his head, and murmured something Orson didn't catch. Then
he gracefully swept off the white cap, revealing a narrow crest
of curly blond hair that stood up like a rooster's comb. "I am
Henry Palamountain." His voice, clear and colorless in the way
of West Coast voices, suggested a radio announcer. His hand-
shake was metallically firm and seemed to have a pinch of malice in it. Like Orson, he wore glasses. The thick lenses emphasized the hyperthyroid bulge of his eyes and their fishy,
searching expression.

"Orson Ziegler," Orson said.

"I know."

Orson felt a need to add something adequately solemn,
standing as they were on the verge of a kind of marriage. "Well,
Henry"—he lamely lowered the other suitcase to the floor—"I
guess we'll be seeing a lot of each other."

"You may call me Hub," the roommate said. "Most people
do. However, call me Henry if you insist. I don't wish to dimin-
ish your dreadful freedom. You may not wish to call me any-

thing at all. Already I've made three hopeless enemies in the dormitory."

Every sentence in this smoothly enunciated speech bothered Orson, beginning with the first. He himself had never been given a nickname; it was the one honor his classmates had withheld from him. In his adolescence he had coined nicknames for himself—Orrie, Ziggy—and tried to insinuate them into popular usage, without success. And what was meant by "dreadful freedom"? It sounded sarcastic. And why might he not wish to call him anything at all? And how had the roommate had the time to make enemies? Orson asked irritably, "How long have you *been* here?"

"Eight days." Henry concluded every statement with a strange little pucker of his lips, a kind of satisfied silent click, as if to say, "And what do you think of *that*?"

Orson felt that he had been sized up as someone easy to startle. But he slid helplessly into the straight-man role that, like the second-best bed, had been reserved for him. "That *long*?"

"Yes. I was totally alone until the day before yesterday. You see, I hitchhiked."

"From *Oregon*?"

"Yes. And I wished to allow time enough for any contingency. In case I was robbed, I had sewed a fifty-dollar bill inside my shirt. As it turned out, I made smooth connections all the way. I had painted a large cardboard sign saying 'Harvard.' You should try it sometime. One meets some very interesting Harvard graduates."

"Didn't your parents worry?"

"Of course. My parents are divorced. My father was furious. He wanted me to fly. I told him to give the plane fare to the Indian Relief Fund. He never gives a penny to charity. And, of course, I'm old. I'm twenty."

"You've been in the Army?"

Henry lifted his hands and staggered back as if from a blow. He put the back of his hand to his brow, whimpered "Never," shuddered, straightened up smartly, and saluted. "In fact, the Portland draft board is after me right now." With a preening tug of his two agile hands—which did look, Orson realized, old: bony and veined and red-tipped, like a woman's—he broadened his foulard. "They refuse to recognize any conscientious objectors except Quakers and Mennonites. My bishop agrees with them. They offered me an out if I'd say I was willing to work in a hospital, but I explained that this released a man for combat duty and if it came to that I'd just as soon carry a gun. I'm an excellent shot. I mind killing only on principle."

The Korean War had begun that summer, and Orson, who had been nagged by a suspicion that his duty was to enlist, bristled at such blithe pacifism. He squinted and asked, "What *have* you been doing for two years, then?"

"Working in a plywood mill. As a gluer. The actual gluing is done by machines, but they become swamped in their own glue now and then. It's a kind of excessive introspection—you've read *Hamlet?*"

"Just *Macbeth* and *The Merchant of Venice.*"

"Yes. Anyway. They have to be cleaned with solvent. One wears long rubber gloves up to one's elbows. It's very soothing work. The inside of a gluer is an excellent place for revolving Greek quotations in your head. I memorized nearly the whole of the *Phaedo* that way." He gestured toward his desk, and Orson saw that many of the books were green Loeb editions of Plato and Aristotle, in Greek. Their spines were worn; they looked read and reread. For the first time, the thought of being at Harvard frightened him. Orson had been standing between his suitcases and now he moved to unpack. "Have you left me a bureau?"

"Of course. The better one." Henry jumped on the bed that had not been slept in and bounced up and down as if it were a trampoline. "And I've given you the bed with the better mattress," he said, still bouncing, "and the desk that doesn't have the glare from the window."

"Thanks," Orson said.

Henry was quick to notice his tone. "Would you rather have my bed? My desk?" He jumped from the bed and dashed to his desk and scooped a stack of books from it.

Orson had to touch him to stop him, and was startled by the tense muscularity of the arm he touched. "Don't be silly," he said. "They're exactly alike."

Henry replaced his books. "I don't want any bitterness," he said, "or immature squabbling. As the older man, it's my responsibility to yield. Here. I'll give you the shirt off my back." And he began to peel off his lumberjack shirt, leaving the foulard dramatically knotted around his naked throat. He wore no undershirt.

Having won from Orson a facial expression that Orson himself could not see, Henry smiled and rebuttoned the shirt. "Do you mind my name being in the upper slot on the door? I'll remove it. I apologize. I did it without realizing how sensitive you would be."

Perhaps it was all a kind of humor. Orson tried to make a joke. He pointed and asked, "Do I get a spinning wheel, too?"

"Oh, *that*." Henry hopped backward on one bare foot and became rather shy. "That's an experiment. I ordered it from Calcutta. I spin for a half hour a day, after Yoga."

"You do Yoga, too?"

"Just some of the elementary positions. My ankles can't take more than five minutes of the Lotus yet."

"And you say you have a bishop."

The roommate glanced up with a glint of fresh interest. "Say. You listen, don't you? Yes. I consider myself an Anglican Christian Platonist strongly influenced by Gandhi." He touched his palms before his chest, bowed, straightened, and giggled. "My bishop hates me," he said. "The one in Oregon, who wants me to be a soldier. I've introduced myself to the bishop here and I don't think he likes me, either. For that matter, I've antagonized my adviser. I told him I had no intention of fulfilling the science requirement."

"For God's sake, why *not*?"

"You don't really want to know."

Orson felt this rebuff as a small test of strength. "Not really," he agreed.

"I consider science a demonic illusion of human *hubris*. Its phantasmal nature is proved by its constant revision. I asked him, 'Why should I waste an entire fourth of my study time, time that could be spent with Plato, mastering a mass of hypotheses that will be obsolete by the time I graduate?' "

"My Lord, Henry," Orson exclaimed, indignantly defending the millions of lives saved by medical science, "you can't be serious!"

"Please. Hub. I may be difficult for you, and I think it would help if you were to call me by my name. Now let's talk about you. Your father is a doctor, you received all A's in high school —I received rather mediocre grades myself—and you've come to Harvard because you believe it affords a cosmopolitan Eastern environment that will be valuable to you after spending your entire life in a small provincial town."

"Who the hell told you all this?" The recital of his application statement made Orson blush. He already felt much older than the boy who had written it.

"University Hall," Henry said. "I went over and asked to see your folder. They didn't want to let me at first, but I explained that if they were going to give me a roommate, after I had specifically requested to live alone, I had a right to information about you, so I could minimize possible friction."

"And they *let* you?"

"Of course. People without convictions have no powers of resistance." His mouth made its little satisfied click, and Orson was goaded to ask, "Why did *you* come to Harvard?"

"Two reasons." He ticked them off on two fingers. "Raphael Demos and Werner Jaeger."

Orson did not know these names, but he suspected that "Friends of yours?" was a stupid question, once it was out of his mouth.

But Henry nodded. "I've introduced myself to Demos. A charming old scholar, with a beautiful young wife."

"You mean you just went to his house and pushed yourself *in*?" Orson heard his own voice grow shrill; his voice, rather high and unstable, was one of the things about himself that he liked least.

Henry blinked, and looked unexpectedly vulnerable, so slender and bravely dressed, his ugly, yellowish, flat-nailed feet naked on the floor, which was uncarpeted and painted black. "That isn't how I would describe it. I went as a pilgrim. He seemed pleased to talk to me." He spoke carefully, and his mouth abstained from clicking.

That he could hurt his roommate's feelings—that this jaunty apparition had feelings—disconcerted Orson more deeply than any of the surprises he had been deliberately offered. As quickly as he had popped up, Henry dropped to the floor, as if through a trapdoor in the plane of conversation. He resumed spinning. The method apparently called for one thread to be wound around the big toe of a foot and to be kept taut by a kind of absentminded pedal motion. While engaged in this, he seemed hermetically sealed inside one of the gluing machines that had incubated his garbled philosophy. Unpacking, Orson was slowed and snagged by a complicated mood of discomfort. He tried to remember how his mother had arranged his bureau drawers at home—socks and underwear in one, shirts and handkerchiefs in another. Home seemed infinitely far from him, and he was dizzily conscious of a great depth of space beneath his feet, as if the blackness of the floor were the color of an abyss. The spinning wheel steadily chuckled. Orson's buzz of unease circled and settled on his roommate, who, it was clear, had thought earnestly about profound matters, matters that Orson, busy as he had been with the practical business of being a good student, had hardly considered. It was also clear that Henry had thought unintelligently. This unintelligence ("I received rather mediocre grades myself") was more of a menace than a comfort. Bent above the bureau drawers, Orson felt cramped in his mind, able neither to stand erect in wholehearted contempt nor to lie down in honest admiration. His mood was complicated by the repugnance his roommate's physical presence aroused in him. An almost morbidly clean boy, Orson was haunted by glue, and a tacky ambience resisted every motion of his unpacking.

The silence between the roommates continued until a great bell rang ponderously. The sound was near and yet far, like a heartbeat within the bosom of time, and it seemed to bring with it into the room the muffling foliation of the trees in the Yard,

which to Orson's prairie-honed eyes had looked tropically tall
and lush; the walls of the room vibrated with leaf shadows, and
many minute presences—dust motes, traffic sounds, or angels
of whom several could dance on the head of a pin—thronged
the air and made it difficult to breathe. The stairways of the
dormitory rumbled. Boys dressed in jackets and neckties
crowded the doorway and entered the room, laughing and calling "Hub. Hey, Hub."

"Get up off the floor, dad."

"Jesus, Hub, put your shoes on."

"Pee-*yew.*"

"And take off that seductive sarong around your neck."

"Consider the lilies, Hub. They toil not, neither do they spin,
and yet I say unto you that Solomon in all his glory was not
arrayed like one of these."

"Amen, brothers!"

"Fitch, you should be a preacher."

They were all strangers to Orson. Hub stood and smoothly
performed introductions.

In a few days, Orson had sorted them out. That jostling
conglomerate, so apparently secure and homogeneous, broke
down, under habitual exposure, into double individuals: roommates. There were Silverstein and Koshland, Dawson and
Kern, Young and Carter, Petersen and Fitch.

Silverstein and Koshland, who lived in the room overhead,
were Jews from New York City. All Orson knew about non-
biblical Jews was that they were a sad race, full of music,
shrewdness, and woe. But Silverstein and Koshland were always clowning, always wisecracking. They played bridge and
poker and chess and Go and went to the movies in Boston and
drank coffee in the luncheonettes around the Square. They
came from the "gifted" high schools of the Bronx and Brook-
lyn respectively, and treated Cambridge as if it were another
borough. Most of what the freshman year sought to teach them
they seemed to know already. As winter approached, Koshland
went out for basketball, and he and his teammates made the
floor above bounce to the thump and rattle of scrimmages with

a tennis ball and a wastebasket. One afternoon, a section of ceiling collapsed on Orson's bed.

Next door, in Room 12, Dawson and Kern wanted to be writers. Dawson was from Ohio and Kern from Pennsylvania. Dawson had a sulky, slouching bearing, a certain puppyish facial eagerness, and a terrible temper. He was a disciple of Anderson and Hemingway and himself wrote as austerely as a newspaper. He had been raised as an atheist, and no one in the dormitory incited his temper more often than Hub. Orson, feeling that he and Dawson came from opposite edges of that great psychological realm called the Midwest, liked him. He felt less at ease with Kern, who seemed Eastern and subtly vicious. A farm boy driven by an unnatural sophistication, riddled with nervous ailments ranging from conjunctivitis to hemorrhoids, Kern smoked and talked incessantly. He and Dawson maintained between them a battery of running jokes. At night Orson could hear them on the other side of the wall keeping each other awake with improvised parodies and musical comedies based on their teachers, their courses, or their fellow-freshmen. One midnight, Orson distinctly heard Dawson sing, "My name is Orson Ziegler, I come from South Dakota." There was a pause, then Kern sang back, "I tend to be a niggler, and masturbate by quota."

Across the hall, in 15, lived Young and Carter, Negroes. Carter was from Detroit and very black, very clipped in speech, very well dressed, and apt to collapse, at the jab of a rightly angled joke, into a spastic giggling fit that left his cheeks gleaming with tears; Kern was expert at breaking Carter up. Young was a lean, malt-pale colored boy from North Carolina, here on a national scholarship, out of his depth, homesick, and cold. Kern called him Br'er Possum. He slept all day and at night sat on his bed playing the mouthpiece of a trumpet to himself. At first, he had played the full horn in the afternoon, flooding the dormitory and its green envelope of trees with golden, tremulous versions of languorous tunes like "Sentimental Journey" and "The Tennessee Waltz." It had been nice. But Young's somber sense of tact—a slavish drive toward self-effacement that the shock of Harvard had awakened in him—soon cancelled these harmless performances. He took to hiding from the sun, and at night the furtive spitting sound from across the hall seemed to Orson, as he struggled into sleep, music drowning in shame. Carter always referred to his roommate as "Jonathan," mouthing the syllables fastidiously, as if he were pronouncing the name of a remote being he had just learned about, like Rochefoucauld or Demosthenes.

Cattycorner up the hall, in unlucky 13, Petersen and Fitch kept a strange household. Both were tall, narrow-shouldered, and broad-bottomed; physiques aside, it was hard to see what they had in common, or why Harvard had put them together. Fitch, with dark staring eyes and the flat full cranium of Frankenstein's monster, was a child prodigy from Maine, choked with philosophy, wild with ideas, and pregnant with the seeds of the nervous breakdown he was to have, eventually, in April. Petersen was an amiable Swede with a transparent skin that revealed blue veins in his nose. For several summers he had worked as a reporter for the Duluth *Herald*. He had all the newsman's tricks: the side-of-the-mouth quip, the nip of whiskey, the hat on the back of the head, the habit of throwing still-burning cigarettes onto the floor. He did not seem quite to know why he was at Harvard, and in fact did not return at the end of the freshman year. But, while these two drifted toward their respective failures, they made a strangely well-suited couple. Each was strong where the other was helpless. Fitch was so uncoördinated and unorganized he could not even type; he would lie on his bed in pajamas, writhing and grimacing, and dictate a tangled humanities paper, twice the requested length and mostly about books that had not been assigned, while Petersen, typing with a hectic two-finger system, would obligingly turn this chaotic monologue into "copy." His patience verged on the maternal. When Fitch appeared for a meal wearing a coat and tie, the joke ran in the dormitory that Petersen had dressed him. In return, Fitch gave Petersen ideas out of the superabundance painfully cramming his big flat head. Petersen had absolutely no ideas; he could neither compare, contrast, nor criticize St. Augustine and Marcus Aurelius. Perhaps having seen, so young, so many corpses and fires and policemen and prostitutes had prematurely blighted his mind. At any rate, mothering Fitch gave him something practical to do, and Orson envied them.

He envied all the roommates, whatever the bond between them—geography, race, ambition, physical size—for between himself and Hub Palamountain he could see no link except forced cohabitation. Not that living with Hub was superficially unpleasant. Hub was tidy, industrious, and ostentatiously considerate. He rose at seven, prayed, did Yoga, spun, and was off to breakfast, often not to be seen again until the end of the day. He went to sleep, generally, at eleven sharp. If there was noise in the room, he would insert rubber plugs in his ears, put a black mask over his eyes, and go to sleep anyway. During the day, he kept a rigorous round of appointments: he audited two courses in addition to taking four, he wrestled three times a week for his physical-training requirement, he wangled tea invitations from Demos and Jaeger and the Bishop of Massachusetts, he attended free evening lectures and readings, he associated himself with Phillips Brooks House and spent two afternoons a week supervising slum boys in a Roxbury redevelopment house. In addition, he had begun to take piano lessons in Brookline. Many days, Orson saw him only at meals in the Union, where the dormitory neighbors, in those first fall months when their acquaintance was crisp and young and differing interests had not yet scattered them, tended to regroup around a long table. In these months there was often a debate about the subject posed under their eyes: Hub's vegetarianism. There he would sit, his tray heaped high with a steaming double helping of squash and lima beans, while Fitch would try to locate the exact point at which vegetarianism became inconsistent. "You eat eggs," he said.

"Yes," Hub said.

"You realize that every egg, from the chicken's point of reference, is a newborn baby?"

"But in fact it is not unless it has been fertilized by a rooster."

"But suppose," Fitch pursued, "as sometimes happens—which I happen to know, from working in my uncle's henhouse

in Maine—an egg that *should* be sterile has in fact been fertilized and contains an embryo?"

"If I see it, I naturally don't eat that particular egg," Hub
said, his lips making that satisfied concluding snap.

Fitch pounced triumphantly, spilling a fork to the floor with
a lurch of his hand. "But *why*? The hen feels the same pain on
being parted from an egg whether sterile or fertile. The embryo
is unconscious—a vegetable. As a vegetarian, you should eat it
with special relish." He tipped back in his chair so hard he had
to grab the table edge to keep from toppling over.

"It seems to me," Dawson said, frowning darkly—these dis-
cussions, clogging some twist of his ego, often spilled him into a
vile temper—"that psychoanalysis of hens is hardly relevant."

"On the contrary," Kern said lightly, clearing his throat and
narrowing his pink, infected eyes, "it seems to me that there, in
the tiny, dim mind of the hen—the minimal mind, as it were—
is where the tragedy of the universe achieves a pinpoint focus.
Picture the emotional life of a hen. What does she know of
companionship? A flock of pecking, harsh-voiced gossips. Of
shelter? A few dung-bespattered slats. Of food? Some flecks of
mash and grit insolently tossed on the ground. Of love? The
casual assault of a polygamous cock—cock in the Biblical
sense. Then, into this heartless world, there suddenly arrives, as
if by magic, an egg. An egg of her own. An egg, it must seem to
her, that she and God have made. How she must cherish it, its
beautiful baldness, its gentle luster, its firm yet somehow fragile, softly swaying weight."

Carter had broken up. He bent above his tray, his eyes tight
shut, his dark face contorted joyfully. "Puhleese," he gasped at
last. "You're making my stomach hurt."

"Ah, Carter," Kern said loftily, "if that were only the worst
of it. For then, one day, while the innocent hen sits cradling
this strange, faceless, oval child, its little weight swaying softly
in her wings"—he glanced hopefully at Carter, but the colored
boy bit his lower lip and withstood the jab—"an enormous
man, smelling of beer and manure, comes and tears the egg
from her grasp. And why? Because *he*"—Kern pointed, arm
fully extended, across the table, so that his index finger, orange

with nicotine, almost touched Hub's nose—*"he,* Saint Henry Palamountain, wants more eggs to eat. 'More eggs!' he cries voraciously, so that brutal steers and faithless pigs can continue to menace the children of American mothers!"

Dawson slammed his silver down, got up from the table, and slouched out of the dining room. Kern blushed. In the silence, Petersen put a folded slice of roast beef in his mouth and said, chewing, "Jesus, Hub, if somebody else kills the animals you might as well eat 'em. They don't give a damn anymore."

"You understand nothing," Hub said simply.

"Hey, Hub," Silverstein called down from the far end of the table. "What's the word on milk? Don't calves drink milk? Maybe you're taking milk out of some calf's mouth."

Orson felt impelled to speak. *"No,"* he said, and his voice seemed to have burst, its pitch was so unsteady and excited. "As anybody except somebody from New York would know, milch cows have weaned their calves. What I wonder about, Hub, is your shoes. You wear leather shoes."

"I do." The gaiety left Hub's defense of himself. His lips became prim.

"Leather is the skin of a steer."

"But the animal has already been slaughtered."

"You sound like Petersen. Your purchase of leather goods— what about your wallet and belt, for that matter?—encourages the slaughter. You're as much of a murderer as the rest of us. More of one—because you think about it."

Hub folded his hands carefully in front of him, propping them, almost in prayer, on the table edge. His voice became like that of a radio announcer, but an announcer rapidly, softly describing the home stretch of a race. "My belt, I believe, is a form of plastic. My wallet was given to me by my mother years ago, before I became a vegetarian. Please remember that I ate meat for eighteen years and I still have an appetite for it. If there were any other concentrated source of protein, I would not eat eggs. Some vegetarians do not. On the other hand, some vegetarians eat fish and take liver extract. I would not do this. Shoes are a problem. There is a firm in Chicago that makes non-leather shoes for extreme vegetarians, but they're very expensive and not comfortable. I once ordered a pair. They killed my feet. Leather, you see, 'breathes' in a way no synthetic substitute does. My feet are tender; I have compromised. I apologize. For that matter, when I play the piano I encourage the slaughter of elephants, and in brushing my teeth, which I must do faithfully because a vegetable diet is so heavy in carbohydrates, I use a brush of pig bristles. I am covered with blood, and pray daily for forgiveness." He took up his fork and resumed eating the mound of squash.

Orson was amazed; he had been impelled to speak by a kind of sympathy, and Hub had answered as if he alone were an enemy. He tried to defend himself. "There are perfectly wearable shoes," he said, "made out of canvas, with crêpe-rubber soles."

"I'll look into them," Hub said. "They sound a little sporty to me."

Laughter swept the table and ended the subject. After lunch Orson walked to the library with the beginnings of indigestion; a backwash of emotion was upsetting his stomach. There was a growing confusion inside him he could not resolve. He resented being associated with Hub, and yet felt attacked when Hub was attacked. It seemed to him that Hub deserved credit for putting his beliefs into practice, and that people like Fitch and Kern, in mocking, merely belittled themselves. Yet Hub smiled at their criticism, took it as a game, and fought back in earnest only at Orson, forcing him into a false position. Why? Was it because in being also a Christian he alone qualified for serious rebuke? But Carter went to church, wearing a blue pin-striped suit with a monogrammed handkerchief peaked in the breast pocket, every Sunday; Petersen was a nominal Presbyterian; Orson had once seen Kern sneaking out of Mem Chapel; and even Koshland observed his holidays, by cutting classes and skipping lunch. Why, therefore, Orson asked himself, should Hub pick on him? And why should he care? He had no real respect for Hub. Hub's handwriting was childishly large and careful and his first set of hour exams, even in the course on Plato and Aristotle, had yielded a batch of C's. Orson resented being condescended to by an intellectual inferior. The knowledge that at the table he had come off second best galled him like an unfair grade. His situation with Hub became in his head a diagram in which all his intentions curved off at right angles and his strengths inversely tapered into nothing. Behind the diagram hung the tuck of complacence in Hub's lips, the fishy impudence of his eyes, and the keenly irksome shape and tint of his hands and feet. These images—Hub disembodied—Orson carried with him into the library, back and forth to classes, and along the congested streets around the Square; now and then the glaze of an eye or the flat yellowish nail of a big toe welled up distinctly through the pages of a book and, greatly magnified, slid with Orson into the unconsciousness of sleep. Nevertheless, he surprised himself, sitting one February afternoon in Room 12 with Dawson and Kern, by blurting, "I hate him." He considered what he had said, liked the taste of it, and repeated, "I hate the bastard. I've never hated anybody before in my life." His voice cracked and his eyes warmed with abortive tears.

They had all returned from Christmas vacation to plunge into the weird limbo of reading period and the novel ordeal of midyear exams. This was a dormitory, by and large, of public-school graduates, who feel the strain of Harvard most in their freshman year. The private-school boys, launched by little Harvards like Exeter and Groton, tend to glide through this year and to run aground later on strange reefs, foundering in alcohol, or sinking into a dandified apathy. But the institution demands of each man, before it releases him, a wrenching sacrifice of ballast. At Christmas, Orson's mother thought he looked haggard, and set about fattening him up. On the other hand, he was struck by how much his father had aged and shrunk. Orson spent his first days home listening to the mindless music on the radio, hours of it, and driving through farmland on narrow straight roads already banked bright with plowed snow. The South Dakota sky had never looked so open, so clean; he had never realized before that the high dry sun that made even sub-zero days feel warm at noon was a local phenomenon. He made love to his girl again, and again she cried. He said to her he blamed himself, for ineptitude; but in his heart he blamed her. She was not helping him. Back in Cambridge, it was raining, raining in January, and the entryway of the Coop was full of gray footprints and wet bicycles and Radcliffe girls in slickers and sneakers. Hub had stayed here, alone in their room, and had celebrated Christmas with a fast.

In the monotonous, almost hallucinatory month of rereading, outlining, and memorizing, Orson perceived how little he knew, how stupid he was, how unnatural all learning is, and how futile. Harvard rewarded him with three A's and a B. Hub pulled out two B's and two C's. Kern, Dawson, and Silverstein did well; Petersen, Koshland, and Carter got mediocre grades; Fitch flunked one subject, and Young flunked three. The pale Negro slunk in and out of the dorm as if he were diseased and marked for destruction; he became, while still among them, a rumor. The suppressed whistling of the trumpet mouthpiece was no longer heard. Silverstein and Koshland and the basketball crowd adopted Carter and took him to movies in Boston three or four times a week.

After exams, in the heart of the Cambridge winter, there is a grateful pause. New courses are selected, and even the full-year courses, heading into their second half, sometimes put on, like a new hat, a fresh professor. The days quietly lengthen; there is a snowstorm or two; the swimming and squash teams lend the sports pages of the *Crimson* an unaccustomed note of victory. A kind of foreshadow of spring falls bluely on the snow. The elms are seen to be shaped like fountains. The discs of snow pressed by boots into the sidewalk by Albiani's seem large precious coins; the brick buildings, the arched gates, the archaic lecterns, and the barny mansions along Brattle Street dawn upon the freshman as a heritage he temporarily possesses. The thumb-worn spines of his now familiar textbooks seem proof of a certain knowingness, and the strap of the green book bag tugs at his wrist like a living falcon. The letters from home dwindle in importance. The hours open up. There is more time. Experiments are made. Courtships begin. Conversations go on and on; and an almost rapacious desire for mutual discovery possesses acquaintances. It was in this atmosphere, then, that Orson made his confession.

Dawson turned his head away as if the words had menaced him personally. Kern blinked, lit a cigarette, and asked, "What don't you like about him?"

"Well"—Orson shifted his weight uncomfortably in the black but graceful, shapely but hard Harvard chair—"it's little things. Whenever he gets a notice from the Portland draft board, he tears it up without opening it and scatters it out the window."

"And you're afraid that this incriminates you as an accessory and they'll put you in jail?"

"No—I don't know. It seems exaggerated. He exaggerates everything. You should see how he prays."

"How do you know how he prays?"

"He shows me. Every morning, he gets down on his knees and *throws* himself across the bed, his face in the blanket, his arms way out." He showed them.

"God," Dawson said. "That's marvellous. It's medieval. It's more than medieval. It's Counter-Reformation."

"I mean," Orson said, grimacing in realization of how deeply he had betrayed Hub, "I pray, too, but I don't make a show of myself."

A frown clotted Dawson's expression, and passed.

"He's a saint," Kern said.

"He's *not,*" Orson said. "He's not intelligent. I'm taking Chem I with him, and he's worse than a child with the math. And those Greek books he keeps on his desk, they look worn because he bought them second-hand."

"Saints don't have to be intelligent," Kern said. "What saints have to have is energy. Hub has it."

"Look how he wrestles," Dawson said.

"I doubt if he wrestles very *well,*" Orson said. "He didn't make the freshman team. I'm sure if we heard him play the piano, it'd be awful."

"You seem to miss the point," Kern said, eyes closed, "of what Hub's all about."

"I know goddam well what he thinks he's all about," Orson

said, "but it's fake. It doesn't go. All this vegetarianism and love of the starving Indian—he's really a terribly cold bastard. I think he's about the coldest person I've ever met in my life."

"I don't think Orson thinks that; do you?" Kern asked Dawson.

"No," Dawson said, and his puppyish smile cleared his cloudy face. "That's not what Orson the Parson thinks."

Kern squinted. "Is it Orson the Parson, or Orson the Person?"

"I think Hub is the nub," Dawson said.

"Or the rub," Kern added, and both burst into grinding laughter. Orson felt he was being sacrificed to the precarious peace the two roommates kept between themselves, and left, superficially insulted but secretly flattered to have been given, at last, a nickname of sorts: Orson the Parson.

Several nights later they went to hear Carl Sandburg read in New Lecture Hall—the four adjacent roommates, plus Fitch. To avoid sitting next to Hub, who aggressively led them into a row of seats, Orson delayed, and so sat the farthest away from the girl Hub sat directly behind. Orson noticed her immediately; she had a lavish mane of coppery red hair which hung down loose over the back of her seat. The color of it, and the abundance, reminded him, all at once, of horses, earth, sun, wheat, and home. From Orson's angle she was nearly in profile; her face was small, with a tilted shadowy cheekbone and a pale prominent ear. Toward the pallor of her profile he felt an orgasmic surge; she seemed suspended in the crowd and was floating, a crest of whiteness, toward him. She turned away. Hub had leaned forward and was saying something into her other ear. Fitch overheard it, and gleefully relayed it to Dawson, who whispered to Kern and Orson; *"Hub said to the girl, 'You have beautiful hair.'"*

Several times during the reading, Hub leaned forward to add something more into her ear, each time springing spurts of choked laughter from Fitch, Dawson, and Kern. Meanwhile, Sandburg, his white bangs as straight and shiny as a doll's wig of artificial fiber, incanted above the lectern and quaintly

strummed a guitar. Afterward, Hub walked with the girl into
the outdoors. From a distance Orson saw her white face turn
and crumple into a laugh. Hub returned to his friends with the
complacent nick in the corner of his mouth deepened, in the
darkness, to a gash.

It was not the next day, or the next week, but within the
month that Hub brought back to the room a heap of red hair.
Orson found it lying like a diaphanous corpse on a newspaper
spread on his bed. "Hub, what the hell is this?"

Hub was on the floor playing with his spinning wheel.
"Hair."

"Human hair?"

"Of course."

"Whose?"

"A girl's."

"What happened?" The question sounded strange; Orson
meant to ask, "What girl's?"

Hub answered as if he had asked that question. "It's a girl I
met at the Sandburg reading; you don't know her."

"This is *her* hair?"

"Yes. I asked her for it. She said she was planning to cut it all
off this spring anyway."

Orson stood stunned above the bed, gripped by an urge to
bury his face and hands in the hair. "You've been *seeing* her?"
This effeminate stridence in his voice: he despised it and only
Hub brought it out.

"A little. My schedule doesn't allow for much social life, but
my adviser has recommended that I relax now and then."

"You take her to movies?"

"Once in a while. She pays her admission, of course."

"Of *course.*"

Hub took him up on his tone. "Please remember I'm here on
my savings alone. I have refused all financial assistance from
my father."

"Hub"—the very syllable seemed an expression of pain—
"what are you going to do with her hair?"

"Spin it into a rope."

"A *rope*?"

"Yes. It'll be very difficult; her hair is terribly fine."

"And what will you do with the rope?"

"Make a knot of it."

"A *knot*?"

"I think that's the term. I'll coil it and secure it so it can't come undone and give it to her. So she'll always have her hair the way it was when she was nineteen."

"How the hell did you talk this poor girl into it?"

"I didn't talk her into it. I merely offered, and she thought it was a lovely idea. Really, Orson, I don't see why this should offend your bourgeois scruples. Women cut their hair all the time."

"She must think you're insane. She was humoring you."

"As you like. It was a perfectly rational suggestion, and my sanity has never been raised as an issue between us."

"Well, *I* think you're insane. Hub, you're a *nut*."

Orson left the room and slammed the door, and didn't return until eleven, when Hub was asleep in his eye mask. The heap of hair had been transferred to the floor beside the spinning wheel, and already some strands were entangled with the machine. In time a rope was produced, a braided cord as thick as a woman's little finger, about a foot long, weightless and waxen. The earthy, horsy fire in the hair's color had been quenched in the process. Hub carefully coiled it and with black thread and long pins secured and stiffened the spiral into a disc the size of a small saucer. This he presented to the girl one Friday night. The presentation appeared to satisfy him, for, as far as Orson knew, Hub had no further dates with her. Once in a while Orson passed her in the Yard, and without her hair she scarcely seemed female, her small pale face fringed in curt tufts, her ears looking enormous. He wanted to speak to her; some obscure force of pity, or hope of rescue, impelled him to greet this wan androgyne, but the opening word stuck in his throat. She did not look as if she pitied herself, or knew what had been done to her.

Something magical protected Hub; things deflected from him. The doubt Orson had cast upon his sanity bounced back onto himself. As spring slowly broke, he lost the ability to

sleep. Figures and facts churned sluggishly in an insomniou
mire. His courses became four parallel puzzles. In mathema
ics, the crucial transposition upon which the solution pivote
consistently eluded him, vanishing into the chinks between th
numbers. The quantities in chemistry became impishly unsta
ble; the unbalanced scales clicked down sharply and the syste
of interlocked elements that fanned from the lab to the far sta
collapsed. In the history survey course, they had reached th
Enlightenment, and Orson found himself disturbingly im
pressed by Voltaire's indictment of God, though the lecture
handled it calmly, as one more dead item of intellectual history
neither true nor false. And in German, which Orson had take
to satisfy his language requirement, the words piled on re
morselessly, and the existence of languages other than Englisl
the existence of so many, each so vast, intricate, and opaque
seemed to prove cosmic dementia. He felt his mind, which wa
always more steady than quick, grow slower and slower. H
chair threatened to adhere to him, and he would leap up i
panic. Sleepless, stuffed with information he could neither for
get nor manipulate, he became prey to obsessive delusions; h
became convinced that his girl in South Dakota had taken u
with another boy and was making love to him happily, Orso
having shouldered the awkwardness and blame of taking he
virginity. In the very loops that Emily's ballpoint pen describe
in her bland letters to him he read the pleased rotundity, th
inner fatness of a well-loved woman. He even knew the man. I
was Spotted Elk, the black-nailed Chippewa, whose impassiv
nimbleness had so often mocked Orson on the basketball cour
whose terrible ease and speed of reaction had seemed so unjus
and whose defense—he recalled now—Emily had often under
taken. His wife had become a whore, a squaw; the scraggl
mute reservation children his father had doctored in the charit
clinic became, amid the sliding transparencies of Orson's min
his own children. In his dreams—or in those limp elisions o
imagery which in the absence of sleep passed for dreams—h
seemed to be rooming with Spotted Elk, and his roommate
who sometimes wore a mask, invariably had won, by under
handed means, the affection and admiration that were righ

fully his. There was a conspiracy. Whenever Orson heard Kern and Dawson laughing on the other side of the wall, he knew it was about him, and about his most secret habits. This ultimate privacy was outrageously invaded; in bed, half-relaxed, he would suddenly see himself bodily involved with Hub's lips, Hub's legs, with Hub's veined, vaguely womanish hands. At first he resisted these visions, tried to erase them; it was like trying to erase ripples on water. He learned to submit to them, to let the attack—for it was an attack, with teeth and sharp acrobatic movements—wash over him, leaving him limp enough to sleep. These dives became the only route to sleep. In the morning he would awake and see Hub sprawled flamboyantly across his bed in prayer, or sitting hunched at his spinning wheel, or, gaudily dressed, tiptoeing to the door and with ostentatious care closing it softly behind him; and he would hate him—hate his appearance, his form, his manner, his pretensions with an avidity of detail he had never known in love. The tiny details of his roommate's physical existence—the wrinkles flickering beside his mouth, the slightly withered look about his hands, the complacently polished creases of his leather shoes—seemed a poisonous food Orson could not stop eating. His eczema worsened alarmingly.

By April, Orson was on the verge of going to the student clinic, which had a department called Mental Health. But at this point Fitch relieved him by having, it seemed, his nervous breakdown for him. For weeks, Fitch had been taking several showers a day. Toward the end he stopped going to classes and was almost constantly naked, except for a towel tucked around his waist. He was trying to complete a humanities paper that was already a month overdue and twenty pages too long. He left the dormitory only to eat and to take more books from the library. One night around nine, Petersen was called to the phone on the second-floor landing. The Watertown police had picked Fitch up as he was struggling through the underbrush on the banks of the Charles four miles away. He claimed he was walking to the West, where he had been told there was enough space to contain God, and proceeded to talk with wild animation to the police chief about the differences and affinities between Kierkegaard and Nietzsche. Hub, ever alert for an opportunity to intrude in the guise of doing good, went to the hall proctor—a spindly and murmurous graduate student of astronomy engaged, under Harlow Shapley, in an endless galaxy count—and volunteered himself as an expert on the case, and even conferred with the infirmary psychologist. Hub's interpretation was that Fitch had been punished for *hubris*. The psychologist felt the problem was fundamentally Oedipal. Fitch was sent back to Maine. Hub suggested to Orson that now Petersen would need a roommate next year. "I think you and he would hit it off splendidly. You're both materialists."

"I'm *not* a materialist."

Hub lifted his dreadful hands in half-blessing. "Have it your way. I'm determined to minimize friction."

"Dammit, Hub, all the friction between us comes from *you.*"

"How? What do I do? Tell me, and I'll change. I'll give you the shirt off my back." He began to unbutton, and stopped, seeing that the laugh wasn't going to come.

Orson felt weak and empty, and in spite of himself he cringed inwardly, with a helpless affection for his unreal, unreachable friend. "I don't know, Hub," he admitted. "I don't know what it is you're doing to me."

A paste of silence dried in the air between them.

Orson with an effort unstuck himself. "I think you're right, we shouldn't room together next year."

Hub seemed a bit bewildered, but nodded, saying, "I told them in the beginning that I ought to live alone." And his hurt eyes bulging behind their lenses settled into an invulnerable Byzantine stare.

One afternoon in middle May, Orson was sitting stumped at his desk, trying to study. He had taken two exams and had two to go. They stood between him and release like two towering walls of muddy paper. His position seemed extremely precarious: he was unable to retreat and able to advance only along a very thin thread, a high wire of sanity on which he balanced above an abyss of statistics and formulae, his brain a firmament of winking cells. A push would kill him. There was then a hurried pounding-up the stairs, and Hub pushed into the room carrying cradled in his arm a metal object the color of a gun and the size of a cat. It had a red tongue. Hub slammed the door behind him, snapped the lock, and dumped the object on Orson's bed. It was the head of a parking meter, sheared from its post. A keen quick pain cut through Orson's groin. "For God's sake," he cried in his contemptible high voice, "what's *that*?"

"It's a parking meter."

"I *know,* I can *see* that. Where the hell did you *get* it?"

"I won't talk to you until you stop being hysterical," Hub said, and crossed to his desk, where Orson had put his mail. He took the top letter, a special delivery from the Portland draft board, and tore it in half. This time, the pain went through Orson's chest. He put his head in his arms on the desk and whirled and groped in the black-red darkness there. His body was frightening him; his nerves listened for a third psychosomatic slash.

There was a rap on the door; from the force of the knock, it could only be the police. Hub nimbly dashed to the bed and hid the meter under Orson's pillow. Then he pranced to the door and opened it.

It was Dawson and Kern. "What's up?" Dawson asked, frowning as if the disturbance had been created to annoy him.

"It sounded like Ziegler was being tortured," Kern said.

Orson pointed at Hub and explained, "He's castrated a parking meter!"

"I did not," Hub said. "A car went out of control on Mass. Avenue and hit a parked car, which knocked a meter down. A crowd gathered. The head of the meter was lying in the gutter, so I picked it up and carried it away. I was afraid someone might be tempted to steal it."

"Nobody tried to stop you?" Kern asked.

"Of course not. They were all gathered around the driver of the car."

"Was he hurt?"

"I doubt it. I didn't look."

"You didn't *look*!" Orson cried. "You're a great Samaritan."

"I am not prey," Hub said, "to morbid curiosity."

"Where were the police?" Kern asked.

"They hadn't arrived yet."

Dawson asked, "Well why didn't you wait till a cop arrived and give the meter to him?"

"Why should I give it to an agent of the State? It's no more his than mine."

"But it *is,*" Orson said.

"It was a plain act of Providence that placed it in my hands," Hub said, the corners of his lips dented securely. "I haven't decided yet which charity should receive the money it contains."

Dawson asked, "But isn't that stealing?"

"No more stealing than the State is stealing in making people pay money for space in which to park their own cars."

"Hub," Orson said, getting to his feet. "You give it back or we'll both go to jail." He saw himself ruined, the scarcely commenced career of his life destroyed.

Hub turned serenely. "I'm not afraid. Going to jail under a totalitarian regime is a mark of honor. If you had a conscience, you'd understand."

Petersen and Carter and Silverstein came into the room. Some boys from the lower floors followed them. The story was hilariously retold. The meter was produced from under the pillow and passed around and shaken to demonstrate the weight of pennies it contained. Hub always carried, as a vestige of the lumberjack country he came from, an intricate all-purpose pocket knife. He began to pry open the little money door. Orson came up behind him and got him around the neck with one arm. Hub's body stiffened. He passed the head of the meter and the open knife to Carter, and then Orson experienced sensations of being lifted, of flying, and of lying on the floor, looking up at Hub's face, which was upside down in his vision. He scrambled to his feet and went for him again, rigid with anger and yet, in his heart, happily relaxed; Hub's body was tough and quick and satisfying to grip, though, being a wrestler, he somehow deflected Orson's hands and again lifted and dropped him to the black floor. This time, Orson felt a blow as his coccyx hit the wood; yet even through the pain he perceived, gazing into the heart of this marriage, that Hub was being as gentle with him as he could be. And that he could try in earnest to kill Hub and be in no danger of succeeding was also a comfort. He renewed the attack and again enjoyed the tense defensive skill that made Hub's body a kind of warp in space through which his own body, after an ecstatic instant of contention, was converted to the supine position. He got to his feet and would have gone for Hub the fourth time, but his fellow-freshmen grabbed his arms and held him. He shook them off and without a word returned to his desk and concentrated down into his book, turning the page. The type looked extremely distinct, though it was trembling too hard to be deciphered.

The head of the parking meter stayed in the room for one night. The next day, Hub allowed himself to be persuaded (by the others; Orson had stopped speaking to him) to take it to the Cambridge police headquarters in Central Square. Dawson and Kern tied a ribbon around it, and attached a note: "Please take good care of my baby." None of them, however, had the nerve to go with Hub to the headquarters, though when he came back he said the chief was delighted to get the meter, and had thanked him, and had agreed to donate the pennies to the local orphans' home. In another week, the last exams were over. The freshmen all went home. When they returned in the fall, they were different: sophomores. Petersen and Young did not come back at all. Fitch returned, made up the lost credits, and eventually graduated *magna cum* in History and Lit. He now teaches in a Quaker prep school. Silverstein is a biochemist, Koshland a lawyer. Dawson writes conservative editorials in Cleveland, Kern is in advertising in New York. Carter, as if obliged to join Young in oblivion, disappeared between his junior and senior years. The dormitory neighbors tended to lose sight of each other, though Hub, who had had his case shifted to the Massachusetts jurisdiction, was now and then pictured in the *Crimson*, and once gave an evening lecture, "Why I Am an Episcopalian Pacifist." As the litigation progressed, the Bishop of Massachusetts rather grudgingly vouched for him, and by the time of his final hearing the Korean War was over, and the judge who heard the case ruled that Hub's convictions were sincere, as witnessed by his willingness to go to jail. Hub was rather disappointed at the verdict, since he had prepared a three-year reading list to occupy him in his cell and was intending to memorize all four Gospels in the original Greek. After graduation, he went to Union Theological Seminary, spent several years as the assistant rector of an urban parish in Baltimore, and learned to play the piano well enough to be the background music in a Charles Street cocktail lounge. He insisted on wearing his clerical collar, and as a consequence gave the bar a small celebrity. After a year of overriding people of less strong convictions, he was allowed to go to South Africa, where he worked and preached among the Bantus until the government requested that he leave the country. From there he went to Nigeria, and when last heard from—on a Christmas card, with French salutations and Negro Magi, which arrived, soiled and wrinkled, in South Dakota in February—Hub was in Madagascar, as a "combination missionary, political agitator, and soccer coach." The description struck Orson as probably facetious, and Hub's childish and confident handwriting, with every letter formed individually, afflicted him with some of the old exasperation. Having vowed to answer the card, he mislaid it, uncharacteristically.

Orson didn't speak to Hub for two days after the parking-meter incident. By then, it seemed rather silly, and they finished out the year sitting side by side at their desks as amiably as two cramped passengers who have endured a long bus trip together. When they parted, they shook hands, and Hub would have walked Orson to the subway kiosk except that he had an appointment in the opposite direction. Orson received two A's and two B's on his final exams; for the remaining three years at Harvard, he roomed uneventfully with two other colorless pre-med students, named Wallace and Neuhauser. After graduation, he married Emily, attended the Yale School of Medicine, and interned in St. Louis. He is now the father of four children and, since the death of his own father, the only doctor in the town. His life has gone much the way he planned it, and he is much the kind of man he intended to be when he was eighteen.

He delivers babies, assists the dying, attends the necessary meetings, plays golf, and does good. He is honorable and irritable. If not as much loved as his father, he is perhaps even more respected. In one particular only—a kind of scar he carries without pain and without any clear memory of the amputation —does the man he is differ from the man he assumed he would become. He never prays.

A Short Trip Home

by F. Scott Fitzgerald

I was near her, for I had lingered behind in order to get the
short walk with her from the living room to the front door.
That was a lot, for she had flowered suddenly and I, being a
man and only a year older, hadn't flowered at all, had scarcely
dared to come near her in the ten days we'd been home. Nor
was I going to say anything in that walk of ten feet, or touch
her; but I had a vague hope she'd do something, give a gay little
performance of some sort, personal only in so far as we were
alone together.

She had magic suddenly in her pink palms, in the twinkle of
the short hairs on her neck, in the sure, clear confidence that at
about eighteen begins to deepen and sing in attractive American girls. She was nearly complete, yet the dew was still on her.

Already she was sliding into another world—the world of
Joe Jelke and Jim Cathcart waiting for us now in the car. In
another year she would pass beyond me forever.

As I waited, feeling the others outside in the snowy night,
feeling the excitement of Christmas week and the excitement of
Ellen here, blooming away, filling the room with "sex appeal"
—a wretched phrase to express a quality that isn't like that at
all—a maid came in from the dining room, spoke to Ellen quietly and handed her a note. Ellen read it and her eyes lit up, as
when the current grows strong on rural circuits, and glowed off
into space. Then she gave me an odd look—in which I probably
didn't show—and without a word, followed the maid into the
dining room and beyond. I sat turning over the pages of a
magazine for a quarter of an hour.

Joe Jelke came in, red-faced from the cold, his white silk
muffler gleaming at the neck of his fur coat. He was a senior at

New Haven; I was a sophomore. He was prominent, a member of Scroll and Keys, and, in my eyes, very distinguished and handsome.

"Isn't Ellen coming?"

"I don't know," I answered discreetly. "She was all ready."

"Ellen!" he called. "Ellen!"

He had left the front door open behind him and a great cloud of frosty air rolled in from outside. He went halfway up the stairs—he was familiar in the house—and called again, till Mrs. Baker came to the banister and said that Ellen was below. Then the maid, a little excited, appeared in the dining-room door.

"Mr. Jelke," she called in a low voice.

Joe's face fell as he turned toward her, sensing bad news.

"Miss Ellen says for you to go on to the party. She'll come later."

"What's the matter?"

"She can't come now. She'll come later."

He hesitated, confused. It was the last big dance of vacation, and he was mad about Ellen. He had tried to give her a ring for Christmas, and failing that, got her to accept a gold mesh bag that must have cost two hundred dollars. He wasn't the only one—there were three or four in the same wild condition, and all in the ten days she'd been home—but his chance came first, for he was rich and gracious and "white headed"—at that moment the desirable boy of St. Paul. To me it seemed impossible that she could prefer another, but the rumor was she'd described Joe as "much too perfect." I suppose he lacked mystery for her, and when a man is up against that with a young girl who isn't thinking of marriage—

"She's in the kitchen," Joe said angrily.

"No, she's not." The maid was defiant and a little scared. "She is."

"She went out the back way, Mr. Jelke."

"I'm going to see."

I followed him. The Swedish servants washing dishes looked up sideways at our approach and an interested crashing of pans marked our passage through. The storm door, unbolted, was flapping in the wind and as we walked out into the snowy yard we saw the tail light of a car turn the corner at the end of the back alley.

"I'm going after her," Joe said slowly. "I don't understand this at all."

I was too awed by the calamity to argue. We hurried to his car and drove in a fruitless, despairing zigzag all over the residence section, peering into every machine on the streets. It was half an hour before the futility of the affair began to dawn upon him—St. Paul is a city of almost three hundred thousand people—and Jim Cathcart reminded him that we had another girl to stop for. Like a wounded animal he sank into a melancholy mass of fur in the corner, from which position he jerked upright every few minutes and waved himself backward and forward a little in protest or despair.

Jim's girl was ready and impatient, but after what had happened her impatience didn't seem important. She looked lovely though. That's one thing about Christmas vacation—the excitement of growth and change and adventure in foreign parts transforming the people you've known all your life. Joe Jelke was polite to her in a daze—he indulged in one burst of short, loud, harsh laughter by way of conversation—and we drove to the hotel.

The chauffeur approached it on the wrong side—the side on which the line of cars was not putting forth guests—and because of that we came suddenly upon Ellen Baker just getting out of a small coupé. Even before we came to a stop, Joe Jelke had jumped excitedly from the car.

Ellen turned toward us, a faintly distracted look—perhaps of surprise, but certainly not of alarm—in her face; in fact, she didn't seem very aware of us. Joe approached her with a stern, dignified, injured and, I thought, just exactly correct reproof in his expression. I followed.

Seated in the coupé—he had not dismounted to help Ellen out—was a hard thin-faced man of about thirty-five with an air of being scarred, and a slight sinister smile. His eyes were a sort of taunt to the whole human family—they were the eyes of an animal sleepy and quiescent in the presence of another species. They were helpless yet brutal, unhopeful yet confident. It was as if they felt themselves powerless to originate activity, but infinitely capable of profiting by a single gesture of weakness in another.

Vaguely I placed him as one of the sort of men whom I had been conscious of from my earliest youth as "hanging around" —leaning with one elbow on the counters of tobacco stores, watching, through heaven knows what small chink of the mind, the people who hurried in and out. Intimate to garages, where he had vague business conducted in undertones, to barber shops and to the lobbies of theaters—in such places, anyhow, I placed the type, if type it was, that he reminded me of. Sometimes his face bobbed up in one of Tad's more savage cartoons, and I had always from earliest boyhood thrown a nervous glance toward the dim borderland where he stood, and seen him watching me and despising me. Once, in a dream, he had taken a few steps toward me, jerking his head back and muttering: "Say, kid" in what was intended to be a reassuring voice, and I had broken for the door in terror. This was that sort of man.

Joe and Ellen faced each other silently; she seemed, as I have said, to be in a daze. It was cold, but she didn't notice that her coat had blown open; Joe reached out and pulled it together, and automatically she clutched it with her hand.

Suddenly the man in the coupé, who had been watching them silently, laughed. It was a bare laugh, done with the breath—just a noisy jerk of the head—but it was an insult if I had ever heard one; definite and not to be passed over. I wasn't surprised when Joe, who was quick-tempered, turned to him angrily and said:

"What's your trouble?"

The man waited a moment, his eyes shifting and yet staring, and always seeing. Then he laughed again in the same way. Ellen stirred uneasily.

"Who is this—this—" Joe's voice trembled with annoyance.

"Look out now," said the man slowly.

Joe turned to me.

"Eddie, take Ellen and Catherine in, will you?" he said quickly. . . . "Ellen, go with Eddie."

"Look out now," the man repeated.

Ellen made a little sound with her tongue and teeth, but she didn't resist when I took her arm and moved her toward the side door of the hotel. It struck me as odd that she should be so helpless, even to the point of acquiescing by her silence in this imminent trouble.

"Let it go, Joe!" I called back over my shoulder. "Come inside!"

Ellen, pulling against my arm, hurried us on. As we were caught up into the swinging doors I had the impression that the man was getting out of his coupé.

Ten minutes later, as I waited for the girls outside the women's dressing room, Joe Jelke and Jim Cathcart stepped out of the elevator. Joe was very white, his eyes were heavy and glazed, there was a trickle of dark blood on his forehead and on his white muffler. Jim had both their hats in his hand.

"He hit Joe with brass knuckles," Jim said in a low voice. "Joe was out cold for a minute or so. I wish you'd send a bellboy for some witch hazel and court plaster."

It was late and the hall was deserted; brassy fragments of the dance below reached us as if heavy curtains were being blown aside and dropping back into place. When Ellen came out I took her directly downstairs. We avoided the receiving line and went into a dim room set with scraggly hotel palms where couples sometimes sat out during the dance; there I told her what had happened.

"It was Joe's own fault," she said, surprisingly. "I told him not to interfere."

This wasn't true. She had said nothing, only uttered one curious little click of impatience.

"You ran out the back door and disappeared for almost an hour," I protested. "Then you turned up with a hard-looking customer who laughed in Joe's face."

"A hard-looking customer," she repeated, as if tasting the sound of the words.

"Well, wasn't he? Where on earth did you get hold of him, Ellen?"

"On the train," she answered. Immediately she seemed to

regret this admission. "You'd better stay out of things that aren't your business, Eddie. You see what happened to Joe."

Literally I gasped. To watch her, seated beside me, immaculately glowing, her body giving off wave after wave of freshness and delicacy—and to hear her talk like that.

"But that man's a thug!" I cried. "No girl could be safe with him. He used brass knuckles on Joe—brass knuckles!"

"Is that pretty bad?"

She asked this as she might have asked such a question a few years ago. She looked at me at last and really wanted an answer; for a moment it was as if she were trying to recapture an attitude that had almost departed; then she hardened again. I say "hardened," for I began to notice that when she was concerned with this man her eyelids fell a little, shutting other things—everything else—out of view.

That was a moment I might have said something, I suppose, but in spite of everything, I couldn't light into her. I was too much under the spell of her beauty and its success. I even began to find excuses for her—perhaps that man wasn't what he appeared to be; or perhaps—more romantically—she was involved with him against her will to shield someone else. At this point people began to drift into the room and come up to speak to us. We couldn't talk anymore, so we went in and bowed to the chaperons. Then I gave her up to the bright restless sea of the dance, where she moved in an eddy of her own among the pleasant islands of colored favors set out on tables and the south winds from the brasses moaning across the hall. After a while I saw Joe Jelke sitting in a corner with a strip of court plaster on his forehead watching Ellen as if she herself had struck him down, but I didn't go up to him. I felt queer myself —like I feel when I wake up after sleeping through an afternoon, strange and portentous, as if something had gone on in the interval that changed the values of everything and that I didn't see.

The night slipped on through successive phases of paper caps and cardboard horns, amateur tableaux and flashlights for the morning papers. Then was the grand march and supper, and about two o'clock some of the committee, dressed up as reve-

nue agents, pinched the party, and a facetious newspaper was
distributed, burlesquing the events of the evening. And all the
time out of the corner of my eye I watched the shining orchid
on Ellen's shoulder as it moved like Stuart's plume about the
room. I watched it with a definite foreboding until the last
sleepy groups had crowded into the elevators, and then, bundled to the eyes in great shapeless fur coats, drifted out into the
clear dry Minnesota night.

2

There is a sloping midsection of our city which lies between
the residence quarter on the hill and the business district on the
level of the river. It is a vague part of town, broken by its climb
into triangles and odd shapes—there are names like Seven Corners—and I don't believe a dozen people could draw an accurate map of it, though everyone traversed it by trolley, auto or
shoe leather twice a day. And though it was a busy section, it
would be hard for me to name the business that comprised its
activity. There were always long lines of trolley cars waiting to
start somewhere; there was a big movie theater and many small
ones with posters of Hoot Gibson and Wonder Dogs and Wonder Horses outside; there were small stores with Old King
Brady and the Liberty Boys of '76 in the windows, and marbles, cigarettes and candy inside; and—one definite place at
least—a fancy costumer whom we all visited at least once a
year. Sometime during boyhood I became aware that one side
of a certain obscure street there was blackly questionable, and
all through the district were pawnshops, cheap jewelers, small
sporting clubs and gymnasiums and somewhat too blatantly
run-down saloons.

The morning after the Cotillion Club party, I woke up late
and lazy, with the happy feeling that for a day or two more
there was no chapel, no classes—nothing to do but wait for
another party tonight. It was crisp and bright—one of those
days when you forget how cold it is until your cheek freezes—
and the events of the evening before seemed dim and far away.
After luncheon I started downtown on foot through a light,

pleasant snow of small flakes that would probably fall all afternoon, and I was about half through that halfway section of
town—so far as I know, there's no name for it—when suddenly
whatever idle thought was in my head blew away like a hat and
I began thinking hard of Ellen Baker. I began worrying about
her as I'd never worried about anything except myself before. I
began to loiter, with an instinct to go up on the hill again and
find her and talk to her; then I remembered that she was at a
tea, and I went on again, but still thinking of her, and harder
than before. Right then the affair opened up again.

It was snowing, I said, and it was four o'clock on a December afternoon, when there is a promise of darkness in the air
and the street lamps are just going on. I passed a combination
pool parlor and restaurant, with a stove loaded with hot dogs in
the window, and a few loungers hanging around the door. The
lights were on inside—not bright lights but just a few pale yellow ones high up on the ceiling—and the glow they threw out
into the frosty dusk wasn't so bright that you weren't tempted
to stare inside. As I went past, thinking hard of Ellen all this
time, I took in the quartet of loafers out of the corner of my
eye. I hadn't gone half a dozen steps down the street when one
of them called to me, not by name but in a way clearly intended
for my ear. I thought it was a tribute to my raccoon coat and
paid no attention, but a moment later whoever it was called to
me again in a peremptory voice. I was annoyed and turned
around. There, standing in the group not ten feet away and
looking at me with the same half sneer on his face with which
he'd looked at Joe Jelke, was the hard, thin-faced fellow of the
night before.

He had on a black fancy-cut coat, buttoned up to his neck as
if he were cold. His hands were deep in his pockets and he wore
a derby and high button shoes. I was startled, and for a moment I hesitated, but I was most of all angry, and knowing that
I was quicker with my hands than Joe Jelke, I took a tentative
step back toward him. The other men weren't looking at me—I
don't think they saw me at all—but I knew that this one recognized me; there was nothing casual about his look, no mistake.

"Here I am. What are you going to do about it?" his eyes seemed to say. ·

I took another step toward him and he laughed soundlessly, but with active contempt, and drew back into the group. I followed. I was going to speak to him—I wasn't sure what I was going to say—but when I came up he had either changed his mind and backed off, or else he wanted me to follow him inside, for he had slipped off and the three men watched my intent approach without curiosity. They were the same kind—sporty, but, unlike him, smooth rather than truculent; I didn't find any personal malice in their collective glance.

"Did he go inside?" I asked.

They looked at one another in that cagy way; a wink passed between them, and after a perceptible pause, one said:

"Who go inside?"

"I don't know his name."

There was another wink. Annoyed and determined, I walked past them and into the poolroom. There were a few people at a lunch counter along one side and a few more playing billiards, but he was not among them.

Again I hesitated. If his idea was to lead me into any blind part of the establishment—there were some half-open doors farther back—I wanted more support. I went up to the man at the desk.

"What became of the fellow who just walked in here?"

Was he on his guard immediately, or was that my imagination?

"What fellow?"

"Thin face—derby hat."

"How long ago?"

"Oh—a minute."

He shook his head again. "Don't know him," he said.

I waited. The three men from outside had come in and were lined up beside me at the counter. I felt that all of them were looking at me in a peculiar way. Feeling helpless and increasingly uneasy, I turned suddenly and went out. A little way down the street I turned around and took a good look at the place, so I'd know it and could find it again. On the next corner

I broke impulsively into a run, found a taxicab in front of the hotel and drove back up the hill.

Ellen wasn't home. Mrs. Baker came downstairs and talked to me. She seemed entirely cheerful and proud of Ellen's beauty, and ignorant of anything being amiss or of anything unusual having taken place the night before. She was glad that vacation was almost over—it was a strain and Ellen wasn't very strong. Then she said something that relieved my mind enormously. She was glad that I had come in, for of course Ellen would want to see me, and the time was so short. She was going back at half-past eight tonight.

"Tonight!" I exclaimed. "I thought it was the day after to-morrow."

"She's going to visit the Brokaws in Chicago," Mrs. Baker said. "They want her for some party. We just decided it today. She's leaving with the Ingersoll girls tonight."

I was so glad I could barely restrain myself from shaking her hand. Ellen was safe. It had been nothing all along but a moment of the most casual adventure. I felt like an idiot, but I realized how much I cared about Ellen and how little I could endure anything terrible happening to her.

"She'll be in soon?"

"Any minute now. She just phoned from the University Club."

I said I'd be over later—I lived almost next door and I wanted to be alone. Outside I remembered I didn't have a key, so I started up the Bakers' driveway to take the old cut we used in childhood through the intervening yard. It was still snowing, but the flakes were bigger now against the darkness, and trying to locate the buried walk I noticed that the Bakers' back door was ajar.

I scarcely know why I turned and walked into that kitchen. There was a time when I would have known the Bakers' servants by name. That wasn't true now, but they knew me, and I was aware of a sudden suspension as I came in—not only a suspension of talk but of some mood or expectation that had filled them. They began to go to work too quickly; they made unnecessary movements and clamor—those three. The parlor maid looked at me in a frightened way and I suddenly guessed she was waiting to deliver another message. I beckoned her into the pantry.

"I know all about this," I said. "It's a very serious business. Shall I go to Mrs. Baker now, or will you shut and lock that back door?"

"Don't tell Mrs. Baker, Mr. Stinson!"

"Then I don't want Miss Ellen disturbed. If she is—and if she is I'll know of it—" I delivered some outrageous threat about going to all the employment agencies and seeing she never got another job in the city. She was thoroughly intimidated when I went out; it wasn't a minute before the back door was locked and bolted behind me.

Simultaneously I heard a big car drive up in front, chains crunching on the soft snow; it was bringing Ellen home, and I went in to say good-bye.

Joe Jelke and two other boys were along, and none of the three could manage to take their eyes off her, even to say hello. She had one of those exquisite rose skins frequent in our part of the country, and beautiful until the little veins begin to break at about forty, and the cold had lit it to a lovely flame, like the thrilling flush of children after their cold baths in the evening. She and Joe had reached some sort of reconciliation, or at least he was too far gone in love to remember last night; but I saw that though she laughed a lot she wasn't really paying any attention to him or any of them. She wanted them to go, so that there'd be a message from the kitchen, but I knew the message wasn't coming—that she was safe. There was talk of the Pump and Slipper dance at New Haven and of the Princeton Prom, and then, in various moods, we four men left and separated quickly outside. I walked home with a certain depression of spirit and lay for an hour in a hot bath thinking that vacation was all over for me now that she was gone; feeling, even more deeply than I had yesterday, that she was out of my life.

And something eluded me, some one more thing to do, something that I had lost amid the events of the afternoon, promising myself to go back and pick it up, only to find that it had

escaped me. I associated it vaguely with Mrs. Baker, and now I
seemed to recall that it had poked up its head somewhere in the
stream of conversation with her. In my relief about Ellen I had
forgotten to ask her a question regarding something she had
said.

The Brokaws—that was it—where Ellen was to visit. I knew
Bill Brokaw well; he was in my class at Yale. Then I remem-
bered and sat bolt upright in the tub—the Brokaws weren't in
Chicago this Christmas; they were at Palm Beach!

Dripping, I sprang out of the tub, threw an insufficient union
suit around my shoulders and sprang for the phone in my
room. I got the connection quickly, but Miss Ellen had already
started for the train.

Luckily our car was in, and while I squirmed, still damp,
into my clothes, the chauffeur brought it around to the door.
The night was cold and dry, and we made good time to the
station through the hard, crusty snow. I felt queer and insecure
starting out this way, but somehow more confident as the station loomed up bright and new against the dark, cold air. For
fifty years my family had owned the land on which it was built
and that made my temerity seem all right somehow. There was
always a possibility that I was rushing in where angels feared to
tread, but that sense of having a solid foothold in the past made
me willing to make a fool of myself. This business was all
wrong—terribly wrong. Any idea I had entertained that it was
harmless dropped away now; between Ellen and some vague
overwhelming catastrophe there stood me, or else the police
and a scandal. I'm no moralist—there was another element
here, terribly dark and frightening, and I didn't want Ellen to
go through it alone.

There are three competing trains from St. Paul to Chicago
that all leave within a few minutes of half-past eight. Hers was
the Burlington, and as I ran across the station I saw the grating
being pulled over and the light above it go out. I knew, though,
that she had a drawing room with the Ingersoll girls, because
her mother had mentioned buying the ticket, so she was, literally speaking, tucked in until tomorrow.

The C., M. & St. P. gate was down at the other end and I

raced for it and made it. I had forgotten one thing, though, and that was enough to keep me awake and worried half the night. This train got into Chicago ten minutes after the other. Ellen had that much time to disappear into one of the largest cities in the world.

I gave the porter a wire to my family to send from Milwaukee, and at eight o'clock next morning I pushed violently by a whole line of passengers, clamoring over their bags parked in the vestibule, and shot out of the door with a sort of scramble over the porter's back. For a moment the confusion of a great station, the voluminous sounds and echoes and crosscurrents of bells and smoke struck me helpless. Then I dashed for the exit and toward the only chance I knew of finding her.

I had guessed right. She was standing at the telegraph counter, sending off heaven knows what black lie to her mother, and her expression when she saw me had a sort of terror mixed up with its surprise. There was cunning in it too. She was thinking quickly—she would have liked to walk away from me as if I wasn't there, and go about her own business, but she couldn't. I was too matter-of-fact a thing in her life. So we stood silently watching each other and each thinking hard.

"The Brokaws are in Florida," I said after a minute.

"It was nice of you to take such a long trip to tell me that."

"Since you've found it out, don't you think you'd better go on to school?"

"Please let me alone, Eddie," she said.

"I'll go as far as New York with you. I've decided to go back early myself."

"You'd better let me alone." Her lovely eyes narrowed and her face took on a look of dumb-animal-like resistance. She made a visible effort, the cunning flickered back into it, then both were gone, and in their stead was a cheerful reassuring smile that all but convinced me.

"Eddie, you silly child, don't you think I'm old enough to take care of myself?" I didn't answer. "I'm going to meet a man, you understand. I just want to see him today. I've got my ticket East on the five o'clock train. If you don't believe it, here it is in my bag."

"I believe you."

"That man isn't anybody that you know and—frankly, I think you're being awfully fresh and impossible."

"I know who the man is."

Again she lost control of her face. That terrible expression came back into it and she spoke with almost a snarl:

"You'd better let me alone."

I took the blank out of her hand and wrote out an explanatory telegram to her mother. Then I turned to Ellen and said a little roughly:

"We'll take the five o'clock train East together. Meanwhile you're going to spend the day with me."

The mere sound of my own voice saying this so emphatically encouraged me, and I think it impressed her, too; at any rate, she submitted—at least temporarily—and came along without protest while I bought my ticket.

When I start to piece together the fragments of that day a sort of confusion begins, as if my memory didn't want to yield up any of it, or my consciousness let any of it pass through. There was a bright, fierce morning during which we rode about in a taxicab and went to a department store where Ellen said she wanted to buy something and then tried to slip away from me by a back way. I had the feeling, for an hour, that someone was following us along Lake Shore Drive in a taxicab, and I would try to catch them by turning quickly or looking suddenly into the chauffeur's mirror; but I could find no one, and when I turned back I could see that Ellen's face was contorted with mirthless, unnatural laughter.

All morning there was a raw, bleak wind off the lake, but when we went to the Blackstone for lunch a light snow came down past the windows and we talked almost naturally about our friends, and about casual things. Suddenly her tone changed; she grew serious and looked me in the eye, straight and sincere.

"Eddie, you're the oldest friend I have," she said, "and you oughtn't to find it too hard to trust me. If I promise you faithfully on my word of honor to catch that five o'clock train, will you let me alone a few hours this afternoon?"

"Why?"

"Well"—she hesitated and hung her head a little—"I guess everybody has a right to say—good-bye."

"You want to say good-bye to that—"

"Yes, yes," she said hastily; "just a few hours, Eddie, and I promise faithfully that I'll be on that train."

"Well, I suppose no great harm could be done in two hours. If you really want to say good-bye—"

I looked up suddenly and surprised a look of such tense and palpable cunning in her face that I winced before it. Her lip was curled up and her eyes were slits again; there wasn't the faintest touch of fairness and sincerity in her whole face.

We argued. The argument was vague on her part and somewhat hard and reticent on mine. I wasn't going to be cajoled again into any weakness or be infected with any—and there was a contagion of evil in the air. She kept trying to imply, without any convincing evidence to bring forward, that everything was all right. Yet she was too full of the thing itself— whatever it was—to build up a real story, and she wanted to catch at any credulous and acquiescent train of thought that might start in my head, and work that for all it was worth. After every reassuring suggestion she threw out, she stared at me eagerly, as if she hoped I'd launch into a comfortable moral lecture with the customary sweet at the end—which in this case would be her liberty. But I was wearing her away a little. Two or three times it needed just a touch of pressure to bring her to the point of tears—which, of course, was what I wanted—but I couldn't seem to manage it. Almost I had her—almost possessed her interior attention—then she would slip away.

I bullied her remorselessly into a taxi about four o'clock and started for the station. The wind was raw again, with a sting of snow in it, and the people in the streets, waiting for busses and street cars too small to take them all in, looked cold and disturbed and unhappy. I tried to think how lucky we were to be comfortably off and taken care of, but all the warm, respectable world I had been part of yesterday had dropped away from me. There was something we carried with us now that was the enemy and the opposite of all that; it was in the cab beside us, the streets we passed through. With a touch of panic, I wondered if I wasn't slipping almost imperceptibly into Ellen's attitude of mind. The column of passengers waiting to go aboard the train were as remote from me as people from another world, but it was I that was drifting away and leaving them behind.

My lower was in the same car with her compartment. It was an old-fashioned car, its lights somewhat dim, its carpets and upholstery full of the dust of another generation. There were half a dozen other travelers, but they made no special impression on me, except that they shared the unreality that I was beginning to feel everywhere around me. We went into Ellen's compartment, shut the door and sat down.

Suddenly I put my arms around her and drew her over to me, just as tenderly as I knew how—as if she were a little girl—as she was. She resisted a little, but after a moment she submitted and lay tense and rigid in my arms.

"Ellen," I said helplessly, "you asked me to trust you. You have much more reason to trust me. Wouldn't it help to get rid of all this, if you told me a little?"

"I can't," she said, very low—"I mean, there's nothing to tell."

"You met this man on the train coming home and you fell in love with him, isn't that true?"

"I don't know."

"Tell me, Ellen. You fell in love with him?"

"I don't know. Please let me alone."

"Call it anything you want," I went on, "he has some sort of hold over you. He's trying to use you; he's trying to get something from you. He's not in love with you."

"What does that matter?" she said in a weak voice.

"It does matter. Instead of trying to fight this—this thing—you're trying to fight me. And I love you, Ellen. Do you hear? I'm telling you all of a sudden, but it isn't new with me. I love you."

She looked at me with a sneer on her gentle face; it was an expression I had seen on men who were tight and didn't want to be taken home. But it was human. I was reaching her, faintly and from far away, but more than before.

"Ellen, I want you to answer me one question. Is he going to be on this train?"

She hesitated; then, an instant too late, she shook her head.

"Be careful, Ellen. Now I'm going to ask you one thing more, and I wish you'd try very hard to answer. Coming West, when did this man get on the train?"

"I don't know," she said with an effort—"in Pittsburgh, I think. He spoke to me just after we left Pittsburgh, back in the observation car."

Just at that moment I became aware, with the unquestionable knowledge reserved for facts, that he was just outside the door. She knew it, too; the blood left her face and that expression of low-animal perspicacity came creeping back. I lowered my face into my hands and tried to think.

We must have sat there, with scarcely a word, for well over an hour. I was conscious that the lights of Chicago, then of Englewood and of endless suburbs, were moving by, and then there were no more lights and we were out on the dark flatness of Illinois. The train seemed to draw in upon itself; it took on an air of being alone. The porter knocked at the door and asked if he could make up the berth, but I said no and he went away.

After a while I convinced myself that the struggle inevitably coming wasn't beyond what remained of my sanity, my faith in the essential all-rightness of things and people. That this person's purpose was what we call "criminal," I took for granted, but there was no need of ascribing to him an intelligence that belonged to a higher plane of human, or inhuman, endeavor. It was still as a man that I considered him, and tried to get at his essence, his self-interest—what took the place in him of a comprehensible heart—but I suppose I more than half knew what I would find when I opened the door.

When I stood up Ellen didn't seem to see me at all. She was hunched into the corner staring straight ahead with a sort of film over her eyes, as if she were in a state of suspended animation of body and mind. I lifted her and put two pillows under her head and threw my fur coat over her knees. Then I knelt beside her and kissed her two hands, opened the door and went out into the hall.

I closed the door behind me and stood with my back against it for a minute. The car was dark save for the corridor lights at each end. There was no sound except the groaning of the couplers, the even click-a-tick of the rails and someone's loud sleeping breath farther down the car. I became aware after a moment that he was standing by the water cooler just outside the men's smoking room, his derby hat on his head, his coat collar turned up around his neck as if he were cold, and his hands in his coat pockets. When I saw him, he turned and went into the smoking room, and I followed. He was sitting in the far corner of the long leather bench; I took the single armchair beside the door.

As I went in I nodded to him and he acknowledged my presence with one of those terrible soundless laughs of his. But this time it was prolonged, it seemed to go on forever, and rather to cut it short than to deal in hollow amenities, I asked: "Where are you from?" in what I tried to make a casual tone of voice.

He stopped laughing and looked at me narrowly, wondering what my game was. When he decided to answer, his voice was muffled as though he were speaking through a silk scarf, and it seemed to come from a long way off.

"I'm from St. Paul, Jack."

"Been making a trip home?"

He nodded.

"Just a short trip?" I pursued.

Again he nodded impatiently. Then he took a long breath and spoke in a hard, menacing voice:

"You better get off at Fort Wayne, Jack."

He was dead. He was dead as hell—he had been dead all along, but what force had flowed through him, like blood in his veins, out in St. Paul, was leaving him. Now a new outline—the outline of him dead—was coming through the palpable figure that had knocked down Joe Jelke.

He spoke again, with a sort of jerking effort:

"You get off at Fort Wayne, Jack, or I'm going to bump you

off." He moved his hand in his coat pocket and showed me the outline of a revolver.

I shook my head. "You can't touch me," I answered. "You see, I know." His terrible eyes shifted over me quickly, trying to determine whether or not I did know. Then he gave a snarl and made as though he were going to jump to his feet.

"You climb off here or else I'm going to get you, Jack!" he cried hoarsely. The train was slowing up for Fort Wayne and his voice rang loud in the comparative quiet, but he didn't move from his chair—he was too weak, I think—and we sat staring at each other while workmen passed up and down outside the window banging the brakes and wheels, and the engine gave out loud mournful pants up ahead. No one got into our car. After a while the porter closed the vestibule door and passed back along the corridor, and we slid out of the murky yellow station light and into the long darkness.

What I remember next must have extended over a space of five or six hours, though it comes back to me as something without any existence in time—something that might have taken five minutes or a year. There began a slow, calculated assault on me, wordless and terrible. I felt what I can only call a strangeness stealing over me—akin to the strangeness I had felt all afternoon, but deeper and more intensified. It was like nothing so much as the sensation of drifting away, and I gripped the arms of the chair convulsively, as if to hang on to a piece in the living world. Sometimes I felt myself going out with a rush. There would be almost a warm relief about it, a sense of not caring; then, with a violent wrench of the will, I'd pull myself back into the room.

Suddenly I realized that from a while back I had stopped hating him, stopped feeling violently alien to him, and with the realization, I went cold and sweat broke out all over my head. He was getting around my abhorrence, as he had got around Ellen coming West on the train; and it was just that strength he drew from preying on people that had brought him up to the point of concrete violence in St. Paul, and that, fading and flickering out, still kept him fighting now.

He must have seen that faltering in my heart, for he spoke at once, in a low, even, almost gentle voice: "You better go now."

"Oh, I'm not going," I forced myself to say.

"Suit yourself, Jack."

He was my friend, he implied. He knew how it was with me and he wanted to help. He pitied me. I'd better go away before it was too late. The rhythm of his attack was soothing as a song: I'd better go away—*and let him get at Ellen.* With a little cry I sat bolt upright.

"What do you want of this girl?" I said, my voice shaking.

"To make a sort of walking hell of her."

His glance held a quality of dumb surprise, as if I was punishing an animal for a fault of which he was not conscious. For an instant I faltered; then I went on blindly:

"You've lost her; she's put her trust in me."

His countenance went suddenly black with evil, and he cried: "You're a liar!" in a voice that was like cold hands.

"She trusts me," I said. "You can't touch her. She's safe!"

He controlled himself. His face grew pale and bland, and I felt that curious weakness and indifference begin again inside me. What was the use of all this? What was the use?

"You haven't got much time left," I forced myself to say, and then, in a flash of intuition, I jumped at the truth: "You're sinking. You've only got a few hours. Your body is lying dead back in Pittsburgh. That's as far as you can go."

His face contorted, lost all semblance of humanity, living or dead. Simultaneously the room was full of cold air and with a noise that was something between a paroxysm of coughing and a burst of horrible laughter, he was on his feet, reeking of shame and blasphemy.

"Come and look!" he cried. "I'll show you—"

He took a step toward me, then another and it was exactly as if a door stood open behind him, a door yawning out to an inconceivable abyss of darkness and corruption. There was a scream of mortal agony, from him or from somewhere behind, and abruptly the strength went out of him in a long husky sigh and he wilted to the floor. . . .

How long I sat there, dazed with terror and exhaustion, I

don't know. The next thing I remember is the sleepy porter shining shoes across the room from me, and outside the window the steel fires of Pittsburgh breaking the flat perspective of the night. There was something extended on the bench also— something too faint for a man, too faint for a man, too heavy for a shadow. Even as I perceived it, it faded off and away.

Some minutes later I opened the door of Ellen's compartment. She was asleep where I had left her. Her lovely cheeks were white and wan, but she lay naturally—her hands relaxed and her breathing regular and clear. What had possessed her had gone out of her, leaving her exhausted but her own dear self again.

I made her a little more comfortable, tucked a blanket around her, extinguished the light and went out.

3

When I came home for Easter vacation, almost my first act was to go down to the billiard parlor near Seven Corners. The man at the cash register quite naturally didn't remember my hurried visit of three months before.

"I'm trying to locate a certain party who, I think, came here a lot some time ago."

I described the man rather accurately, and when I had finished, the cashier called to a little jockeylike fellow who was sitting near with an air of having something very important to do that he couldn't quite remember.

"Hey, Shorty, talk to this guy, will you? I think he's looking for Joe Varland."

The little man gave me a tribal look of suspicion. I went and sat near him.

"Joe Varland's dead, fella," he said grudgingly. "He died last winter."

I described him again—his overcoat, his laugh, the habitual expression of his eyes.

"That's Joe Varland you're looking for all right, but he's dead."

"I want to find out something about him."

"What you want to find out?"

"What did he do, for instance?"

"How should I know? He used to come in here once in a while and shoot pool."

"Look here! I'm not a policeman. I just want some kind of information about his habits. He's dead now and it can't hurt him. And it won't go beyond me."

"Well"—he hesitated, looking me over—"he was a great one for traveling. Somebody told me he died on a train"—I started—"wait a minute now—who was it told me that? Anyhow, he was in New York sick and he tried to come home. They took him off the train with pneumonia at Pittsburgh and he died there."

I nodded. Broken pieces of the puzzle began to assemble in my head.

"Why was he a lot on trains?"

"How should I know, fella?"

"If you can use ten dollars, I'd like to know anything you may have heard on the subject."

"Well," said Shorty reluctantly, "all I know is they used to say he worked the trains."

"Worked the trains?"

"He had some racket of his own he'd never loosen up about. He used to work the girls traveling alone on the trains. Nobody ever knew much about it—he was a pretty smooth guy—but sometimes he'd turn up here with a lot of dough and he let 'em know it was the janes he got it off of."

I thanked him and gave him the ten dollars and went out, very thoughtful, without mentioning that though a part of Joe Varland had been taken off the train at Pittsburgh, another part of him had made a last trip home. Ellen wasn't West for Easter, and even if she had been I wouldn't have gone to her with the information, either—at least I've seen her almost every day this summer and we've managed to talk about everything else. Sometimes, though, she gets silent about nothing and wants to be very close to me, and I know what's in her mind.

Of course she's very popular and coming out this fall and I have two more years at New Haven; still, things don't look as impossible as they did a few months ago. She belongs to me in a way—even if I lose her she belongs to me. She'll always know I love her and that she might need me, and sometimes those are powerful considerations. I'm going to take her out to a dance at the club tonight, and perhaps sometime during the evening she'll get silent and a little frightened and want me close to her. Who knows? Anyhow, I'll be there—I'll always be there.

HOUSEPARTY

by Walter Bernstein

The small room was crowded, but the boy managed to get through without spilling the drink he held in his hand.

"Hello," he said to the girl on the window seat. "Here's your drink."

The girl looked at him and then looked at her watch. "You're late," she said. "Last time you were faster."

"I couldn't help it," the boy said. "The place is filling up."

The girl accepted the glass and took a long drink. She looked up at the boy and took another drink. Then she set the glass down. "What do they put this Scotch in with—an eye dropper?" she asked.

"I'll get you some more."

"No, never mind." She turned to look out of the window.

"That's the library," the boy said.

"Your friend told me. I guess he wanted me to get the idea. He told me five times. Look," she said, "there's a clock on the other side of that tower, too, isn't there?"

"Sure," said the boy. "Four of them."

"Does it keep the same time as this one?"

"Sure."

The girl looked triumphant. "How do you know?" she asked.

"Well—" the boy said. He was a trifle uneasy. "Well, I guess it does."

"You ought to find out," the girl insisted. "You really ought to find out. That clock on the other side might be slow. If you can only see one clock at a time, how do you know it isn't slow?"

"I guess you don't know," said the boy. "You have to take their word for it."

"I'd find out if I were you," said the girl, shaking her head slowly. She took another drink. "You really ought to know." She looked out of the window, then turned back to the boy. "What do they call this place again?"

"Dartmouth," said the boy.

"That's a silly name," said the girl. She finished her drink. "Do you think you could get me another one of these with some Scotch in it?"

"Sure," said the boy. He took the glass and started through the crowd. The girl put her nose against the pane and looked out of the window.

After a while, the boy came back, holding the drink above his head so it wouldn't be spilled. He tapped the girl on the shoulder. "Hello," he said. "I'm back."

The girl looked at him. "Go away," she said. "I never heard of you."

"I'm your date," said the boy. "I'm bringing you another drink."

The girl peered at him. "So you are," she said. She took the drink and returned to the window.

"I got a little more Scotch this time," the boy said.

The girl turned around. "You're cute," she said.

The boy blushed. "Look," he said, "are you having a good time?"

"I'm having a wonderful time," the girl said. "I am having a simply wonderful time." Her eyes were very large and bright.

"I'm glad," said the boy. He sat down and took hold of her hand. The girl looked at his hand holding hers and then up at his face. She looked at his hand again and took another drink. The boy held on to her hand and leaned forward. "Do you really dance in a chorus?" he said.

"When I'm working," the girl said. "They call us chorus girls." She put her head next to his. "Who squealed?"

"Oh, no one." The boy was emphatic. "My sister told me. Remember? You know my sister. She introduced us in New York."

The girl nodded. "I know your sister." She hiccuped gently. "Little bitch."

The boy released her hand and sat up straight. Seeing his startled expression, the girl put her fingers to her mouth. "There I go again, always belching in public," she said. She leaned toward the boy. "Pardon me."

"Sure," said the boy. "Sure." He sat up very straight.

The girl was beating out a rhythm on the glass with her fingernails, watching the crowd. "How long do you have to stay in this place?" she asked.

"No special time," said the boy. "We can leave now if you want."

"Not here," said the girl. "I mean in college."

"Oh. Four years. I have one to go."

"That's a long run." She drained her glass and looked at the boy. "You're cute," she said. She put down the glass and took up his hands. "You have nice hands."

The boy gave her hands a slight squeeze. "So have you," he said, but the girl had turned away.

"You touch that glass," she was saying to a girl about to sit down, "and I'll lay you out like a rug." She retrieved the glass and held it out to the boy. "How about another drink?"

"Sure," said the boy. He took the glass and moved into the crowd. As he was pouring the liquor, another boy came over and put an arm around his shoulders.

"How're you doing?" he asked.

The boy spilled a little soda into the glass and started back toward the window.

"Fine," he called back. "Fine." He dodged someone carrying a tray. "She's a cinch," he said.

A Student in Economics

by George Milburn

All of the boys on the third floor of Mrs. Gooch's approved rooms for men had been posted to get Charlie Wingate up that afternoon. He had to go to see the Dean. Two or three of them forgot about it and two or three of them had other things to do, but Eddie Barbour liked waking people up. Eddie stuck his weasel face in at Charlie's door just as the alarm clock was giving one last feeble tap. The clock stood on the bottom of a tin washpan that was set upside down on a wooden chair beside the bed. The alarm had made a terrific din. Eddie had heard it far down the hall. The hands showed two o'clock. Pale needles from a December sun were piercing the limp green window shade in a hundred places.

Eddie Barbour yelled, "Aw right, Charlie! Snap out of it!" He came into the chilly room and stood for a moment staring vaguely at the ridge of quilts on the sagged iron bed. The only sound was the long, regular sough of Charlie Wingate's breathing. He hadn't heard a thing. Eddie made a sudden grab for the top of the covers, stripped them back and began jouncing the sleeper by the shoulders. Charlie grunted every time the bed springs creaked, but he nuzzled his pillow and went on sleeping. Eddie went over to the study table where a large, white-enameled water pitcher stood and he came back to the bed with the water, breathing giggles. He tipped the water pitcher a little and a few drops fell on the back of Charlie's neck without waking him. Eddie sloshed the icy water up over the pitcher's mouth. A whole cupful splashed on Charlie's head. Charlie sat up quickly, batting his arms about, and Eddie Barbour whinnied with laughter.

"Arise, my lord, for the day is here," he said, going across and ceremoniously raising the crooked window shade. Charlie sat straight up among the rumpled quilts with his head cocked on one side, staring dully. He had slept with his clothes on. He sat up in bed all dressed, in a soldier's brown uniform, all but his shoes and roll puttees.

"You got army today?" Eddie asked, putting the pitcher down.

Charlie looked at him for a moment and blinked. Then he said in a voice stuffy with sleep, "Naw. I had army yesterday. I got army make-up today." He worked his mouth, making clopping noises.

"What time you got army make-up, Charlie? When you come in from class you said get you up because you had to go see the Dean at two-thirty."

"Yeah, I do have to go see the Dean at two-thirty. But I got army make-up too. I got to make up drill cuts from three till six." All at once he flopped back down on the bed, sound asleep again.

"Hey!" Eddie cried, jumping forward. "Come out of that! Wake up there, Charlie! You can't sleep no more if you got to see the Dean at two-thirty. You just about got time to make it." He jerked him back up in bed.

"Screw the Dean," Charlie said; "two hours' sleep ain't enough."

"Is two hours all the sleep you got last night?"

"Where you get the 'last night'? I worked all night last night. I had classes till noon. Two hours' sleep was all I got today. And darn little more yesterday or the day before. When is Sunday? Sunday's the first day I'm due to get any real sleep. Two hours' sleep is not enough sleep for a man to get."

He plumped his stockinged feet onto the cold floor and got up stiffly. He went over to the washstand, where he picked up his toothbrush and toothpaste and a bar of soap and slowly took his face towel down from beside the warped looking-glass. He came back to where his shoes lay and stood looking at the toilet articles in his hands as if he had forgotten what he meant to do with them. He dumped them on the bed, took the pan with the alarm clock on it and set it on the floor. Then he sat down on the chair and picked up one of the heavy army shoes, held it and felt it and studied it carefully before he put it on. He put on the other shoe with equal deliberation and stood up without lacing either of them. He took his things up from the bed and started off for the bathroom, his loose shoes clogging. Eddie Barbour followed him down the drafty hall.

The creosote disinfectant that Mrs. Gooch used in her bathrooms gave off a strong odor. "Dag gum bathroom smells just like a hen coop," Charlie said thickly as he stood in front of the white-specked mirror twisting his face. He wouldn't need a shave for another day. He had a fairly good-looking face, tan and thin, with ringlets of black hair tumbling down over his forehead. His large ears stuck straight out. He looked at his image with dark eyes made narrow by two purplish puffs under them, and he yawned widely.

Eddie Barbour stood leaning against the jamb of the bathroom door. He said, "You ought to try and get more sleep, Charlie."

"Are you telling *me*?" Charlie said, running water in the face bowl. Eddie Barbour was a freshman too.

2

Charlie Wingate came walking along University Boulevard toward the campus, hunched up in his army overcoat. The raw December wind whipped his face and made him feel wide awake. He passed a bunch of fraternity men pitching horseshoes in the drive beside the K.A. house. Two or three, sprucely dressed, gave him impersonal glances as he passed. They did not speak, and he walked past self-consciously, seeing them without looking toward them.

When he reached the business section opposite the campus he turned in at the white-tiled front of The Wigwam. The noon rush was over and Nick was not at the cash register. A few noon "dates" were still sitting in the booths along the wall. Charlie walked straight back along the white-tile counter and sat down on the end stool. Red Hibbert was standing by the coffee urns reading the sports section. When Charlie sat down

Red folded his newspaper slowly and came over to wait on him. Charlie sat with his cheeks resting on the heels of his hands.

"How's it, Chollie, old boy, old boy?" Red Hibbert said.

"Not bad. Give me a cup of javy without and a couple of them Grandma's oatmeal cookies over there, Red. Where's Nick?"

Red scooted the plate with the cookies on it down the glassy white counter top and came along with the cup of black coffee. "This is Nick's day for Kiwanis," he said. "It looks to me like you'd stay home and get some sleep once in a while. You're dyin' on your feet."

"I am going to get some sleep Sunday, don't you never worry. I have to go see the Dean this afternoon. And I got make-up drill at three o'clock. I've got to make up some drill cuts."

"What you got to go see the Dean about?"

"I don't know what about; here's all it said." Charlie reached in his overcoat pocket and pulled out a jagged window envelope and a mimeographed postal card. He pushed the envelope across the counter along with the postal card. "I got that other in the morning mail too."

Red took the printed form from the Dean of Men's office out of the envelope and glanced at it. Then he picked up the postal card. It was headed,

FOURTH AND FINAL NOTICE

You are hereby summoned to appear before the chairman of the Student Senate Committee on Freshman Activities, Rm 204 Student Union Bldg., not later than 4 P.M., Friday afternoon. It will be to your advantage not to ignore this summons as you have three previous ones. This is positively the last opportunity you will be given to rectify your delinquency. Should you fail to appear this time, steps will be taken to bring you.

(signed)   Aubrey H. Carson, Chrmn
Com. on Frshmn Actvts.

Red waggled the postal card. "What you going to do about this?"

"Tear it up like I did the others, I guess. I know what they want. They want to try and make me buy one of them damn' freshman caps."

"Take a tip from me, Charlie: I'd go see them. It won't hurt nothing, and it might be a lot easier on you in the long run."

"Hell, what can they do?"

"Plenty. They could sick the Black Hoods onto you."

"Ah! The Black Hoods, that bunch of amateur ku kluckers!"

"Call 'em amateurs if you want to, Charlie, but it wasn't only but last Friday night they took that little Jew-boy, Sol Lewis, out of the rooming house where I stay. It look to me like they did a pretty professional job on him. They used the buckle-end of a belt on him. They claim he was a stool pigeon for the University."

"Stool pigeon! Ah, you know that guy wasn't a stool pigeon, Red."

"We-ell, I'm not saying one way or the other. Anyhow, that's what you're up against when you take to fooling with that Student Committee on Freshman Activities, Charlie."

"Prexy claimed in his opening address at the first of school that he had put a stop to these masked frats and all this hazing."

"Yeah, he said he had; but how's he going to put a stop to the Black Hoods? He can't kick out all the biggest shots in the University, can he? All the big shots on the campus are Black Hoods. Football stars and fellas like that. You won't see the President kicking guys like that out of the University."

"Maybe not, but—why, hell, that freshman cap business is nothing but a racket. That's all it is. Damn' if I let 'em scare me into paying a dollar for a little old sleazy green cloth cap!"

"O.K., Charlie; I guess you know what you want to do."

"Anyway, how could I get around to see that committee before four o'clock this afternoon, and see the Dean at two-thirty, and go to make-up drill from three till six? I'll be late to drill and get bawled out by the captain again. The captain's already about to flunk me for cuts. That's what's getting me down—Military. It's this Military that's getting me down."

"Jees, I don't know, Charlie; seems like I get a bigger kick out of army than I do any other course I got. They sure learn you more in army than they do in anything else *in* this University."

"Yeow, you learn plenty in army, all right. But what I don't like is the compulsory part. I don't think they ought to be allowed to make it compulsory for freshmen and sophomores. That's just like they had it over in Germany before they got rid of the Kaiser."

The red-haired boy gave him a startled look. He frowned heavily. "Charlie," he exclaimed, "where are you getting all these radical ideas you been spouting around here lately?" Charlie peered at him. Red's face was set in earnestness.

"Why, that's not a radical idea," Charlie said, pushing back his empty coffee cup. "That's just a plain historical fact, that's all that is. I don't see where they got any right to make Military Training compulsory. This is supposed to be a *free* country. That compulsory stuff is what Mussle-leany and birds like that pull."

"But, Charlie, it's all for your own benefit. The University is just looking out after your own interests."

"How do you figure they're looking out for *my* interests?"

"Well, for one thing, when the next war comes we'll all be officers, us fellas that got this training in college. We'll go right into the regular army as officers. There's where we'll have the edge on guys that never did take advantage of a college education. Person'ly, when the next war comes along, I'm not hankerin' after any front-line trenches. And you know darn' well they're not going to stick their college-trained officers into front-line trenches to get shot. So there's where I figure us guys in R.O.T.C. will have a big advantage."

"Yeah, you might be right, at that, Red. But I'm not kicking about R.O.T.C. It's just the compulsory part I'm kicking against."

Red perked his head and scowled impatiently. "Charlie, they *got* to make it compulsory. If it wasn't compulsory, how many of the fellas would enroll in it? They have to make Military compulsory in order to give the fullest benefits. What good could they do if only a few of the fellas was taking it?"

"Anyway, I know some it's not compulsory for," Charlie said stubbornly. "Last night there was a Phi Gam pledge in here bragging about how he got out of Military. He told them at the first of school he didn't want to take Military. They told him he *had* to take it—required of all able-bodied freshmen. Couldn't get his degree without it. So he had to go buy his army shoes. Well, he got the shoe store to send the bill to his old man. His old man is one of these they call 'em pacifists. When his old man gets the bill for his kid's army shoes, maybe you think he don't get the President of this University on long distance and tell him where to head in it. And this kid didn't have to take Military, neither. His old man's a big shot lawyer in the City."

"Yeah, but you got to have pull to get away with that, Charlie."

"That's what I mean, Red. You can get away with plenty in this University if you got the pull."

3

Charlie Wingate loped up the steps of the Administration Building, hurried through the revolving doors, and walked past hissing steam radiators down the long hall to the Dean of Men's office. He was ten minutes late. Before he opened the frosted-glass door he took out a pair of amber-colored spectacles and put them on. Then he went in and handed his summons to the secretary.

"The Dean will see you in a moment," she said. "Please take a chair."

Charlie sat down and gave an amber-hued glance about the outer office. Three dejected freshmen, holding their green caps, were waiting with him. He recognized none of them, so he picked up a week-old copy of the *Christian Science Monitor* and started to read it. But the room was warm and he immediately went to sleep. He had his head propped back against the wall. The newspaper slipped down into his lap. His amber-colored glasses hid his eyes and no one could see that they were closed.

He was awakened by the secretary shaking him. She was smiling and the freshmen were all snickering.

"Wake up and pay for your bed, fella!" one of the freshmen called, and everyone laughed heartily.

"I sort of drowsed off. It's so nice and warm in here," Charlie said, apologizing to the pretty secretary.

The Dean of Men got up as he entered and, with his eyes on the slip bearing Charlie's name, said, "Ah, this is Charles Wingate, isn't it?" He grasped Charlie's hand as if it were an honor and pressed a button under the edge of his desk with his other hand. The secretary appeared at the door. "Miss Dunn, will you bring in Wingate's folder—Charles W-i-n-g-a-t-e. How do you like college by now, Wingate? Eyes troubling you?"

"Pretty well, sir. Yes, sir, a little. I wear these glasses."

The secretary came back with the folder and the Dean looked through it briefly. "Well, Wingate, I suppose you're anxious to know why I sent for you. The unpleasant truth is, Wingate, you don't seem to be doing so well in your college work. Your freshman adviser conferred with you twice about this, and this week he turned your case over to me. My purpose, of course, is to help you. Now, to be quite frank, Wingate, you're on the verge of flunking out. Less than a third of the semester remains, and you have a failing grade in English 101, conditional grades in Psychology 51 and Military Training; three hours of F and four hours of D, almost half your total number of hours. On the other hand, you have an A average in Spanish and a B in Economics 150. Wingate, how do you account for your failing English when you are an A student in Spanish?"

"To tell you the truth, sir, I got behind on my written work in English, and I've never been able to catch up. And I don't really have to study Spanish. My father is a railway section foreman in my home town, and he's always had a gang of Mexicans working for him. I've been speaking Mexican ever since I was a kid. It's not the pure, what they call Castilian, Spanish, but I probably know almost as much Spanish as my professor."

"How about this B in Economics? That's a fairly high grade."

"Yes, sir. Doctor Kenshaw—he's my Ec professor—doesn't give exams. Instead he gives everyone a B until he calls for our term papers. We don't recite in his class. We just listen to him lecture. And the grade you get on your term paper is your semester grade."

"Ah! What you students term a pipe course, eh, Wingate?"

"Not exactly, sir. We have to do a lot of outside reading for the term paper. But I'm counting on keeping that B in Ec."

"That's fine, Wingate. But it appears to me that it's high time you were getting busy on some of these other grades, too. Why can't you dig in and pull these D's up to B's, and this F up to at least a C? You've got it in you. You made an unusually high grade on your entrance exams, your record shows. Graduated from high school with honors. What's the trouble, Wingate? Tell me!"

"I don't know, sir, except I work at night and—"

"Oh, I see it here on your enrollment card now. Where do you work?"

"I work nights for Nick Pappas, down at The Wigwam."

"How many hours a night do you work?"

"Ten hours, sir. From nine till seven. The Wigwam stays open all night. I eat and go to eight o'clock class when I get off."

"Very interesting, Wingate. But don't you suppose that it would be advisable to cut down a bit on this outside work and attend a little more closely to your college work? After all, that's what you're here for, primarily—to go to college, not work in a café."

"I couldn't work fewer hours and stay in school, sir. I just barely get by as it is. I get my board at The Wigwam, and I pay my room rent, and I've been paying out on a suit of clothes. That leaves only about a dollar a week for all the other things I have to have."

"Wingate, shouldn't you earn more than that, working ten hours?"

"I get the regular, first-year-man rate, sir. Twenty cents an hour. It's set by the University. Nick takes out a dollar a day for board. Pays me five dollars a week in cash."

"Can't you arrange for a little financial support from home?"

"No, sir, I'm afraid I couldn't. I have two brothers and two sisters at home younger than I am. It wouldn't be right for me to ask my father to send money out of what he makes."

"But surely you could get out and land something a little more lucrative than this all-night restaurant job, Wingate."

"No, sir. Twenty cents an hour is standard rate for working students, and I haven't found anything better. Nick says he has at least thirty men on the waiting list for this job I have."

"Well, there's this about it, Wingate. The University is here, supported by the taxpayers of this State, for the purpose of giving the young men and women of this State educational opportunities. The University is not here for the purpose of training young men to be waiters in all-night restaurants. And, so far as I can see, that's about all you are deriving from your University career. So it occurs to me that you should make a choice: either find some way to devote more attention to your college work or drop out of school altogether. We are very loath to encourage students who are *entirely* self-supporting. And yet, I will admit that I know any number of first-rate students who are entirely self-supporting. There's Aubrey Carson, for example. Quarterback on the football team, delegate to the Olympics, president of the Student Senate, and he's a straight A student. Aubrey Carson was telling me only last week that he hasn't had any financial assistance from home since he enrolled as a freshman. Aubrey is a fine example of the working student."

"Yes, sir; but look at the job Carson has. He works for a big tobacco company, and all he has to do is hand out Treasure Trove cigarettes to other students. The tobacco company pays him a good salary for passing out samples of their cigarettes."

"Why, Wingate, you surely must be mistaken about that. I don't believe Aubrey Carson smokes. In fact, I know he doesn't smoke. He's one of the finest all-round athletes in this country."

"No, sir; I don't say he smokes either. But that's the straight stuff about his job with the cigarette company. They figure it's a good advertisement to have a popular guy like Aubrey Carson passing out Treasure Troves. Sort of an endorsement."

"All the same, Wingate, it doesn't reflect a very good attitude on your part, criticizing the way one of your fellow students earns his college expenses."

"Oh, I didn't mean to criticize him, sir. I was only saying—"

"Yes, yes, I know; but all this is beside the point. We're here to discuss the state of your grades, Wingate. The fact is, you are on probation right now. As you must know, any student who is passing in less than half his work is automatically suspended from the University and must return to his home. Now one F more and out you'll go, Wingate. That's just being frank with you."

"I'd hate to have to go back home like that, sir."

"Well, you'd have to. If you flunk out, the University authorities are obliged to see that you return to your home immediately."

"I'd hate that, sir. I'd hate to go back home and have to live off my family, and that's probably what I'd have to do. I had a letter from Mother yesterday, and she says that nearly all the boys who graduated from high school with me are still there, loafing on the streets and living off their old folks. I don't like that idea. Mother's proud of me because I'm working my way through college. You know there are not many jobs to be had nowadays, sir, and I'd hate to have to go back home and loaf."

"It *is* a problem, I'll confess, Wingate. But what's the point in your coming to the University and working all night in a café and then flunking your class work? Moreover, your freshman adviser reports that you make a practice of sleeping in class. Is that true?"

"Well, yes, sir. I suppose I do drop off sometimes."

"Pretty impossible situation, isn't it, Wingate? Well, I've given you the best advice I can. Unless you can alter your circumstances I suggest that you withdraw from the University at once. We have six thousand other students here who need our attention, and the University has to be impartial and impersonal in dealing with these problems. Unless you can find some means to avoid flunking out I suggest withdrawing before-hand."

"Withdrawal would be a disgrace to me, sir. If I withdrew and went back home now, everyone at home would say that I had been expelled. You know how small towns are."

"Ah, now, Wingate, when you begin dealing with small-town gossip, I fear you're really getting outside my province. But I should think you'd prefer honorable withdrawal to flunking out."

"I believe I'll try to stick it through, sir. I'll try to remove the conditional grades, and maybe I can luck through on my finals."

"I hope you can, Wingate. As long as you feel that way about it, good luck to you." The Dean of Men stood up. Charlie stood up too. The Dean put out his hand and showed his teeth in a jovial smile and bore down hard on Charlie's knuckles. "I'm counting on you strong, old man," he said, encircling Charlie's shoulders with his left arm. "I know you have the stuff and that you'll come through with flying colors one of these days."

"Thank you, sir," Charlie said, grinning tearfully while the Dean gave his shoulder little pats. He edged toward the door as soon as the Dean released him, but when he reached it he hesitated and pulled the postal card out of his pocket. "Oh, pardon me, sir, but there's something I forgot to ask you. I got this in the mail today. I've been a little bothered about what to do about it."

The Dean of Men took the mimeographed card and read it quickly. "Why, I should say that you ought to go see what they want, Wingate. You shouldn't ignore things of this sort, you know. It's all a part of the normal activities of college life. No reason for antagonizing your fellow-students by ignoring a request of this kind."

"All right, sir; I'll go see them."

"Why, to be sure, go see them! Always keep in mind that the University is a social as well as an educational institution, Wingate."

4

Room 204, Student Union Building, was a newly finished
rather barren office that smelled dankly of lime in the fresh
plaster. It was fitted with a metal desk painted to imitate
painted walnut, a large brass spittoon, a square metal waste-
paper basket, a green metal filing cabinet, a large bank calen-
dar, a huge pasteboard shipping case, and Aubrey H. Carson
who had the freshman cap concession.

Charlie Wingate hesitantly opened the door and saw Aubrey
H. Carson tilted back in a chair, his feet on the metal walnut
desk, reading a copy of *Ballyhoo*.

"Co-ome in! Co-ome in!" Aubrey Carson called loudly without putting down his magazine. "All right, old timer. What's
on your mind?"

Charlie held out the mimeographed card. Carson held his
magazine a moment longer before accepting the card. He
shoved his hat down over one eye, turning the card, looking
first at the back, then at the name on the front. "Um-m-m," he
grunted. He reached over to a drawer in the filing cabinet without taking his feet down and flipped through the cards. He
looked at the name on the postal card again, pulled a card out
of the file, and drew his thick lips up into a rosette. He looked
at the file card in silence.

"Wingate," he said at last in a severe tone, "you have been
dilatory. Indeed, Wingate, I might even go so far as to say you
have been remiss. At the beginning of this semester you applied
for and received a refund on your student ticket fee. That signi-
fies that you have not attended a single football game this season, and that you have no intention of honoring any of the
University's athletic spectacles with your presence this season.
Also, the record discloses that you did not register at the
Y.M.C.A. freshman mixer. Neither did you respond to polite
solicitation for a trifling monetary pledge to the Memorial Sta-
dium Fund. And, most heinous offense of all, Wingate, we find
that you have yet to pay in one dollar for your freshman cap
prescribed by your seniors and purveyed to you on a non-profit
basis by the Student Committee on Freshman Activities. And

et, Wingate, I find you duly enrolled and attending classes in his here now University. Wingate, what possible excuse do you aave for such gross neglect of University tradition? Speak up!"

Charlie said meekly, "Well, I work nights and it's hard for ne to get here in the daytime, and I can't afford to buy a cap."

"What's this!" Carson exclaimed, jerking his legs down from he desk top and banging the desk with two flat hands. "Why, ƴoy, this is treason! You mean you can't afford *not* to buy a ƴreshman cap."

"No, I just came to tell you that a dollar has to go a long way with me and that I need every cent I earn to stay in school. So I wish you'd please excuse me from buying a freshman cap."

Carson's lean, florid face suddenly became rigid and he stuck ais jaw out with his lower teeth showing and, in spite of his narcelled taffy pompadour and his creased tailored suit, he again looked very much as he did in all the sporting section ᴘhotographs. "See here, Wingate," he said, hard-lipped, "you're still a freshman at this University. You'll have to wait another year before you can start saying what you will do and won't do, see? Now we've been patient with you. You've been in school here three months without putting on a freshman cap. Ɔo you realize that over eighty-five per cent of the freshman ᴄlass came in here and bought their caps before the first week of school ended? Now who do you think *you* are, Wingate—Mr. Ɔod? You're going to get you a cap, and you're going to wear ᴛ. See? No ifs, ands, or buts about it. And if you don't leave his office with a green cap on your head then I don't mind elling you that we've got ways of getting one on you before another day passes."

"Well, if I buy one it's going to put me in a bad hole. All the money I've got is what I saved out to pay my room rent this week."

"Listen, fella, if we let horsefeathers like that go here, half he freshman class wouldn't be wearing freshman caps right now. Now I've said all I'm going to to you. Do you want your green cap now or will you wait till later? That's all I want to know. I don't aim to give you any high-pressure sales talk on something that's already been decided for you. Take it or leave it."

Carson reached over into the large pasteboard box, groped far down in it, and brought forth a small green monkey cap. He tossed it on the desk. Charlie Wingate stuck his forefinger in his watch pocket and pulled out a small pad of three carefully folded dollar bills. He unfolded them and laid one on the desk and picked up the cap. Carson put the dollar in his pocket and stood up.

Charlie stood holding his cap. He scuffed the cement floor with his shoe toe and began doggedly, "The only thing is—"

"Aw, that's O.K., Wingate, old man," Carson said suavely. "No hard feelings whatsoever." He held out a freshly opened pack of cigarettes. "Here, have a Treasure Trove on me before you go."

5

That night all the stools along the counter at The Wigwam were filled when Charlie Wingate came in, still dusty from the drill field. He got himself a setup back of the counter and went into the kitchen. He moved about the steam-table, dishing up his dinner. He dragged a stool over to a zinc-covered kitchen table and sat down to eat. The kitchen was warm and steamy and the air was thick with the odors of sour chili grease and yellow soap melting in hot dishwater. Charlie's fork slipped through his fingers, and he began nodding over his plate.

Fat Kruger, the night dishwasher and short-order cook, yelled, "Hey, there, wake up and pay for your bed!" Charlie jerked his head up and looked at the ponderous, good-humored cook with half-lidded eyes. "Why'n't you try sleeping in bed once in a w'ile, Charlie?" Fat said in a friendly tone. "You're going to kill yourself if you don't watch out, trying to go without sleep."

"Don't worry, Fat. I can take it," Charlie said.

Almost two hours had to pass before it would be the hour for him to come on, but not time enough for him to walk back to his room and catch a nap, so he took the book on which he had to make an outside reading report in Economics 150 and went up to the last booth to study until nine o'clock. He fell asleep and he did not wake up until Red Hibbert, going off, shook him and told him that it was almost time for him to come on. He closed his book and went back to the washroom. The acrid stench of the mothballs that Nick used to deodorize the latrine cleared his head. He took down his apron and tied it on over his army breeches. Then he slipped into a white coat.

The usual black-coffee addicts came dribbling in. When the telephone rang, Charlie answered it, jotting down short orders to go. The delivery boy came in and went out and banged off on his motorcycle with paper bags full of "red hots" and nickel hamburgers and coffee in paper cylinders. The Wigwam's white tile shone under the inverted alabaster urns. There was a pale pink reflection in the plate-glass window as the Neon sign outside spelled and re-spelled "Wigwam Eats. Open All Night." A party of drunken Betas came in at ten-thirty and seated themselves noisily in the last booth. They tossed Charlie's economics book out into the aisle with a whoop, and he came and picked it up and took their orders in silence while they kidded him about his flap ears and the grease on his white coat. At eleven o'clock the last whistle at the University power house blew for the closing hour, and a couple of lingering "dates" scurried out. Finally the drunks left, after one had been sick in a corner of the booth. The delivery boy came coasting up at midnight and checked in and roared away again on his motorcycle. The long small hours began inching past.

At one o'clock Charlie finished cleaning up the drunk's mess and he had cleared off the last of the tables. The Wigwam was empty, so he opened the book he must read for Ec 150. He had read a few lines when a bunch of girls from the Theta house down the street came charging in, giggling and talking in gasps and screams, their fur coats clutched over their sleeping pajamas. It was long after the closing hour, and they told Charlie to keep an eye out for the University night watchman. They took up the two back booths and they consulted The Wigwam's printed menu card without failing to read aloud the lines "Nick (Pericles) Pappas," "We Employ Student Help Exclusively," and "Please Do Not Tip. A Smile Is Our Reward" with the customary shrieks. Nearly all ordered filet mignon and French fries, which were not on the menu, but two or three ordered pecan waffles and coffee, which were. When he had served their orders Charlie went back to his book again, but the low buzz of their talk and their sudden spurts of laughter disturbed him and he could not read. At a quarter of two they began peering round corners of their booths. They asked Charlie in stage-whispers if the coast were clear.

Charlie went to the door and looked out on the street and beckoned widely with his arm. They trooped out with their fur coats pulled tight, their fur-trimmed silken mules slapping their bare heels. Charlie went on back to clear away their dishes. They had left about thirty cents as a tip, all in cents and nick-els. The coins were carefully imbedded in the cold steak grease and gluey syrup and putty-colored cigarette leavings on their plates. Charlie began stacking the plates without touching the money. He carried the dirty dishes back and set them through the opening in the kitchen wall. Fat Kruger came to the open-ing and Charlie went back to his book.

Fat called, "Hey, Charlie, you leavin' this tip again?"

"You're damn right, I'm leaving it!" Charlie said. "I can get along without their tips. They leave it that way every time. I guess they think I'll grabble on their filthy plates to get a lousy thirty cents. It takes a woman to think up something like that."

"Charlie, you're too proud. I don't see where you can afford to be so proud. The way I figure it, thirty cents is thirty cents."

"Hell, I'm not proud, Fat. I just try to keep my self-respect. When those sorority sows come in and plant their tips in the dirt and grease of their plates, damn' if I'll lower myself to grub it out."

He sat down on a counter stool with the economics book before him, trying to fix his mind on it. He read a page. The print became thin blurred parallels of black on the page. His eyelids kept drooping shut and he propped the muscles with his palms at his temples, trying to keep his eyes open. His head jerked forward and he caught it and began reading again. Soon his face lowered slowly through his hands and came to rest on the open book.

Fat Kruger came through the kitchen swinging door and tiptoed up front. Fat stood grinning, watching Charlie sleep. Cramped over with his head on the counter, Charlie snored softly. Fat gave his head a gentle shove, and Charlie started up to catch his balance.

"For God sakes, guy, you're *dead*!" Fat howled. "Don't you never get no sleep except like that?"

"What time is it?" Charlie said, yawning and arching his back.

"Half-past two."

"Jees, is that all?"

"Charlie, go back there and lay down on the kitchen table. I'll watch the front for you. Nobody'll be coming in for a while."

As he was talking old Uncle Jim Hudson ambled in, a bundle of sweaters, overcoats, and grizzled dewlaps, his black timeclock slung over one shoulder by a leather lanyard. Uncle Jim laid his long, nickeled flashlight carefully on the counter and eased himself onto a stool. He ordered a cup of black coffee and in a lecherous wheeze began telling dirty stories selected from his twenty years' experience as a campus night-watchman. Fat Kruger nickered loudly after each telling, and Charlie jerked his eyes open and smiled sleepily. It was three-thirty when Uncle Jim left. Charlie opened his book again.

"Charlie, I wouldn't put my eyes out over that damn' book if I was you, when you're dyin' for sleep," Fat said.

"I've got to get it read, Fat. It's my outside reading in Economics and the whole semester grade depends on it. It's the hardest book to keep your mind on you ever saw. I've been reading on it for over a month and I'm only half through, and he's going to call for these reports any day now. If I flunk Ec I flunk out of school."

"Why mess with reading it? I know a guy over at the Masonic Dorm who'll read it and write your report for two bucks. He writes all my English themes for me, and I'm making a straight A in English. He only charges fifty cents for short themes and two bucks for term papers. You ought to try him."

"Hell, Fat, you get five dollars a week from home. Where am I going to get two dollars for hiring a guy to read this book?"

"Charlie, I just can't figure you out. You never do get any real sleep. You sure must want a college education bad. It don't look to me like you would figure it's worth it."

"Oh, it's worth it! It's a big satisfaction to my folks to have me in college. And where can a man without a college degree get nowadays? But I'll tell you the truth, I didn't know it was going to be like this when I came down here last fall. I used to read *College Humor* in high school, and when fellows came home from University for the holidays, all dressed up in snappy clothes, talking about dates and football and dances, and using college slang—well, I had a notion I'd be like that when I got down here. The University publicity department sent me a little booklet showing how it was easy to work your way through college. So here I am. I haven't had a date or been to a dance or seen a football game since I enrolled. And there are plenty of others just like me. I guess I'm getting a college education, all right—but the only collegiate thing I've been able to do is go to sleep in class."

"How you get by with sleeping in class, Charlie?"

"I wear those colored spectacles and prop myself, and the profs can't see I've got my eyes closed."

Fat waggled his heavy face mournfully. "Boy, it sure is tough when a man don't get his sleep."

"Yeah, it is," Charlie said, looking down at his book again. "I'll get a break pretty soon, though. I'd rather chop off a hand than to flunk out of University before I'd even finished one semester."

6

The tardiest of the hundred students enrolled in Dr. Sylvester C. O. Kenshaw's Economics 150 straggled into the lecture room and made their ways to alphabetically-assigned chairs with much scuffling and trampling of toes and mumbled apologies. Ec 150, renowned as a pipe course, was always crowded. Doctor Kenshaw was the celebrated author of seven textbooks on economics, five of which his students were required to buy each semester. Doctor Kenshaw's national reputation as an economist permitted him to be erratic about meeting his classes, but fame had never dimmed his fondness for student flattery. The only students who ever flunked Ec 150 were those who gave affront to Doctor Kenshaw by neglecting to buy his textbooks or by not laughing at his wit or by being outrageously inattentive to his lectures.

Doctor Kenshaw was late that morning. Charlie Wingate sat in his chair on the back row in an agony of waiting. He had on his amber glasses and he could fall asleep as soon as Doctor Kenshaw opened his lecture. But he had to stay awake until then. There was a slow ache in the small of his back. The rest of his body was numb. He had not taken off his army shoes for twenty hours, and his feet were moist and swollen. Every time he shifted position his arms and legs were bathed in prickling fire. He kept his eyes open behind the amber lenses, watching the clock. Small noises of the classroom came to him as a low, far-off humming.

When the clock on the front wall showed nine after eleven the seated class began stirring as if it were mounted on some eccentric amusement-park device. Excited whispers eddied out on the warm air of the steam-heated lecture room. "He's giving us another cut! He's not meeting this class today!" "He's got one more minute to make it!" "Naw; six more! You have to wait fifteen minutes on department heads."

There was a seething argument on this point, but when the clock showed fourteen minutes after eleven a bold leader sprang up and said, "Come on, everybody!" All but five or six especially conscientious students rose and milled after him toward the door. Charlie Wingate followed, thoroughly awakened by the chance of getting to bed so soon. The leader yanked the door open and Doctor Kenshaw stumbled in, all out of breath, his eyeglasses steamed, his pointed gray beard quivering, a vain little man in a greenish-black overcoat.

"Go back to your seats!" Doctor Kenshaw commanded

sternly as soon as he could get his breath. He marched over to his lecture table and plunked down his leather briefcase. He took off his overcoat and began wiping the steam from his eyeglasses while the students hurried back to their chairs. "It does seem to me," he said, his voice quavering with anger, "that it would be no more than courteous for this class to await my arrival on those rare occasions when I am delayed. Day after day you come lagging into my classes, and I have always been extremely lenient in giving credit for attendance, no matter how tardy your arrival. Certainly it is no more than my privilege to ask that you wait for me occasionally."

A few students exchanged meaningful glances. They meant, "Now we're in for it. The old boy has on one of his famous mads."

"Today, I believe I shall forego delivering my prepared lecture," Doctor Kenshaw went on in a more even voice, but with elaborate sarcasm, "and let *you* do the talking. Perhaps it would be meet to hear a few outside reading reports this morning. All of you doubtless are aware that these reports were due last week, although I had not expected to call for them at once. I trust that I have impressed you sufficiently with the importance of these reports. They represent to me the final result of your semester's work in this course. The grades you receive on these reports will be your grades for the semester. Let us begin forthwith. When your name is called, you will rise and read your report to the class." He opened his roll book.

"Mr. Abbott!" he called. Mr. Abbott stammered an excuse. Doctor Kenshaw passed coldly on to Miss Adams, making no comment. All through the A's it was the same. But with the B's an ashen, spectacled Miss Ballentyne stood up and began reading in a droning voice her report on *The Economic Consequences of the Peace.* Obviously Doctor Kenshaw was not listening to her. His hard little eyes under craggy brows were moving up one row and down the other, eager for a victim. On the back row, Charlie Wingate's propped legs had given way and he had slipped far down into his seat, fast asleep. When Doctor Kenshaw's preying eyes reached Charlie they stopped moving. Someone tittered nervously and then was silent as

Doctor Kenshaw jerked his head round in the direction of the noise. Miss Ballentyne droned on.

When she had finished, Doctor Kenshaw said dryly, "Very good, Miss Ballentyne, very good, indeed. Er—ah—would someone be kind enough to arouse the recumbent young gentleman in the last row?"

There was a murmur of laughter while everyone turned to look at Milton Weismann nudging Charlie Wingate. Doctor Kenshaw was running down the list of names in his small record book. Milton Weismann gave Charlie another stiff poke in the ribs, and Charlie sprang up quickly. Everyone laughed loudly at that.

"Mr.—ah—*Wingate,* isn't it? Mr. Wingate, your report."

"Pardon me, sir?"

"Mr. Wingate, what was the title of the book assigned to you for report in this class?"

"Theory of the Leisure Class by Veblen, sir."

"Ah, then, that's the explanation. So you were assiduously engaged in evolving your own theory of the leisure class. Is that right, Mr. Wingate? You have evidently concluded that Economics 150 is the leisure class."

The class rocked with laughter. Doctor Kenshaw, pleased with his pun and flattered by the response to it, found it hard to keep his face straight. Suddenly he was back in good humor. "Mr. Wingate's theory is quite apparently one to which the majority of this class subscribes. Now I try to be lenient with students in this class. Surely no one could describe me as a hard taskmaster. But I resent your implication that I have been too easy-going. Now these reading reports were assigned to you last September, and you have had ample time to prepare them. I'll not call for any more of them today, but at the next session of this class I expect every one of these papers in. As for you, Mr. Wingate, if you'll see me directly after class, I'll be glad to hear any explanation or apology that you may wish to make. I want most of all to be fair. I have always given every student the benefit of the doubt until a student deliberately flouts me with his indifference. But I am capable of being quite ruthless, I assure you."

"Thank you, sir," Charlie mumbled. He suffered a slow torture, trying to keep awake until the class bell rang. He rolled his hot, red-veined eyes up with drunken precision to see the clock. Fifteen minutes had to pass before the bell would ring.

When the bell rang the class arose quickly and began clumping out. Several co-eds and men, politickers and apple-polishers wangling for A's, crowded about the lecture table. Doctor Kenshaw always remained behind after each class to accept their homage. But today he looked up over the heads of the eager group. He silenced their inane questions and flagrant compliments by placing his right forefinger against his thin, unsmiling lips. "Sh-h-h!" he said. The apple-polishers turned their heads in the direction of his gaze and then, giggling softly, tiptoed away. When the last had gone out, Doctor Kenshaw unscrewed his fountain pen and opened his roll book. He ran his finger down the list until he came to "Wingate, C." and in the space opposite under "Smstr Grd" he marked a precise little F.

A whiffling snore escaped Charlie Wingate in the back of the room. Doctor Kenshaw looked back across the varnished chair rows with a frown of annoyance. He took his overcoat from its hanger, slipped into it, and strapped up his briefcase. He jammed on his hat and strode out of the lecture room, slamming the door. The noise made a hollow echo in the empty room, but it did not disturb Charlie Wingate. He slept on behind his amber glasses.

All Problems Are Simple

by Allan Seager

The door of the closet was stuck. It was a sliding panel and it stuck because it was new. The newness of the whole place struck Dr. Holloway's nostrils as he tugged at the handle, an acrid smell of fresh paint and, curiously, mothballs. The door opened a foot. Dr. Holloway shoved his hat through the opening and laid it on the shelf of the closet. There were even three naked black wire hangers in the closet, and, turning, he saw a single fresh daffodil in a glass tube on his desk. Somebody had thought of everything. In the old building his office had been a little slot beneath a staircase with a desk, two chairs, no windows, and an electric bulb dangling from a cord over his head. Painted on the frosted glass of the door that he always had to keep open if he wanted any air were the words *Student Counselor, A. E. Holloway.* On the door of his new office, there was only a gray aluminum number and a student had to look him up on the building directory in the lobby as if he were an executive of a large corporation. The University Counseling Service was at last amounting to something.

Dr. Holloway sat down at his desk, a small *moderne* article in the shape of a kidney. He had an appointment at eleven and the long hand of the electric clock covered the stud that indicated five minutes past. All students were late; it was an axiom. He reached into a drawer and took out the student's dossier. A sophomore, Miss Ottilie Schroeder. Inside were several folders containing all the relevant information: the application from high school with grades and reasons for applying, Psychological Tests A, B, and C given on entrance as a freshman, Aptitude Test, Rorschach Test, a Physical Examination report, data from Health Service showing illnesses, psychic and physical, incurred during residence as a student, and, of course, the semester grade sheets. There was also a folder intended for notes taken by the Counselor during previous consultations but it was blank.

While Dr. Holloway officially and publicly had great respect for the University Agencies who had got up this mass of forms and the high, tense pitch of organization they showed, he knew that in practice he did not need them. As he thumbed through the papers all he was looking for was the photograph and the note from the Assistant Dean. The rest of the stuff was not important.

He found the picture, a blond girl with freshly curled bobbed hair, smiling in a frantic amiability. She had buck teeth and blotches of acne barely hidden by rouge and powder. The Assistant Dean's note said that she was flunking German 31 according to the mid-semester grade reports. This was all the information Dr. Holloway needed, this and her home town. It made students feel good if he could mention their home towns. He looked up Miss Schroeder's. It was Manchester. He tossed the dossier back into the drawer, looked at the clock, and lit a cigarette.

The mothball smell, he decided, came from the new window drapes. They were the color of plug tobacco. The carpeting was beige and the chairs were upholstered in turquoise blue. The chairs had tapering legs and the laminated framework of the back and seat looked like the jawbone of an ass. On the wall hung a reproduction of a John Marin watercolor but Dr. Holloway thought it was only a lot of smudges. Still, the office was done up very smartly. If only counseling weren't such a bore.

Behind him the door opened a little, then closed. It was the student he was waiting for, Miss Schroeder. She was wretched and afraid and she had not yet been able to find courage to knock and come in.

Holloway was by the window irritably picking at a spot of paint left on the glass. Counseling was a bore, a part-time bore; teaching was a supreme bore; and certainly the research papers on Thomas Traherne and Sir Thomas Browne he whacked out in his carrell at the library were a bore. He was a seventeenth-century man and whenever he thought of Traherne and Browne, he felt warm and clever because he could remember that night in his senior year, fourteen years before, banging on a bar in Scollay Square when he had said, "I'm going out for the two-mile run. Nobody goes out for that." It was true then; the literature of the seventeenth century had no special popularity with scholars at the time. But he, Art, later, of course, Arthur Holloway, had prowled through them early, a mess of dusty quartos. He had got a head start in the two-mile and now he had only to wait for a couple of the old guys to die off and he would be head man in the field. But it was still a bore. He hated to read.

Where he shone was at faculty meetings, club luncheons, and, above all, at the great conventions of his caste, the annual meetings of the learned societies. Thanks to a memory course he had taken, he never forgot a name. He was civil to all, and, beneath a disguise of manly camaraderie, obsequious to all who could do him any good. For, hidden under the ennui of his daily round, Art Holloway entertained a vision. He wanted to be a Dean. He was a little like a businessman who wants to be a millionaire—he did not know exactly what he would do when he became one but it was his deepest ambition, and he had an oblique, unacknowledged belief that a Deanship would offset his wife's money. You could take a few drops of iodine every day in a glass of water, he had heard, and in the vision he saw himself walking across the campus, his hair and mustache still its pristine brown (from the iodine), and people would say, "Good morning, Dean," and they would think how young and vigorous he looked for a man so high up. Also, when his wife shooed him upstairs and into his tail coat on nights when Milstein or Horowitz was playing in town, he would be able to say to her coarsely, vigorously, "The hell with that. I'm going to bed." He had never liked music.

At last there was a knock. He turned around, shouting, "Come in, Miss Schroeder!" The door opened and she came in, glancing miserably up at him once, then back at the floor. "Sit down. It's swell of you to come in so promptly." She missed the irony completely and sat down on the blue chair with her feet close together, her head bowed, picking at a fingernail. The blond hair hung in stringy unwound spirals. She wore a sweater and skirt, both black and covered with wisps of white fuzz. She certainly had a rough case of acne. There was no sorority pin on her bosom, he noticed.

"Well, how do you like our new offices, Miss Schroeder? The old building was never like this, eh?" he said loudly.

She looked up smiling with her lip pulled down over her buck teeth and shook her head.

"How are things going? You're looking well, better than the last time I saw you," he said, leaning back in his chair with his hands clasped behind his head (Informality of Pose). "How are things at home in Manchester?" (Note of Personal Solicitude.)

"All right," she said without looking up.

"Your work seems to be quite satisfactory. Three C's on the mid-semester exams. There's only German 31. What happened there?"

She shook her head again, gulping and swallowing.

"Is everything all right? Health good? You like your room-mate? Feel perfectly free to tell me everything." She did not say a word but her fingers wreathed and wove themselves together constantly in her lap. "Perhaps you feel some resistance to the language because the Germans were our enemies. We must forget our enmity to them; the war is over. Germany is a beautiful country. I traveled there before the war. Nuremberg, Rothenburg, Munich. *München war damals eine schöne Stadt.*" Munich had been a beautiful city. He recalled eagerly all the *Ausschänker* where you could sit at a little table and buy the potato salad and the beer radishes and *Hofbräu, Löwenbräu, Tomasbräu, Augustinerbräu,* all those wonderful beers. "You mustn't scorn the language. The Germans have been a great people."

"I know," she said. "My people were German. My grandfather was born in Essen."

"Well, then. It's part of your inheritance. How does it come you are flunking it?"

She threw up her head and spoke very rapidly in a high,

choking voice, " '*ch kann nicht studieren. 'ch habe keine Freunde. 'ch stehe ganz allein, immer ganz allein.*"

This was a little too fast for Dr. Holloway's German. He stood up. "I'm sorry. You're hysterical. I didn't catch . . ."

The angry defiance was gone. She was sniffling and sobbing. "I can't study. I can't do any work. I haven't any friends. I haven't had a date since I came to college."

Dr. Holloway looked down at the top of her head as it bobbed up and down with her sobs, the limp yellowish hair swaying a little. It was sex again, the old story. About every third babe had some gripe about her sex life.

"I'll tell you what you do," he said in a warm friendly voice. "You start going to church. There are a lot of social activities around a church. You'll meet somebody there as sure as the world. You mustn't be shy. You have to go halfway in your social life, you know." With that face she'll have to go seven-eighths, he thought. He waited a moment until she had finished blowing her nose. "Will you do that, Miss Schroeder?"

She looked at him and nodded.

"And we'll get that German up by the end of the term, won't we? As well as you seem to know it, it shouldn't be . . ."

"May I go now, Dr. Holloway?"

"Why, that's about all I had to say. You know how it is—a flunk's a flunk . . ." She interrupted him by starting for the door. "Glad you came in, Miss Schroeder. Stop in any time." The door closed after her.

It was just eleven-thirty by the electric clock. He had polished that one off in fifteen minutes. There was one more to go before lunch. He took out a second dossier labeled "Raymond Burch." Burch, he discovered, was a junior and a veteran, a former infantry sergeant, twenty-five years old. Holloway felt a tingle of annoyance. Veterans did not handle easily. Other students you had to treat like bright children but veterans somehow you had to treat as men and it bothered him. He glanced through the dossier. Burch, it seemed, was an orphan with no place of residence but the university; his service was spent in the ETO; and the Assistant Dean's note said that Burch was flunking every course because he seldom visited his classes. The

Assistant Dean thought Burch was drinking heavily. Burch's photograph showed a thin coffin-shaped face with light eyes and another glance at the service record told him that Burch had a Purple Heart and a Silver Star.

Holloway had somehow expected that Burch's wound scars would be on his legs or torso, some place that would be decently covered. Instead there was a half-inch of shiny pink wrist showing below the left sleeve of Burch's coat; there was no hand. Holloway could not take his eyes off it for a moment.

"Shot off in the Battle of the Huertgen Forest, sir," Burch said, holding up the stump impassively. "Shrapnel."

"You—you're going to have a prosthetic device, aren't you?" The photograph had been a good likeness. Burch's eyes were red as if he had perhaps been crying. Otherwise he was the same as his picture.

"One of these fake hands with a glove on it? No, sir."

"Sit down, Mr. Burch. Sit down," Holloway said nervously, standing up himself (Psychological Dominance of Height). Burch sat down and Holloway walked up and down with the Assistant Dean's note in his hand.

"Mr. Burch . . ." he began.

"Yes, sir?" Burch interposed. When the veterans had first returned from the war, Holloway had been flattered to be addressed like an officer but he had learned to detect the bogus civility of these emphasized "sirs."

"The Dean's Office say you are flunking every subject. They say you don't come to class."

"No, sir."

"Why? How is that?"

"Drink, sir."

This stopped Holloway but he did not like to seem at a loss. He said, "Uh—you mean—"

"Just whisky, sir."

An intimation that Burch was playing him for and like a fish struck Holloway. He said sharply, "Well, what are you going to do about it? You keep on this way and you'll be out of school in June. What are you going to do?"

"Stop drinking. Study hard. Go to class every day. Sir." Burch rattled this off with insulting promptness.

Holloway stopped walking and looked at Burch. Burch looked back. They both knew that, theoretically, since Burch had given the right answer, the interview should end but Holloway could not let him go yet. He glanced at the clock.

"Cigarette, Mr. Burch?" Holloway held out a pack.

"Thank you, sir."

Holloway snapped open his lighter. "I don't think you believe it but we're here to try and help you. You're spending your time and the government's money. It seems to me that you ought not to waste either one by turning into a rummy. What's the matter? What's on your mind?"

Burch had been sitting with his hand on his knee looking straight ahead, waiting, it seemed, with patience. Now he looked up at Holloway with his light eyes, paused a moment thoughtfully, made a wrong judgment, and said, "Suppose I tell you? What then?"

"If it's combat fatigue, we . . ."

"It's not combat fatigue," Burch said with a soft scorn.

"Whatever it is, if something's riding you, we've got some good men over at Health Service, doctors who . . ."

"Psychiatrists."

"Yes. Why? Don't you like psychiatrists? They can discover . . ."

"I *know* what's the matter with me."

"Do you want to talk about it? I don't want to pry into your personal . . ." (Ostensible Kindness).

"Sure. I'll talk about it." For the next few minutes Burch sat with his hand on his knee, the ash growing longer on his cigarette, staring straight ahead of him, talking. "I was stationed in Munich after the war. I knew a girl. She was a Polish DP. She had been in the camp at Dachau. She was one beautiful dame and the only scars she had were on her back where they didn't show in the daytime. She said there was a girl in the camp with her and this girl was pregnant. They waited until her time came and the pains had started and then they tied her feet together and hung her head down from the limb of a tree. My girl saw this from a window." There was a pause. The ash fell off Burch's cigarette onto the beige carpet. Burch looked up at Holloway, took a heavy breath, and said, "That's what's the matter with me." He looked back into whatever distances lay before him and said, "I keep thinking about it."

"I'm sure your sympathy for that poor girl does you every credit but . . ."

"Oh, I don't think about her much anymore. It's the guys that did it I think about."

Holloway, a Doctor of Philosophy, was honestly puzzled. "How? In what way?"

Burch said patiently, "Why, I'm a man. They're men. I figure a man has more in common with any other man than he has differences."

"Yes. Certainly."

"But what I want to know is, have I got *that* in common? I went through the camp at Dachau. I saw the limb of that tree. I used to drive a big semi for Interstate Transport before the war. Now I'm a college boy and that's why. Maybe I find out here, huh?"

"This is a philosophical question, Burch. You can't answer it all of a sudden like this. I'll tell you what you do. Why don't you duck over to Health Service and have a talk with them. And try to stay off the sauce until sundown every day at least, will you?"

Burch sat perfectly still, saying nothing.

Across the street from the Hofbräuhaus in Munich, Holloway remembered, there had been a little open-air stage for street vaudeville. It was called the Dachauerl Platzl and the men had worn *Lederhosen* and little green hats with shaving brushes, happy fat men, smiling plump women, dancing and singing, and right across the street for only eighteen pfennigs a liter of that wonderful beer. In a spasm of exasperation, Holloway said, "But you have to accept the fact that people are cruel."

Burch stood up. "Jesus, I thought maybe you guys knew something." He spun violently around on one heel and walked out. The door was slowed down by an automatic device or it would have slammed.

Dr. Holloway glanced at the clock as he swept Burch's papers into the drawer of his desk. He had wound it all up by five minutes to twelve. He went to the closet, jerked the door open, and took his hat. In the pleasant sunshine he walked leisurely toward the Faculty Club. By arriving promptly at twelve he might just get in a word or two with the Vice-President of the university, who usually lunched there. He might even suggest that they lunch together. It would be noticed.

Fear of Math

by Peter Cameron

In order to enter the MBA program at Columbia in the fall, I had to take calculus in the summer. I was offered two options: an eight-week, slow-paced course or a three-week intensive. Although the last math course I took was trigonometry my junior year in high school, I chose the three-week course, on the principle that things you are scared of are things you shouldn't dwell on too long. I'd finish calculus in July, spend August at the beach, and start school with a tan.

The first Monday of class, the air-conditioning was broken. I had made the mistake of wearing a denim dress, and as the morning progressed, I felt the back of it getting wetter and wetter. The teacher must have known about the air-conditioning because he was wearing khaki shorts and a white T-shirt. He didn't look at all like a teacher—he looked more like a very old Boy Scout or a very young forest ranger. No one knew he was the teacher until he started teaching, which he did hesitantly, almost apologetically. I could tell right away he had never taught before.

The class met from nine to twelve and then from twelve-thirty to three-thirty. By noon the blackboard was so dusty from erased equations the teacher had to wash it with a sponge and a bucket of water. I went outside and sat on the front steps of the building and ate my tabbouleh-and-pita-bread sandwich. I read over my notes, which already filled about half of the new notebook I'd bought in Lamston's that morning. I couldn't make any sense of them. I'd have to write neater.

The air conditioner in the hall worked, so I went back up and stood outside the classroom door and drank from a water fountain. I had to lean way down into the curved white basin to reach the weak spurt of water.

When I stood back up the forest ranger was standing beside me holding his bucket of chalky water.

"Will you do me a favor?" he asked.

"What?" I said.

"Will you dump this in the women's room? The men's is locked."

"Sure," I said.

Instead of handing me the bucket, he started walking down the hall. I followed him. Outside the women's room he gave me the bucket and opened the door. He held it open and watched me pour the water down the sink.

He took the bucket back, and we walked down the hall. "You were smart," I said, "to wear shorts."

He looked down at his shorts, as if he had forgotten he was wearing them. He opened the door of the hot classroom and we went in. We were the only ones there. I sat at the desk I had chosen in the morning—in the back row—and he began filling the blackboard with new, harder, equations.

I was subletting an apartment from a friend of mine, Alyssa. Actually, I wasn't subletting it: her parents owned it, and she had gone to Europe for the summer, so I was staying there, paying the bills, watering the ferns, and feeding the two long-haired, exotic, nasty cats.

It was a huge apartment. The more I saw other people's apartments the more I began to realize how extraordinary this one was: it was full of space. The living room was as big as most apartments, with its two leather couches facing one another across from the fireplace. There was a long hall with a thin Persian runner unraveling along the wooden floor, two bedrooms, an eat-in kitchen, and even a pantry full of glass hutches in which hung dozens of globular wineglasses, like a laboratory.

The evening after the first day of class, I was trying to make cucumber soup without a recipe or a blender when the phone rang. It was an old-fashioned black wall phone in the pantry, where it always seemed to ring louder on account of the glass.

"Hello," I said.

"Is Julie there?" a man asked.

"This is Julie," I said. I never say "This is she." Something about speaking that properly unnerves me.

"Julie? This is Stephen?"

"Stephen?" I repeated. I didn't know any Stephens in New York. I didn't know any men here, actually, except for Ethan, my older sister Debbie's creepy ex-husband, and a cute man named Gerry I met a few nights before in the greengrocer's. I'd helped him pick out a cantaloupe.

"From calculus," the man said.

"Oh," I said. "Which one are you?"

"The teacher," he said. "The one who stands in front."

I laughed, and so did he, then I stopped laughing because I suddenly thought he must be calling to tell me I'd have to drop the class. They must have some system where they weed the hopeless students out immediately. I saw my whole career—business school, New York, executive suites, tailored suits—going down the drain. And so quickly.

"What do you want?" I said rudely.

"I don't know," he said. "To see how I did. I've never taught calculus before."

"Really?" I said. "Never?"

"Well, not for six straight hours."

"Oh," I said.

"So how was I?"

"I've never taken calculus," I said. "Not even an hour. I'm the wrong person to ask."

"Did you understand everything?"

"No," I said.

"Oh. Maybe I should go slower." Then he paused, and said, "Do you want to go out for dinner sometime?"

"Dinner?" I said, as if this was a complicated theorem that needed some explaining.

"Well," he said. "Maybe just a drink."

"No," I said. "Dinner's fine. Dinner's good."

* * *

Stephen and I ate dinner the next night in the garden of a restaurant, under a dogwood tree. White blossoms fell into my soup and across the lavender tablecloth when the wind blew. We had met outside the restaurant, and for a minute I didn't recognize him. I had only seen Stephen in his Boy Scout shorts, and that was the only way I could picture him. He didn't look as cute in his green fatigue pants and pink oxford shirt. He could have been anyone.

"So," Stephen said, once our small talk had been run through and our soup delivered. "End my suspense. Why are you taking calculus?"

"I have to," I said. "I'm going to business school."

"I knew it," Stephen said. "Everyone's going to business school. My mother's going to business school."

"Did you teach her calculus?"

"No. I got my math genes from her. My father's mathematically illiterate. He's a painter."

"So am I," I said.

"What, a painter?"

"No," I said. "An illiterate."

"Oh," he said. "Well, you can still learn calculus. It just takes longer."

"Can I learn it by September?"

"Sure. If you get a tutor."

"A tutor?"

"Well, yeah. You're going to have to devote all your time to learning calculus. It's a new way of thinking for people like you. We're talking twelve-hour days, seven days a week."

"Why am I doing this?" I said. "It sounds horrible."

"I don't know," Stephen said. "Why are you doing this?"

I spooned my soup, pushing the blossoms aside.

"I don't know," I finally said. "I felt like my life was going nowhere, like it needed a big change. I've been living in Michigan," I said, as if that explained things.

"Where?"

"Ann Arbor. I went to school there."

"What did you study? I assume it wasn't math."

"French. I can hardly speak it anymore."

"What did you do with a French major?"

"Nothing. I was stenciling wicker furniture. I was making pretty good money, for Ann Arbor, at least, but I got sick of it. There was nowhere to go. So I figured I needed an MBA."

I didn't mention that my boyfriend, Tim, made the wicker furniture and that I had lived with him for five years and been engaged for one of them (the fourth). Most of going to business school had to do with breaking with Timmy.

The waiter came and took our soup away.

"I don't know," I said. "Do you think this is all a big mistake?"

"Fools can get MBA's," Stephen said.

"But they have math genes," I said.

"You have math genes," Stephen said. "They just have to be aroused."

I laughed.

"No, really," he said. "They're there. It's like Pygmalion. I could take you on. I'll transform you into a math whiz."

The leaves of the dogwood tree started shaking above us. I looked up and saw the sky glowing as if the sun had set all over, not in just one spot. I could feel the drops of rain above us, falling: heavy, sooty drops. I stood up and put my bag over my shoulder.

"What's the matter?" said Stephen. He thought I was leaving.

"It's going to rain," I said. "Look."

We were the first couple in the empty restaurant, and we got a table right inside the terrace doors. Watching the rain fall in the deserted garden, I felt wise and intuitive and in touch, if not with calculus, at least with the weather.

The next night—the third night of class—my official tutelage began. Stephen arrived at my door with a calculator and a bunch of freesias.

"This is some building," he said. "The elevator is about the size of my apartment."

"It's not mine," I said. "I'm subletting it."

"Oh," Stephen said. "And I thought I had found an heiress."
He handed me the flowers.

"Then you should meet Alyssa." I went into the kitchen but
Stephen walked into the living room, then down the hall, and
into the kitchen through the pantry. "Do you want something
to drink? All I really have is beer and cranberry juice."

"I'll just have water," Stephen said. He took an overturned
glass from the dish drain and filled it from the tap. I had been
nervous about this rendezvous, but there was something reassuring about watching Stephen's Adam's apple bob as he
gulped the water: he did it as if he'd been drinking water in my
kitchen for years.

Stephen was a better tutor than a teacher. He began by asking me what I didn't understand. I said just about everything,
so we started at the beginning and as he explained things I
asked questions, not letting him continue until I understood.
We moved from the dining-room table to the living-room
couch, and when I finally felt like I understood the first three
days of calculus—about one o'clock in the morning—I put my
calculus book on the floor and my feet on the couch. We were
sitting on opposite ends of the leather couch, facing each other,
our legs entangled between us. He was the kind of person, I
noticed, whose second toe is longer than his big toe. My toes
are perfectly proportional, and I set a standard by them.

"You have very long toes," I said. I touched them. "They're
kind of ugly."

Stephen yawned and peered down his body at his toes. "It
comes with the math genes," he said. "It's part of the package."

When I was growing up, my father was an engineer for
NASA, and my mother taught home economics. Now they're
both retired and are in business together. They've bought a
series of what my father calls "exploitable" houses—barns and
shacks and even abandoned churches—which they live in and
jointly convert into luxurious summer homes and then resell
for no small profit. My father does the outside and my mother
the inside, or, as they put it, my father builds the nest and my

mother feathers it. They are never in one house for more than a
year. My mother gets attached to some of them, but my father
insists on selling them. He thinks it's important for people their
age to keep moving, as if you'd petrify if you lived in the same
house for a few years.

I went up to see them—and the boathouse they were restor-
ing in upstate New York—the first weekend of calculus, although Stephen thought I should stay in New York and study.
I told him I'd study at the lake. I intended to: I packed my
huge calculus book in my knapsack, and even did a few problems on the plane, but by the time I switched to a six-seater in
Syracuse, calculus didn't seem to matter anymore. In the city,
with the straight streets and glass walls and constant noise,
calculus could be accommodated, but in the tiny plane, gliding
over trees and lakes all fading away beneath me into the growing darkness, calculus faded away, too. The numbers and ar-
rows and symbols seemed foolish, so I put my book away and
watched the lights come on in the houses below.

Saturday morning I helped my mother upholster a dock that
extended around two sides of the house. My parents were con-
verting it into a veranda, covering it with grass-colored indoor-
outdoor carpeting. My mother was treading water, outfitted
with flippers, mask, snorkel, and staple gun. She looked like
Jacques Cousteau. Her job was to swim under the dock and
affix the carpeting to the underside; I was supposed to hold it in
place and smooth out the wrinkles.

My job was easy. I found the best way to hold the carpet flat
and in place was to just lie on the section we were working on. I
unhitched my bathing-suit straps and opened my calculus
book. I could hear my mother slurping around in the water
beneath me, attacking the dock with her staple gun. When she
pulled the carpet for a snugger fit, my mechanical pencil rolled
off into the weedy water.

In a few minutes my mother swam out from under the dock.
She raised the mask so it stuck out from the top of her bathing
cap, and crossed her tanned arms on the dock.

"I lost my pencil," I said. "It rolled off."

My mother looked at my calculus book and said, "Can you really do that stuff?"

"Not yet," I said. "It's supposed to click and all make sense at some point."

"The only nice thing about being an old woman is that I was spared new math. I remember when I had to teach metric conversion I was a loony case. Your father had to do a guest lecture on the metric system. We made vichyssoise. All the girls fell in love with him. They had never seen a man cook before. What ever happened to all that?"

"What?"

"The metric system. Don't you remember? We were supposed to convert. They even had commercials on TV about it: 'America Goes Metric.' What happened?"

"I don't know," I said. "I guess they gave up."

"I like inches," my mother said. "I'd miss inches. It's too bad we're not closer to New York. Daddy could help you with your calculus. He used to help Debbie."

"My teacher says it's all genetic," I said. "He thinks my math genes just have to be aroused."

"Aroused?" My mother pushed away from the dock and floated on her back. The skirt of her bathing suit fanned out around her thighs. I looked up into the bright sky and closed my eyes. The first night Stephen and I slept together, he whispered numbers into my ear: long, high numbers—distances between planets, seconds in a life. He spoke as if they were poetry, and they became poetry. Later, when he fell asleep, I leaned over him and watched, trying to picture a mathematician's dreams. I concluded that Stephen must dream in abstract, cool designs like Mondrian paintings.

"Have you heard from Tim?" my mother asked.

"No," I said. I could feel the green turf pressing into my cheek and hear my mother making tiny splashing sounds, listlessly circumventing the lily pads. "We're not calling each other."

"Don't you wonder how he is?"

I opened my eyes. My mother was treading water, moving

her arms and legs very gracefully and slowly, making the least possible effort to stay afloat.

"Actually," I said, "I'm seeing someone else."

"Already? Who?"

"You don't know him," I said.

"Well, I assume I don't know him. That's why I'm asking."

"The teacher," I said.

"The calculus teacher? The geneticist?"

"Yes," I said.

"Oh, honey," my mother said. She sounded sad. "Just remember you're on the rebound. Be careful. Especially with a calculus teacher."

"I'm not on the rebound."

"What do you call it, then?" My mother picked a piece of duckweed out of the water, fingered it, then tossed it a few feet away. A small fish rose and mouthed the surface of the water, nipping at it. I thought for a moment. I sat up and put my legs in the water. The fish swam away. I was mad at my mother for bringing up Tim, as I had been doing a pretty good job of forgetting about him.

"It's not a rebound," I said. "It's a new life. It has nothing to do with Ann Arbor or Timmy or wicker."

But my mother wasn't listening. She was looking at the bottom of the lake. "Look," she said. "Your pencil." She did a quick surface dive. I watched her white legs kick down into the dark water. In a moment she popped back up, and tossed my pencil onto the dock.

Stephen and I had, in our one short week together, established a ritual. We went out together after class for a beer. The middle of the afternoon, I discovered, was a nice time to frequent bars. I'd never much liked them at night in Ann Arbor when they were noisy and crowded and dark and sticky. But in the afternoon no one played the jukebox, the sun shone in the open door, and the people in the soap operas swam through their complicated lives on the TV above the bar like fish in an aquarium.

Stephen was drawing a diagram on a soggy cocktail napkin,

trying, as always, to explain something I didn't understand. I was half watching him and half watching a large white cat thread himself through the legs of the bar-stools, savoring the touch of each leg against his fur.

"See," Stephen said, pushing the napkin across the table. I looked at it but couldn't make any sense of it, so I turned it around.

"No," Stephen said. "This way." He turned it back around.

Something about the blurry diagram on the cocktail napkin depressed me. I couldn't believe it had come to be an important part of my life. It had no message for me. I leaned back against the vinyl booth.

"Can we forget about it for a while?" I said.

"Sure." Stephen crumpled the napkin and punted it to the floor with his fingers. "What's the matter?" he asked.

"I've been thinking," I said. "Maybe this is a bad idea."

"What?"

"This," I said. "Us."

"Oh," said Stephen. "Why?"

"I just feel like I should get through this myself. I mean I think I should pass calculus by myself and then we can decide if we want to see each other."

"But you can't pass calculus by yourself. You need a tutor."

"I'll get another tutor," I said.

"It's too late to get another tutor. We just have one more week. Julie, you know, no one expects you to pass calculus yourself. It's not some big deal. This isn't the Girl Scout merit-badge contest."

"I know," I said. "I can't explain. I just think this is wrong."

Stephen drained his beer glass. "Why won't you let me help you?" he asked.

"I told you," I said. "I think it's wrong."

"But it's not wrong. There's nothing wrong about it. You just want to get rid of me."

I didn't say anything. I watched the cat. We sat there for a moment. I felt like I was making a terrible mistake, only I wasn't sure what it was: if it had to do with love or calculus. I felt I was probably losing on both counts.

* * *

I don't think I've worked at anything as hard as I worked at calculus the next week. The exam was scheduled for one o'clock on the last Friday of class; we had a review session in the morning. I asked two questions. Stephen answered them.

I was sitting on the front steps of the math building rereading my notes when he came out. He stood beside me. "Come on," he said. "I'm taking you out to lunch."

"I can't," I said. "I have to study."

He leaned over and pulled my spiral notebook out of my hands. "If you don't know it now," he said, "you never will."

We went across the street to the bar with the slinking white cat. We had a nice lunch. We didn't mention calculus.

I finished the exam before the allotted time was up, which I thought might be a good sign. I couldn't tell. I had no idea how I did. I handed it in and took the subway home. I showered and began packing, because I was going up to the lake to see my parents for the weekend. I was just going out the door when the phone rang. I debated answering it. Most of the calls were still for Alyssa, and I had turned the answering machine on. But it's hard not to answer a ringing phone.

It was Stephen, telling me I had failed the exam and, consequently, the course. For a second I was actually shocked, and then I realized how absurd the whole thing was, my ever thinking I could pass calculus, get an MBA, live in New York. I stood for a moment looking at Alyssa's ridiculous accumulation of crystal. I couldn't speak.

"Julie?" Stephen said. "Are you listening?"

"Yes," I said.

"Listen," he said. "I explained the situation to Foster." Foster was the chairman of the department and a dean at the business school. His eleven-year-old daughter sat next to me in class. She was taking calculus, she told me, for fun.

"You explained the situation?"

"I just told him you almost passed—you almost did—and that you needed the grade to start the program."

"What program?" I asked.

"The MBA," Stephen said.

"Oh," I said. "I've changed my mind about that. I'm not getting an MBA."

"What?" said Stephen. "Are you crazy?"

I was starting to cry, so I didn't say anything.

"Julie? What are you talking about? Why don't we go out to dinner and talk about this?"

"I can't," I said. "I'm going up to my parents'."

"Listen," said Stephen. "Are you listening?"

"I'm not deaf, Stephen."

"I'm going down to the registrar. I'm going to register you for the August session. I don't even teach it, so it will be O.K. We won't talk about it now. But think about it."

I told him I would think about it; I told him I would call him when I got back on Sunday. I hung up. I stood in Alyssa's pantry. I thought, If I were the kind of person who broke things I would break a glass, or maybe several. I thought, Maybe I should break some even though I'm not that type of person. It would be therapeutic. But I didn't break any. It wasn't worth the effort of cleaning it up, which I would have done, immediately.

Then I started thinking about Stephen. I wished he hadn't called me. He must have started grading my exam the moment I left. Now he was going down to the registrar, at this very moment. He was being so nice. It made me feel guilty and selfish and mean.

I ordered two gin-and-tonics at once from the steward because I wanted two drinks and was afraid he wouldn't make it up the aisle twice by the time we got to Syracuse. They tasted great, and after a while even the fields below us looked trustworthy and harmless, as though if we crashed they'd just reach up and hold us as we fell.

My father was waiting in his Army-surplus jeep at the airport. I threw my knapsack in the back and climbed in the front and we took off. It seemed like he was driving a little too quickly down the tree-lined road; the wind seemed to rush past awfully fast. The sun was finally setting but the light lingered all over the sky.

"I failed my exam," I shouted to my father.

"Oh, honey," he shouted back. "Can you take it again?"

"Maybe. I'll see on Monday."

We drove a little farther in silence and then turned down the dirt road that goes through the woods to the boathouse.

"Your mother's a little upset," my father said, not looking at me.

"Why? What happened?"

"We had a little argument."

Because my parents never argued in front of me, I thought they never argued. "About what?" I asked.

My father sighed and downshifted. "Your mother wants to settle down. She wants to buy a condominium somewhere." He said "condominium" as if it were a carcinogen.

"Oh," I said.

"I like the way we live. I think it's good for us. I think eventually we should think about settling down in one place. But why now? Look at this—" He motioned out at the land that fell away to the lake that lay as still as a mirror between the trees. "A year ago we didn't know this existed," he said. "I just like finding new things. Making new things."

We pulled into the barn where he parked the jeep, but neither of us made a move to get out.

"I hate to tell you this, honey," my father said. "But I just thought you should know. Mom is in bed. She got kind of upset."

"Oh," I said. My poor father. He sat in his jeep, feeling bad.

"Maybe you should go up and talk to her." For the first time he looked at me. There was just enough light left in the barn for me to see the tears, not falling from his eyes, but sitting in them, glistening.

The electricity in the boathouse was limited to the kitchen, so the rest of the house was dark. I climbed the spiral staircase my father had built to the bedroom. My mother was sitting in bed with her hands folded on the quilt she'd made from scraps of dresses she'd sewn for me and my sister when we were little. Whenever I see the quilt, I can picture some of the dresses, although they were all alike: tiny Peter Pan collars, the fronts smocked, skirts puffed out from the waist. I don't know what happened to them. I wish I still had one or two, just to look at. I sat on the other side of the bed.

"Hi," I said. I leaned over and kissed her. She smiled at me, knowing how silly the situation was: her in bed, me coming to her—it was all wrong, all reversed.

"Did Daddy tell you about our disagreement?" she asked.

I said yes.

She looked out the porthole window my father had installed in the crook of the roof, but it was too dark to see anything.

"I'm sorry now I made such a fuss," she said. "It's just that I can't keep doing this. It's not that I don't have the energy or the will. It's just that I can't keep making things and leaving them behind. Does that seem wrong?"

"No," I said. "Of course not."

She looked at me. "Your father loved you kids, adored you, but he was so happy when you went away to school and he retired. We could finally take off and do things and not be tied down, and it was great for a while but now I'm sick of it. I'm sorry but I'm plain sick of it."

I thought, Don't tell me this, don't say any of this. I don't want to know you're unhappy. And then for the second time that day I felt mean and selfish. My mother sighed and looked back out the window.

I stood up. "Do you want anything from downstairs?"

"No, thanks." She turned away from the window, trying to smile. "How was your exam? I forgot all about it."

"O.K.," I said. "I passed."

A month later, I did pass calculus. It was almost easy the second time. I didn't see Stephen very much; he wasn't teaching so he wasn't really around. When we did see each other we felt awkward: without calculus we had little to share, and for all the hours we had spent together, we didn't seem to know each other very well.

That same week, my parents told me they were separating, at least until they could decide upon a way of life that was "mutually enjoyable." I was surprised and a little ashamed to find that I felt more relieved than upset. While I was growing up I had always been so proud of them, and my intact home, but at some point—and I didn't know when—all that had lost its terrible importance.

They finished work on the boathouse and sold it to a movie star. Over Labor Day weekend, my father went off to Maine to look for a very dilapidated, very large farm. My mother came to see me in New York. We went out to dinner and celebrated my passing calculus. My mother waited until the bottle of champagne was empty and we were drinking brewed decaffeinated coffee before she talked about the separation.

"I feel very brave doing this," she said. "I feel foolish, too, but I do feel brave. And it's nice that it can end like this, with no hard feelings. We really do understand each other. Of course it helps that it's a very specific problem—not something about how we feel about each other."

"But doesn't that make it harder?"

"What?"

"Still feeling the same," I said. "I mean, I'd think if you hated each other it would be easier."

My mother stroked the tablecloth, forming and then smoothing wrinkles. Her hands were covered with tiny cuts and scratches, and I noticed she was still wearing her wedding ring.

"No," she said. "Although I don't know why. I guess I like to think things have changed more than failed. I don't know. Does that make any sense?"

"Yes," I said.

"Debbie doesn't understand at all. She's worried about me. She wants me to move to Allentown."

"What are you going to do?" I asked.

She opened her pocketbook and took out a brochure for condominiums on a golf course in South Carolina. There were pictures of buildings nestled in the rough along green fairways, and floor plans of different models.

"No two are alike," my mother said. "I'm going down next week to look at them."

"They look nice," I said.

"The best thing about them is that I can pick out everything myself: the carpeting, the drapes, the Congoleum, the Formica, the appliances—even the shelf paper."

"That's great." I said. There was a moment when I thought my mother was about to start crying, so I studied the brochure. When I looked up, she seemed O.K.

"And they do all the work," my mother said. "Everything. They even fill the ice trays before you move in."

My mother left for South Carolina on Tuesday, and Wednesday was registration for the fall semester of business school. For a few panic-stricken moments at breakfast, I thought about not going—about getting out of New York while I was ahead. I could go down and help my mother move into her condominium. But that morning I realized that if I went uptown and registered for accounting and statistics and behavioral management and whatever else, I'd be done with all these second thoughts.

It hasn't been quite like that, of course, but it hasn't been bad. Sometimes I see Stephen around in the late afternoon, and we go across the street to our bar. Now it gets dark while we sit there, but it's still nice. Stephen always asks me if I need help. I tell him no. After the ordeal of calculus, business school is manageable.

Where All Things Wise and Fair Descend

by Irwin Shaw

He woke up feeling good. There was no reason for him to wake up feeling anything else.

He was an only child. He was twenty years old. He was over six feet tall and weighed 180 pounds and had never been sick in his whole life. He was number two on the tennis team and back home in his father's study there was a whole shelf of cups he had won in tournaments since he was eleven years old. He had a lean, sharply cut face, straight black hair that he wore just a little long, which prevented him from looking merely like an athlete. A girl had once said he looked like Shelley. Another, like Laurence Olivier. He had smiled noncommittally at both girls.

He had a retentive memory and classes were easy for him. He had just been put on the dean's list. His father, who was doing well up North in an electronics business, had sent him a check for $100 as a reward. The check had been in his box the night before.

He had a gift for mathematics and probably could get a job teaching in the department if he wanted it upon graduation, but he planned to go into his father's business.

He was not one of the single-minded educational wizards who roamed the science departments. He got A's in English and history and had memorized most of Shakespeare's sonnets and read Roethke and Eliot and Ginsberg. He had tried marijuana. He was invited to all the parties. When he went home, mothers made obvious efforts to throw their daughters at him.

His own mother was beautiful and young and funny. There were no unbroken silver cords in the family. He was having an affair with one of the prettiest girls on the campus and she said she loved him. From time to time he said he loved her. When he said it he meant it. At that moment, anyway.

Nobody he had ever cared for had as yet died and everybody in his family had come home safe from all the wars.

The world saluted him.

He maintained his cool.

No wonder he woke up feeling good.

It was nearly December, but the California sun made a summer morning of the season and the girls and boys in corduroys and T-shirts and bright-colored sweaters on their way to their ten-o'clock classes walked over green lawns and in and out of the shadows of trees that had not yet lost their leaves.

He passed the sorority house where Adele lived and waved as she came out. His first class every Tuesday was at ten o'clock and the sorority house was on his route to the arts buildings in which the classroom was situated.

Adele was a tall girl, her dark, combed head coming well above his shoulder. She had a triangular, blooming, still-childish face. Her walk, even with the books she was carrying in her arms, wasn't childish, though, and he was amused at the envious looks directed at him by some of the other students as Adele paced at his side down the graveled path.

" 'She walks in beauty,' " Steve said, " 'like the night/Of cloudless climes and starry skies;/And all that's best of dark and bright/Meet in her aspect and her eyes.' "

"What a nice thing to hear at ten o'clock in the morning," Adele said. "Did you bone up on that for me?"

"No," he said. "We're having a test on Byron today."

"Animal," she said.

He laughed.

"Are you taking me to the dance Saturday night?" she asked.

He grimaced. He didn't like to dance. He didn't like the kind of music that was played and he thought the way people danced these days was devoid of grace. "I'll tell you later," he said.

"I have to know today," Adele said. "Two other boys've asked me."

"I'll tell you at lunch," he said.

"What time?"

"One. Can the other aspirants hold back their frenzy to dance until then?"

"Barely," she said. He knew that with or without him, Adele would be at the dance on Saturday night. She loved to dance and he had to admit that a girl had every right to expect the boy she was seeing almost every night in the week to take her dancing at least once on the weekend. He felt very mature, almost fatherly, as he resigned himself to four hours of heat and noise on Saturday night. But he didn't tell Adele that he'd take her. It wouldn't do her any harm to wait until lunch.

He squeezed her hand as they parted and watched for a moment as she swung down the path, conscious of the provocative way she was walking, conscious of the eyes on her. He smiled and continued on his way, waving at people who greeted him.

It was early and Mollison, the English professor, had not yet put in an appearance. The room was only half full as Steve entered it, but there wasn't the usual soprano-tenor turning-up sound of conversation from the students who were already there. They sat in their chairs quietly, not talking, most of them ostentatiously arranging their books or going through their notes. Occasionally, almost furtively, one or another of them would look up toward the front of the room and the blackboard, where a thin boy with wispy reddish hair was writing swiftly and neatly behind the teacher's desk.

"Oh, weep for Adonais—he is dead!" the red-haired boy had written. "Wake, melancholy Mother, wake and weep!"

Yet wherefore? Quench within their burning bed
Thy fiery tears, and let thy loud heart keep
Like his a mute and uncomplaining sleep;
For he is gone where all things wise and fair
Descend. Oh, dream not that the amorous Deep
Will yet restore him to the vital air;
Death feeds on his mute voice, and laughs at our despair.

Then, on a second blackboard, where the boy was finishing the last lines of another stanza, was written:

> He has outsoared the shadow of our night;
> Envy and calumny and hate and pain,
> And that unrest which men miscall delight;
> Can touch him not and torture not again;
> From the contagion of the world's slow stain
> He is secure, and now can never mourn
> A heart grown cold, a head grown grey in vain;

Professor Mollison came bustling in with the half-apologetic smile of an absentminded man who is afraid he is always late. He stopped at the door, sensing by the quiet that this was no ordinary Tuesday morning in his classroom. He peered nearsightedly at Crane writing swiftly in rounded chalk letters on the blackboard.

Mollison took out his glasses and read for a moment, then went over to the window without a word and stood there looking out, a graying, soft-faced, rosy-cheeked old man, the soberness of his expression intensified by the bright sunlight at the window.

"Nor," Crane was writing, the chalk making a dry sound in the silence,

> when the spirit's self has ceased to burn,
> With sparkless ashes load an unlamented urn.

When Crane had finished, he put the chalk down neatly and stepped back to look at what he had written. A girl's laugh came in on the fragrance of cut grass through the open window and there was a curious hushing little intake of breath all through the room.

The bell rang, abrasively, for the beginning of classes. When the bell stopped, Crane turned around and faced the students seated in rows before him. He was a lanky, skinny boy, only nineteen, and he was already going bald. He hardly ever spoke in class and when he spoke, it was in a low, harsh whisper.

He didn't seem to have any friends and he never was seen with girls and the time he didn't spend in class he seemed to spend in the library. Crane's brother had played fullback on the football team, but the brothers had rarely been seen together, and the fact that the huge, graceful athlete and the scarecrow bookworm were members of the same family seemed like a freak of eugenics to the students who knew them both.

Steve knew why Crane had come early to write the two verses of Shelley's lament on the clean morning blackboard. The Saturday night before, Crane's brother had been killed in an automobile accident on the way back from the game, which had been played in San Francisco. The funeral had taken place yesterday, Monday. Now it was Tuesday morning and Crane's first class since the death of his brother.

Crane stood there, narrow shoulders hunched in a bright tweed jacket that was too large for him, surveying the class without emotion. He glanced once more at what he had written, as though to make sure the problem he had placed on the board had been correctly solved, then turned again to the group of gigantic, blossoming, rosy California boys and girls, unnaturally serious and a little embarrassed by this unexpected prologue to their class, and began to recite.

He recited flatly, without any emotion in his voice, moving casually back and forth in front of the blackboards, occasionally turning to the text to flick off a little chalk dust, to touch the end of a word with his thumb, to hesitate at a line, as though he had suddenly perceived a new meaning in it.

Mollison, who had long ago given up any hope of making any impression on the sun-washed young California brain with the fragile hammer of nineteenth-century Romantic poetry, stood at the window, looking out over the campus, nodding in rhythm from time to time and occasionally whispering a line, almost silently, in unison with Crane.

" '. . . an unlamented urn,' " Crane said, still as flat and unemphatic as ever, as though he had merely gone through the two verses as a feat of memory. The last echo of his voice quiet now in the still room, he looked out at the class through his thick glasses, demanding nothing. Then he went to the back of the room and sat down in his chair and began putting his books together.

Mollison, finally awakened from his absorption with the sunny lawn, the whirling sprinklers, the shadows of the trees speckling in the heat and the wind, turned away from the window and walked slowly to his desk. He peered nearsightedly for a moment at the script crammed on the blackboards, then said, absently, "On the death of Keats. The class is excused."

For once, the students filed out silently, making a point, with youthful good manners, of not looking at Crane, bent over at his chair, pulling books together.

Steve was nearly the last one to leave the room and he waited outside the door for Crane. *Somebody* had to say something, do something, whisper "I'm sorry," shake the boy's hand. Steve didn't want to be the one, but there was nobody else left. When Crane came out, Steve fell into place beside him and they went out of the building together.

"My name is Dennicott," Steve said.

"I know," said Crane.

"Can I ask you a question?"

"Sure." There was no trace of grief in Crane's voice or manner. He blinked through his glasses at the sunshine, but that was all.

"Why did you do that?"

"Did you object?" The question was sharp but the tone was mild, offhand, careless.

"Hell, no," Steve said. "I just want to know why you did it."

"My brother was killed Saturday night," Crane said.

"I know."

" 'The death of Keats. The class is excused.' " Crane chuckled softly but without malice. "He's a nice old man, Mollison. Did you ever read the book he wrote about Marvell?"

"No," Steve said.

"Terrible book," Crane said. "You really want to know?" He peered with sudden sharpness at Steve.

"Yes," Steve said.

"Yes," Crane said absently, brushing at his forehead, "you

would be the one who would ask. Out of the whole class. Did
you know my brother?"

"Just barely," Steve said. He thought about Crane's brother,
the fullback. A gold helmet far below on a green field, a number (what number?), a doll brought out every Saturday to do
skillful and violent maneuvers in a great wash of sound, a photograph in a program, a young, brutal face looking out a little
scornfully from the page. Scornful of what? Of whom? The
inept photographer? The idea that anyone would really be interested in knowing what face was on that numbered doll? The
notion that what he was doing was important enough to war-
rant this attempt to memorialize him, so that somewhere, in
somebody's attic fifty years from now, that young face would
still be there, in the debris, part of some old man's false memory of his youth?

"He didn't seem much like John Keats to you, did he?"
Crane stopped under a tree, in the shade, to rearrange the
books under his arm. He seemed oppressed by sunshine and he
held his books clumsily and they were always on the verge of
falling to the ground.

"To be honest," Steve said, "no, he didn't seem much like
John Keats to me."

Crane nodded gently. "But I knew him," he said. "I knew
him. And nobody who made those goddamned speeches at the
funeral yesterday knew him. And he didn't believe in God or in
funerals or those goddamned speeches. He needed a proper
ceremony of farewell," Crane said, "and I tried to give it to
him. All it took was a little chalk, and a poet, and none of those
liars in black suits. Do you want to take a ride today?"

"Yes," Steve said without hesitation.

"I'll meet you at the library at eleven," Crane said. He waved
stiffly and hunched off, gangling, awkward, ill-nourished, thin-
haired, laden with books, a discredit to the golden Coastal leg-
end.

They drove north in silence. Crane had an old Ford without
a top and it rattled so much and the wind made so much noise
as they bumped along that conversation would have been al-

most impossible, even if they had wished to talk. Crane bent over the wheel, driving nervously, with an excess of care, his long pale hands gripping the wheel tightly. Steve hadn't asked where they were going and Crane hadn't told him. Steve hadn't been able to get hold of Adele to tell her he probably wouldn't be back in time to have lunch with her, but there was nothing to be done about that now. He sat back, enjoying the sun and the yellow, burnt-out hills and the long, grayish-blue swells of the Pacific beating lazily into the beaches and against the cliffs of the coast. Without being told, he knew that this ride somehow was a continuation of the ceremony in honor of Crane's brother.

They passed several restaurants alongside the road. Steve was hungry, but he didn't suggest stopping. This was Crane's expedition and Steve had no intention of interfering with whatever ritual Crane was following.

They rocked along between groves of lemon and orange and the air was heavy with the perfume of the fruit, mingled with the smell of salt from the sea.

They went through the flecked shade of avenues of eucalyptus that the Spanish monks had planted in another century to make their journeys from mission to mission bearable in the California summers. Rattling along in the noisy car, squinting a little when the car spurted out into bare sunlight, Steve thought of what the road must have looked like with an old man in a cassock nodding along it on a sleepy mule, to the sound of distant Spanish bells, welcoming travelers. There were no bells ringing today. California, Steve thought, sniffing the diesel oil of a truck in front of them, has not improved.

The car swerved around a turn, Crane put on the brakes and they stopped. Then Steve saw what they had stopped for.

There was a huge tree leaning over a bend of the highway and all the bark at road level on one side of the tree had been ripped off. The wood beneath, whitish, splintered, showed in a raw wound.

"This is the place," Crane said, in his harsh whisper. He stopped the engine and got out of the car. Steve followed him and stood to one side as Crane peered nearsightedly through

his glasses at the tree. Crane touched the tree, just at the edge
of the wound.

"Eucalyptus," he said. "From the Greek, meaning well covered; the flower, before it opens having a sort of cap. A genus of
plants of the N. O. Myrtaceae. If I had been a true brother," he
said, "I would have come here Saturday morning and cut this
tree down. My brother would be alive today." He ran his hand
casually over the torn and splintered wood, and Steve remembered how he had touched the blackboard and flicked chalk
dust off the ends of words that morning, unemphatically, in
contrast with the feel of things, the slate, the chalk mark at the
end of the last "s" in Adonais, the gummy, drying wood.
"You'd think," Crane said, "that if you loved a brother enough
you'd have sense enough to come and cut a tree down, wouldn't
you? The Egyptians, I read somewhere," he said, "were believed to have used the oil of the eucalyptus leaf in the embalm-
ing process." His long hand flicked once more at the torn bark.
"Well, I didn't cut the tree down. Let's go."

He strode back to the car, without looking back at the tree.
He got into the car behind the wheel and sat slumped there,
squinting through his glasses at the road ahead of him, waiting
for Steve to settle himself beside him. "It's terrible for my
mother and father," Crane said, after Steve had closed the door
behind him. A truck filled with oranges passed them in a thun-
derous whoosh and a swirl of dust, leaving a fragrance of a
hundred weddings on the air. "We live at home, you know. My
brother and I were the only children they had, and they look at
me and they can't help feeling, If it had to be one of them, why
couldn't it have been *him?* and it shows in their eyes and they
know it shows in their eyes and they know I agree with them
and they feel guilty and I can't help them." He started the
engine with a succession of nervous, uncertain gestures, like a
man who was just learning how to drive. He turned the car
around in the direction of Los Angeles and they started south.
Steve looked once more at the tree, but Crane kept his eyes on
the road ahead of him.

"I'm hungry," he said. "I know a place where we can get
abalone about ten miles from here."

They were sitting in the weather-beaten shack with the windows open on the ocean, eating their abalone and drinking beer. The jukebox was playing *Downtown*. It was the third time they were listening to *Downtown*. Crane kept putting dimes into the machine and choosing the same song over and over again.

"I'm crazy about that song," he said. "Saturday night in America. Budweiser Bacchanalia."

"Everything all right, boys?" The waitress, a fat little dyed blonde of about thirty, smiled down at them from the end of the table.

"Everything is perfectly splendid," Crane said in a clear, ringing voice.

The waitress giggled. "Why, that sure is nice to hear," she said.

Crane examined her closely. "What do you do when it storms?" he asked.

"What's that?" She frowned uncertainly at him.

"When it storms," Crane said. "When the winds blow. When the sea heaves. Then the young sailors drown in the bottomless deeps."

"My," the waitress said, "and I thought you boys only had one beer."

"I advise anchors," Crane said. "You are badly placed. A turn of the wind, a twist of the tide, and you will be afloat, past the reef, on the way to Japan."

"I'll tell the boss," the waitress said, grinning. "You advise anchors."

"You are in peril, lady," Crane said seriously. "Don't think you're not. Nobody speaks candidly. Nobody tells you the one-hundred-percent honest-to-God truth." He pushed a dime from a pile at his elbow, across the table to the waitress. "Would you be good enough to put this in the box, my dear?" he said formally.

"What do you want to hear?" the waitress asked.

"Downtown," Crane said.

"Again?" The waitress grimaced. "It's coming out of my ears."

"I understand it's all the rage," Crane said.

The waitress took the dime and put it in the box and *Downtown* started over again.

"She'll remember me," Crane said, eating fried potatoes covered with ketchup. "Everytime it blows and the sea comes up. You must not go through life unremembered."

"You're a queer duck, all right," Steve said, smiling a little, to take the sting out of it, but surprised into saying it.

"Ah, I'm not so queer," Crane said, wiping ketchup off his chin. "I don't behave like this ordinarily. This is the first time I ever flirted with a waitress in my life."

Steve laughed. "Do you call that flirting?"

"Isn't it?" Crane looked annoyed. "What the hell is it if it isn't flirting?" He surveyed Steve appraisingly. "Let me ask you a question," he said. "Do you screw that girl I always see you with around the campus?"

Steve put down his fork. "Now, wait a minute," he said.

"I don't like the way she walks," Crane said. "She walks like a coquette. I prefer whores."

"Let's leave it at that," Steve said.

"Ah, Christ," Crane said, "I thought you wanted to be my friend. You did a friendly, sensitive thing this morning. In the California desert, in the Los Angeles Gobi, in the Camargue of Culture. You put out a hand. You offered the cup."

"I want to be your friend, all right," Steve said, "but there're limits . . ."

"The word friend has no limits," Crane said harshly. He poured some of his beer over the fried potatoes, already covered with ketchup. He forked a potato, put it in his mouth, chewed judiciously. "I've invented a taste thrill," he said. "Let me tell you something, Dennicott, friendship is limitless communication. Ask me anything and I'll answer. The more fundamental the matter, the fuller the answer. What's your idea of friendship? The truth about trivia—and silence and hypocrisy about everything else? God, you could have used a dose of my brother." He poured some more beer over the gobs of ketchup on the fried potatoes. "You want to know why I can say Keats and name my brother in the same breath?" he asked challengingly, hunched over the table. "I'll tell you why. Because he had a sense of elation and a sense of purity." Crane squinted thoughtfully at Steve. "You, too," he said, "that's why I said you would be the one to ask, out of the whole class. You have it, too—the sense of elation. I could tell—listening to you laugh, watching you walk down the library steps holding your girl's elbow. I, too," he said gravely, "am capable of elation. But I reserve it for other things." He made a mysterious inward grimace. "But the purity—" he said. "I don't know. Maybe you don't know yourself. The jury is still out on you. But I knew about my brother. You want to know what I mean by purity?" He was talking compulsively. Silence would have made memory unbearable. "It's having a private set of standards and never compromising them," he said. "Even when it hurts, even when nobody else knows, even when it's just a tiny, formal gesture, that ninety-nine out of a hundred people would make without thinking about it."

Crane cocked his head and listened with pleasure to the chorus of *Downtown,* and he had to speak loudly to be heard over the jukebox. "You know why my brother wasn't elected captain of the football team? He was all set for it, he was the logical choice, everybody expected it. I'll tell you why he wasn't, though. He wouldn't shake the hand of last year's captain, at the end of the season, and last year's captain had a lot of votes he could influence any way he wanted. And do you know why my brother wouldn't shake his hand? Because he thought the man was a coward. He saw him tackle high when a low tackle would've been punishing, and he saw him not go all the way on blocks when they looked too rough. Maybe nobody else saw what my brother saw or maybe they gave the man the benefit of the doubt. Not my brother. So he didn't shake his hand, because he didn't shake cowards' hands, see, and somebody else was elected captain. That's what I mean by purity," Crane said, sipping at his beer and looking out at the deserted beach and the ocean. For the first time, it occurred to Steve that it was perhaps just as well that he had never known Crane's brother, never been measured against that Cromwellian certitude of conduct.

"As for girls," Crane said. "The homeland of compromise,

the womb of the second best—" Crane shook his head emphatically. "Not for my brother. Do you know what he did with his first girl? And he thought he was in love with her, too, at the time, but it still didn't make any difference. They only made love in the dark. The girl insisted. That's the way some girls are, you know, darkness excuses all. Well, my brother was crazy about her, and he didn't mind the darkness if it pleased her. But one night he saw her sitting up in bed and the curtains on the window moved in the wind and her silhouette was outlined against the moonlight, and he saw that when she sat like that she had a fat, loose belly. The silhouette, my brother said, was slack and self-indulgent. Of course, when she was lying down it sank in, and when she was dressed she wore a girdle that would've tucked in a beer barrel. And when he saw her silhouette against the curtain, he said to himself, This is the last time, this is not for me. Because it wasn't perfect, and he wouldn't settle for less. Love or no love, desire or not. He, himself, had a body like Michelangelo's David and he knew it and he was proud of it and he kept it that way, why should he settle for imperfection? Are you laughing, Dennicott?"

"Well," Steve said, trying to control his mouth, "the truth is, I'm smiling a little." He was amused, but he couldn't help thinking that it was possible that Crane had loved his brother for all the wrong reasons. And he couldn't help feeling sorry for the unknown girl, deserted, without knowing it, in the dark room, by the implacable athlete who had just made love to her.

"Don't you think I ought to talk about my brother this way?" Crane said.

"Of course," Steve said. "If I were dead, I hope my brother could talk like this about me the day after the funeral."

"It's just those goddamned speeches everybody makes," Crane whispered. "If you're not careful, they can take the whole idea of your brother away from you."

He wiped his glasses. His hands were shaking. "My goddamned hands," he said. He put his glasses back on his head and pressed his hands hard on the table, so they wouldn't shake.

"How about you, Dennicott?" Crane said. "Have you ever

done anything in your whole life that was unprofitable, damaging, maybe even ruinous, because it was the pure thing to do, the uncompromising thing, because if you acted otherwise, for the rest of your life you would remember it and feel shame?"

Steve hesitated. He did not have the habit of self-examination and had the feeling that it was vanity that made people speak about their virtues. And their faults. But there was Crane, waiting, himself open, naked. "Well, yes . . ." Steve said.

"What?"

"Well, it was never anything very grandiose . . ." Steve said, embarrassed, but feeling that Crane needed it, that in some way this exchange of intimacies helped relieve the boy's burden of sorrow. And he was intrigued by Crane, by the violence of his views, by the almost comic flood of his reminiscence about his brother, by the importance that Crane assigned to the slightest gesture, by his searching for meaning in trivialities, which gave the dignity of examination to every breath of life. "There was the time on the beach at Santa Monica," Steve said, "I got myself beaten up and I knew I was going to be beaten up . . ."

"That's good," Crane nodded approvingly. "That's always a good beginning."

"Oh, hell," Steve said, "it's too picayune."

"Nothing is picayune," said Crane. "Come on."

"Well, there was a huge guy there who always hung around and made a pest of himself," Steve said. "A physical-culture idiot, with muscles like basketballs. I made fun of him in front of some girls and he said I'd insulted him, and I had, and he said if I didn't apologize, I would have to fight him. And I was wrong, I'd been snotty and superior, and I realized it, and I knew that if I apologized, he'd be disappointed and the girls'd still be laughing at him—so I said I wouldn't apologize and I fought him there on the beach and he must have knocked me down a dozen times and he nearly killed me."

"Right." Crane nodded again, delivering a favorable judgment. "Excellent."

"Then there was this girl I wanted—" Steve stopped.

"Well?" Crane said.

"Nothing," Steve said. "I haven't figured it out yet." Until now he had thought that the episode with the girl reflected honorably on him. He had behaved, as his mother would have put it, in a gentlemanly manner. He wasn't sure now that Crane and his mother would see eye to eye. Crane confused him. "Some other time," he said.

"You promise?" Crane said.

"I promise."

"You won't disappoint me, now?"

"No."

"O.K.," Crane said. "Let's get out of here."

They split the check.

"Come back again sometime, boys," the blond waitress said. "I'll play that record for you." She laughed, her breasts shaking. She had liked having them there. One of them was very good-looking, and the other one, the queer one with the glasses, she had decided, after thinking about it, was a great joker. It helped pass the long afternoon.

On the way home, Crane no longer drove like a nervous old maid on her third driving lesson. He drove very fast, with one hand, humming *Downtown,* as though he didn't care whether he lived or died.

Then, abruptly, Crane stopped humming and began to drive carefully, timidly, again. "Dennicott," he said, "what are you going to do with your life?"

"Who knows?" Steve said, taken aback by the way Crane's conversation jumped from one enormous question to another. "Go to sea, maybe, build electronic equipment, teach, marry a rich wife . . ."

"What's that about electronics?" Crane asked.

"My father's factory," Steve said. "The ancestral business. No sophisticated missile is complete without a Dennicott supersecret what-do-you-call-it."

"Nah," Crane said, shaking his head, "you won't do that. And you won't teach school, either. You don't have the soul of a didact. I have the feeling something adventurous is going to happen to you."

"Do you?" Steve said. "Thanks. What're you going to do with *your* life?"

"I have it all planned out," Crane said, "I'm going to join the forestry service. I'm going to live in a hut on the top of a mountain and watch out for fires and fight to preserve the wilderness of America."

That's a hell of an ambition, Steve thought, but he didn't say it. "You're going to be awfully lonesome," he said.

"Good," Crane said. "I expect to get a lot of reading done. I'm not so enthusiastic about my fellow man, anyway, I prefer trees."

"What about women?" Steve asked. "A wife?"

"What sort of woman would choose me?" Crane said harshly. "I look like something left over after a New Year's party on skid row. And I would only take the best, the most beautiful, the most intelligent, the most loving. I'm not going to settle for some poor, drab Saturday-night castaway."

"Well, now," Steve said, "you're not so awful." Although, it was true, you'd be shocked if you saw Crane out with a pretty girl.

"Don't lie to your friends," Crane said. He began to drive recklessly again, as some new wave of feeling, some new conception of himself, took hold of him. Steve sat tight on his side of the car, holding on to the door, wondering if a whole generation of Cranes was going to meet death on the roads of California within a week.

They drove in silence until they reached the university library. Crane stopped the car and slouched back from the wheel as Steve got out. Steve saw Adele on the library steps, surrounded by three young men, none of whom he knew. Adele saw him as he got out of the car and started coming over to him. Even at that distance, Steve could tell she was angry. He wanted to get rid of Crane before Adele reached him. "Well, so long," Steve said, watching Adele approach. Her walk *was* distasteful, self-conscious, teasing.

Crane sat there, playing with the keys to the ignition, like a man who is always uncertain that the last important word has been said when the time has come to make an exit.

"Dennicott," he began, then stopped, because Adele was

standing there, confronting Steve, her face set. She didn't look at Crane.

"Thanks," she said to Steve. "Thanks for the lunch."

"I couldn't help it," Steve said. "I had to go someplace."

"I'm not in the habit of being stood up," Adele said.

"I'll explain later," Steve said, wanting her to get out of there, away from him, away from Crane, watching soberly from behind the wheel.

"You don't have to explain anything," Adele said. She walked away. Steve gave her the benefit of the doubt. Probably she didn't know who Crane was and that it was Crane's brother who had been killed Saturday night. Still . . .

"I'm sorry I made you miss your date," Crane said.

"Forget it," Steve said. "She'll get over it."

For a moment he saw Crane looking after Adele, his face cold, severe, judging. Then Crane shrugged, dismissed the girl.

"Thanks, Dennicott," Crane said. "Thanks for coming to the tree. You did a good thing this afternoon. You did a friendly thing. You don't know how much you helped me. I have no friends. My brother was the only friend. If you hadn't come with me and let me talk, I don't know how I could've lived through today. Forgive me if I talked too much."

"You didn't talk too much," Steve said.

"Will I see you again?" Crane asked.

"Sure," said Steve. "We have to go back to that restaurant to listen to *Downtown* real soon."

Crane sat up straight, suddenly, smiling shyly, looking pleased, like a child who has just been given a present. If it had been possible, Steve would have put his arms around Crane and embraced him. And with all Crane's anguish and all the loneliness that he knew so clearly was waiting for him, Steve envied him. Crane had the capacity for sorrow and now, after the day Steve had spent with the bereaved boy, he understood that the capacity for sorrow was also the capacity for living.

"Downtown," Crane said. He started the motor and drove off, waving gaily, to go toward his parents' house, where his mother and father were waiting, with the guilty look in their

eyes, because they felt that if one of the sons had to die, they would have preferred it to be him.

Steve saw Adele coming back toward him from the library steps. He could see that her anger had cooled and that she probably would apologize for her outburst. Seeing Adele suddenly with Crane's eyes, he made a move to turn away. He didn't want to talk to her. He had to think about her. He had to think about everything. Then he remembered the twinge of pity he had felt when he had heard about the fat girl erased from her lover's life by the movement of a curtain on a moonlit night. He turned back and smiled in greeting as Adele came up to him. Crane had taught him a good deal that afternoon, but perhaps not the things Crane had thought he was teaching.

"Hello," Steve said, looking not quite candidly into the young blue eyes on a level with his own. "I was hoping you'd come back."

But he wasn't going to wake up, automatically feeling good, ever again.

Judith Kane

by Elizabeth Spencer

It must have been Thursday when I first came to Mrs. Hollo-way's and certainly it was June. It had to be Thursday because the first three days of the week I was busy working for that professor, typing his thesis notes, checking his sources, and keeping his office in order. It wasn't Friday because I wanted to settle in my new quarters before the weekend, when somebody might ask me to the movies or a party or something. I know absolutely that it was June, because that was when the summer term began at the university. Since my dormitory had closed for lack of students to stay in it, I had to find somewhere off campus to stay.

A Thursday in June. Sometime in the late 'thirties. Money was all-important. A dollar was a dollar. The professor I worked for was paying me, and by working hard on my own I could get a couple of courses ticked off and my family wouldn't have to keep me in school quite so long. Times were hard and everyone had to work to get ahead. My education had to be given me somehow, but I must understand that because of it my sisters were going around in hand-me-down clothes, the house needed a coat of paint, and the fence was falling down. I knew it all, in all its earnest truth and rightness, and had will-ingly put my nineteen-year-old girl-shoulder to the wheel where it belonged; yet I was sulky, too. In those pre-war days, going to summer school was something between a reformatory sen-tence and having to get a job as a waitress.

Having paid the cab, I stood on the curb for a good long minute or so in my limp dirndl skirt and white blouse, dirty from moving things out of the dormitory closet, with suitcases beside me on the grass along with grocery store cartons filled with odds and ends, coat hangers tied together by the hooks, my old rag doll, and patchwork pillows stuffed around some books on the English Renaissance. It was afternoon and the sun was straight in my eyes as I shielded my face with one hand and looked at the house I was coming to take a room in, a large three-story white frame house with verandas and balconies, turret and shade tree, holes neatly bored in every step to let the rain water through, and wrought-iron foot scraper clamped to the floor right by the fresh hemp doormat. Mrs. Holloway's house on Knowlton Place.

The maid let me in, helping me get everything upstairs, trudging good-naturedly with me time after time through the hot front yard into the cooler interior where I was cheered by a renewed vision of built-in columned fireplace with mirror set above, glassed-in bookcases in dark-stained oak, dark-bannistered staircase with a creaking step or two, and a cool pitcher of lemonade set out on the landing. I had remembered all this from the time I came to see the room and take it; now I found it all the same. I sat on the bed in my small front room before unpacking, comforted by the hominess of Mrs. Holloway's. A breeze blew through the windows, which overlooked the street. It touched my hot brow and damp hair.

It's better than the dormitory, I thought. *There could be worse places, even if I don't want to go to summer school.*

A door must have closed in the hallway behind me, but I didn't hear it. My own door was open, and I felt a presence behind me and turned around with a start.

"Just moved in?"

Looks like it, I would have cracked to anybody I knew. Instead, I nodded politely, then did a real double take. The girl who was standing there was somebody I knew and had known for a long time. She didn't know me at all. The only reason I knew her was the same reason everybody knew her; she was so beautiful, tall and put together like a Greek statue, with cornsilk hair brushed back and hanging or drawn up in a swirl behind. The boys all talked about her for obvious reasons, admiring her and wishing they had a chance to date her and all; and the girls all wanted to look like her. Now, there she stood, at closer range than I had ever seen her, in a loose blue house-coat, just out of the shower, with the air of someone who had been in this house a long time.

"Judith Kane!" I said. "I didn't know you lived here."

"I thought I was going to be alone all summer," she said. "Everybody left but me."

"You just about will be," I said, "except on weekends. I've got so much work to do I expect I may even have to sleep in the library."

"I used to work there," she said, "after I graduated."

"What do you do now?" I asked, after telling her my name and who I worked for. I was hardly conscious of what words I was using, her looks were so astonishing. I know all this about how they say Southern girls are so pretty and how they come pouring out of little towns and from way up in the hills to get elected Miss Pickle Queen and Miss Watermelon Queen, Miss Centennial Year, Miss America, Maid of Cotton, Miss Universe, and so on. All true, but not all that interesting. Nothing of this related to Judith Kane. She wasn't cute or pretty, her measurements weren't for contests or advertising copy, but for aesthetics; she was, simply, a creation.

"Do?" she repeated. "Not much of anything, I guess. That's just the trouble. Welcome, anyway. I'd help you unpack but don't have time."

The reason she didn't have time was because she had a date. I soon heard the front door close and by going to the window to look could see her go off across the street with a lean, sandy-haired guy, who moved out beside her to where a blue-green Pontiac convertible stood shimmering beside the curb. The doors went *chunk* and *chunk* and the car accelerated silently like a lioness which has sighted the prey. Judith's white shoes, her lime-green summer dress and scrolled-up hair, made me feel the way I looked, tired and unattractive. I had sat brooding the whole time she was dressing. Whoever came to take me somewhere, any fool could plainly see, was bound to get interested in her. I felt I had no looks or clothes or any asset to hold a candle to hers. Personally speaking, the prospects of this summer didn't give me a lot to rave about.

But, as the days went by, I saw I had been hasty, at least as regards Judith Kane.

Judith was twenty-four, that was the first thing to cheer me. Though to admit to being that old seemed a shame, she evidently didn't mind, for Mrs. Holloway knew it and told me. "Not that it's any of my business," she said, giving me my mail. "All I wonder is what's she still doing around here, not going to school or anything." The boys who came around sometimes on weekends to take me to the movies seemed able to survive the sight of her after all. One said she was a knockout all right, and let it go at that; another said he'd heard she was expensive. She was friendly with them in a harmless, open way, and might run up from the basement in an old skirt with a scarf around her head and some warm ironing over her arm, making no effort to please anybody. She told me once in passing that boys without money were of no interest to her. I guess the boy with that Pontiac must have had financial resources, all right. Seen close to, I found him not so much attractive as well turned-out. The possession of the right articles meant a lot to him—you could tell that by the way he opened the car door—and Judith said he had good taste. Once he brought her a bottle of champagne and they sat down on Mrs. Holloway's front porch in the swing drinking it. She poured out some in a fruit juice glass from the kitchen and ran upstairs to give it to me. "It's champagne," she said. "Take some." I was under a reading lamp, bent over a book with my hair in pins. *This is not the way to drink champagne,* I thought, and finished it off like Alka-Seltzer. The boy's name was Grant Exum, I now remember, and somebody in summer school mentioned him one day, again in connection with his car, which was the fanciest thing around, and further said that he wanted to marry Judith Kane, but his parents wouldn't let him marry anybody till he finished law school. "Money families," whoever was telling this remarked, "are always bossy. Po' folks are a whole lot easier." The memory drifts back after so many years: sitting out gossiping in a group on the library steps, with sun glossing the empty summer campus, far and wide.

I then concluded that Judith stayed around on account of

Grant Exum, holding a job downtown in a small branch library
which, with summer hours, took up scarcely half her time. It
could not have paid her very much or interested her very much.
In the afternoons I came in from work, toiling up the stairs to
my room. She would generally have been home for an hour or
so, and would be reading out in the corridor, where a breeze
drew, smoking a cigarette with her hair up, or sometimes sipping some of Mrs. Holloway's lemonade. She seldom said anything, and often never even looked up: it was rather like passing
a garden statue, and it became disconcerting only when she did
speak. To hear "Hi, there" or "How's it going?" was almost as
startling as her first appearance had been. She read T. S. Eliot,
Auden, Mann, Proust—a lot of highbrow things—with concen-
tration, paying that close sort of attention that does not seem to
have enjoyment or future conversation anywhere in mind, the
matter being more urgent than that. I was in literature, too, but
might as well have been analyzing Tennessee rainwater for all
she would care to talk to me about. But I finally came to realize, the first couple of weeks having gone by like this, that
Judith Kane's life, like her extraordinary looks, was no more to
me than Mrs. Holloway's, or the house which had somehow
managed to absorb both of them into it; for, if the downstairs
with its starched antimacassars and glass-front bookshelves and
sanded-glass ornaments belonged to Mrs. Holloway, the upstairs—white-curtained, smooth, simple, immaculate, and quiet
—had long been Judith's and hers was the rocking chair that I,
finding it empty in the hallway, dropped into one afternoon
when I arrived home early from work.

The heat was severe that summer. I watched the white curtains swell and thought that I was tired thinking of anything
that came out of books or went into them. I thought I would be
glad to think of nothing, for one whole year at least. But all I
had ahead were a few free weeks in August and September
before the round began again. And there was still some of July
and August yet to go.

I heard Judith come in, stop for the mail, and start upstairs,
and I lingered, rocking and comfortable in the afternoon

breeze, before getting up to go to my room and give her favorite place to her, as obviously I had no business there. But rounding the landing and seeing me, she made a gesture that indicated I should stay where I was, and as a further surprise, sat down on the edge of the cot Mrs. Holloway kept out in the hallway and offered me a cigarette, lighting one for herself. She had on a white linen dress with sea horses worked on the front in dark brilliant thread. I never saw a dress like it, before or since.

"Do you want to hear a story?" she began. "I feel I've just got to tell somebody, I don't know why. It happened last spring —you won't tell? That's a stupid thing to ask. What I mean is, if you tell, get it right and don't make it sound silly."

The remark revealed nothing so much as how she thought of me—not me so much personally, I believed, as girls of my average sort—but being curious, I decided not to object. At that point I would have listened to anyone's story, to anything at all that didn't come out of a book.

It had happened one early morning back in the spring, before I had moved in. There were only some elderly ladies across from her, now graduated from a teachers' college nearby and gone back to wherever they came from, no one in the front rooms but an occasional overnight guest. Judith had been standing in her own room at the window looking down on the little garden of the tall brown house next door, wearing nothing and brushing her hair. It was then she felt suddenly drawn, compelled, to look up instead of down and saw in the attic window above a young man leaning close to the glass and watching her. He was sprawled facedown on a bed or bunk and his face wore the expression of one who breathes the air of paradise. She had the distinct feeling that he was exactly where he always spent this hour of the morning, had been there not once, not twice or a dozen times, but morning after morning for perhaps a year, perhaps for the entire three years she had lived there.

"But do you always," I asked her, "stand there without any clothes on and brush your hair? Even in the winter?"

"I guess I do, quite a lot. Yes, I hadn't thought of it so much —but I did for a long time make a habit of it. I don't go near that window now, and as he saw me look up that time he hasn't been back either—at least, I've never seen him. I've not seen him even on this street again since that day."

"Well, who is he?" I asked her. "Did you recognize him?"

To me this all seemed rather funny and I almost laughed, but at this point she became terribly serious and tried twice to go on but her voice, so much in control ordinarily that it seemed a cool comment on anything that could possibly be brought up, like a water sprinkler passing over a lawn, faded out twice when she tried to speak. She essayed another cigarette, but her hands shook so violently, she had to give up.

"I saw him today." She finally got it out. Her anguish at this point was so intense it got across to me something of the force the experience had had for her. I began to feel uneasily that I might have done better to stick to books.

"I've got to tell somebody," she went on. "I've felt for months that I was losing my mind. I couldn't see myself in a psychiatrist's office; in the first place, can't afford it. I began to see that boy's face everywhere—car hops, movie ushers, students on the bus, taxi drivers—for a while, every face could make me look at it at a certain distance, but once the distance lessened and it wouldn't be that face, after all, I would get a sick dizzy feeling, and wild . . . wild!" She laughed. "There was a shoe clerk once. . . . But it's no use remembering them all. A lot of stupid pickups, when they noticed. Somebody to get rid of."

"But," I said, though I hesitated to become practical, "wouldn't it have been simple just to go next door and ask who the boy was—or maybe get somebody to do it for you?"

She hardly heard me, remarking after a long silence, "I did go there once. Nobody was in, but the door was open. So I went all the way upstairs, up to the attic. There's only that one room plus a nightmarish kind of storage place, trunks and old pictures, a box full of tennis stuff, a rack of old dresses and suits. He isn't there anymore, nobody is. Nobody saw me. I went there and came back here and then wondered if I dreamed it all. I wondered if I was dreaming when I came back and was actually still up in that attic. And next I wondered if I were both places and could look down at myself, in my own room."

"Good Lord," I said, and saw there wasn't any end to thoughts like that. "But you saw him. You said you met him today."

"He crossed the street by the grill and I was coming out, so we met."

"Then what happened?"

"His name is Yancey Clements. He teaches swimming and gym at the Y. On weekends he keeps the desk there. Sometimes he works àt a high school gym over in the east of the city. He used to be a paper boy."

At the end of this recital, I broke out laughing, but she did not hear me laugh. She had turned pale and her makeup seemed to be too strong for her face. Crazy as it all might sound to me, it had succeeded in stirring her as ordinary things did not.

"So did you talk to him?" I asked.

"Oh, he knew right away why I stopped him. I felt he understood everything in a minute, even before I spoke or got across the street with him. He said he'd moved from that house. I think he decided to move the day I looked up. Then he said he wouldn't see me."

"So that finishes that," I said.

"It doesn't finish anything. Why do you think that? I begged him. Indeed I did. Finally, he gave in. He's going to have a drink with me, tonight, and we'll talk, something will happen to break it up for me. I've got to break it up, you see. It's got into everything."

She had wandered nervously about the cot, and had reached the pair of windows through which the breeze was now blowing more strongly. The white sheer curtains, standing out, blew around her, and she looked hectic and for the first time I thought this house could not really contain her, a big friendly old comfortable innocent house like this. She was threatening it already, and had been for a long time.

* * *

Singular though it was, I for some reason did not mention this conversation to anyone for a time, nor did I receive any further confidence from Judith. I did not, for one thing, see her, even in passing. At the weekend she went off early with the law student in the Pontiac and did not reappear till Monday.

When I finally talked about her, it was to a graduate student named Scott Crawford—older even than twenty-four, I guess—who worked near me in the library and sometimes asked me over to the grill for coffee, or across from the campus to a café for a beer. This time, evening being nearly on us, it was across the street we went, and that was how I happened to come out with it all. It would have been surprising if I hadn't, though, for I had been confiding just about everything I had on my mind to Scott Crawford, for about a year now, and he talked a lot to me too, seeming to enjoy it, for we used to laugh a lot together.

"So what happened when she saw him?" he asked me.

"Well, I don't know yet," I said.

"It's funny your telling me," he said.

"Well," I said, "I knew you knew her slightly."

"Slightly! What gave you that impression? I used to go with her."

"I didn't know that."

"I was never so in love in my life."

"I didn't know that either," I said.

"I know you didn't, or you wouldn't have mentioned her current problem, I don't think. At least, not in the way you did, like a curious thing. It is a curious thing. But once you understand her tendencies, then it gets pretty clear. She broke everything off with me. Reason? She couldn't see herself as a professor's wife in some pokey little college town. She has this idea about herself, about her own image. Being intelligent and looking like that, I guess you think it's just a happy miracle. Well, maybe it ought to be a happy miracle, but how is she not to realize it? And realizing it, how is she not to ask herself the main question: What's good enough? What's great enough? What could possibly be good or great enough for Judith Kane? Not that she'd come right out with it, nothing blunt or corny.

But if she doesn't say it to herself, she's letting the mirror say it, forty times a day. Do I think she was right to give me up? Sure, I think she was right. I agree with her."

I had to grin a little because he said this last in the self-amused way he had, half-bitterness, half-gaiety, that made him engaging and showed his intelligence to me much more than the doctor's dissertation he was slaving over, trying to get it done before school was out, so he could qualify for a higher salary somewhere. I would probably never read it anyway. Scott Crawford smoked a pipe and carried masses of stuff around with him, to stoke it and clean it and light it and so on. He worked on this pipe as hard as some men work on cars. Picking all his junk off the table took about five minutes at the least, and during all this time he thought steadily on about the state of affairs at Mrs. Holloway's.

I, meantime, thought on about him, about what I knew of him, that is. He lived near the East Campus, two blocks over toward the park, in an apartment with thin walls and sprung furniture. His wife was rather pretty but had begun to look tired of the life there. Her heart was set on having a house someday. He sometimes asked a few of us over to have a beer and talk about things. The baby had cried with a heat rash the last time I was there. That was June, I remembered, thinking it must by now be about melted away like a snail, but he said it was all right. That he was attractive, everyone agreed; though that he was completely unconcerned about it, all could see. He was respected by the faculty, and I once overheard a professor say that he had a classical, unsentimental mind. He spoke with a harsh, backcountry R, almost like a Yankee, and this gave a clean, intellectual turn to his speech, and drew the kind of attention to it that clarity always commands.

That night, when we got out on the street where the evening was still coming slowly on through the lingering heat from pavement and grass, I could sense the direction of his thoughts, like seeing the segment of a path. "No good will come of it," he said, and shook himself together for going back to the library and getting down to his grind. As we approached a parting of ways within the library foyer, he threw an arm around me. "Look, honey, you find out what happened, hear?"

I didn't say I would or wouldn't, just ran up the steps away from him, wishing I'd never mentioned Judith Kane. Had she confided in me because she had learned somehow that I knew Scott Crawford? I wondered. Whether the answer was yes or no, I just was not going to go into it any further, just as I was not going to conclude that Scott had married his wife Ruth on the rebound, or let it interest me in the least that he was never going to be really happy now. Having been so terribly, gorgeously, deeply in love with Judith. What business was it of mine? I had wasted time over there talking and would have to work till ten instead of nine. I ran down the hall to plunge into a mass of stacked-up carbons on onionskin with footnotes two thirds the way up every page, and ran smack into my professor, who had come back over for a book.

"What's the matter with you?" he asked.

"Nothing," I said, breathing beer upon him, without a doubt.

"Must be good," he said, an automatic phrase. He never really noticed anything that wasn't down in print.

What he was working on was a treatise on Hawthorne's ideas of good and evil. He kept me working along with him to verify footnotes and I had to wade through a lot of old musty New England sermons, too, copying out parts that might have some bearing on his train of thought. The odd thing was that this man seemed so mild and inattentive—he could never get my name straight—I wondered if he ever would have thought there was any such thing as good and evil if he hadn't come across the words in books. Ideas did excite him, though. He once came in just bursting with something which had come to him while walking past the grill, namely, that the great white squid in *Moby Dick* might have been deliberately used by Melville to symbolize love and goodness, just as the white whale was nemesis and evil. He was heatedly explaining this to me, and I couldn't help but think what his wife had to listen to while cooking supper. "A squid?" I said. "You mean those awful things like octopuses?" It sort of took the wind out of his sails, putting it that way.

I chose to ignore Scott Crawford's request to check up on Judith Kane. Wouldn't that have made me more of a go-between than ever? I didn't want to be one.

Then one late middle of the night I woke and couldn't sleep, the heat was so intense and not a breath of air was stirring. The sheet stuck to my back, and I could hear the tap drip from the kitchen downstairs, and somewhere way off a motor grinding, trying to start on a rundown battery. I got up to run water over my wrists and put a wet cloth on the back of my neck and do all the other little things they cheerfully advise in the newspaper columns when you're stifling to death, and when I went through the hall past the cot and rocking chair there sat Judith, smoking.

"Sit down," she said. "We'll whisper. Have a cigarette."

"It's not only too hot to smoke; it's too hot to breathe," I said.

"True," she said, lighting a fresh one off the stub.

"So what happened?" I asked her. "Did you see the gym teacher?"

"He didn't come. I looked him up the next day at the Y and he just got angry. He said he didn't come because he didn't want to."

"So he was just a peeper and starer, after all," I said. Why couldn't she stop it?

"I don't believe it," she answered at once, with the quickness of anger, or fear. "I don't believe that for a minute."

"But isn't he a lot younger than—" I paused, "younger than we are?"

"Oh, sure." She laughed in a hushed clear way, and seemed in such a perfectly good humor with herself I couldn't think but that another person was suffering like this somewhere and she was describing it all. "I wasn't considering matrimony," she said. "He knows how I feel; he knows it all. He just doesn't care. He saw me as I am, and he does not care. It's all I can hear, all the time. A voice inside, on a record as big as the moon. Would you like to live like that?"

"I'd stop it," I said. "Shut it off."

"How?"

"Just do it," I said. "Do it anyway."

"I can't," she said. "I just can't."

She did look, even in the dark, terribly thin. She had begun to look like a *Vogue* model. I asked then if she still had her job —she said she had given it up. I wondered what she was living on, but guessed she hadn't eaten anything in days and did nothing but smoke, read, and drink lemonade. The law student had called about a million times, but she never would come to the phone, and even he had given up. She made me think there must be times when the world is separated from yourself with something like a wall of glass that you cannot find a foothold on, and what if the key to the one gate in it is in the possession of something which calls itself Yancey Clements and works at the Y?

"Just to talk to him would make me feel better," she said, in a calmer tone. "He won't even do that. I'm a mass of neuroses," she laughed, "and everything I do or think is in a world by itself and can't get out."

"Maybe you ought to just try going out and eating a lot of good food," I suggested. "Starting with breakfast in the morning."

She seemed to give me up, and snuffing out her final cigarette, wadding the pack for hurling in the wastebasket, she started back to her room. "What's it to you?" she asked, good-humoredly, as always. "What should it be to you?"

Her door closed, and I had never once mentioned Scott Crawford. I had clammed up dead to the world around his name.

The next morning Mrs. Holloway stopped me at the door. She wanted to know what on earth was the matter with Judith. Was she sick? If so, why not see a doctor? She had taken her chance, when Judith was in the bath one day, to peek into that room, and could hardly see anything through smoke so thick it looked like a gambling house. There were choked ashtrays islanded around and shoals of books, and the bed looked to have had a wild cat in it. I said I didn't know anything about it, I was always working. But I had heard the mounting anxiety in her voice and knew her mild, widowed world was being shaken, trembling like a great big web that's all carefully worked out to hold in every part. Next thing the house would shake, for they'd be at each other in some final way.

After lunch I went over to the Y and asked for Yancey Clements. They said he wasn't working there right now but was out doing some sort of gym teaching or other in a high school in the east of the city. That was how I happened to be on the bus in the early afternoon heat riding to a strange part of town where they had, miraculously, tiny friendly houses with small front yards, small plots of flowers, windows open, radios going. How nice, I kept thinking. How nice it is.

The high school, a large, dark brick building, was summer-empty. From the gym, way out in the back wing, I heard somebody bouncing a basketball. There was the usual acrid smell, the deep thumbed-book smells, chalk, blackboards, erasers, and floor polish smells, but all breathed over and subdued by summer, and back near the gym door, overriding everything, were the sweat smells of basketball uniforms, along with the sound of the ball spanking harder and harder in the silence of the building. I was sure the boy with the basketball would turn out to be Yancey Clements, but I was wrong.

He was only a stringy high school boy in a moth-eaten red jersey and blue trunks too big for him, whamming the ball at the floor as though he'd never done another thing in his life. I thought I would have to go and take the ball away from him to get his attention, but he finally looked up. "I'm looking for Yancey Clements," I said, or shouted, over the sound of the ball. "Is he here, or not?" The boy jerked his head. Then Yancey himself stepped out of a small dark doorway that led back of the stands into the lockers, beyond a doubt.

I knew right away this really was Yancey because I had seen him, I now realized, from time to time at the hamburger place near the Y. He must have just showered and dressed because he had on a pair of old cotton trousers and a clean white shirt. He was blond with a shock of hair that came up like a rooster's comb, and he had a very funny face, with protuberant teeth that crossed each other in front, a high bridged nose, and gray-blue eyes. He was absolutely humorless and he came straight to me before I could speak and said, "Don't think I don't know why you're here."

Good Lord, I thought, *he thinks I'm after him, too.*

"Listen, you come over with me," he said. "I was just going for a Coke."

We crossed the street, which was empty, and sat down in the drugstore. He ordered Cokes for both of us, and when they came he stuck a pair of straws in his bottle, and then did the same for me, in the manner of one making an enormous concession, and behaving like a gentleman if it killed him. "I prefer a glass with ice in it," I almost said, but not wanting to throw him into a rage, I let it go.

"That girl is nuts," he said. "I don't care about seeing her. I told her that. I just don't care. She's beautiful, but she's nuts. Look at the trouble I've gone to. You think I like living over here? I couldn't stay over there and have her hanging around, that's a positive fact."

"But look," I said, "I'm sure she'd be different from what you think if you'd only talk to her. She might be reasonable and very sweet, and get over it all just over a Coke in the drugstore —like this, for instance. What harm would there be in trying? She laughs about it all herself," I added.

"Oh, she does?"

"You did start it," I said. "And now she feels awful. If only you were a little kind—"

"Kind!" He bit his lip stubbornly; he was nervous and tough, and no one should have said "kind" to him.

I rode back on the bus; I was the only person on it besides the bus driver and a colored maid who rode only four stops, and looked out the window the whole time, daydreaming. It was when we got on the long hill going from one side of the city to the other (and what with very little traffic at that hour of the afternoon, the bus went flying along, reeling, bounding and rattling over the rough uneven brick and asphalt) that all the

:olored beads began to fall off my hat. It was an old hat, and I ~~ad~~ had found it in the college office where I worked, having left it ~~here~~ there after church last Easter. It was the only hat I owned; I ~~ad~~ had had it since high school. It was navy blue straw with a ~~unch~~ bunch of large varicolored glass beads sewed on the band, and ~~t~~ it went with everything and was never out of style and showed ~~10~~ no age at all except that I had often in moments of stress ~~eached~~ reached up and twisted the wire which threaded the beads to-~~gether~~ gether, and I must undoubtedly have twisted it several times ~~hat~~ that day or else the wire had about died of old age, because ~~every~~ every time the bus hit another bump in the road another bead ~~ell~~ fell off on the floor. They made a terrible racket rolling and ~~umbling~~ tumbling around, and as the hill was steep, several rolled all the ~~vay~~ way down the aisle and up around the driver's feet. He stopped ~~he~~ the bus at the bottom of the hill. "Listen, miss," he said, "do ~~vou~~ you want these things?"

"Well, no, I guess not," I said. It just seemed like too much ~~rouble~~ trouble; and besides, how would I get them back on? He began ~~o~~ to pick them up anyway.

"I thought at first you were throwing them," he said. "There ~~vere~~ were some kids in here, throwing some marbles the other day. ~~One~~ One or two people tripped up on them. Them things," he said, "are worse'n banana peel, and if you think of old people and ~~ll~~ all . . ."

"I wasn't throwing anything," I said. "It was an accident."

That night I saw Scott Crawford, or rather he saw me. He ~~came~~ came all the way over to my office in the library where I had to ~~work~~ work that evening to make up for the afternoon.

"How is Judith?" he asked me. We had gone out to sit on the ~~steps~~ steps of the library by then, and it was a calm, full late summer ~~night~~ night, so rich and sweet it wouldn't do to think too much about ~~t~~ it. There were the low mountains outside the city, covered with ~~neavy~~ heavy late summer green, and the long roads that went tilting ~~hrough~~ through them, winding on forever.

"I don't want to hear about it anymore," I said. "I don't ~~want~~ want to talk about it. I've done the best I could." I told him ~~about~~ about Yancey Clements.

"She's run up a blind alley and won't believe it," he said.

"Can't you understand it? That minute she looked up and saw
him watching, blank as a mirror, but as if a mirror could look
back, admire, finally possess . . ."

He had clenched his hand beside me in the dark and before I
knew it, I had grasped it, trying to get the fingers open and
relaxed. "I wish I'd never mentioned her," I said. "We always
had such a good time till she got into everything. Why don't
you just stop it?"

"Stop it?" He did unclench his hand, take mine, and give it
an affectionate squeeze, which went through me deep and clear.
But it was only affection; that was all. "Stop it how? How?"

She was almost present then, his thought of her had summoned her before us both, alive in the strong disaster of her
looks, which his intelligence and wit and everything I admired
about him could only multiply until she had wrapped him up in
a million ways and drawn him endlessly down. She, too, he was
saying, with fine logic, had fallen for herself; it was not Yancey
Clements she wanted, only that the lightning stroke of his look
had thrown her off-balance, maybe for good and all.

"If you don't stop it," I said, "it's just going to go on down
forever, like the bottomless pit. Isn't it?"

At long last, he agreed. "You're right. I'm going to let it go."
He got up and walked away, vanished into the night among the
thick tree shadows. I wanted to run after him, had wanted to
maybe for months now, but all this of Judith had trapped and
denied my own feelings for him. They rose now, swept over me
and fell; my heart ran after him, but I never moved at all. The
words I might have said had all been taken.

He came to the house the next afternoon. I was upstairs
working so did not see him on the street, and he must have just
walked in without knocking, because no one challenged him or
went to the door. I heard his first step down below and knew
what had happened. The whole house knew it too, that ramified
abode of women, women, women, over the long years. Turret to
basement, it had needed this for a long time, that stride in the
hall, that step on the stairs. Out in the upstairs corridor, I
heard him blundering, trying one door after another, saying

"Judith? Judith?" Then he found her. "Who?" she said, and then with a low cry, filled with surprise, opening toward joy, "Scott? Oh, Scott!" She must have risen then, out of her ruins, to go to him. I heard her stumble, fall and get up, or be lifted up by him.

Judith came to my room after he left. It was just at twilight. The spell was broken; as if to prove it, there had even been some rain. She had emerged at last, with new purpose, to bathe and dress, had put up her hair, got makeup on, stained her shoes fresh as chalk, and slipped into the lime-green dress, which hung on her limbs like a nightgown or a robe.

"You did it," she said, reflectively. "It was all because you talked to him about me, wasn't it? But one thing," she continued, leaning in the doorway. "One thing. You've got to understand it. I didn't know you knew him."

"It's a lie," I said. "A lie! You must have known, you had to know! You used me to make him come back. You can't deny it!"

She shook her lovely head; it was gaunt and rapacious now as some tall white bird, one with a great latent wingspread for long flight. Where would she lead him to, where would she drop him when she moved furiously on to some other high perch, to astonish and confound whoever found her there? My heart filled up with dread. For him, I guess; that was where the dread started, but it had a way of spreading: it was more than just for him.

"Don't look at me like that," she said, raising her hand uneasily to touch her hair. "Why are you looking that way?"

"How could he do it, come here, come to you, when he knows about Yancey Clements? You were ready to crawl to that awful boy, that peeper, that vile, stupid, no-account . . ." I couldn't go on. But the questions forced themselves up anyway, kept rising to my lips. "Are they so much alike to you, you can't tell the difference? How could you want them both? How could you?"

Her head had snapped back, and her features strained to the force of my innocent words, as though I were striking her. I saw this, and stopped. In the silence (in which she could have turned and walked away but did not), I saw suddenly appear before my eyes identical streaks of tears from the corners of her eyes downward.

"I don't know," she whispered at last. "Oh, believe me, I don't know why."

I turned back to my work table, on which papers and books had been scrambled about and ink spilled, a great mess. "It's his most important time," I said. "Right at the end. Exams and all."

"You cared for him, didn't you?"

"Yes, but I . . ." I nodded, and with a strong, releasing sigh that shook me, confessed it. "Yes."

She melted from the threshold, vanished. She had taken that from me, too, I realized, had come for it and easily taken it, my one privacy. She had had to have it, and so had demanded it.

She went out shortly after, going toward whatever place he had said; bone-thin and swift, moving—inexorable, indifferent, and sublime—toward him, as he desired. I watched through the window till I could no longer see her, and only the empty street was there, lit by street lights.

Sentimental Education

by Harold Brodkey

He was very tall, six feet three, and gangling. He had a small head, curiously shaped (his roommate, Dimitri, sometimes accused him of looking like a wedge of cheese), and a hooked nose. He wanted to be a professor in the field of comparative philology, and he believed in Beauty. He studied all the time, and there were moments when he was appalled by how hard he worked. He was known for his crying in movies. He was not unathletic.

Somehow, he had become convinced that he was odd and that only odd girls liked him, pitiable girls who couldn't do any better, and this singed his pride.

It was his fate that this particular night he should see a girl walking up the steps of Widener Library. She was of medium height and had black hair cut short; she was wearing a light-colored coat that floated behind her because she was walking so fast, nearly running, but not quite; and the curve of her forehead and the way her eyes were set took Elgin's breath away. She was so pretty and carried herself so well and had a look of such healthy and arrogant self-satisfaction that Elgin sighed and thought here was the sort of not odd girl who could bestow indescribable benefits on any young man she liked—and on his confidence. She was that very kind of girl, that far from unhappy, that world-contented kind, he believed would never fall for him.

She carried her books next to her bosom. Elgin's eyes followed her up the steps; and then his head turned, his nostrils distended with emotion; and she was gone, vanished into Widener.

"Surely this year," he thought, looking up at the sky. "Now

that I'm almost nineteen." He stretched out his arms, and the leaves on the trees, already growing dry at the approach of autumn, rustled in the breezes.

He thought about that girl once or twice in the days that followed, but the longing for her didn't really take root until he saw her again, two weeks later, at a Radcliffe Jolly-Up in Cabot Hall. It was in one of the dimly lit common rooms, where couples were indefatigably dancing in almost total darkness. Elgin was swaying in place (he was not a good dancer) with a girl who helped him on his German when he caught sight of his Widener Library vision. When the next dance began, he wound through the couples looking for her, to cut in on her, but when he drew near her, he turned and walked over to the wall, where he caught his breath and realized he was frightened.

This was the stroke that fatally wounded him. Knowing he was frightened of that girl, he longed for her, the way men who think they are cowards long for war so they can prove they're not. Or perhaps it was some other reason. The girl had a striking appearance; there was her youth and her proud, clean look to recommend her.

But whatever the reason, he did begin to think about her in earnest. She rose up in clouds of brilliant light in his head whenever he came across certain words in his reading. ("Mistress" was one, "beautiful" another; you can guess the rest.) He did a paper on "The Unpossessable Loved One in Troubadour Poetry." When he walked through the Yard on his way to classes, his eyes revolved nervously and never rested, searching all the faces on all the walks in the hope of seeing her. In fact, on his walks to classes he looked so disordered that a number of his friends asked him if he was feeling ill, and it pleased Elgin, after the first two times this happened, to reply that he was. He was ill with longing.

At night, before going to the dining hall for supper, he would put on his bathrobe and slip down to the pool in the basement of Adams House. There, under the wooden beams, he would swim angrily from one end of the pool to the other, faster and faster, until his arms ached. Then he would take a cold shower.

When he slept, he dreamed of carnage, horses, and speeding

automobiles. He went to French movies and ground his knees against the seat in front of him. He laughed at himself, and decided to break this absurd habit he had got into of thinking all the time about this girl he had never met, but he didn't quite succeed. At last, he admitted to himself that he was in love with her; and one night, sleeping in his lower bunk while Dimitri breathed heavily over his head, he had tears in his eyes because he was so foolish and did desire that girl whom he had seen the two times mentioned and only twice more besides.

Having resigned himself—in imitation of Dante—to a state of perpetual longing, he felt calmer and looked at the world with sad, scholarly eyes. But his equilibrium was delicate, and in December Dimitri began having an affair with a Radcliffe girl named Felicia. Upperclassmen could have girls in their room in the afternoon if they signed them in with the campus policeman who sat in a little room near the main entrance of their house, and signed them out when they left. There was always the chance the policeman would come to the room and check up, but even so on gray December afternoons Dimitri, all bundled up, would come searching through Widener for Elgin and ask him not to come home until after six o'clock because Dimitri was taking Felicia to the room. Then Elgin would sit in front of his books, numbed, unable to read, with fine beads of sweat standing out on his upper lip and forehead.

Once he came back to the room and found Dimitri lying in front of a fire in the fireplace; the fire was being fed by Dimitri's lecture notes. "Oh God, it's you. How I hate your ugly face!" Dimitri said, but Elgin knew what he meant; at that moment, being Elgin and not Felicia was a blasphemy. He tiptoed through the room to hang up his coat and tiptoed out again.

In January, immediately after exams, Elgin came down with flu. He was exhausted. When he was well again, it seemed to him that he had been washed clean and purified. He hardly thought about that girl at all.

But one sunny, cold morning in February Elgin saw her standing in front of Sever Hall. She was wearing long blue woolen socks, and she was talking to a pock-marked boy in a raccoon overcoat. Elgin suddenly turned and went into Sever and waited in the hall until the bell rang. The girl came in, and Elgin followed her upstairs and into a classroom; he sat three rows in back of her. It was a course given by Professor Bush on Metaphysical Poets of the Seventeenth Century. And that afternoon Elgin went and got permission to transfer from The Victorian Novel to that class.

The girl's name was Caroline Hedges and she came from Baltimore. She was a horsewoman of considerable ability. She spent a good deal of her time on clothes, not ever being quite sure where true elegance lay. She was inclined to buy pale colors, blouses one size too large for her, and tweeds. She was easily embarrassed. She read a good deal, her favorite books being *The Charterhouse of Parma, Anna Karenina,* and *Madame Bovary.*

She was very proud and easily moved by appeals to her courage. She considered she'd had a happy childhood, and she liked her family (although she could not help looking down on them a little because their name was not famous in the history of America). When she was ten, she had briefly loved a cousin of hers, who was twelve, and who had taken her to the National Museum of Art in Washington and told her the names of the great painters.

At Radcliffe, her freshman year, she discovered that she had been sheltered, compared to most of the other girls, and she felt young and slightly ashamed of herself. This gave her a look of great purity, and she was something of a belle. But late in the spring of her freshman year she stayed up all one night, obsessed and genuinely moved by the fact that she was intelligent and hadn't really known it before. She had just found it out by noticing that section men and assistant professors and sometimes full professors liked to hear her talk in class. From that night on, she limited her dating and threw herself into studying.

"It is poetry that I love," she wrote in her diary. "It is hard for me to explain why. Once when I was staying with Aunt Kitty in New York I went for a walk in Central Park when it was snowing. In the zoo I saw the Bactrian camel standing in the middle of its pen. It was holding its head straight up in the air with its mouth open and its tongue out and the snowflakes were falling on it. Perhaps he never saw snow before. I'm not exactly sure where Bactria is or what its climate is like—perhaps it was remembering snow. That is how I feel about poetry."

Another entry read, "My mother writes and asks me if I still see Louis Du Pont whom she thought such a charming boy. How can Mother think anyone so plump is charming?"

Early in April of her junior year, she wrote, "Today in Metaphysical Poetry, we discussed the tradition of Platonic Love in Jacobean England. A boy named Elgin Smith spoke brilliantly, I thought. He described the winters the young people spent in those vast country houses, twenty or so young people visiting in one house, with two or three chaperons, and snow everywhere. They sang and gave masques and such things. Because young people are so hot-blooded, it was necessary to devise a code of courtship to restrain them, for marriages of alliance had to be made later. Needless to say, it didn't work, Platonic Love, I mean, and it was much more often written about than observed. I do so admire brilliance and wish that I had some. This young man had the oddest voice. It is positively nasal and twangs and twangs. I wanted to put my hand over his mouth and tell him 'Sh-h-h.' He is terribly intense and nervous. He has borrowed a pencil from me several times, and he asked me to have coffee with him once. I said I couldn't, but next time he asks, I will accept. I long for some really intelligent friends."

When you consider the combustibility of the emotions of these two young people, it is hardly surprising that within two weeks of their first long conversation together they were trembling when they talked, and found themselves oppressed whenever silences fell. The impulse to discuss this state of affairs with each other kept recurring, but they fought it, until one afternoon when they were sitting in the Cambridge Common and having a cigarette together before separating for dinner.

All through the Common, young mothers were sitting,

bored, by baby carriages, and beneath the trees, newly come to leaf, children were climbing on the old cannon. Abraham Lincoln was brooding under his canopy, and trolleys clanged on Massachusetts Avenue.

"Elgin," Caroline said, "we've talked about a hundred things, a thousand things, I bet."

"Yes."

"But we've never talked about what we think of each other."

"No," he said, twisting his fingers together. "I guess we never have."

"I—I don't approve of it, actually," Caroline said. "Analyzing things and all. Some things are better left unsaid."

"I agree," Elgin said. The words seemed to explode on his lips, leaving a faintly surprised look on his face.

"Do you?" Caroline said. For her part, she was having difficulty hanging on to her poise.

"There isn't much people can say that hasn't been said before," Elgin said with finality. Then he added, "It's my reading. I've read so much I guess I'm a little jaded."

"I see," said Caroline. "Well, it's a fascinating subject."

"Yes," said Elgin, "it is."

They sat in silence for several seconds, both of them on the verge of speaking, but Elgin was frightened and Caroline was disconcerted, as if her ideas of what could happen had been trampled on and left for dead.

"Let's get started back," Elgin said. Caroline rose and the two of them walked on toward Radcliffe, past the Hotel Continental. At the corner, Caroline said, "You coming by this evening?"

Elgin nodded.

Caroline reached out and shook Elgin's hand, which was a strange thing for her to do.

"Caroline!" Elgin said sharply.

"Yes."

"Let's go have dinner together."

"Where? I thought you were broke."

"The Chinese restaurant."

"All right, if I have enough money." She opened her purse

and looked; she and Elgin went Dutch most places. "I've got two dollars and some change." They linked arms and walked back to the Common.

"I think Vaughan is a little bit of a bore," Caroline said. "Really, the language has deteriorated so much since Donne."

They sat down on the same bench where they had sat before.

Elgin said, "I assume since our conversation fifteen minutes ago it would be terrible if I talked about the way I feel about you."

"Oh, no," said Caroline. "Go right ahead."

"Well, they're very strong."

"I'd more or less guessed that," Caroline said, unable to make her voice sound normal.

"But I never mentioned it before," Elgin said, "because I didn't want anything to come up that might make you want to stop seeing me."

"I understand," Caroline said. "That was very subtle of you."

"Please shut up," Elgin said. "I'm trying to get something out and it's very hard. I want you to know I'm not just chasing you or anything like that."

"Oh?"

"I saw you last fall. You were going into Widener. It was—you know—at first sight."

"Elgin!"

"It was. I only took Metaphysical Poetry because you were taking it. Caroline, I have deep feelings about you."

Caroline felt an intense sense of relief. "Well, I always thought so," she said. "But I wasn't sure." Then she realized Elgin was trembling. "Elgin, what's wrong?"

A child ran by with a red disintegrator pistol. "You're not angry?" Elgin asked.

"Of course not!" she said ringingly.

"You're not going to tell me that the most I can expect is your friendship? And if I expect more we oughtn't to see each other anymore?"

There was silence. "I hadn't thought this far," Caroline said. She thought it was much more decent if she didn't have to mention her feelings; she felt trapped. "Well, Elgin, I'll tell you, I certainly don't want to stop seeing you." She moved her legs until they were spread ungracefully. "But, really, I think . . . we ought to be careful and not get, oh, I don't know, sloppy, if you know what I mean."

"I don't mind that," Elgin said. He swallowed. "But is it all right— Is it all right, Caroline, if I show how I feel a little more?" His voice rose and quivered with longing.

"I don't know what you mean."

"You do."

"Honestly, Elgin, I—"

"You do!"

"I suppose so. . . . Yes. Do show it. Let's be honest. For God's sake, who can it hurt? Yes, let's not be priggish."

To her astonishment and delight, Elgin caught her hand and pressed it to his lips.

They hadn't kissed then, nor did they kiss each other for several days afterward. It was a tacit confession that they suspected the presence of passion, and in such cases, if one is at all practical, one stands back, one dawdles, one doesn't rush in to confront the beast in its lair. Or to put it another way, one doesn't go tampering with the floodgates. What they did, after this conversation, was suddenly to become lighthearted. They made jokes; Caroline stole Elgin's notebook from his hands and made him chase her; they discussed Metaphysical Poetry. And when this lightness and gaiety had eased their suspicion and their fright was in abeyance, Caroline decided she wanted Elgin to kiss her.

She was walking up Garden Street in late afternoon, and the sunlight was clear and golden. There was a light wind that ruffled her hair, and she was striding along, passing any number of couples, Harvard boys and Radcliffe girls, some with their arms around each other's waists, some holding hands, some just walking side by side. Caroline decided then, in a single flash; and the next minute her cheeks began to glow and she pushed happily at her hair, which kept blowing across her eyes.

At seven o'clock that evening, Elgin arrived at Cabot Hall to pick her up. He was wearing his shabby tweed jacket and khaki pants and a striped tie. Caroline came downstairs wearing her prettiest sweater, a pink cashmere. Her hair was carefully brushed and she wore lipstick, so Elgin knew something was up.

"I'd sort of like to go to a movie tonight," she said. "I've got enough money for both of us if you're flat."

Elgin told her he had a little cash. They settled on the U.T. —the University Theatre in Harvard Square.

"I'm in the mood for gangsters," Caroline said as they emerged from Cabot into the spring evening.

The sky between the trees was purple, a deep, stirring plum color. Caroline put her arm through Elgin's, and they strode briskly through the Quad toward Garden Street, and then through the Common—one of a number of couples, in a long, irregular procession stretching from the Radcliffe dormitories to Harvard Square.

"I finished my paper on Donne," Elgin said.

Caroline laughed inconsequently, and Elgin laughed, too, for no good reason.

They passed through the middle of the Common, by Lincoln's statue, where a lamp cast a ghostly white glare on leaves and benches and the surface of the walk. Caroline's charming face swam into the light, shadows fell across it, and Elgin closed his eyes.

Caroline pressed his hand. They hurried.

All during the movie, they sat holding both of each other's hands, and their shoulders touching. Entwined and tangled like that, they giggled together whenever the movie became particularly violent. They couldn't stop giggling after a while, as the death toll in the movie mounted. When the movie ended, they left and Elgin bought Caroline a chocolate ice-cream cone at St. Clair's and they walked down to the Charles River.

The Charles looked placid, and glimmered as it quietly flowed under its bridges; the lights of Eliot House were reflected in its surface. Caroline put her head on Elgin's shoulder. They breathed in unison, the two of them, standing on the bank

of the river, and then Elgin said, "It's clumsy to ask, but, Caroline, do you really . . . or . . . would I . . ." He missed her
lips, kissing her cheek instead, and he was holding her so
tightly that she couldn't move and correct his mistake. But a
minute later he corrected his error himself. They both had difficulty breathing. "I love, I love you, I love you," he whispered.

It sounded beautiful in the moonlight, the river ran quietly
beneath the bridge, and Caroline was glad she had let him kiss
her.

After that they took to kissing each other a good deal. They
met every afternoon at Widener. When one of them broke off
work, the other would break off, too, and they would both go
downstairs. Along either side of the steps rose large stone arms,
which looked as if they should be surmounted by statues, but
they were bare, and in spring, in the afternoons, on both of
them there would usually be people sitting, sometimes alone,
sometimes in pairs. Here Elgin and Caroline would sit and look
out over the Yard toward the Chapel.

At four-thirty, they would go to Massachusetts Avenue and
have a cup of coffee in one of the luncheonettes. Usually they
separated then, Caroline to go to Cabot Hall, Elgin to Adams
House, for supper, but some evenings, when they had the
money, they had dinner together at a Chinese restaurant near
the Square, where the food was very cheap. (Elgin didn't like
taking her to Adams House on the nights when girls were allowed in the dining hall, because it reminded him that he was
young and ineffectual and under the control of an institution.)
In the evenings, they studied, either in the library or in one of
the common rooms at Cabot, and at nine o'clock when the
library closed, they would walk down to the riverbank. Elgin
had an old raincoat that he wore, and they used that to spread
on the grass, to sit on. They sat side by side and shared long,
rather tender kisses. At first on these expeditions they talked
about poetry, but after a while conversation began to seem disagreeable, and they sat in silence.

Then they began to leave off studying at Widener earlier in
the afternoon, at three-thirty, or even three. Caroline liked go-

ing with Elgin to the Boston Museum of Fine Arts, and they would look at the pictures and, when their feet were tired, go and sit in the Fens, the park just behind the Museum, which has a rose garden at one end of it. Caroline wanted Elgin to lose his Middle Western pronunciation, and the excuse they used for these jaunts was that this was time spent in teaching Elgin how to speak. He would bring a book, Bacon's *Essays,* or Montaigne's, or Jeremy Taylor's *Sermons,* or Johnson's *Rasselas*—good, sturdy books, with sentences so rich that sometimes Elgin's voice grew fuzzy with the pleasure he felt reading them.

"Always, all-ways, not oll-wez," Caroline would say.

"Wait, Caroline, just wait a bit, listen to this," and he would read another rolling, rhetorical period. "Isn't that gorgeous?"

"Not gorgcous," Caroline would say. "That's not the right word somehow."

"Oh, it is in this case," Elgin would say. "It's absolutely exact."

And Caroline, struggling not to be moved, would say, "I suppose. I suppose, just barely."

Then Elgin started reading Colette and Boccaccio. Now, when silence fell, something seemed to be lying beside them on the grass, breathing softly. Glances, trees, the movements of people in the park suddenly split off from the commonsensical, taken-for-granted world and became strange. Caroline frowned more and more often, turned into something very like a nag. She made Elgin buy new ties and have his shoes reheeled. Often, in the afternoons, she would take him to St. Clair's and make him drink freshly squeezed orange juice. When it was raining, she still insisted they go for walks because it was good for Elgin. She took to proofreading all his papers and typing them over for him because he was a poor and careless typist. One day, Elgin read to her the story in Boccaccio of the young girl who used to tell her mother that she wanted to sleep in the garden in order to hear the nightingale sing, but the girl met her lover in the garden—*he* was the nightingale. Elgin read this story to Caroline in an intense and quavering voice. For a week afterward, Caroline walked back and forth to classes hearing in her head the phrase "listening to the nightingale." Finally, the phrase came to stand for so much, it aroused such deep tumult in her and made her feel so lonely and deprived, that one night Elgin came back to his room, woke Dimitri from a sound sleep, and asked him to stay away from the room the next afternoon.

It turned out that Elgin and Caroline were both virgins.

Their first dip in sensual waters left them nonplussed. They didn't know what to make of it. They tried to persuade themselves that something had really happened, but the minute it was over, they couldn't believe they had ever done such a thing. They rushed into further experiences; they broke off in the middle of embraces and looked at each other, stunned and delighted. "Is this really happening?" they both asked at different times, and each time the other said, "No," and they would laugh. They knew that nothing they did was real, was actual. They had received a blow on the head and were prey to erotic imaginings, that was all. But at the same time they half realized it was true, they *were* doing these things, and then the fact that they, Caroline and Elgin, shared such intimacy dazed and fascinated them; and when they were together, they tried to conceal it, but this indescribable attraction they felt for each other kept making itself known and draining all the strength from their bodies. They tried to make jokes about themselves and this odd little passion they felt. "We're unskilled labor," Elgin said. "You know, I'm just giving in because you're irresistible," Caroline said. She always pretended that she was completely dispassionate about sex. It just happened that she was susceptible to Elgin's entreaties. But he was too shy to entreat unless she encouraged him, and Caroline often felt like the worst kind of hypocrite. The truth of the matter is, they were caught up in a fever of their senses.

Caroline would have her lunch in Cabot Hall, locked in an impenetrable haze of daydreaming, not even hearing the girls chattering around her. She would walk to Widener, and if boys she knew stopped her to talk, she would stare at them stonily, afraid the boy might guess her feelings for Elgin and think they applied to him. She would run up the stairs of Widener, past the Sargent murals, petrified that Elgin might not be waiting 'or her. Every day this fear grew worse; but every day he was :here, sitting at one of the long wooden tables in the reading :oom, beneath the great coffered ceiling, and the look on his 'ace when he caught sight of her would make Caroline smile giddily, because she had never known before what a miraculous power she had over men.

They managed a wry stiffness when they were in public. They spoke to each other in tones of the crudest good-fellow-ship. Elgin called her "Girl." "Girl, you finished with that book?" Caroline called Elgin "Cheese." "No, Cheese. Don't rush me." They didn't hold hands or touch. They thought they fooled everyone, but everyone who knew them guessed, and they both told their roommates. In fact, they wanted to talk about what was happening to them to everyone; this news was always on the tip of their tongues; and so they got into the habit of suddenly breaking off conversations with their friends when the impulse to confess grew too strong to be contained a moment longer, and all their friends thought they were becoming very queer and difficult indeed.

Each afternoon that they met in Widener started on this high level of confusion and rapidly ran downhill. The minute hand of the clock over the door of the reading room jerked every sixty seconds, marking off a whole minute in one movement, and at two-thirty they were no longer capable of speech. Elgin would be pale or flushed. He would draw breath irregularly through a mouth he couldn't quite close, or through distended nostrils, and this phenomenon would fascinate Caroline, except that she couldn't look at him for too long without feeling the most awful pain in her head. Finally, Elgin would gasp, "Well?"

"I'm finished," Caroline would say in the weakest voice imaginable.

They would walk in silence to Adams House, and Elgin would sign Caroline in at the policeman's room. In silence they would mount the stairs, and Elgin would unlock the door of his room, and then they would fall into each other's arms, sometimes giggling with relief, sometimes somber, sometimes almost crying with the joy of this privacy and this embrace.

Then, later, both of them dressed and their faces scrubbed, Caroline, like an addict, would descend on Elgin's bureau and haul out his torn and buttonless shirts. She didn't know how to sew, but she thought she did, and she sat on Elgin's couch, smiling to herself, softly humming, and sewed buttons on wrong. Elgin tried to study, but his moods whirled and spun him around so that one minute he'd be reading quietly and the next minute he'd be striding up and down the room on the worn carpet, wringing his hands or else waving them aloft and denouncing the College and the American Educational System, full of rage, but not knowing with what or why, and forced to let it out any way he could, while Caroline, faintly bored, ignored him mostly and sewed.

Every once in a while, Caroline would cry. Then she would be unable to dress properly, and she'd drag around the room with her hair badly combed, her shoes off, looking slatternly, and say, "I don't know what's wrong with me. Actually, nothing's wrong with me." But every few minutes tears would course down her cheeks. Nor did she know why she cried; she was as innocent of understanding herself as she was of understanding Elgin.

Sometimes they quarrelled. Once, it was because Caroline wouldn't use Elgin's towel.

"If you loved me, you'd use it."

"I'd adore to use *your* towel," Caroline said, "but *this* towel is dirty."

Elgin thought her preposterous; she called Elgin a boor and slammed out of the room. She reached the bottom of the stairs and started back up and heard Elgin coming down. Neither of them said a word; they didn't apologize or mention this episode again. They went for a walk along the riverbank and talked about Metaphysical Poetry.

On Saturdays, Elgin took Caroline to the Harvard courts to play tennis. Caroline had fine ankles and legs, and while they walked to the courts, Elgin kept stealing glances at them, which made Caroline nervous. She was a good tennis player, as good as Elgin, but he could throw her off her game by charging the net and yelling at her, "I've got you now!" This would rattle her so she'd completely miss the ball, and then she would laugh with exasperation.

When he served, he made a point of calling the score in a loud, cheerful, teasing voice: "Thirty–love!" He'd say the "love" in such a way that Caroline would blush, and then she would try to drive the ball directly at him, and most of the time it went out of bounds.

One afternoon, they were in each other's arms in Elgin's room. Elgin was whispering, "I love you, Caroline. I love you so much," and someone knocked on the door. The sound seemed to blind Elgin, who squeezed his eyes closed, as tightly as he could. The knock was repeated a second time, and a third, echoing in the small room. Then the footsteps retreated.

Elgin got up and fetched cigarettes and towels for them both. They leaned back on the couch, at opposite ends, wrapped in towels, and smoked. They didn't mention the fact that they were afraid it had been the campus policeman and they would be expelled. They discussed whether or not they were depraved.

"We are," Caroline said. "Otherwise, we wouldn't be so ashamed."

"We don't have to be ashamed," Elgin said. "We only pretend we are anyway, to be polite."

"You're a rebel," Caroline said gloomily. "You can say that. But I'm a conformist. I'm basically a nice girl. I *am* ashamed."

The pressure of details, the maze of buttons, hooks, and zippers that they had to make their way through to that condition which pleased them best, kept forcing them to be self-conscious. They couldn't believe that what they were doing was real, and yet it was real, as they well knew the minute they separated, when the memory of their last encounter would descend on both of them, occupying their minds, and unfitting them for any occupation except dreaming of the next encounter. At night, lying in his bunk, Elgin would try to sleep, but he'd think of Caroline, and slowly, like a leaf curling in a salt solution, he would twist under his covers until his knees were even with his chest, and this was a tortured, involuntary movement of longing he could no more control than he could control his thoughts. He would try to do his reading for his courses:

"In the early years of this century, I moved to London, feeling that Ireland and my love for Ireland were too distracting for my poetry." And then right on the printed page would appear "CAROLINE," in capital letters, and Elgin would rub his face foolishly with both hands, twisting his mouth and his cheeks and his nose.

He didn't believe that Caroline loved him as much as he loved her, or at least that she desired him as much as he did her, and this made him sullen. He picked on her. He told her she wasn't as smart as she thought she was; people treated her as if she were intelligent only because she was pretty. He would accuse her of pettiness, and she would agree with him, confess that she had an awful character, and while he was consoling her, their embraces would begin.

Elgin would be hurt whenever Caroline was the first to point out that it was time to go and have dinner. Caroline would eye the clock, but Elgin would pretend he was so entranced with Caroline he didn't know what time it was. The minutes would tick by, and Caroline would grow gayer and gayer, trying to ignore the time, while Elgin, beetling, thin, and sardonic, refused to say the words that would release her.

Elgin became frightened. He was so frightened he couldn't eat. He was afraid of losing Caroline, of failing his courses because he couldn't study unless she was sitting beside him where he could reach out and touch her every few minutes. The thought of what it would be like if any of the quarrels they had should turn serious worried him until he was sick. Finally, looking gray and haggard, he suggested to her one afternoon that the two of them should run off and get married.

"Elgin, don't. Don't let's talk about that. You know we can't."

Elgin shrugged and looked disheartened. "I don't like self-pity," he said. "But I admit I have some. Oh, yes. I pity myself a lot. Imagine, here I am, in love with a common, ordinary, conventional girl like you."

Caroline supported her head with her hands. "Oh, Elgin," she said, "you're being cruel. You know we're awfully young.

And just because we got carried away—there's no need, really, to . . . It's our animal appetites mostly, you know. . . ."

Elgin wanted to say something bitter but her last remark stopped him. *"Your* animal appetites, too?"

"Yes."

He was so happy he forgot his feelings had been hurt.

Sometimes, she and Elgin went out with Felicia and Dimitri. Caroline could not now bear girls she thought were virgins; they made her uneasy, and she would not go on a double date with Dimitri and Felicia until Elgin swore they were lovers, too. Elgin spent more than one afternoon telling her that almost all the girls at Radcliffe and all other colleges had slept with somebody. "The percentage is very high," he said.

They went boating twice at Marblehead. Dimitri had a car, which Elgin borrowed—an old, weak-lunged Ford—and they would wheeze up to Marblehead and rent a dinghy and be blown around the bay, with the sunlight bright on Caroline's hair and the salt air making them hungry and the wind whipping up small whitecaps to make the day exciting.

Caroline wrote in her diary, "His back is so beautiful. It has such a lovely shape. It's so defenseless. I like to put my ear against his back and listen to his heart—I think it's his heart I hear. It's funny he is not more handsome in his clothes, but that only makes him seem more beautiful to me, I think. I feel I would like to give birth to him. Sometimes, I want to crawl into his pocket and be carried like a pencil. I never let him see how strongly I feel. I am a dreadful person, dreadful. . . ."

Elgin wrote her a letter.

"Dear Caroline, Isn't it funny to have me writing a letter to you when I see you every day? But just imagine how it would seem later if we looked back and saw that we had never written each other how we felt.

"You, Caroline Hedges, are the greatest love of my life, just as you are the first.

"I don't suppose, you being a girl, that you know what it's like to love a girl like you, but if you knew how dependent men are on women, you might understand. Not that men can't survive alone, but they don't seem to really amount to anything until they have a woman they love.

"Reading over what I have just written, I see that everything I've said applies only to the selfish side of love. I guess that's a dead giveaway about me. But as for you, kid, just knowing you is rather awe-inspiring."

Sometimes, there would be birds singing in the ivy outside the window of Elgin's room. Sometimes, Elgin would sing to Caroline; he had a sweet, insecurely pitched voice, and his singing would give them both pleasure. Sometimes, seeing Elgin walk across the room unclothed would make all the breath leave Caroline's body, and she would not even be conscious of her gasp or that he heard her. One afternoon, Elgin went into the bathroom to get Caroline a glass of water. She was lying in the lower bunk, lapped in shadows, and she saw him come back into the room and she said weakly, "I love you, Elgin." It was the first time she had said it, that proud, stubborn girl. Elgin heard her; he stopped in his tracks and he put his head back. "God," he said. "This is the happiest moment I ever had."

Now there was no bar to their intimacy, and they talked. Elgin was relentless about asking questions: "What do you think about money? What is your father like? Are you fond of him?"

At first, Caroline was cautious. "Well, I think there's a minimum amount of money people should have. . . . My father is sort of nice. He's shallow, I guess. He doesn't seem to have very strong emotions. He works for an insurance company. I used to like him a lot; I still do. . . . I think I feel sorry for him."

"What do you mean by that?" Elgin asked. He handed her a cigarette and lit it for her. "Tell me everything about yourself. Be honest. I've never known anyone as well as I know you."

Caroline cupped her hands over her mouth. "I think he loves me, and now I love you, and I think that's sad. That he's older . . . Should we be talking like this, Elgin?"

"Why not? Who else can we talk to?"

Then it all began to come out, her feelings toward her father, toward her mother, toward money. Caroline wanted a nice house and a large family; she looked down a little on people who weren't well off. When she felt exhausted from telling Elgin these things, she asked him questions.

"My mother's very possessive," he said. "If we got married, I think we'd have in-law problems. I want to be a famous scholar. I don't disapprove of campus politics. I know I should, but I don't. Isn't that shameful?"

"This isn't dignified, talking like this," Caroline said. "I don't want to do it anymore."

She was frightened. Having admitted she loved Elgin, she felt naked, and these conversations only made her feel worse. She kept hoping she and Elgin would reach some stability together, but it never came. She still was frightened when she ran up the stairs of Widener that he wouldn't be waiting for her. She wondered why she couldn't get used to this situation, why the pleasures she was drawn into didn't lose their elements of pain—indeed, why the elements of pain grew steadily worse, until she dreaded seeing Elgin and had to force herself to get out of bed in the morning and go through her day. She couldn't help thinking that what she was with comparative strangers was much pleasanter than what she was with Elgin. With him she was capricious, untruthful, often sharp-tongued, giddy with emotions that came and went, and while one emotion might be ennobling, having six or seven in the space of an hour was undignified and not decent at all. She had always believed that a woman ought to walk very straight, write a firm hand, keep house and entertain well—in short, be like those friends of her mother's whom she most admired. The fact that she was young didn't seem any excuse at all for her not being like those women, and now she said to herself, "I'm wild. That's all there is to that."

She decided she was inordinately sexual. Elgin caught her in Widener reading a book describing the great courtesans of the nineteenth century, La Belle Otero and Lola Montez. She believed that Elgin would inevitably forsake her because she had lost all her dignity and mystery, and she boasted to him that he would never forget her, even if he married some pasty-faced virgin. Elgin couldn't calm her; in fact, he was more than half persuaded that she *was* unusually passionate when she said she was, and he became uneasy with her. Caroline began to wear a little too much lipstick and to walk not in her habitual erect fashion but slouching and swaying her hips. She drank and smoked more, and when she got high, she would look at Elgin through lowered eyelids and kiss him in a knowing—a childishly knowing—way. And all of this humbled Elgin, who felt Caroline was a great enigma and that she was drawing away from him. One night, they were sitting on the riverbank and Caroline put her hands on Elgin's head and drew him to her, and Elgin pulled away desperately. "I don't want you to kiss me like that!"

"What's wrong?" Caroline asked haughtily. "Am I too much woman for you?"

Elgin's eyes grew moist. "I don't know what you do to me," he said miserably. "I'm ready to cry. I didn't think we were having *that* kind of an affair."

In the darkness, he saw Caroline's eyelids descend. Then a shudder passed over her face. He decided to stake everything rather than have Caroline frighten him into helplessness.

He grabbed her arm. "Listen, you've got to get hold of yourself. You're acting like an ass."

Caroline was motionless.

"You're ruining everything," Elgin said.

"You have too many illusions about me," Caroline said coldly. She pulled away from his grasp and lay down on his old, battered raincoat and put her hands under her head. "There are a lot of things you don't know about me. I didn't want to tell you I loved you because I wanted to hold you. There, what do you think of that?"

Elgin hit himself on the chest. "You think that's bad? Well, I always intended to seduce you, right from the beginning. God!" He lay down, too, on the damp grass, two feet away from her, and he put his hands under his head.

Lying like that, they quarrelled in this peculiar way, libeling themselves, lowering the object of love in the other's eyes.

"I think it's loathsome that we sleep together," Caroline said. "I feel like a you-know-what."

"I hate seeing you every day," Elgin said. "Not because of

you but because I'm always afraid you'll see through me. Also, I miss having free time to study—that's how cold-blooded I am."

There was a full moon that night, and its light was no chillier than what these two young people said about themselves. But after a while Elgin rolled over and took Caroline in his arms. "Please don't hate me."

"I don't hate you. I love you."

"I love you, too. God, it's hell!"

They decided to be more sensible. The next day they didn't meet in Widener. Elgin stayed in his room, and at three o'clock the phone rang.

"It's me—Caroline."

"Oh God, you called. I was praying you would. Where are you?"

"In the drugstore on the corner." There was silence. "Elgin," she said at last, "did you have any orange juice today?"

He ran, down the stairs, along the sidewalk, to the drugstore, to have his orange juice.

One day, Elgin told Caroline he was going to stay home and play poker with some of the boys in his entry. Caroline said that was a good idea. She had to write her mother; for some reason, her letters home had got her mother all upset, and she wanted to take some time and calm the old biddy down. "Poor thing," said Caroline. "She's had such an empty life, and I'm so important to her." Then she smiled a thin, nervous smile. "Of course, when I think how stupid she is, I wonder what I'll find to say to her."

Elgin played poker. He lost four dollars and sixty cents. At eleven-thirty, he excused himself from the game and went out on the street. He walked hurriedly, jogging part of the distance, until he stood on the sidewalk across from Cabot Hall, looking up at the light in Caroline's room. Finally, a shadow passed over the window, and Elgin felt what he could only describe as anguish.

He looked in the gutter until he found a pebble, and then he hurled it at Caroline's window. It struck. The shadow appeared again, standing quite still. At that moment, a policeman rounded the corner. Elgin thrust his hands in his pockets and walked up the street. The policeman stopped him.

"Hey, buddy, did you just throw something at that building?"

"No, Officer." Elgin was sweating and looked so pitiable the officer said, "I guess it was a trick of the light."

When Caroline asked him if he had come by Cabot the night before, he denied it.

The next day, he and Caroline went up to his room. As Elgin closed the door, Caroline threw herself onto the couch. She looked pale and unhappy, and she was making a face, preparing herself for what was coming. But Elgin walked over and stood next to the couch and said, "Caroline, we've got to be chaste. God!" he cried. "It's not easy to say this, and if your feelings get hurt, I don't know what I'll do!"

"They're not hurt."

"I want you to be happy," he said, looking down at her. "I think we ought to get married."

"We're under age, Elgin—you know that. Our parents won't let us."

"We'll tell them you're pregnant. We'll do something."

Caroline jumped up. "But I don't want to marry you! You won't make me happy. I'm scared of you. You don't have any respect for me. I don't know how to be a good wife."

"Listen, Caroline, we haven't done the right thing. You want to have children?"

A pink, piteous flush covered Caroline's face. "Oh," she said.

"We ought to get married," he said doggedly. "It won't be easy, but otherwise we'll never be happy. You see, what we didn't figure out is the teleology of the thing. We don't have a goal. We have to have a goal, do you see?"

"Elgin, we can't be foolish. If we really love each other, we have to be very practical or else we'll just cause each other very needless pain."

They looked at each other, pure at last, haloed by an urge to sacrifice.

"I may not be right for you," Caroline whispered. "We'll

wait. We'll wait until fall. We'll have the summer to think things over."

Elgin frowned, not liking to have his sacrifice ignored. "I'm willing to marry you," he said.

"No, it's not right," said Caroline. "We're too young. We couldn't have children now. We're too ignorant. We'd be terrible parents." How it pained her to say this!

"If you feel that way," Elgin said, "I think we ought to plan to break up. Nothing sudden," he added, to ease the sudden twinge that was twisting his stomach. "When school's over."

Caroline hesitated, but it seemed to her dreamlike and wonderful to be free of this febrile emotion. And atonement would be so wonderful. . . . At the same time, she was hurt. "All right," she said with dignity. "If you want."

Elgin turned away from her. "Caroline, tell me one thing," he said with his back to her. "Emotionally, would you like to marry me?"

"Yes."

"God!" he said. "You're so practical!"

"I'm not!" she cried. "I can't help it." She wrung her hands. "If you tried to carry me off, I wouldn't resist," she said. "But if you ask me, I think—I think—"

He didn't have to marry her; he wouldn't have to worry about supporting her; he hadn't lost his career. Elgin felt irrepressible relief welling up in him. "God, how we love each other."

Caroline laughed. "It's true." She laughed a little more. "It's so true!" She threw her arms around his neck and kissed him.

Of course, they didn't stick to Elgin's plan of breaking up when school ended. They decided they would take a vacation from each other, and meet in the fall, when college began again, as friends. This agreement seemed to remove a great weight from them. They had only two weeks of the reading period and three weeks of exams left to be together, but they resumed some of their old habits—the walks between classes, for instance, and the trips to the Boston Museum of Fine Arts—and they even took to reading stories aloud again, preferring Chekhov and Colette. The sweetness and the sadness of their predicament were what they loved, and they threw themselves into the role of well-disciplined lovers with all their energy. Hardly a day passed without their thinking of some new gesture toward each other. Elgin gave flowers to Caroline; she bought him cuff links and books of poetry. Elgin left off suspecting that he was being made a fool of, and was actually gentlemanly, opening doors for Caroline and lighting her cigarettes. Caroline was ladylike and concealed her moods. They engaged in roughhouse; Elgin pulled her hair and she pummelled him when they sat on the riverbank. They were chaste. They referred sometimes to the times when they had listened to the nightingale, and while the chastity didn't come easily to them, the act of sacrifice did. Elgin put on weight, and his face regained its color. "My goodness," Caroline said. "I think knowing me has improved your looks." It seemed they had found the secret of being happy together, in the imminence of separation, and while they didn't understand the paradox, they knew it was true.

But as their five last weeks passed, they discovered why it was true. All the pain of the relationship was now bound up with the parting and not with the things they did to each other. "It's dreadful," Caroline said. "I have feelings. They're like heavy mice that come out of holes and sit in my stomach and weigh me down."

They had been so proud of themselves, so free and relaxed and peaceful together, and now, when they saw what this parting was going to be like, all their vivacity and happiness flagged, they lost interest in talking to each other, and all they wanted was to get it over with.

On the last day of exams, they went up to Elgin's room at six o'clock. Elgin had bought a bottle of champagne and rented two glasses. Caroline was all dressed up because she was going to catch a train for Baltimore at nine o'clock. She had on a small hat, which she kept eyeing in the mirror. Poor Elgin was nervous about opening the champagne. "It's imported," he said. "I don't want to sound tight, but if half of it explodes or comes out in foam, I won't be happy." Caroline laughed, but when the cork popped, she turned very serious. She was afraid of what Elgin would toast; she was afraid it would ruin her self-possession.

Elgin slowly poured the champagne into the two glasses. Then the two young people, alone in the room, picked up their glasses and held them together. "To our reunion in the fall," Elgin said. "God knows what it will be like." They drank.

Caroline put her glass down. "Let's play a record and dance," she said. Elgin put on a Cole Porter L.P., and he and Caroline circled around the room, dodging the furniture, pausing to take occasional sips of their champagne. At six-thirty, they went downstairs and ate in the dining hall.

By seven-fifteen, they were back upstairs in Elgin's room, sitting on the bunk, kissing each other with a dry, intense helplessness. At quarter of eight, Caroline said she had to go. Elgin pulled away from her; she had taken off her hat, and her dress, made of some pretty gray-blue material, was hopelessly rumpled. With his hands, he set her just so on the bunk. Then he took out his pocket comb and combed her hair. "There," he said.

"Do I look prettier now?" Caroline asked.

"Yes," Elgin said.

They walked downstairs and out the door of Adams House. When they reached the sidewalk, Caroline said, "I don't want you to come with me. I want to go back to the dorm alone. All right?"

Elgin nodded.

"I'll write you from Europe," Caroline said. "Goodbye," she said and walked away, up the sidewalk; she tried to walk crisply but her feet dragged because she felt tired. Slowly, the hoped-for sense of relief was coming; she was free of Elgin, she had herself back, but not all of herself. Elgin still held some of her, and she would never get it back except when he was beside her.

Elgin sat on the steps in front of Adams House and buried his face in his hands. "God!" he said to himself. "I love her." And he wondered what would become of them now.

The Famous Toboggan of Laughter

by Ella Leffland

"Whenever I see a picture of the Eiffel Tower, it always reminds me of Paris."

I didn't bother answering. I didn't like her. Anyway, she was already past me, halfway down the boat deck. She was always in a big hurry, Mayo, never waited for a response. She was reckless, too. The first day out she climbed halfway up the ladder to the pilothouse just for laughs, and having only one arm, she almost fell off. Every night she drank with the drinkers or smoked pot with the pot smokers, stumbling into our cabin at dawn and making extra noise for the benefit of our other cabinmate, a retired missionary woman in her seventies. Mayo was my age, nineteen or twenty. I made no pretense of liking her, but she seemed to be the star of our student crowd even though, or maybe because, her rudeness was breathtaking, the kind that hits you in the solar plexus. There was always a lot of laughter and stomping of feet around her. Even Miss Shatswell, our cabinmate, seemed drawn to her.

Miss Shatswell had melancholy eyes. Her long, thin hands were full of condolence. When she spooned up custard or soup at the dining table she seemed to be soothing a great culinary flaw built into the universe. When she looked out at the ocean she seemed to see only the ships that had sunk and the sailors that had drowned. She always dropped dark quotes from Ecclesiastes.

Watching us play shuffleboard, she would tell the loser compassionately, "The race is not to the swift, nor the battle to the strong." When a stout Frenchman sat down on a folding chair and broke it Miss Shatswell hurried over to him as he tried to fix it, and said with feeling, "That which is crooked cannot be made straight." And once by the pool she singled out Mayo in her bikini, looked at the stump of her arm, and, with her eyes moist, told her, "That which is wanting cannot be numbered."

There was a silence around the pool. Then Mayo barked, "Pull the nails out of your hands, lady," and jumped into the water with a big splash. Her friends clapped, but Miss Shatswell's gentle smile was unperturbed.

In the Cherbourg customs shed, at the end of the crossing, I saw Miss Shatswell threading her way through the crowd toward Mayo, and I saw Mayo's eyes narrow. The old lady looked at her for a moment; then her special smile filled her face. It was the most radiantly pitying smile I ever saw. She laid her long fingers on the girl's shoulder.

An obscenity burst from Mayo's lips. Still smiling, Miss Shatswell melted back into the crowd. She was on her way to the Passion Play in Oberammergau.

I was on my way to Paris for the summer between my junior and senior years at college. I found the cheapest room I could near the Place St.-Michel, and went out to the cafés. Within a week I had met enough interesting people to keep me busy. The sun shone, and everything was fine. Then a sullen, clammy rain began to fall.

One day I saw Mayo again. She was coming down the street toward me under a big black umbrella. I crossed the street, but she crossed, too.

"What time is it?" she asked peremptorily.

I consulted my watch. "Three," I said, and she walked off leaving me with my arm in the air. I saw her again a few days later as I came out of my hotel room, but this time she didn't speak. The third time I saw her was in Notre Dame Cathedral. She was eating a pomegranate and spitting the seeds on the floor. It was cold in the church.

"He must have had rheumatism," she said, coming over to me.

"Who?"

"Quas."

"Who?"

"Quasimodo. The Hunchback," she said loudly, adding,

"Jesus, it's cold." And tossing her pomegranate core into the open shoulder bag of a nearby tourist, she sauntered out, pausing to give a skeptical glance at the rose window.

The next day there was a knock at my door, and Mayo walked in with a newspaper under her arm.

"Shooting a picture down on the Costa Brava. Want to be an extra? *Extras,"* she shouted into my surprised silence. "And don't look at my arm, anybody can pass in a crowd scene. It's some crazy American picture shooting in Spain for tax reasons. You're wondering why I don't wear a prosthesis."

She had taken off her coat, and was wearing one of the slightly soiled sleeveless blouses she favored, exposing the stump, which was three or four inches long and very white.

"I don't like those hook things, and artificial hands get discolored. Satisfied? Or now I guess you want to know how I lost it. Right? Okay. Went for a ride a couple years ago. Car rammed into me. I was thrown out on the road, the arm stayed in the car."

For the first time since I had met her I felt that my look of cool dislike was out of place. I searched for something to say, but came up with only, "Gee."

"Great dialogue!" she snapped, adding, "Does it disgust you? The stump, I mean."

I nodded. "The way you always draw attention to it, to shock people."

"That's tough. Now look, page six." She shoved a week-old London tabloid under my nose.

"Do you go in for this kind of journalism?" I asked, feeling the cheap print smear under my thumb.

"Myself, no. But the concierge doesn't care what quality he hangs in the WC. From the Manchester *Guardian,* which goes a long way, to the flimsiest Fleet Street yellow sheet. Never a French paper, always English. He's either an Anglophile or an Anglophobe, hard to tell which."

I could tell she had practiced that one, and I found myself giving a proper audience smile. I didn't like her, yet she did have something.

"I don't want to go to Spain," I told her, giving the paper back.

She shrugged, going to the mirror and taking a tube of lipstick from her bag. "Gotta meet a guy. Big Hungarian. Wears a cloak. Very smashing." The lipstick gave her face the only color it had. It was a small heart-shaped face with regular features. The skin under the eyes was gray, as though she had stayed up every night since puberty. The eyes were gray, too, with long lashes. She was pretty, but she didn't strike you as pretty.

"I don't remember your name," she said, blotting her lips with the back of her hand.

"Judith. How did you find me?"

"Saw you come out of this hole once. So I asked downstairs for the American girl with the big nose. No problem."

I touched my nose. "You're really a charmer."

"Whenever I see a picture of Madrid, I can't help thinking of Spain," she said with a smile, going out the door. She came back a minute later. "You don't like me, do you?"

"Does anybody?"

"Oh, you'd be surprised," she laughed, and shut the door.

A few days later I received a note from her.

"Dear Judith," she wrote, "I've contracted an amusing chest cold and can't go out. Have you changed your mind about Spain? I was in San Sebastián once with this guy, Terrance. It was winter, lots of fog. We went up this big hill on the outskirts. There's a posh white restaurant at the top, and a crazy amusement place called the Grand Labyrinth. We almost died in the Labyrinth, it was so terrific. But I want to go farther south now. Reconsider. Mayo."

I bought some fruit and went to her address, finding a surprisingly high-class pension. Her room was large, messy—books, clothes, and pomegranate cores strewn everywhere—and filled with a dozen American students. I had interrupted a girl who was reading aloud from a small English-French phrase book, seated on the edge of the unmade bed, her clear pink face shining like a nun's. I took her for the type whose washcloth would have a neatly printed little name tag sewn in the corner.

"These are useful phrases for the visitor to France," she explained to me, and read on in a warm, tremulous voice. " 'This is not what I asked for. It is too hot. Too cold. Help! Fire! Thief! Who are you? I shall call a policeman. I am hungry; tired; ill . . .' "

Ignoring the laughter, Mayo was walking around the room looking for something. "Move over," she ordered the girl on the bed, and she found what she was looking for, a bottle of cough medicine. "Seat must be as numb as your head," she muttered. The girl gave her a charming smile. I suppose what was beginning to fascinate me was the predictability of Mayo's obnoxiousness. I wondered when, if ever, she would slip up.

When the group left she slammed the door after them. "Met that ass in a bookstore once and can't shake her," she said. "Today she brings up a bunch of rubbernecks I don't even know. Know her type. Crooked seams offend her. But not on me. Vulgar language offends her. But not from me. Thinks she's a goddamn angel of mercy."

"Here, I brought you some fruit," I said, and she took the bag and flung it down on the table.

"What'd you come to Europe for anyway?" she asked.

"I don't know. I wanted to see Paris."

She shook her head angrily. "I don't know what the hell I'm doing here."

"You must have been here before. You mentioned San Sebastián."

"Hell, I've been in Europe a year. Lived in London first. All the time I was there I had this fantastic desire to be in Dublin. So I went. Had a ball. Met this guy Terrance. He had blond hair, a brown mustache, and a red beard. Colorful guy. And he had this thing for San Sebastián. So we went. We had this fantastic time. Greatest time of my life. He was a very smashing guy. At first. But he got to be a bore. Too possessive. So I ditched him. I had this fantastic desire to be in Paris. And my family said I was frittering my time away and withdrew my allowance. So I had to go back. You've got parents?"

"Sure, of course I've got parents."

"You oughta have mine. My mother's always cutting off my allowance so I have to come home. Then she hangs on me and tells me how she worries about me. I bet. She wishes I'd been totaled, like the car, instead of leaving an arm in it. Anyway, I persuaded them I'd get into the Sorbonne. I've got this fantastic IQ. But Paris is dead in the summer. I want to go to Spain."

"I want to stay here."

"What for?"

"I told you, I like Paris. Besides, I've made friends here."

"So have I. God, have I got friends."

"Frankly, I'm surprised."

"I'm not." And she said cheerfully, "But you—you really don't like me, do you?"

I reflected. "I don't know, in a way I guess I wouldn't be here if I didn't."

She shot me a furious and disappointed look. "I thought you were different. Angel of mercy! Try to be honest for once in your Christian middle-class life. Don't put me on. Don't tell me you like me."

"Don't worry," I told her, "I *do* think you're obnoxious. I'm only here because I find you interesting. I mean your approach to life. As a person I dislike you. That's the truth."

"That's better," she said. "Anyway, you're in the same boat. That's one ugly nose."

"I'm taking my fruit back. Your parents are loaded, buy your own." And I took the fruit and left.

I came across her occasionally after that in cafés. She was usually with a group of friends. She now wore an artificial hand made of plastic. It was yellowed and dead-looking. When people were introduced to her she always shook hands with that hand, and watched their faces as their fingers came in contact with the cold plastic. Her friends always laughed, and this relieved the stranger, who would laugh, too. Then she stopped wearing it; I guess the novelty wore off.

One evening a few weeks after I had taken my fruit back she appeared at my room. It was very cold and damp.

"Come to Spain," she said. "None of this crappy cold weather."

"I don't want to go to Spain. Leave me alone."

"Well, I'm going," she said.

"Good for you."

"I'm going down to that movie they're shooting. I want some excitement."

"What do you want more excitement for? You always seem to have a lot of people around you."

"On *their* terms, baby, *their* terms." She was silent for a moment. "I'm leaving tomorrow. I want to leave this with you, this I cherish." She pulled a slip of green paper from her pocket and handed it to me. I looked at it.

WILL YoU HAVE SoME FUN?
If so, Ladies a nd Gentlemen,
Come In a nd See The
    GRAND LABYRINTH
A Voyage to Italy a nd Egypt
The Sun Bath
The Invisible Man
oRPHEE IN HELL
A LoVE AFFLICTIoN
A Midsummer Night's Dream
THE FAMoUS ToBoGGAN oF LAUGHTER
A nd other merry entertainments that
    everybody
Should not fail to visit the
    GRAND LABYRINTH
everything in it is amusement, joy a nd
    gaiety.

"That's the place you mentioned in your letter," I said. "In San Sebastián."

"That's right."

"What do you want me to have it for?"

"I don't know. I might get killed in Spain or something."

"Why should you get killed?"

"How do I know? Christ, don't you know anything about accidents? Nobody expects an accident."

As she went to the door she paused. "Everybody thinks I've had lovers for years. But I'll tell you something—I only had a lover once, last winter, in San Sebastián."

"That multicolored Irishman?"

"Yeah, Terrance. He was smashing."

"I thought you said—"

"I know, I know, I wound up hating him. He suffocated me with his ardor."

"Oh."

The door closed.

After she had gone I realized she had finally broken her predictability and forgotten to be obnoxious.

She was back in nine days. She was sunburned and she looked good, and she was not obnoxious.

"How was Spain?" I asked.

"A gas. Only the picture was canceled."

"You didn't get killed, anyway."

"Naw, I didn't get killed."

She paced up and down my room.

"Every time I see a picture of the Colosseum," she said, "I'm always reminded of Rome."

"You're going to Italy."

She stopped her pacing. "Everybody in this world is a Miss Shatswell."

"Who's that?" I had forgotten.

"I don't care if they're French, Spanish, American, or what, they're all Miss Shatswells. Now I'm gonna go meet the Italian Miss Shatswells. What the hell." She turned to me. "Well, I've got to zoom, got to meet a guy, a big sculptor . . ."

"Very smashing?"

"You've still got the Grand Labyrinth, I hope?"

I found it for her. "It must mean a lot to you," I said, "that little piece of paper. Don't you want me to keep it for you till you get back from Italy?"

"You might be gone by then." She gave it a long look. "I'll tell you something, that's where I had my affair. With Terrance. Right there in the Grand Labyrinth, right under the Famous Toboggan of Laughter."

"You did it in a crowd?"

"Naw, of course not. It was winter, the place was deserted.

Just this old caretaker puttering around. He opened the place up for us, and we had it all to ourselves. There was this fantastic foggy, silvery light coming through all these little windows, I can never forget that light. And I was standing there, looking at the Famous Toboggan of Laughter, and it was all lit up by that light. It was the most beautiful thing I ever saw. All in a second we got down under it, under the table." She stuffed the slip of paper into her bag, gave a quick wave, and went out the door.

I spent the last two weeks with friends at a youth hostel on the Bay of Biscay, near Bayonne. The day before I left Paris I received a postcard of the Colosseum from Mayo. On the back she had scrawled: "Whenever I see a picture of the Vienna Opera House I can't help thinking of Vienna."

I decided that if I got the chance I would make a pilgrimage across the border to the Grand Labyrinth for Mayo.

It turned out that we went into San Sebastián several times— it was only a few miles from Bayonne. The weather was so hot that it was only our last time there that I got up the energy to detach myself from my friends and take the bus to the outskirts, to Mount Igueldo, where the Grand Labyrinth was located. There were few people aboard the funicular that ran to the top.

I walked over to the small building and found "Grand Labyrinth" painted over the door in blue letters. Sitting by the door, an old man in a black uniform with gold braid was dozing. I asked for a ticket, and he woke with a start. He took my money and gave me a ticket and, with a deep, courteous nod, watched me as I went in.

The room was as uninteresting as a dentist's waiting room. In it were a half-dozen neatly spaced tables, each with a cardboard box on it. A series of small windows ran along the walls and the sun poured through them.

The old man had come inside and was leaning against the wall. "Enjoy yourself, señorita," he said. "Take your time and see everything."

I walked over to the first box. One side was removed, to

simulate a theater stage. The old man announced loudly, "The Sunbather."

Under a painted yellow sun, lying on her stomach, was a nude lady shaped like a tube of toothpaste. A fly sat reflectively on one buttock.

"Look at the next one," the old man said. There was a huge joke in his voice, and I looked with interest at the next box, entitled "The Invisible Man." The floor of the box was painted green, the sides blue. There was nothing in it.

The old man chuckled and moved from his station against the wall. He followed a few paces behind me as I went on, reading each caption aloud and waiting for my response.

" 'A Love Affliction,' " he announced.

I looked at the small figure of a lady whose paper hair had turned green with time. She held a bent cardboard knife to her bosom.

"Look at her face," he urged.

Her mouth was drawn down to her chin, her eyebrows were fiercely knotted, and a chain of faded blue tears decorated both cheeks.

"She looks very unhappy," I said.

"And so she should. She is suffering from a love affliction."

The next box was "The Famous Toboggan of Laughter." Several tiny, well-bundled figures sat on a small blue toboggan made of cardboard. The little faces were all but consumed by enormous smiles expressing the very ultimate in excitement and delight, and the tails of their caps all stood straight out to indicate that they were going at a great clip.

"You like this one?" the old man asked when I had looked at it for several minutes.

"Yes. It's very happy."

"I think it's probably my best."

"Did you make these scenes?"

"Every one."

"That's quite an accomplishment."

"Go on, señorita, look at the rest." And as we walked along he said, "Nowadays it's all cinema and television. Who cares for the Grand Labyrinth? You're the first person to buy a ticket in three days."

"Still," I said, "your fame has spread. I heard about the Grand Labyrinth in Paris."

"Did you?" he asked, his eyebrows going up. "Did you really?"

"Yes, the person who told me was very enthusiastic."

"Who was the person? Not a Frenchman. The French are the worst—jaded."

"No, an American."

"Ah, an American. Like yourself, señorita, if I may presume. Much is said against your countrymen, but I have always found them to be soulful. What did this one tell you, precisely?"

"She was very enthusiastic about the Toboggan of Laughter."

"A woman of taste. Was she a woman of taste?"

"Well, she's well read, intelligent."

"Tell me, was the memory fresh, or had it lingered for several seasons?"

"I think she'd been here about eight months before, in the winter."

"In the winter? But the Labyrinth is closed in the winter."

I had completed my tour, and somehow I was anxious to leave before he recalled Mayo. "Thank you very much," I said. "Your Labyrinth has lived up to all my expectations."

"In the winter it is closed," he repeated, and paused for a moment. "But wait—wait. Your friend, does she—forgive me for mentioning it—does she have only one arm?"

I nodded.

"I remember her very well. Indeed, it was in the winter . . . in January, during the fog . . ."

"She mentioned that," I said, approaching the door.

"I was outside . . . I came around the building from the garden, not able to see a foot ahead of me for the fog, and all at once I ran right into them . . ."

"Them?" I said, stopping. Then perhaps Terrance wasn't a fantasy. I realized that was what I had really thought.

"She had her sweetheart with her," he said.

"Did he have a red beard?" I asked.

"A red beard. Imagine crashing into them unexpectedly, a man with a big red beard and a girl—forgive me again—with only one arm. It gave a jolt."

"And he—he wasn't a nothing sort of fellow, was he? He was big and good-looking?"

"Oh, he was a good-looking boy, very tall, with fine eyes."

I looked back at the Toboggan, at the floor beneath it. "And he liked her? He seemed to like her?"

"He couldn't take his eyes off her."

For a moment I could see the fogged, silver light coming through the windows, and felt the winter stillness.

"And they spent a long time in here?" I asked.

"Over an hour. They were so interested they wanted to stay on, so I went back to the garden. When they gave back the key I saw that they had been very impressed."

"They were, they were." I smiled.

"They cheered up my whole winter," he said, following me outside. "You tell her that if you see her again."

He seated himself before the door again. I waved good-bye, and he waved back, ending the gesture with a little salute. I went back to the funicular, feeling suddenly, unaccountably sad.

The funicular clanged to a stop at the bottom of the hill, and the few tourists got out and stood on the corner to wait for the bus. I could picture Mayo and Terrance standing on this very corner waiting for the same bus.

After twenty minutes the bus finally drew up, the same one I had come out in—ancient, rattling, packed to capacity as all Spanish buses—and we jammed our way aboard. I struggled toward a strap and stood hanging on to it, and all I could see was Mayo pushing through the crowd with her stump, forcing a gap between her and Terrance. I saw her fixing her narrowed eyes on his fervent ones, and seeing in them the fire of pity she saw everywhere in this world of Miss Shatswells—only stronger, hotter, more unforgivable than any before.

The Tea Time of Stouthearted Ladies

by Jean Stafford

"As I tell Kitty, this summer job of hers is really more a vacation with pay than work. What wouldn't *I* give to be up there in the mountains away from the hurly-burly of this town! They have a lake right there below the main lodge where the girls can cool off after they serve lunch. And quite often they can have the horses to trot off here, there, and the other place—go down to Brophy, for instance, and have a Coke. They can help themselves to the books in the lounge, play the Victrola, sit in the sun and get a good tan. They go to the square dances and dance with the dudes as if they were dudes themselves, and if there's a home movie they're invited to come and view. Mrs. Bell and Miss Skeen are very democratic along those lines and when they first hired Kitty, when she was just fourteen, they told me they didn't look on their employees as servants but as a part of the family."

"Not my idea of work," agreed Mrs. Ewing, and made a hybrid sound, half deprecating giggle, half longing sigh. "Some different from *our* summers, what with those scorching days in August and no let-up in the way of a breeze. Oh, I'm by no means partial to summer on the plains. And all those pesky grasshoppers spitting tobacco juice through the screens onto your clean glass curtains, to say nothing of the fuss-budget old schoolmarms—give me a dude any day of the week sooner than Miss Prunes and Prisms from Glenwood Springs still plugging away at her M.A. after fifteen years. Kitty's in luck all right."

Lucky Kitty Winstanley, home from her last class for the day at Nevilles College, stood in the middle of her small, shadowy bedroom, her arms still full of books, and listened to the voices in the kitchen below her. She visualized her mother and the turnip-shaped, bearded neighbor as they lingered in the bright hollow of the dying May afternoon. Their ration of icebox cookies eaten, their pale, scalding coffee drunk, they would be sitting in the breakfast nook, facing each other through spotless, rimless spectacles. Their tumid hands mutilated by work would be clasped loosely on the tulip-patterned oilcloth and their swollen feet would be demurely crossed as they glibly evaluated the silver lining of the cloud beneath which they and their families lived, gasping for every breath. It was out of habit, not curiosity, that Kitty listened; she knew all their themes by heart and all of them embarrassed her. She listened with revulsion, with boredom, pity, outrage, and she moved stealthily so that they would not know she had come home.

Each afternoon, in one house or another along this broad, graveled street, there was such an imitation tea party in such a fiercely clean kitchen as Mrs. Winstanley's when two women or more established themselves in speckless cotton dresses in the breakfast nooks for a snack and a confab. United in their profession, that of running boardinghouses for college students, and united more deeply but less admissibly in hardship and fatigue and in eternal worry over "making ends meet," they behaved, at this hour of day that lay tranquilly between the toasted peanut-butter sandwiches of lunch and the Swedish meatballs of dinner, like urban ladies of leisure gossiping after a matinee. Formal, fearful of intimacy lest the full confrontation with reality shatter them to smithereens, they did not use each other's first names, asked no leading questions; it was surprising that they did not wear gloves and hats. They did not refer, even by indirection, to personal matters, not to the monotonous terror of debt that kept them wakeful at night despite the weariness that was their incessant condition, or to the aching disappointment to which they daily rose, or to their hopeless, helpless contempt for their unemployed husbands who spent their days in the public park, clustering to curse the national dilemma or scattering to brood alone upon their individual despair.

Valorously, the landladies kept their chins up, rationalized; they "saw the funny side of things," they never said die. One would not guess, to listen to their light palaver, that they had been reduced to tears that same morning by the dunning of the grocer and the coal man and had seen themselves flung into debtors' prison for life. To hear their interchange of news and commentary on their lodgers, one might have thought they were the hostesses of prolonged, frolicsome houseparties. The cancer was invisible, deep in their broken, bleeding hearts.

They sat at the social hour of four to five in the kitchens because their parlors were either rented out or were used as a common room by the lodgers, but even in this circumstance they contrived to find expansive consolation. Often Mrs. Winstanley, sitting at attention on the stark bench, had said, "I can relax so much better in a kitchen." Did she think, her daughter wondered, that the repetition of this humbug was one day going to make it true? She sometimes went on from there to say, "When I was a girl back home in Missouri, we used to call our kitchen 'the snuggery,' and we used it more than any other room in the house." As she complacently glanced around, her manner invited her caller to believe that she saw a Boston rocker and braided rugs, copper spiders hanging on white-washed walls, a fireplace with a Dutch oven and cherry settles in the inglenooks, and a mantel crowded with pewter tankards and historic guns. In fact, the caller looked on a room all skin and bones: a coal-oil range with gaunt Queen Anne legs, a Hoosier cabinet ready to shudder into pieces, a linoleum rug worn down to gummy blackness save in the places that were inaccessible to feet and still showed forth its pattern of glossy bruises—a room, in short, in which there was nothing to recommend itself to the eye except the marmalade cat and the sunshine on the windowsill in which he slept.

But the neighbor conspiratorially played the game with her hostess, gladly breathed in these palliative fibs without which the ladies would have spent their days in tears. In one way or another, they had all "come down in the world," but they had descended from a stratum so middling, so snobbish, and so uncertain of itself that it had looked on penury as a disgrace and to have joked about it would have been as alien to their upright natures as it would have been to say aloud the name of a venereal disease. They had come to Adams, this college town in the Rocky Mountains, from the South and the Midwest and New England, most of them driven there by tuberculosis in one member of the family, and now that the depression had slid to its nadir and there were no jobs for their husbands, they had taken up this hard, respectable work.

They bore their shame by refusing to acknowledge its existence: except in the bitter caverns of the night when they reproached their husbands in unflagging whispers, too soft for the boarders to hear but not too soft for their own sons and daughters. For years, Kitty had heard these static diatribes coming up through the hot-air register from her parents' bedroom off the kitchen; sometimes they lasted until the coyotes howled at sunup in the foothills. Rarely did her ruined father answer back; all the charges were true, brutally unfair as they were, and he had nothing to say for himself. He was a builder, but no one was building houses these days; he had only one lung and so he could not work in the mines. The oppressive facts of the depression and of his illness testified to his innocence, but his misery, so long drawn out and so unrelieved, had confused him until he was persuaded that he was jobless because he was no good at his work and he believed his wife when she, cruel out of fear, told him that if he had a little more gumption they would not have to live this way, hand to mouth, one jump ahead of the sheriff. Kitty hated her father's unmanliness (once she had seen him cry when a small roof-repairing job that he had counted on was given to someone else, and she had wanted to die for disgust) and she equally hated her mother for her injustice; and she hated herself for hating in them what they could not help.

In the daytime, the woe and bile were buried, and to her lodgers Mrs. Winstanley was a cheery, cherry-cheeked little red hen who was not too strict about quiet hours (their portable phonographs and radios drove Kitty nightly to the library) or about late dates.

With her friends, she liked to talk of her lodgers and of theirs: of their academic failures and successes ("I wasn't a bit surprised when Dolores got a con in psych," Kitty once heard

Mrs. Ewing say, using the patois as self-confidently as if it were her own. "She told me herself that she hadn't cracked a book all term," and Mrs. Winstanley, au courant and really interested, replied, "But won't those A's in oral interp and business English bring her average up?"); they talked of the girls' love affairs, their plans for holidays, their clothes, their double dates. Gravely and with selfless affection, they told each other facts and sometimes mildly looked for overtones and meanings. Once, Kitty heard her mother say, "Helen went to the Phi Delt tea dance on Thursday with the boy in Mrs. McInerney's single front, but she didn't have a good time at all. She said afterward she was sorry that she had turned down an invitation to go to the show at the Tivoli, even though everyone said it was punk. Of course, I didn't ask any questions, but between you and me and the gatepost I think she was simply cutting off her nose to spite her face by going to the dance instead of keeping her regular date with her steady. Jerry Williams, that is, that big tall engineer with the Studebaker."

They liked to speculate on the sort of homes their students came from; someone's mother's diabetes, someone's younger brother's practical jokes, someone else's widowed father's trip to Mexico were matters that mattered to them. They counted it an equal—and often thrilling—trade if one landlady, offering to her interlocutor the information that one of her girls or boys had been elected to Phi Beta Kappa, got in return the news that Helen or Joyce or Marie had been "pinned" with his Chi Psi pin by a prominent member of the football team.

It was not often that they discussed their own sons and daughters who were working their way through college, but when they did their applause was warm. They were, said the landladies, a happy-go-lucky bunch of kids (though serious in their studies) despite the fact that they did not belong to fraternities and sororities (and were known, therefore, as Barbarians) and could not have exactly the clothes they wanted ("But they keep warm!" the ladies cried. "And when you come right down to it, what else are clothes for?") and had to think twice about spending a nickel on a Coca-Cola. They mouthed their sweet clichés like caramels: "Anything you work hard for means so much more than something just handed to you on a silver platter." "Our children's characters will be all the better for their having gone to the School of Hard Knocks." "For these youngsters of ours, Mrs. Ewing, the depression is a blessing in disguise."

With this honorable, aggressive, friendly mendacity, they armed themselves against the twilight return of their gray-faced husbands from the park and of their edgy children, exhausted from classes and study and part-time jobs and perpetually starved for status (they loathed the School of Hard Knocks, they hated being Barbarians) and clothes (a good deal of the time they were *not* warm) and fun. The husbands ate early, fed like dogs in the kitchen, and then, like dogs, they disappeared. Kitty's father spent his evenings in the furnace room where, under a weak light, he whittled napkin rings. But the landladies' sons and daughters, at the end of the day, became maids or footmen to the students whom they had earlier sat next to in Latin class or worked with on an experiment in chemistry. Kitty Winstanley, setting a plate of lamb stew in front of Miss Shirley Rogers, rejoiced that the girl had flubbed her translation in French and had got a scathing jeer from the instructor, but it was cold comfort because this did not detract at all from the professional set of Miss Rogers's fine blond hair or the chic of her flannel skirt and her English sweater on which, over her heart, was pinned the insignia of her current fiancé. Sometimes in the kitchen, as Kitty brought out dirty dishes or refilled the platter of meat, her mother whispered angrily, "Don't look so down in the mouth! They'll go eat some place where they can find a cheerful smile and then what will we do?" Blackmailed, Kitty set her lips in a murderous grin.

A little work never hurt anyone, the landladies assured each other, and if it was not Mrs. Winstanley yearning to trade places with Kitty in the debonair life she led as waitress and chambermaid at the Caribou Ranch, it was Mrs. Ewing, similarly self-hypnotized, enumerating the advantages that accrued to her asthmatic son in nightly setting up pins in a bowling alley. What a lark she made of it! And what a solemn opportunity. It was a liberal education in itself, according to his

mother, for Harry Ewing to mingle until one in the morning
with coal miners and fraternity boys, a contrast of class and
privilege she found profoundly instructive. A cricket match on
the playing fields of Eton would not seem to offer more in the
demonstration of sportsmanship than a bowling tournament
between the Betas and the ATOs at the Pay Dirt Entertainment
Hall. And, again, a stranger might have thought that Harry
was only slumming when Mrs. Ewing spoke, with a sociolo-
gist's objectivity, of the low mentality and lower morality of the
men from the mines and the scandalous girls they brought with
them on Ladies' Night. She never touched upon the sleep that
Harry lost or on those occasions when a doctor had to be summoned on the double to give the pin boy an injection of Adren-
alin. "I do believe Harry's outgrowing his asthma," she said
once, although that very morning Kitty had seen him across
the hall in modern European history buffeted suddenly by an
attack so debilitating that he had had to be led out by a monitor.

Kitty sat down at her study table and opened her Renaissance survey book to Donne, shutting her ears against the
voices of the heroines below. But she was distracted and discon-
solate, and the *Divine Poems* fled from her eyes before her mind
could detain them. She turned to stare out of her narrow window at the sweet peas that her father's green thumb had coaxed
to espalier the wall of the garage. Somewhere in the neighborhood, a music student was phrenetically practicing a polonaise,
making villainous mistakes, and somewhere nearer a phonograph was playing "I Wonder Who's Kissing Her Now," the
singer's tribulation throbbing luxuriously in the light spring air.
Beyond the garage, over the tops of the mongrel houses and
through the feathery branches of mountain ash trees, Kitty
could see the red rock terraces of the foothills and the mass of
the range beyond where, in a high, wild, emerald and azure and
bloodstone park, she would spend her summer.

She would not spend it exactly as her mother imagined. She
thought of that lake Mrs. Winstanley so much admired, sight
unseen, where the girls could swim after lunch if they were not
repelled by the mud puppies that abounded in the icy water;

and then she thought of the lambent green pool in the main lodge for the exclusive use of the dudes. She thought of the one spooked and spavined old cow pony the kitchen help could ride if they wanted to go where he contrarily wanted to take them, up in the hot sage where the rattlers were or through thick copses of scratchy chokecherry or over sterile, stubbly fields pitted with gopher holes into which he maliciously stumbled when there was no need; and then she saw in her mind's eye the lively blooded bays and palominos that the dudes rode, never failing, as they mounted, to make some stale, soft-boiled joke about Western saddles. It was true, just as her mother said, that the help was asked to the square dances, only "asked" was not the right word; they had to go to show the Easterners the steps, and there could not have been any dances at all if Wylie, the horse-wrangler, had not been there to call the turns. And it was hardly like going to Paris to go down to Brophy, all but a ghost town, where the only buildings that were not boarded up were a drugstore, a grocery, the post office, a filling station, and a barbershop that was open on Tuesday and Saturday when an itinerant barber came to town. A handful of backward people, most of them named Brophy, lived in battered cabins in the shadows of the ore dumps of extinguished gold mines. In the wintertime, the story was, they often killed each other because they had nothing else to do.

The help at the Caribou blundered out of bed at five o'clock before the sun came up to begin a day that did not end until after nine at night, a day filled, besides work, with the fussy complaints about their cabins and their food from the older guests, pinches and propositions from the randy younger ones (who were not that young). There was ceaseless bickering among the staff who, xenophobic, despised the dudes and, misanthropic, despised each other. The kitchen was ruled by a fat red cook and a thin yellow pantry girl who did not speak to each other although they glared verbosely across the room, the cook from under the lowering hood of her enormous stove, the pantry girl over the counter of her bailiwick, where the smell of rancid butter was everlasting.

Every morning, as the girls and the wranglers drowsed

through their breakfast of flapjacks and side meat, Miss Skeen appeared in the outer doorway of the kitchen, a homicidal German shepherd at her side (his name was Thor and he lived up to it; he had bitten many ankles and had abraded countless others), and boomed through the screen, "Howdy, pardners!" Miss Skeen, a tall and manly woman, combined in her costume the cork helmet of the pukka sahib, the tweed jacket of the Cotswold squire, the close-fitting Levi's and the French-heeled boots of the wry American cowboy, and the silver and turquoise jewelry of the colorful Southwestern aborigine. Her hair was short, her face was made of crags, she spoke in a Long Island basso profundo.

While Miss Skeen gave the men their orders for the day, her partner, Mrs. Bell, entered the kitchen to chirp admonitions to the female servants. Mrs. Bell was stout, small-mouthed, doggishly dewlapped, and she wore the khaki uniform of a Red Cross ambulance driver; her contribution to the Great War still gave her great satisfaction, and her memories of France, which were extensive and fresh, were ever on the tip of her tongue. Quite often she lapsed from Western into Army lingo, called the dining room "the mess hall," asked a guest how he liked his billet, spoke of the wranglers as "noncoms." Her awful greeting was, "Cheerio, boys and girls! Everybody get out of the right side of bed this morning, I hope, I hope?"

The five waitress-chambermaids lived a mile from the main lodge down in a pine-darkened gulch in what had once been a chicken coop and what now Mrs. Bell archly called "the girls' dorm." The door still latched on the outside and the ceilings were so low that no one taller than a child could stand up straight in any of the three small rooms. There was an outhouse, vile and distant; they were so plagued by trade rats that they had to keep everything they could in tin boxes if they did not want to find their money or their letters stolen and replaced by twigs or bluejay feathers. At that altitude it was freezing cold at night, and the laundry stove in which they burned pine knots could not be regulated, so that they had the choice of shivering or being roasted alive. They had a little time off in the afternoon, but, as often as not, Mrs. Bell would dream up some

task for them that she tried to make out was a game: they
would have to go gather columbines for the tables in the dining
room or look for puffballs to put in the pot roast. It was ex-
hausting work; sometimes, after a thronged weekend or a holiday, Kitty's arms ached so much from carrying burdened trays
that she could not sleep, and through the long night listened
anxiously to the animals gliding and rustling like footpads
through the trees.

But, all the same, each spring for the past four years Kitty
had been wild with impatience to get to the Caribou, to get
away from home, from the spectacle of her eaten father and
from her mother's bright-eyed lies, from all the maniacal respectability with which the landladies strait-jacketed the life of
the town. The chicken coop was filthy and alarming, but it was
not this genteel, hygienic house in which she was forced to live
a double life. At the Caribou, she was a servant and she enjoyed
a servant's prerogative of keeping her distance; for instance, to
the rich and lascivious dude, Mr. Kopf, a painter, she had been
respectful but very firm in refusing to pose for him (he wanted
to paint her as Hebe), had said, in a way that left no room for
argument, "I have to rest in my time off, sir." But, at home,
what could she do if a boarder, valuable to her mother for the
rent she paid, asked for help with a translation or the loan of
lecture notes? She could not put the girl, her contemporary and
classmate, in her place by calling her "ma'am," she could do
nothing but supinely deliver the lecture notes together with the
dumplings or lend a hand with *De Amicitia* after she had taken
to the various rooms the underwear and blouses her mother
had washed and ironed.

At the Caribou, there was no one she knew in any other
context. Her fellow waitresses were local mountain girls, so
chastely green that they were not really sure what a college was
and certainly did not care. They never read, but it did not
embarrass them that Kitty did. At Christmas she exchanged
cards with them but they did not exist for her, or she for them,
before the first of June or after Labor Day. And the dudes
whose bathtubs she scoured and whose dietary idiosyncrasies
she catered to came from a milieu so rich and foreign and

Eastern that she could not even imagine it and therefore did not envy it.

Friendless, silent, long and exasperating, the summers, indeed, were no holiday. But she lived them in pride and without woe and with a physical intelligence that she did not exercise in the winter; there in the mountains, she observed the world acutely and with love—at dusk, the saddle horses grazing in the meadow were joined by deer seeking the salt lick; by day the firmament was cloudless and blinding and across the blue of it chicken hawks and eagles soared and banked in perpetual reconnaissance; by night the stars were near, and the mountains on the moon, when it was full, seemed to have actual altitude. On these wonders, Kitty mused, absorbed.

The voices downstairs invaded her trance. She began to calculate in pencil on the margin to the left of "If poisonous minerals . . ." how many more hours there were to come before she got into the rattletrap mail coach that would take her, coughing spastically in its decrepitude, up the rivered canyon and over the quiet passes to her asylum. Her arithmetic did not deafen her. She heard:

"I grant you that the hours are long and the pay is low," her mother said, "but the Caribou attracts big spenders from the East and the tips more than make up for the poor wages. I don't mean your flashy tourists and I don't mean your snobby new rich but simply your settled, well-to-do people, mostly middle-aged and older. Mrs. Bell and Miss Skeen are cultured —went to boarding school in Switzerland as I understand it— and they are ladies and, as a result, they are particular about their clientele—absolutely will not tolerate anything in the least out-of-the-way. For one thing, they don't allow drinking on the premises, and anyone who breaks the rule is given his walking papers without any further ado, I don't care if his name is Astor or John Doe. And with all the beer-drinking and whatnot going on down here when those fast boys come flocking to town from heaven knows where in those convertible roadsters with the cut-outs open and those horns that play a tune, it's a comfort to me to know that my daughter is out of the way of loose living."

"Oh, I agree," said Mrs. Ewing, and Kitty could imagine her nodding her head spiritedly and shaking loose the bone hairpins that held her gray braids in place. "I happen to know that the drinking that goes on in this town is decidedly on the upgrade. In these bowling alleys and so on, they spike the three point two with grain alcohol. And that's the very least of it. There are many, many ether addicts in the frat houses. Oh, I'm telling you, there are plenty of statistics that would make your hair stand on end. D.T.'s and so on among the young."

For a few minutes then the ladies lowered their voices and Kitty could not hear what they said, but she knew the bypath they were joyfully ambling down; they were expounding the theory that beer-drinking led to dope and dope to free love and free love to hydrocephalic, albino, club-footed bastard babies or else to death by abortion.

The fact was that both Mrs. Bell and Miss Skeen were lushes, and they fooled nobody with their high and mighty teetotal rule and their aura of Sen-Sen. The rule was at first a puzzle and a bore to the dudes, but then it became a source of surreptitious fun: outwitting the old girls became as much a part of the routine as fishing or hunting for arrowheads. For the last two years, Kitty Winstanley had acted as middleman between the guests and the bootlegger, Ratty Carmichael. There was local option in the state, but in Meade County where the Caribou lay there was nothing legal to drink but three point two. In an obscure, dry gully back of the cow pasture, Kitty kept her trysts with Ratty (his eyes were feral and his twitching nose was criminal) and gave him handfuls of money and orders for bottles of atrocious brown booze and demijohns of Dago Red. These he delivered at dinnertime when Miss Skeen and Mrs. Bell were in their cabin, The Bonanza, oblivious to everything but their own elation, for which excellent Canadian whisky, bought honorably in Denver, was responsible. Kitty had no taste for this assignment of hers—she was not an adventurous girl—but she was generously tipped by the dudes for running their shady errands and for that reason she put up with the risks of it—being fired, being caught by the revenue officers and charged with collusion.

She smiled, finishing her multiplication. In 283 more hours, immediately after her last examination in final week, she would be putting her suitcase into the mail truck parked behind the post office. And a good many of those hours would be blessedly spent in sleep. Then she'd be gone from this charmless town on the singed plains where the cottonwoods were dusty and the lawns were straw. She'd be gone from the French dolls and baby pillows in the lodgers' rooms. And, in being gone, she would give her mother a golden opportunity to brag to the summer roomers: "Kitty has the time of her life," she could hear her mother say to some wispy, downtrodden school-teacher waif, "up there where the ozone is as good as a drink, as they say."

Now the light was paling on the summit snows. Kitty heard her father's soft-footed, apologetic tread on the back porch and heard Mrs. Ewing brightly say, "Well, I must toddle along now and thanks a million for the treat. My turn next time."

The music student was at work on *The Well-Tempered Clavichord* and the phonograph was playing "The Object of My Affection" as fast as merry-go-round music. And down in the kitchen, as she clattered and banged her pots and pans, Mother Pollyana began to sing "The Stein Song."

The Echo

by Paul Bowles

Aileen pulled out her mirror, which the vibration of the plane shook so rapidly that she was unable to see whether her nose needed powder or not. There were only two other passengers and they were asleep. It was noon; the tropical sun shone violently down upon the wide silver wings and cast sharp reflections on the ceiling. Far below, the uniform green carpet of the jungle moved slowly by. She was sleepy, but she was also excited to be going to a new home. From her handbag she pulled a folded letter which she read again intently, as if to decipher a meaning that did not lie in the sequence of the words. It was in her mother's script:

AILEEN, SWEET—

I must begin (and finish) this before supper. Prue has just gone out for her shower, and that means that by the time she has Luz (the cook) heat the water and can find José (the gardener) to carry it up on the roof to the tank, it will be about an hour. Add to that the time it takes her to do her actual bathing and to dress, and you can see I'll have just about time for a nice chat.

Perhaps I should begin by saying that Prue and I are sublimely happy here. It is absolute heaven after Washington, as you can pretty well imagine. Prue, of course, never could stand the States, and I felt, after the trouble with your father, that I couldn't face anyone for a while. You know how much importance I have always attached to relaxation. And this is the ideal spot for that.

Of course I did feel a little guilty about running off down here without seeing you. But I think the trip to Northampton

would have sealed my doom. I honestly don't believe I could
have stood it. And Prue was nervous about the State Department's passing some new law that would prevent citizens from
leaving the U.S. because of the disturbed conditions, and so on
I also felt that the sooner we got down here to Jamonocal the
more of a home we could make out of the old place, for you to
spend your vacation in. And it *is* going to be beautiful. I won't
drag out my reasons for not letting you know beforehand or it
will sound apologetic, and I know I never have to apologize to
you for anything. So I'll leave that and get on. I'm sure anyway
that the eight months passed very quickly up there for you.

We have had swarms of men working on the house ever since
last October. Mr. Forbes happened to be in Barranquilla for a
new American project in the interior, and I wanted to be sure
of having him supervise the construction of the cantilever in the
foundation. That man is really a prince. They don't come much
finer. He was up again and again, and gave orders down to the
last detail. I felt guilty about making him work so hard, but I
honestly think he enjoyed himself with us girls. In any case it
seemed silly, when one of the best architects in the U.S. was
right here in Colombia and happened to be an old friend, not to
use him when I needed him. Anyway, the old house is now the
old wing and the new part, which is so exciting I can't wait for
you to see it, is built right out over the gorge. I think there's not
likely to be another house like it in the world, if I do say it
myself. The terrace makes me think of an old cartoon in *The
New Yorker* showing two men looking over the edge of the
Grand Canyon, and one is saying to the other: "Did you ever
want to spit a mile, Bill? Now's your chance."

We are all installed. The weather has been wonderful, and if
Luz could only learn a little more about what white people like
to eat and how they like it served, the setup would really be
perfect. I know you will enjoy being here with Prue. She and
you have many things in common, even if you do claim to
"remember not liking her much." That was in Washington and
you were, to put it mildly, at a difficult age. Now, as an adult
(because you really are one by now), you'll be more understanding, I'm sure. She loves books, especially on philosophy

and psychology and other things your poor mother just doesn't
try to follow her in. She has rigged up a kiln and studio in the
old guest house which you probably don't remember. She
works at her ceramics out there all day, and I have all I can do
keeping the house tidy and seeing that the marketing is done.
We have a system by which Luz takes the list to her brother
every afternoon, and he brings the things from town the following day. It just about keeps him fully busy getting up and down
the mountain on his horse. The horse is a lazy old nag that has
done nothing but plod back and forth between house and the
valley all its life, so it doesn't know the meaning of the word
speed. But after all, why hurry down here?

I think you will find everything to your liking, and I'm sure
you won't require more than five minutes to see that Prue is a
dear, and not at all "peculiar," as you wrote in your letter.
Wire me as soon as you receive this, and let me know just what
week you'll be finishing classes. Prue and I will meet you in
Barranquilla. I have a list of things I want you to get me in
New York. Will wire it to you as soon as I hear. Prue's bath
finished. Must close. Love,

MOTHER.

Aileen put the letter away, smiling a little, and watched the
wings diving in and out of the small thick clouds that lay in the
plane's way. There was a slight shock each time they hit one,
and the world outside became a blinding whiteness. She fancied
jumping out and walking on such solid softness, like a character in an animated cartoon.

Her mother's letter had put her in mind of a much earlier
period in her life: the winter she had been taken to visit
Jamonocal. All she could recall in the way of incidents was that
she had been placed on a mule by one of the natives, and had
felt a painful horror that the animal would walk in the wrong
direction, away from the house toward the edge of the gorge.
She had no memory of the gorge. Probably she had never seen
it, although it was only a few paces from the house, through a
short but thick stretch of canebrake. However, she had a clear

memory of its presence, of the sensation of enormous void beyond and below that side of the house. And she recalled the
distant, hollow sound of water falling from a great height, a
constant, soft backdrop of sound that slipped into every moment of the day—between the conversations at mealtimes, in
the intervals of play in the garden, and at night between
dreams. She wondered if really it were possible to remember all
that from the time when she had been only five.

In Panama there was a plane change to be made. It was a
clear green twilight, and she took a short walk beyond the
airport. Parakeets were fighting in the upper branches of the
trees; suddenly they became quiet. She turned back and went
inside, where she sat reading until it was time to go aboard.

There was no one there to meet her when she arrived at
Barranquilla in the early hours of the morning. She decided to
go into town and take a room in the hotel. With her two valises
she stepped outside and looked about for a cab. They had all
gone into town with passengers, but a man sitting on a packing
case informed her that they would soon be coming back. Then
suddenly he said, "You want two ladies?"

"What? No. What do you mean?"

"You want two ladies look for you this night?"

"Where are they?" said Aileen, understanding.

"They want a drink," he answered with an intimate grin.

"Where? Barranquilla?"

"No. Here." He pointed down the dark road.

"Where? Can I walk?"

"Sure. I go you."

"No! No, thanks. You stay here. Thank you. I can go all
right. Where is it? How far?"

"O.K."

"What is it? A bar? What's the name?"

"They got music. La Gloria. You go. You hear music. You
look for two ladies. They drinking."

She went inside again and checked the bags with an airline
employee who insisted on accompanying her. They strode in
silence along the back road. The walls of vegetation on each
side sheltered insects that made an occasional violent, dry noise

like a wooden ratchet being whirled. Soon there was the sound
of drums and trumpets playing Cuban dance music.

"La Gloria," said her escort triumphantly.

La Gloria was a brilliantly lighted mud hut with a thatch-
covered veranda giving onto the road. The juke box was outside, where a few drunken Negroes sprawled.

"Are they here?" she said out loud, but to herself.

"La Gloria," he answered, pointing.

As they came opposite the front of the building, she caught a
glimpse of a woman in blue jeans, and although instantaneously
she knew it was Prue, her mind for some reason failed to accept
the fact, and she continued to ask herself, "Are they here or
not?"

She turned to go toward the veranda. The record had finished playing. The ditch lay in the dark between the road and
the porch. She fell forward into it and heard herself cry out.
The man behind her said, *"Cuidado!"* She lay there panting
with fury and pain, and said, "Oh! My ankle!" There was an
exclamation inside the bar. Her mother's voice cried, "That's
Aileen!" Then the juke box began to scratch and roar again.
The Negroes remained stationary. Someone helped her up. She
was inside the bar in the raw electric glare.

"I'm all right," she said, when she had been eased into a
chair.

"But, darling, where've you been? We've been waiting for
you since eight, and we'd just about given up. Poor Prue's ill."

"Nonsense, I'll recover," said Prue, still seated at the bar.
"Been having a touch of the trots, that's all."

"But, darling, are you all right? This is absurd, landing here
this way."

She looked down at Aileen's ankle.

"Is it all right?"

Prue came over from the bar to shake her hand.

"A dramatic entrance, gal," she said.

Aileen sat there and smiled. She had a curious mental habit.
As a child she had convinced herself that her head was transparent, that the thoughts there could be perceived immediately
by others. Accordingly, when she found herself in uncomfort-

able situations, rather than risk the danger of being suspected
of harboring uncomplimentary or rebellious thoughts, she had
developed a system of refraining from thinking at all. For a
while during her childhood this fear of having no mental privacy had been extended to anyone; even persons existing at a
distance could have access to her mind. Now she felt open only
to those present. And so it was that, finding herself face to face
with Prue, she was conscious of no particular emotion save the
familiar vague sense of boredom. There was not a thought in
her head, and her face made the fact apparent.

Mornings were hard to believe. The primeval freshness,
spilled down out of the jungle above the house, was held close
to the earth by the mist. Outside and in, it was damp and
smelled like a florist's shop, but the dampness was dispelled
each day when the stinging sun burned through the thin cape of
moisture that clung to the mountain's back. Living there was
like living sideways, with the land stretching up on one side and
down on the other at the same angle. Only the gorge gave a
feeling of perpendicularity; the vertical walls of rock on the
opposite side of the great amphitheater were a reminder that
the center of gravity lay below and not obliquely to one side.
Constant vapor rose from the invisible pool at the bottom, and
the distant, indeterminate calling of water was like the sound of
sleep itself.

For a few days Aileen lay in bed listening to the water and
the birds, and to the nearby, unfamiliar, domestic sounds. Her
mother and Prue both had breakfast in bed, and generally appeared just before the midday meal for a few minutes of conversation until Concha brought the invalid's lunch tray. In the
afternoons she thumbed through old magazines and read at
murder mysteries. Usually it began to rain about three; the
sound at first would be like an augmentation of the waterfall in
the distance, and then as its violence increased it came unmis-
takably nearer—a great roar all around the house that covered
every other sound. The black clouds would close in tightly
around the mountain, so that it seemed that night would soon
arrive. She would ring a small bell for Concha to come and

light the oil lamp on the table by the bed. Lying there looking
at the wet banana leaves outside the window, with the rain's
din everywhere, she felt completely comfortable for the precarious moment. There was no necessity to question the feeling, no
need to think—only the subsiding of the rain, the triumphant
emergence of the sun into the steaming twilight and an early
dinner to look forward to. Each evening after dinner her
mother came for a lengthy chat, usually about the servants.
The first three nights Prue had come too, carrying a highball,
but after that her mother came alone.

Aileen had asked to be put into the old part of the house,
rather than into a more comfortable room in the new wing. Her
window looked onto the garden, which was a small square of
lawn with young banana trees on either side. At the far end was
a fountain; behind it was the disordered terrain of the mountainside with its recently cut underbrush and charred stumps,
and still further beyond was the high jungle whose frontier had
been sliced in a straight line across the slopes many years ago to
make the plantation. Here in her room she felt at least that the
earth was somewhere beneath her.

When her ankle ceased to pain her, she began going downstairs for lunch, which was served out on the terrace on a table
with a beach umbrella stuck in its center. Prue was regularly
late in coming from her studio, and she arrived in her blue
jeans, which were caked with clay, with smears of dirt across
her face. Because Aileen could not bring herself to think what
she really felt, which was that Prue was ungracious, ugly, and
something of an interloper, she remained emotionally unconscious of Prue's presence, which is to say that she was polite
but bored, scarcely present in the mealtime conversations.
Then, too, Aileen was definitely uncomfortable on the terrace.
The emptiness was too near and the balustrade seemed altogether too low for safety. She liked the meals to be as brief as
possible, with no unnecessary time spent sipping coffee afterward, but it never would have occurred to her to divulge her
reasons. With Prue around she felt constrained to behave with
the utmost decorum. Fortunately her ankle provided her with a
convenient excuse to get back upstairs to her room.

She soon discovered a tiny patio next to the kitchen where heavy vines with sweet-smelling flowers grew up an arbor that had been placed at one side. The air was full of the humming of hundreds of bees that clung heavily to the petals and moved slowly about in the air. After lunch she would pull a deck chair into the arbor's shade and read until the rain began. It was a stifling, airless spot, but the sound of the bees covered that of the waterfall. One afternoon Prue followed her there and stood with her hands in her hip pockets looking at her.

"How can you take this heat?" she asked Aileen.

"Oh, I love it."

"You do?" She paused. "Tell me, do you really like it here, or do you think it's a bloody bore?"

"Why, I think it's absolutely wonderful."

"Mm. It is."

"Don't you like it?"

Prue yawned. "Oh, I'm all for it. But I keep busy. Wherever I can work, I get on, you know."

"Yes, I suppose so," said Aileen. Then she added, "Are you planning on staying long?"

"What the hell do you mean?" said Prue, leaning backward against the house, her hands still behind her. "I live here."

Aileen laughed shortly. To anyone but Prue it would have sounded like a merry, tinkling laugh, but Prue narrowed her eyes and thrust her jaw forward a bit.

"What's so funny?" she demanded.

"I think you're funny. You're so tied up in knots. You get upset so easily. Perhaps you work too hard out there in your little house."

Prue was looking at her with astonishment.

"God Almighty," she said finally, "your IQ's showing, gal."

"Thank you," said Aileen with great seriousness. "Anyway, I think it's fine that you're happy here, and I hope you go on being happy."

"That's what I came to say to you."

"Then everything's fine."

"I can't make you out," said Prue, frowning.

"I don't know what you're talking about," replied Aileen,

fingering the pages of her book impatiently. "It's the most pointless conversation I've ever had."

"That I *don't* think," Prue said, going into the kitchen.

The same evening, when her mother came for her usual after-dinner chat, she looked a little unhappy.

"You don't seem to be getting on very well with Prue," she said reproachfully, as she sat down at the foot of the bed.

"Why, we get on perfectly well. Oh. You're talking about this afternoon, probably."

"Yes, I am, probably. Really, Aileen. You simply can't be rude to a woman her age. She's my guest, and you're my guest, and you've got to be civil to each other. But she's always civil and I have a feeling you're not."

Aileen caught her breath and said, "I'm your guest . . ."

"I invited you here for your vacation and I want things pleasant, and I don't see the slightest reason why they shouldn't be."

Suddenly Aileen cried, "She's a maniac!"

Her mother rose and quickly left the room.

In the quiet days that followed, the incident was not mentioned by any of them. Aileen continued to haunt the little patio after lunch.

There came a morning sweeter than the rest, when the untouched early mist hung inside her bedroom, and the confusion of shrill bird cries came down with perfect clarity from the uncut forest. She dressed quickly and went out. There was a white radiance in the air that she had never seen before. She walked along the path that led by the native huts. There was life stirring within; babies were crying and captive parrots and songbirds laughed and sang. The path swung into a stretch of low trees that had been planted to shield the coffee bushes. It was still almost nocturnal in here; the air was streaked with chill, and the vegetable odors were like invisible festoons drooping from the branches as she walked through. A huge bright spider walked slowly across the path at her feet. She stood still and watched it until it had disappeared in the leaves at one side. She put her hand over her heart to feel how insistently it was beating. And she listened to its sound in her head for a moment, not wanting to break into its rhythm by starting to walk again. Then she began to walk ahead fast, following the path upward toward the lightest part of the sky. When it came out suddenly onto an eminence directly above the plantation, she could barely discern the cluster of roofs through the mist. But here the sound of the waterfall was stronger; she supposed she was near the gorge, although there was no sign of it. The path turned here and went along rough open ground upward. She climbed at a steady gait, breathing slowly and deeply, for perhaps half an hour, and was surprised to find that the jungle had been cut away on all sides in this portion of the mountainside. For a time she thought the sky was growing brighter, and that the sun was about to break through, but as the path leveled out and she was able to see for some distance ahead, she saw that the mist was even thicker up here than down below.

At certain points there was a steep declivity on each side of the path. It was impossible to see how deeply the land fell away. There were a few nearby plants and rocks, the highest fronds of a tree fern a little beyond, and white emptiness after that. It was like going along the top of a wall high in the air. Then the path would make a wide turn and go sharply upward and she would see a solitary tree above her at one side.

Suddenly she came up against a row of huts. They were less well made than those down at the plantation, and smaller. The mist was full of woodsmoke; there was the smell of pigs. She stood still. A man was singing. Two small naked children came out of the door of one hut, looked at her a moment in terror, and ran quickly back inside. She walked ahead. The singing came from behind the last hut. When she came opposite the hut, she saw that it was enclosed by a tangled but effective fence of barbed wire which left a runway about six feet wide all the way around. A young man appeared from the farther side of the closed-in space. His shirt and pants were tattered; the brown skin showed in many places. He was singing as he walked toward her, and he continued to sing, looking straight into her face with bright, questioning eyes. She smiled and said, *"Buenos dias."* He made a signaling gesture, rather too dramatically. She stopped walking and stood still, looking hesitantly back at the other huts. The young man signaled again and then stepped inside the hut. A moment later he came out, and still staring fascinatedly at her, made more summoning motions. Aileen stood perfectly quiet, not taking her eyes from his face. He walked slowly over to the fence and grasped the wire with both hands, his eyes growing wider as he pressed the barbs into his palms. Then he leaned across, thrusting his head toward her, his eyes fixing hers with incredible intensity. For several seconds they watched each other; then she stepped a little nearer, peering into his face and frowning. At that point with a cry he emptied his mouth of the water he had been holding in it, aiming with force at Aileen's face. Some of it struck her cheek, and the rest the front of her dress. His fingers unclenched themselves from around the wire, and straightening himself, he backed slowly into the hut, watching her face closely all the while.

She stood still an instant, her hand to her cheek. Then she bent down, and picking up a large stone from the path, she flung it with all her strength through the door. A terrible cry came from within; it was like nothing she had ever heard. Or yes, she thought as she began to run back past the other huts, it had the indignation and outraged innocence of a small baby, but it was also a grown man's cry. No one appeared as she passed the huts. Soon she was back in the silence of the empty mountainside, but she kept running, and she was astonished to find that she was sobbing as well. She sat down on a rock and calmed herself by watching some ants demolish a bush as they cut away squares of leaf and carried them away in their mouths. The sky was growing brighter now; the sun would soon be through. She went on. By the time she got back to the high spot above the plantation the mist had turned into long clouds that were rolling away down the mountainside into the ravines. She was horrified to see how near she stood to the ugly black edge of the gorge. And the house looked insane down there, leaning out over as if it were trying to see the bottom. Far below the house the vapor rose up from the pool. She followed the sheer sides of the opposite cliff upward with her eye, all the way to the top, a little above the spot where she stood. It made

her feel ill, and she stumbled back down to the house with her
hand to her forehead, paying no attention to the natives who
greeted her from their doorways.

As she ran past the garden a voice called to her. She turned
and saw Prue washing her hands in the fountain's basin. She
stood still.

"You're up early. You must feel better," said Prue, drying
her hands on her hair. "Your mother's been having a fit. Go in
and see her."

Aileen stared at Prue a moment before she said, "I was going
in. You don't have to tell me."

"Oh, I thought I did."

"You don't have to tell me anything. I think I can manage all
right without your help."

"Help isn't exactly what I'd like to give you," said Prue,
putting her hands into her pockets. "A swift kick in the teeth
would be more like it. How do you think I like to see your
mother worrying about you? First you're sick in bed, then you
just disappear into the goddam jungle. D'you think I like to
have to keep talking about you, reassuring her every ten minutes? What the hell d'you think life is, one long coming-out
party?"

Aileen stared harder, now with unmasked hatred. "I think,"
she said slowly, "that life is pretty awful. Here especially. And
I think you should look once in the mirror and then jump off
the terrace. And I think Mother should have her mind examined."

"I see," said Prue, with dire inflection. She lit a cigarette and
strode off to her studio. Aileen went into the house and up to
her room.

Less than an hour later, her mother knocked at her door. As
she came into the room, Aileen could see she had been crying
only a moment before.

"Aileen darling, I've got something to say to you," she began
apologetically, "and it just breaks my heart to say it. But I've
got to."

She stopped, as though waiting for encouragement.

"Mother, what is it?"

"I think you probably know."

"About Prue, I suppose. No?"

"It certainly is. I don't know how I can ever make it right with her. She told me what you said to her, and I must say I found it hard to believe. How could you?"

"You mean just now in the garden?"

"I don't know where you said it, but I do know this can't go on. So I'm just forced to say this. . . . You'll have to go. I can't be stirred up this way, and I can tell just how it'll be if you stay on."

"I'm not surprised at all," said Aileen, making a show of calm. "When do you want me to leave?"

"This is terribly painful—"

"Oh, stop! It's all right. I've had a vacation and I can get a lot of work done before the term starts. Today? Tomorrow?"

"I think the first of the week. I'll go to Barranquilla with you."

"Would you think I was silly if I had all my meals up here?"

"I think it's a perfect idea, darling, and we can have nice visits together, you and I, between meals."

Now, when the tension should have been over, somehow it was not. During the four nights before she was to leave, Aileen had endless excruciating dreams. She would wake up in the darkness too agonized even to move her hand. It was not fear; she could not recall the dreams. It was rather as if some newly discovered, innermost part of her being were in acute pain. Breathing quickly, she would lie transfixed for long periods listening to the eternal sound of the waterfall, punctuated at great intervals by some slight, nearby nocturnal noise in the trees. Finally, when she had summoned sufficient energy to move, she would change her position in the bed, sigh profoundly, and relax enough to fall back into the ominous world of sleep.

When the final day came, there was a light tapping on her door just after dawn. She got up and unbolted it. Her mother was there, smiling thinly.

"May I come in?"

"Oh. Good morning. Of course. It's early, isn't it?"

Her mother walked across to the window and stood lookin
down at the misty garden.

"I'm not so well today," she said. "I'm afraid I can't tak
you to Barranquilla. I'm not up to getting onto a horse toda
It's just too much, that three-hour trip to Jamonocal, and the
the train and the boat all night. You'll just have to forgive me.
couldn't stand all three. But it won't matter, will it?" she wen
on, looking up at last. "We'll say good-bye here."

"But, Mother, how can I go alone?"

"Oh, José'll go all the way to Barranquilla with you and b
back by Wednesday night. You don't think I'd let you go off b
yourself?"

She began to laugh intensely, then stopped suddenly an
looked pensive.

"I rather hate to be here two nights without him, but I don'
see any other way to get you down there by tomorrow. You ca
go shipside to Panama. There's usually a seat somewhere. Now
breakfast, breakfast. . . ."

Patting Aileen's cheek, she hurried out and downstairs to th
kitchen.

The birds' morning song was coming down from the forest
the mist lay ragged in the tops of the great trees up there
Aileen shifted her gaze to the garden at her feet. Suddenly sh
felt she could not leave; in a sense it was as if she were leavin
love behind. She sat down on the bed. "But what is it?" sh
asked herself desperately. "Not Mother. Not the house. Not th
jungle." Automatically she dressed and packed the remainin
toilet articles in her overnight case. But the feeling was there
imperious and enveloping in its completeness.

She went downstairs. There was the sound of voices and th
clatter of china in the kitchen. Concha and Luz were preparing
her breakfast tray. She went out and watched them until every
thing was ready.

"Ya se va la señorita?" said Concha sadly.

She did not answer, but took the tray from her and carried i
through the house, out onto the terrace, where she set it on th
table. Everything on the terrace was wet with dew and moistur

om the gorge. She turned the chair cushion over and sat down
eat. The sound of the waterfall took her appetite away, but
e thought, "This is the last time." She felt choked with emo-
ons, but they were too disparate and confused for her to be
le to identify any one of them as outstanding. As she sat
ere eating intently, she was suddenly aware that someone was
atching her. She started up and saw Prue standing in the
oorway. She was wearing pajamas and a bathrobe, and in her
and she held a glass of water. She looked very sleepy.

"How are you?" she said, sipping her water.

Aileen stood up.

"We're all up bright and early this morning," Prue went on
heerily.

"I'm—leaving. I've got to go. Excuse me, it's late," mumbled
ileen, glancing about furtively.

"Oh, take your time, gal. You haven't said good-bye to your
nother yet. And José is still saddling the nags. You've got a lot
f grips with you."

"Excuse me," said Aileen, trying to slip past her through the
oorway.

"Well, shake," Prue said, reaching for Aileen's hand.

"Get away!" cried Aileen, struggling to keep clear of her.
'Don't touch me!" But Prue had succeeded in grasping one
rantic arm. She held it fast.

"A dramatic entrance is enough. We don't have to have the
ame sort of exit. Say good-bye to me like a human being." She
wisted the arm a bit, in spite of herself. Aileen leaned against
he door and turned very white.

"Feel faint?" said Prue. She let go of her arm, and holding up
er glass of water, flicked some of it into Aileen's face with her
ingers.

The reaction was instantaneous. Aileen jumped at her with
vicious suddenness, kicking, ripping, and pounding all at once.
The glass fell to the stone floor; Prue was caught off her guard.
Mechanically, with rapid, birdlike fury, the girl hammered at
he woman's face and head, as she slowly impelled her away
from the doorway and across the terrace.

From Prue's lips came several times the word "God." At first she did very little to defend herself; she seemed half asleep as she moved toward the outer edge beneath the onslaught. Then suddenly she threw herself to the floor. Aileen continued to kick her where she lay doubled over, trying to protect her face.

"Nobody! Nobody! Nobody! Nobody can do that to me!" she cried rhythmically as she kicked.

Her voice rose in pitch and volume; she stopped for an instant, and then, raising her head, she uttered the greatest scream of her life. It came back immediately from the black wall of rock across the gorge, straight through the noise of water. The sound of her own voice ended the episode for her, and she began to walk across the terrace.

Concha and Luz stood frightened in the doorway; it was as if they had come to watch a terrible storm pass over the countryside. They stepped aside as Aileen walked through.

Outside the stable, José was whistling as he finished saddling the horses. The valises were already strapped on the burro.

Still in the midst of her deep dream, Aileen turned her head toward the house as they rode past. For a brief second, between the leaves, she saw the two figures of her mother and Prue standing side by side on the terrace, the wall of the gorge looming behind. Then the horses turned and began to descend the trail.